No Slave to Reason

A Mobtown Tale of Blood, Beauty, and Baseball

No Slave to Reason

John Thomas Everett

Braveship BOOKS

Aura Libertatis Spirat

NO SLAVE TO REASON

Braveship Books
www.braveshipbooks.com
Aura Libertatis Spirat

Cover Artwork and Design by Aleksandra Dabic

Book layout by Alexandru Diaconescu
www.steadfast-typesetting.eu

ISBN-13: 978-1-64062-026-1
Printed in the United States of America

*To my wife, Marge, for her honesty, her integrity,
her unerring eye, and the love underneath it all.*

CONTENTS

Acknowledgements

The construction, writing, and research of this story have been a different experience than those I've had with other efforts. There certainly were a number of people who provided not only support, but direct input to what found its way onto a page. And I hope to do them justice here. But the process for me has changed, and I realize that almost any interaction I have with people becomes fodder for my laptop. As a result, I owe a wider debt beyond what I can pay in a few paragraphs. What's more, I have gotten a lot sneakier in gathering input or testing an approach to solving a problem. So, many of my family and friends do not even know that they have helped me. I owe my thanks to them just the same.

Among those I'd like to mention, my wife Marge is at the top. She has been my most stalwart supporter and my most honest critic. This does not always feel like a blessing, but I know it is, and I thank her for it regardless.

Once again, I have to acknowledge my immediate family, John and Jen Everett, Emily and Stephen Hunyadi. Their contributions have come when they least expected it.

I also want to burn a little incense to my brothers Chris Everett, Tim Everett, and Bob Warr whose reviews of drafts have resulted in significant change and whose support has kept me afloat. I have also relied heavily on the comments of my sister, Kate Warr. Kate has been most gracious in letting me harass her directly with particular problems as the plot developed, offering insight that has added greatly to richness of the story.

Others who have been most helpful in the novel's development include my cousin, Randy Everett; his brother, Miles; my good and true friends, Paul Mueller, Mike Lent, Mike Roche, and Tom Taneyhill. Bill and Joanna Mammen also have been good friends and supporters as the novel unfolded.

A tip of my hat goes to Susan Mensch, as well, for introducing me to Mary Elizabeth Garrett. In retrospect, Susan's thoughts were critical in making me realize that a story of 1897 Baltimore without inclusion of the most influential woman living in the city at the time would be a crime.

I'd like to especially thank my re-found friend, Justin Woytowitz, whose artistic mind was invaluable in working out some of the "right-brained" problems I had created for myself. Justin not only has an artistic mind, but, as one of the rising stars among Chesapeake artists, his hands and eyes are pretty damn good as well. (artsbythebaygallery.com and justinwoytowitz.com)

Also, any acknowledgement would be incomplete without extending my appreciation to the Enoch Pratt Library, its staff, its newspaper archives, and its wonderful historical repository, the Maryland Room. If I demonstrated any ability to capture the world of the nineteenth century, it is due in large part to my time spent within the walls of the Maryland Historical Society. The facility, its staff, and its resources are second to none. Please consider supporting this outstanding organization (www.mdhs.org).

Finally, I must mention that the novel owes a great deal of its readability to my editor, Lisa Cerasoli, and her associate, Adrian Muraro. Lisa is a very experienced and talented professional who has the nicest way of correcting glaring abuse of the English language and ignoring gaping holes in one's education. Lisa rules and she may be found on reedsy.com/lisa-cerasoli.

JTE
November 2017

No Slave to Reason's
Cast of Major Characters

Appearing in 1897

Moss Tilghman – ex-slave, student, craftsman, waterman, engineer, chef, savant
Frank Van Sant – managing partner of the Diamond Café
H. Leopold Munsch – neurologist, researcher
Fanny Darlington – actress
Fuzzy Hertzbaugh – doorman for the Academy of Music
Alcott S. Worthy – deceased theater executive
Chauncey Spittle – beat cop, Baltimore City Police
Thomas P. O'Donnell – detective, Baltimore City Police
Enoch Gatch – sergeant, Baltimore City Police
Tunis F. Dean – managing director, the Academy of Music
Mary Elizabeth Garrett – business woman, activist, socialite
Miss Edna May (Klara Drambauer) – comedienne

1897 Baltimore Orioles

Harry Von Der Horst (also Vonderhorst) – brewer, majority owner
Ned (Foxy) Hanlon – manager, minority owner
Wilbert (Uncle Robbie) Robinson – catcher, partner in the Diamond Café
John (Muggsy) McGraw – third baseman, one of the Big Four, partner in the
    Diamond Café
William (Wee Willie) Keeler – rightfielder, one of the Big Four
Hughie Jennings – shortstop, one of the Big Four
Joe Kelley – leftfielder, one of the Big Four

Jack Doyle – first baseman
Heine Reitz – second baseman
Bill Hoffer – pitcher
Joe Corbett – pitcher
Arlie (Doc) Pond – pitcher, physician

Moss Tilghman's Story

Mordecai Stroup – Quaker boatwright
Pastor Lewis – rector, Metropolitan Methodist Episcopal Church
Hattie McQuinn – escaped slave
Joshua McQuinn – escaped slave, son of Hattie McQuinn
Joseph – escaped slave
Esther – escaped slave, wife of Joseph
Felix Barbelin – Jesuit priest, president of St. Joseph's College, mentor/friend
    to Moss
Isaac Myers – business entrepreneur, freedman
Achilles Swann – shanghaied oyster dredger, cook, boxer
Little Lou – shanghaied oyster dredger
Captain Emory – owner/captain of the pilot schooner *Mary Kate*
Caleb Emory – the captain's son
Mr. Workman – the overseer on the *Mary Kate*
Hunter Davidson – commander, Maryland State Oyster Police
Haynie Bradshaw – boxer
Corny Cornish – boxer
Althea Swann – restaurateur
Beatrice Anne (Annie) Rhodes – a lost love
August Williams – Executive Chef, the Rennert House

Any fool knows that working together gets a lot more done than working alone. The human arithmetic of one plus one can often stretch well past two. Our brain is anatomical proof of this. Using only one side can produce some surprising results; but when we use both sides, the surprising can become astonishing.
—Moss Tilghman, 1897

I thought she and I were made for each other. It stands to reason. Opposites attract, don't they?
—Frank Van Sant, 1897

A man who touts the power of reason above all else while ignoring that illogical voice in his head is like a weightlifter who only works one side of his physique. These are complementary human skills that should be developed together.
—Moss Tilghman, 1897

It is through science that we prove, but through intuition that we discover.
—Henri Poincare, 1904

Baltimore
1897

Chapter 1

Howard Street

The bachelor party was already in full roar when Miss Edna May sailed out and moored in the middle of the stage. The lady's bawdy vaudeville act was well-advertised, and the college boys in the first few rows had come fortified and ready to be scandalized. Their hooting and hollering was competing with the Souza march the orchestra was using to open the act. Then the little bald man in the pit raised his baton and gave his band the "pump it up" sign. This blast of brass and string managed to drown out the excited young gentlemen, giving Edna May the opportunity to control the situation. She did so by giving the premed partiers a big smile while spreading her arms wide in welcome and appreciation.

Her gesture had the desired effect and served to exhibit Edna May's obvious charms. She was a frigate of a woman, but her waspish waist offset an impressive prow, allowing landlubbing college boys to dream of the sea.

Edna May was a vision in red. She liked the color, and a lot of it. The entertainer knew well that her admirers thought red signaled easy access. So, she used it as the bark in her barker. She was a milk-bottle-and-baseball carney, reeling in a rube on a first date. She was the Gibson Girl gone bad. She was the woman your mother warned you about and the woman your father kept in his bottom drawer. Her sister, Freida, a spinster who had managed to turn sourness into an art form, charged that if Edna May didn't like the role, she wouldn't have played it for the last twenty years.

Edna May was actually born Klara to Oskar and Itza Drambauer of Highlandtown in East Baltimore. But she loved her stage persona to the degree that she was as much the buxom temptress as she was the dull, working girl who rode the early trolley downtown every morning with the mill workers and the oyster shuckers. From the moment that she walked out onto the Auditorium Theater's stage, she was Miss Edna May, the stuff of masculine dreams. So, it was with genuine pleasure that the star did a suggestive pirouette and finished with a hooker's curtsey that allowed a full look at the goods.

She wore a tight, crimson-striped, shirt-waist blouse with a high collar, puffed sleeves, and not nearly enough buttons. Highlighting her hourglass figure was a wide, black, patent leather belt punctuated with a huge American Beauty rose. Under the belt, she wore a ribbed corset that required a stagehand to use his foot to help tie. The idea was to cause as much speculation as possible as to whether a man could touch his fingers when encircling her waist. She never really understood the appeal of that, but she knew what worked.

Her skirts were a shocking set of silky, wide, crimson cycling bloomers. If your eyes were a little blurry, a malady that many of her admirers suffered, the outfit almost looked like an inverted trumpet, emphasizing her beam and daring to reveal a pair of tiny ankles encased in black silk. These glorious joints were balanced atop cream slippers with square heels, crowned with two more scarlet roses.

Edna May's hair was distantly reminiscent of the red locks she had as a girl, but the color now was the red of a sky at night, and everyone knows what that means come morning. She wore it in a large mass that seemed to be struggling to free itself from an enormous hat full of flowers, ribbons, bird's wings, and other unidentifiable shiny fancies. It was amazing to see it stay on her head as she executed one more deep bow.

"Well, well, well," she began, rubbing her hands together. "It looks like we have a full house tonight. And seeing these boys in the front here, I know that the house is not the only thing full."

With that, she tipped her fist up to her mouth with her thumb extended. This energized the bachelor party even more than they already were, and shouts of "yeah!" came from the revelers.

"I'm told you all want to be medicine men," Edna Mae said, setting up her joke and doing a little shuffle, somehow reminiscent of an Indian dance. "You're from that doctor school up the block. What's it called? John Hopscotch, or something like that, right?"

When the young medical students stopped laughing and jeering, she continued to play with them. "I also hear one of you future proctologists is getting married."

This personal attention from Edna May produced new shouting and a pounding of the back of one of their company. This poor soul looked like he might have been the most schnockered of the bunch, beaming like a fool.

"You know, I applied to work in a doctor's office once, and when we were going over my application, he told me that, on the line marked 'sex,' I should have put 'female,' not 'four times a week.'"

Edna May waited a beat and, while the laughter built, she stuck out her chest and hit them with, "When I told him I wanted to be his medical assistant, he asked me what my qualifications were. I told him that my husband had sold his shotgun. The doctor told me I was hired."

The audience roared. If she had them with those two old jokes, this was going to be easy.

"So, I became a medical assistant, but it wasn't for me. I got into trouble the first day. I brought a basin of boiling water into the patient examination room, just as the doctor asked. But then he went ape and yelled, 'I distinctly said I was going to prick his boil, not boil his...!'"

Edna May trailed off, not finishing the gag. She didn't have to, of course; the audience finished it for her. The comedienne went on to explain that she had to leave the job because the office was full of too many sick people, adding that she didn't like the patients, either.

"One time, I was talking to an old geezer who asked me if the doctor would prescribe something for an erection. I was shocked and told him that the doctor only healed the sick, not raised the dead!"

This groaner got a rim shot from the snare drum and raucous approval from the now warmed-up audience.

"One time, I tried to compliment a new mother on her baby's beautiful hair. Because it was so different from the woman's, I asked if the father had nice, curly hair. The woman told me that she didn't know because he had his hat on at the time."

At this point, she knew that she could say almost anything and the crowd would laugh.

"So, one of you handsome young studs is getting married, huh? Well, my first husband was a pig farmer, and I have to tell you, it was all swine and no roses. So, we divorced and I began dating a professor of English Literature. I remember he asked me if liked Kipling. I told the naughty boy that I didn't know, that I've never kippled before. He shook his finger at me and said that sex is not always the answer. And I said, 'Of course not, it's the question. The answer is yes.'"

Then she delivered this: "That man had a lot of promise, but I didn't marry him. He had an accident and broke it off."

With that, Edna May shifted her hips forward in a fashion that left no mistake as to what was broken off. Her audience was in the aisles. And the orchestra played on.

"My second husband was a road worker. At first, I refused to believe he was a thief, but when I got home, all the signs were there." She paused for the laugh.

"He used to pray to God for one of those fancy new automobiles. I told him God doesn't work that way. So he stole an automobile and prayed for forgiveness." Again she let the joke take hold.

"But it was all over when I caught him snorting cocaine. He told me he doesn't use the stuff, he just likes the way it smells."

Edna May went on with her one-liners for another half-hour, and her audience loved her for it. The gags were a bit moldy, but her timing and presentation were anything but. Salted with sex, her patter was just what her admirers wanted. Her wondrous physique, paired with a repertoire of lewd mannerisms, gave the men in the audience just the hint of sin they were looking for. She capped it all perfectly with another curtsey and a signature exit line that had many standing in applause.

"Please don't think unkindly of me, I'm just a good girl with bad habits," she said with a huge grin and a wave goodbye.

The college boys burst out of the theater, staggering and falling against each other, laughing and inadvertently jostling the other patrons. They were a privileged bunch, dressed in dinner jackets, white shirts with stiff collars, and dark ties. Their attire, once crisp and well-tailored, was now in various stages of disarray. The party had begun in a private room in Baltimore's best hotel and restaurant, the Rennert. There, they dined on Chesapeake delights and drank quality champagne, generating a tab that was sure to elicit acidic comments from their fathers. Hip flasks, charged with Monongahela Rye or Hunter's Pure, were produced in the carriage ride to the show and emptied as Edna May shocked and tickled them. Some were at their limit, especially the young man soon to be married. But other stalwarts wanted to extend the evening and discussed stopping in one of the nearby taverns before heading back to their dorm at Johns Hopkins, just a couple blocks up and across Howard Street.

The nearest café, directly opposite the theaters, was the Diamond, the famous sports palace and watering hole owned by John "Muggsy" McGraw, the star third baseman of the Baltimore Orioles. The young men eyed the glittering, crowded tavern with longing, but they knew the rules. The Diamond was not for them—at least, not yet. One day, they might feel comfortable in there, once they had established themselves, but they knew they had not yet acquired the juice to rub elbows with the place's red-blooded clientele.

In 1897, the Howard Street Theater District was a pulsar, radiating bursts of energy with regularity. Aside from the Diamond, there were plenty of other diversions for young men out on the town—playhouses, beer halls, bars, restaurants, penny arcades, kinetoscope shows, shooting galleries, and even some discreet parlors that offered more personal entertainment. Fun and games abounded, and they drew a wide swathe of humanity.

But there was more to Howard Street than the livelier arts. In an interesting quirk of urban growth, the area also was home to science, including Hopkins University, Baltimore City College, a major hospital, and a wide range of professional offices. Howard Street evolved to bifurcate its art along the right or west side of the street and its science on the left or east side. Noting this split, one young anatomy student, in a moment of clever thought, called the cobblestoned street the corpus callosum of the city, referring to the divide down the middle of the human brain.

As the bachelor party began to dissipate, a few of its hardcore made their way along the street, in, out, and around the area's denizens. They wobbled past well-to-do socialites seeking the unique. Derbied working stiffs out for a night, some even with their wives. Theater people looking to do more than just act. Hard cases haunting the corners, watching the shuffling crowd like wolves eying sheep. Sailors and their doxies. Black men either dressed to the nines or hauling something heavy. Farm boys who would never be able to go home again to stay. All moved in energetic impulses along the pathway that is the gilded dendrite of Howard Street.

It was not long, however, before the boys noticed themselves being followed. As lit as they were, they could easily recall the morning-after stories that circulated in the dorm. Howard Street could be a very dangerous place late at night.

CHAPTER 2

GRAY MATTERS

The notice on the bulletin board was enough of an excuse to avoid studying for various Monday-morning exams. The Johns Hopkins University was offering a free Sunday afternoon lecture by H. Leopold Munsch, MD, renowned brain surgeon and pillar of the staff of Hopkins Hospital. Most of the university's undergraduates would normally shun such an erudite event as if it were dinner with the parents of the girl you just slept with. But Baltimore's vaudeville theaters were closed, and the announcement promised a live demonstration. It was just the thing to give the impression of scholarly interest without requiring too much intellect, an asset lost in the morning fog left by the previous night's revelry.

By one o'clock, the big, tiered classroom was jammed with young men squeezing in the last few hours of the weekend. Some were slowly working their way out of hangovers; those who were not, were afflicted with that special queasiness that rises in ill-prepared students every Sunday afternoon. Nausea, however, was no match for youth since the room could only be called boisterous. The scholars punched each other in the arm, practiced the full nelson on freshmen, played rock-paper-scissors for coins, and laughed in loud bursts while trading rude jokes.

No one expected the lecture to be as entertaining as Miss Edna May's bawdy stand-up at the Auditorium the night before. But Dr. Munsch was supposed to introduce two of his latest patients to the world, and the flyer had proclaimed them "…Amazing savants who were capable of remarkable feats of cerebral dexterity, never evident before post-operative consciousness!" That, at least, sounded somewhat interesting. Anything was better than studying.

At precisely one o'clock, the preeminent physician materialized in the front of the room, seemingly unnoticed by the audience. While he waited for them to quiet, he stood stiffly at a tall podium, arranged a few papers, and glared up at his students. His Van Dyke beard quivered with offense as he pointed it aggressively at the gathered. Behind him hung a heavy, painted canvas illustration of the human brain. The organ's many folds were lined off into various colored sections and sub-areas, and its longitudinal fissure was emphasized to create distinct left and right hemispheres. In front of the doctor, a table held a pitcher of water, two glasses, and various writing and drawing implements. On either side of the podium were two straight-back chairs. Next to the one on the left was a black chalkboard on a wheeled frame. Adjacent to the chair on the right was a large easel, hung with a blank sheet of paper.

The students eventually acknowledged the lecturer's presence and slowly finished whatever important conversation they were having. Just as their noise fell to silence, the double entry at the top of the echeloned seating was pulled open. Because the doors were allowed to slam on their return, all heads swiveled around while the doctor's chin rose even higher in silent, Teutonic fury.

The latecomer was a startling sight. He was a tall, elderly gentleman, well dressed, dignified, and as dark as deepest Africa itself. Recognizing him, several students immediately rose deferentially to offer him their seat. The man made his way down the rows of the gallery to a seat in the middle of the assembly, offering its previous occupant a gracious nod of thanks. More than one student craned to catch the man's eye, hoping for recognition and approval. Instead, the tardy guest directed a small, apologetic smile at Dr. Munsch, who responded with an impatient rattling of his papers.

The speaker rapped sharply on the podium with a long, wooden, rubber-tipped pointer. "Now, if you gentlemen are ready to listen…." His sarcastic emphasis on the word "gentlemen" immediately alienated some of his listeners. Others looked around, knowing that he couldn't have meant them.

"You are about to witness the results of a combination of surgical skill and the amazing restorative power of the human brain. But, as I will demonstrate, the brain works in ways that we do not fully understand. In fact, science just now has embarked on a vast sea of mystery whose shores we cannot yet see. Still, we sail bravely forward, following the currents, observing as we go, confident that science will discover all that there is to discover, as it inevitably shall."

Dr. Munsch's eloquent analogy was lost on the audience. There was some shifting in the seats, some heads placed in hands, and not just a few wiseacre comments, like, "Yeah, and I know what hot air is filling the sails."

The doctor was just warming up.

"If you had prepared for this afternoon's presentation, as I had suggested, you would have read my numerous papers on this wondrous organ. Then, you would know the frontal, the parietal, the occipital and the temporal lobes. And, of course, the cerebellum."

With the mention of each section, the lecturer slapped the pointer against the illustration, more in anger than respect for the subject, making a surprisingly loud pop each time. Two students stopped playing "Hangman" and looked up.

"The continuing, medial cleft that you see here separates the human brain into two distinct cerebral hemispheres."

With even more vigor, he smacked the long rift with his wooden weapon from top to bottom, then rapped the right, then the left hemispheres illustrated in the drawing. He seemed to be getting something out of his system.

"These large areas, right and left, are joined through the corpus callosum, as I'm sure many of you brilliant scholars of anatomy are aware."

Some of the would-be scholars didn't catch the sarcasm, others didn't hear it over their own conversations, and still others would accept any compliment, even if it were insincere.

Dr. Munsch then picked up the beat as he tapped out in rapid fire the various lines and ridges of each section and sub-area on the big drawing of the brain behind him. In singsong condescension, he rattled off the Latin every time the pointer slapped a particular part of the diagram.

"You should also know from your reading that the hemispheres exhibit strong, but not complete, bilateral symmetry in structure. I will demonstrate today, however, that the symmetry is complete when it comes to function. And beyond symmetry, the brain actually compartmentalizes function into one side or the other!"

Again, he used the pointer to support his explanation, pausing for effect. His startling revelation was sure to get their undivided attention. Instead, he received more bottom-shifting and head-supporting. So, he pressed on, impervious to the lack of interest. He cited the latest research on brain function and dropped the names of world-renowned scientists. Then he criticized them, calling them dilettantes and describing their work as merely scratching the surface.

Several students scratched their own surfaces. They didn't know the referenced researchers, of course, because none of them had ever appeared on a playbill. Many did recall with some guilt, however, the need to study for the next day's anatomy exam. They were stuck now without a gracious way to escape, and grace wasn't their longest suit anyway.

"I am here today to tell you that I have gone beyond the scientific efforts of these learned men. I am here to tell you that one side or the other of the brain exhibits specific characteristics—that individual human functions are resident in one side or the other, not both. Progressive science and its standard bearers, like myself, now say that the left side is the home of logical thought; and, on the right, intuition and creativity are resident."

Dr. Munsch ended his comment with great emphasis and once again paused for effect, expecting to see his audience wide-eyed and leaning forward. They were not. Yet, he still let the silence hang a second or two, wanting to spring his intellectual trap at the right moment.

"That's right," he said loudly and confidently. "And this afternoon, I will show you that not only is each hemisphere distinct, but that they are capable of astounding accomplishments when forced to work alone!"

Despite his erudition, when Dr. Munsch looked up once again to his audience, he saw that he had lost them completely. Extended comments were being made out the sides of mouths, muffled laughter could be heard, and closed eyes could be seen scattered throughout the student body. One young man's head was face-down on the desk in front of him. Another slumped sideways and was pushed back by the student he landed upon. The only person in the audience who seemed to be absorbing his words was the black man in the center of the room. He was even taking a note or two.

But this man doesn't count. He is a schwarzer. What is he doing here, anyway? He doesn't belong in a classroom.

Dr. Munsch recalled the tepid reception his lecture and demonstration received the week before from his colleagues at the hospital. Some of those so-called men of science were even hostile to his proposition, calling his work "unfounded." It was the only reason he was even bothering with these feckless undergraduates. He would have a forum for his ideas one way or the other. Many great men were rejected by the established order. He would not let the petty jealousy of his colleagues stand in his way. So, the doctor continued. His demonstration was certain to get attention. He signaled hurriedly to someone standing in the wings.

Immediately, two bulky men in lab coats ushered out onto the stage a sallow woman dressed in a hospital gown. They seated her in the chair to the left of the podium. Her head was down, wrapped in a white linen bandage. Her gray hair, long and oily, hung out from below the wrapping. She was clearly unsteady on her feet and disoriented. She stared through her eyebrows at the rising tiers of students in front of her and gripped the edges of her chair. She looked like she feared attack.

Next, a black man of indeterminate age was escorted out and seated in the chair to the right of the podium. He was dressed and bandaged as the woman was. His eyes could be seen clearly drifting up and to the left, at which point he would drag them back to center, only to have them drift left again. At one point, his look rested on the older man in the gallery. After that, while his eyes still wandered periodically, they always returned to the man in the middle of the tiered seating. This patient seemed a little more in touch than his female counterpart, but that seemed to come and go.

The appearance of the two subjects did bring the students' attention back. The show was about to start.

Gesturing to the woman, the lecturer said, "Allow me to introduce Mrs. Mary Rose Flannigan. Mrs. Flannigan's story is a sad and shocking one. She was working as a charwoman when she arrived home one evening to find her husband inebriated, waving a pistol and threatening suicide. He signaled his serious intent by first shooting the family dog, and then shooting Mrs. Flannigan in the right side of the head. Mr. Flannigan then turned the gun on himself and ended his own ugly, brutal existence."

He now had the audience's full attention.

"Mrs. Flannigan was discovered by the neighbors and rushed to Hopkins, where she came under my care. She was still very much alive when I examined her, but unconscious and suffering from the loss of a great deal of blood. The gunshot all but destroyed the right side of the brain, but the other side, the left side, was fully intact. Within several months, Mrs. Flannigan was conscious again, but able to execute only the most basic functions. It was during postoperative discussions and associated therapy that some very unusual behaviors began to emerge in the patient."

Dr. Munsch glanced up at the students and found them concentrating on the woman. While they were waiting to see the poor soul jump up and do cartwheels across the stage, he mistook this for real scientific interest and was encouraged.

"Allow me to demonstrate."

At this, he signaled the men in white coats. He directed them to turn the chalkboard to the audience, away from Mrs. Flannigan. He then pointed to the first student in the first row.

"You. Give me a four-digit number. Quickly!" he commanded.

The pimpled student started, looked back and forth at his neighbors in desperation, pointed to his chest and stammered, "W-who, me?"

"Yes, yes, of course you. Now hurry!"

The young man was an insect pinned to a lab tray. He stared, bug-eyed and finally said, "Uh, one-five, uh, seven-two."

One of the lab coats wrote this on the chalkboard.

"Now you." Dr. Munsch pointed to another student.

This one managed to get the number, eight-four-two-nine, out in a little less time. By the third and fourth students, the class had gotten the hang of it and, before long, the stage assistant had filled the board with a long string of uninterrupted, incomprehensible numbers.

"Turn the board toward Mrs. Flannigan, gentlemen," the lecturer ordered.

With the wall of numbers in front of her, the doctor asked, "Mrs. Flannigan, do you see the numbers?"

When the woman nodded dumbly, Dr. Munsch directed his helpers to turn the chalkboard back to the audience. She could not have seen the writing for more than a few seconds.

"Now, Mrs. Flannigan," the surgeon said, "can you repeat what you just saw?"

Again, the patient nodded.

"Well, please do so as loudly as you can."

At that, the woman came to life and let out a blood-curdling, involuntary screech. The students jumped out of their seats. Then, in a nerve-plucking voice, Mrs. Flannigan began to rattle off the numbers she had seen. She did it rapidly and in perfect order and when she came to a stop, she let her head drop again and resumed a sort of catatonia.

The students stared with open mouths. A smattering of applause began, but died, seeming somehow inappropriate. A rising buzz filled the room.

"Now, gentleman, I want you to fully erase a quarter of the numbers. Do it randomly. Every time you erase a number, I want you to record it on this easel away from Mrs. Flannigan." The doctor pointed to the paper easel on the right.

When the two assistants had completed their work, Dr. Munsch directed them to turn the incomplete string of numbers back to Mrs. Flannigan.

With the paper easel facing the tiered students, he asked his patient to fill in the blanks. The woman once again came to life with a shriek. And once again, the students jumped. In the same wrenching voice, with no hesitation, she filled in each blank with the correct number. Again, when she finished, she fell back into her semi-comatose state.

The students were amazed and their buzz grew louder. Then, some wag shouted, "It's just a trick of memory!"

"A trick of memory, is it?" The doctor had them. "A simple magician's deceit? I believe you will think differently very shortly."

With that, Dr. Munsch moved around the podium to the chalkboard, erased what was there, and began to enter a complex series of mathematical sentences, full of numbers, symbols, and functions. Turning once again to the audience, he said, "The mathematics scholars among you will recognize the Navier-Stokes equations, a problem in mathematics that is yet to be solved."

He then motioned Mrs. Flannigan to him and extended the chalk to her. She rose to consciousness once again, then stood and stared at the equations. Taking the chalk, the woman began to write slowly at first, and then with increasing speed, she filled the board with her own strings of mathematical functions. A second blackboard was rolled out, and she continued her work on that one as well.

The audience stared in fascination at the woman's furious activity, but Dr. Munsch was not yet finished.

"Now, my young scholars, while Mrs. Flannigan is working on that, I'd like to introduce you to William Johnson." Dr. Munsch pointed to the man sitting on the right.

William Johnson had sat quietly during Mrs. Flannigan's demonstration, and there was little to indicate that he knew she was even there. Even as she wrote one mathematical sentence after another and a third chalkboard was being rolled out, he stared at the audience stolidly.

"Mr. Johnson's story is quite different but just as tragic. Or, maybe not," the lecturer intoned mysteriously. He was starting to enjoy his own show. "William here was a day laborer, a construction worker on the new Howard Street train tunnel, directly below us. A dangerous job, certainly. Two years ago, he was struck in the head by a brick dropped from a great height and he fell into a coma.

He came under my care because of the uniqueness of his injury. The entire left side of William's brain was crushed, yet the right side was undamaged.

"About a year ago, Mr. Johnson emerged from the coma, physically weak, but somehow still sentient, although in a very special way. There are many things that he needs help in doing. However, in this, he needs no help."

With that, the surgeon moved to the paper easel and tore off the used sheet, leaving a large, blank paper surface.

"William, would you like to draw?" he asked the patient.

The man nodded slowly.

"Then, please show us what you see," the doctor pointed to the paper and the table full of pencils, pens, and colored chalk.

Mr. Johnson stood and turned the easel in a way that allowed him to see the audience while working on the paper. Because of the angle, the students could also see what was being produced. He began, first with swift, broad strokes of pencil, then switched to ink and then to the chalk. As he did, an image of the gathered assembly began to take shape. He, like Mrs. Flannigan, fell into a trancelike state, working energetically and mechanically. Only on occasion did he look directly at his subjects. Before long, what emerged was a clear, realistic and artistic rendering of a tiered room full of lively, expressive young men with an older, black man sitting at their center. The assembled were amazed as they watched the busy scene emerge from the man's inner eye.

Dr. Munsch moved to the center of the stage between his two patients, each still working earnestly at their tasks. He spread his arms and gestured to them.

"So, you can see for yourselves, gentlemen, that the human brain is indeed lateralized and that it is capable of incredible feats, even when one side is forced to work alone. Here on the left, a woman with no right hemisphere applying logic in the form of mathematics! On the right, a man with no left hemisphere, demonstrating creativity through art! One side seems to be compensating for the loss of the other. Neither of these people had exhibited a scintilla of these skills prior to their accidents. This has obvious important and untold ramifications for individuals, for medicine, for science, for society itself!"

This aggrandizing statement elicited a growing applause from the students. Some began to stand, then they all stood and clapped, with one exception. The gentleman in the middle of the audience sat quietly with a raised hand, attempting to ask a question.

Dr. Munsch basked in the approbation, even bowed like a showman. However, when he noticed the raised hand, his smile dropped and he backed away from the audience. He quickly directed the white-coated attendants to interrupt Mrs. Flannigan and Mr. Johnson and lead them away. Then, he too disappeared.

As the students filed out clucking about the marvelous things they had just witnessed, the black man remained seated. Again, he ignored those who would catch his eye, and he waited. When all were gone, he made his way down to the stage were William Johnson's artwork had been left. He looked at the effort closely, noticing the clarity of his own presence among the students. He was obviously the focal point of the drawing and the essence of the artist's expression.

The gentleman tore the artwork from the easel, rolled it up, tucked it under his arm, and exited the auditorium.

Chapter 3

Miss Fanny Darlington

I was sitting at a table in the corner of the room, leisurely finishing breakfast and thinking about paying the week's bills. It was early in the morning, but not so early that I wasn't well into my second cup of coffee. It was just me and the Diamond at that hour. I have never been able to decide whether I like the place quiet or raucous. Both have their appeal.

As I reached for a last crumb of cornbread, the most beautiful woman I have ever seen came through the door. She emerged from the kind of bright light that those who claim to have come back from the dead talk about.

It was a chilly morning, but bright and clear for a February in Baltimore. As the sun rose, its light struck the three gigantic, arched windows on the second floor of the Academy of Music directly across the street. The sunshine then caromed in full bolt into the double, cut-glass panels of our front entrance and through the big, stained glass window over it. The Diamond's broad run of Parisian mirrors picked up the shaft and shot it first through the rows of half-empty bottles behind the bar, then over to any number of other reflectors that decorated the now empty saloon. The effect was spectacular. Color. Color everywhere. And she brought the brightest of it in with her. That color tattooed my first sight of Fanny Darlington onto the surface of my heart. All I could do was stare.

The sun's show must have blinded her at first, but stepping uncertainly, she made her way down the two-step entrance into the Diamond's main taproom. Hugging herself from the chill, she looked lost, vulnerable, seeing nothing and wondering about the wisdom of her decision to come in. That look, too, has been etched upon some inner part of me.

17

Speechless, I stood in a scramble and scraped the chair as I did. This made her turn, lean forward, and squint in my direction. There were a lot of feathers floating around somewhere above blond hair and the brim of a big blue hat. I was distracted only for a flash, though, because her eyes drew me hypnotically. They were simultaneously soft and achingly serious.

Expecting at least some sort of greeting and getting none, she hid her discomfort by capturing, then tucking away a rogue wisp of yellow hair. I still said nothing, but not from choice.

"Pardon, me, sir," she said. "I know you don't get many ladies in here, and I hope you'll forgive me, but I need some help. I could find no other gentleman on the street."

Don't get many ladies in here? I thought. What'd she mean by that crack? Now, this woman was beautiful all right, no question about that. But there's no more beautiful thing in the world than the Diamond Café. It was beside the point that she was right about our female clientele.

It didn't take long for me to forgive her, and I finally found my voice. "Yes, yes, come in. You are most welcome, young lady. How can I be of assistance?"

How stupid, oafish! She was about my age, and anyone who saw her would certainly never refer to her as "young lady," unless they were eighty years old. She was young, but she carried herself with a sophistication that demanded respect, not condescension.

As I came to greet her properly, she smiled at me and it felt like I had walked face-first into the back of an iron skillet. What was this alien power she wielded? Normally, I'm not so flummoxed. No one would ever mistake me for a real ladies man, but I've had my successes, as modest as they may be. In fact, women and I get along just great. Still, I stood there like a totem pole as my brain tried to decide what to do next.

A few furrows marred her perfect brow and she hesitated a moment, probably deciding whether the idiot in front of her was capable of helping anyone at all. But she plunged on just the same.

"Sir, my name is Fanny Darlington," she said, extending a gloved hand. "I work across the street."

These words induced an even deeper state of granite in me. As mentioned, what is across Howard Street is the world-renowned Academy of Music and what turned me into a complete stunned ox was her name. Fanny Darlington. It is the name that had been advertised in lights on the theater's huge marquee for the last week. The same name and dazzling songstress that the local dogs had been speculating over just last night!

The lady had been given top billing. I guess that was something, since just the week before, it had been the bigshot Lillian Russell whose name was up there. The large poster by the theater's entrance crowed about Miss Darlington being fresh from a European tour and that tickets for her show were going fast.

To be honest, this meant little to me. I hate most of the stuff that appears on stage, any stage. Give me Union Park and the Orioles' precision baseball any day. It is a mystery to me why Baltimore packs the Academy of Music or the Auditorium next door, or any of the other playhouses in the neighborhood. Regardless of whether it is vaudeville, theater, a troupe of tumblers, a concert artist, or the occasional opera, greasepaint and hot air are not my meat. The last time I was across the street was to see Jacob Schaefer, Champion Billiard Player of the World, in the Auditorium's brand-new rooftop garden. Now that was an exhibition of real skill, exactitude, and geometry. Worth every bit of the four it cost me.

"Sir, are you all right?" she finally asked of me.

"Oh, yes, yes of course," I spit out as life began to flow back into me. I took her hand as if it were a glass butterfly. I'm sure it caused some speculation as to my manhood. So, I hurried to make up for my lack of demonstration. "Please, tell me how I can help."

"Well, I'm already late for rehearsal, the front of the building seems to be locked, and there is a large man lying across the stage door in the alley. I didn't get too close, but he appeared to be quite intoxicated. I was wondering if you would...."

"Say no more, Miss Darlington," I said in a manly voice. "I'll take care of it right now."

As the managing partner and oft-times bouncer of the Diamond, I was quite experienced in this sort of thing. Drunks were my business. Drunks and baseball players—two closely related species of human being. My partners, and the majority owners of the business, were one John McGraw and one Wilbert Robinson. Yes, that's right, the one and only Muggsy McGraw and the accomplished Uncle Robbie of the 1894, 1895, and 1896 World Champion Baltimore Orioles.

Drawing myself up to my full height of five foot eight and a half, I brushed the accumulated crumbs off of my vest, pushed my hair back behind my ears, found my top coat and derby, and escorted the dream back through the Diamond's front doors. Out on the sidewalk, I extended my arm for her to take as I had seen real gentlemen do, and with her hand lying lightly on my forearm, I piloted her out onto the river of cobblestones and over the streetcar tracks of Howard Street.

"A lady of your quality shouldn't have to put up with this, Miss Darlington. I'm so sorry." I knew this sounded even lamer than my earlier utterance.

"It's not your fault, Mr.…ah—"

"Van Sant, Frank Van Sant," I offered. "Please, call me Frank." Even that sounded smarmy.

"Well," she started, not using the familiar I offered her, "there's no reason why you should feel badly. You are a true gentleman to help me."

I did feel bad, or rather, badly. I felt embarrassed for Baltimore, for Howard Street, and for myself. Here Fanny Darlington deigned to perform in my home-town, to honor us, and this is how we treated her?

"You've come all the way to Baltimore to delight us with your terpsichorean skills. You shouldn't have to be exposed to this."

Why was I talking like that? I had never used the word "terpsichorean" in my life before that moment. I don't know where it came from. I was even guessing that it meant singing. It doesn't.

"I'm from Washington, D.C., and I'm an actress," she corrected me.

"All the way down there?" I asked about the thirty-minute train ride. Actress? Maybe I should have read the marquee a little closer.

My latest gaff was not likely to be my last, so I decided to just shut up and enjoy her proximity and the smell of her cologne.

I knew the alley of which she spoke, since it was opposite the Diamond's front window. It was a long, dark passageway that ran between the Academy and the Auditorium and often disgorged an array of chattering chorus girls and extras, escaping through the back stage exits of the two theaters.

We proceeded directly to the door in question, all the way at the end. Sure enough, there was a man lying on his side across the doorway. A very large man. Fat. Expensive overcoat. Spats. A paper bag, spilling an empty shorty of Pikesville Rye, lay nearby.

"Come now, my man. Get up. Time to find your way home." I intoned the closing-hour incantation while tugging at his coat. As I did, he slid down the door a bit and rolled completely over onto his back. It was then that I realized that he was not drunk. He was dead, or perhaps both dead and drunk. Although it was clear one had trumped the other.

The lady gasped and the back of her hand flew to her mouth. Now, I also have had some experience with dead men. Anyone who has spent time in Baltimore has. We have our own means of population control. But my experience was hardly needed, since the round hole in the man's forehead made it plain enough, even for a fragile, protected thing like Miss Fanny Darlington.

"My God, Mr. Van Sant! He's dead," she breathed, stating the obvious. Maybe she wasn't as sharp as she was beautiful. To me, that was not a particular drawback.

"That certainly appears to be the case. Was he alive when you first saw him?"

"Yes. No. I don't know. He was lying just as he was when we walked up."

"Do you know him?" I asked.

"No, of course I don't know him! Why would you ask me that?"

"I'm sorry. I wasn't implying anything. Just curious."

Detective fiction is what I like to do when I'm not running the Diamond or watching the Birds play their "scientific" baseball. I love trying to think through a novel's clues to uncover the writer's web of logic. As a matter of fact, I was just finishing Arthur Conan Doyle's compendium of short stories, *The Adventures of Sherlock Holmes.*

I suggested the lovely Miss Darlington not touch anything and I began to look at the body. Under the overcoat was a well-cut morning coat, sporting a gold watch chain. His shirt collar had been pressed into wings over a white shirt with a stiff front. Onyx studs ran up to a black, four-in-hand tie made up as a neckband, punctuated with a gold stickpin. He obviously was not a victim of a robbery. We pick them cleaner than that in my town.

The small hole in the man's forehead was plain enough, and it was easy to see that he had been shot from the front from close range. Powder burns suggested that maybe a small pistol had been held right up to the head. But there was more. The man had been slugged with something, as well. There was a good-sized dent in his head, but not much blood anywhere.

I then looked around the alley. The usual street trash was salted with empty bottles, cigar butts, and old playbills from the theaters. There were a few busted crates, a couple of empty barrels, and a dilapidated hand truck up against the back wall. I checked for a hat, or maybe a case he had been carrying, but I found nothing of interest. It would have been nice to have spotted a murder weapon or something, as well. Stupid. Who would drop and leave a perfectly good pistol?

The actress stood there, horrified, but riveted on the corpse. Then she said, "You know, Mr. Van Sant, I may have met that poor man before. In the theater. I mean backstage. But I'm not sure. I meet so many people."

I was about to check the victim's pockets when the stage door was pulled open by Old Man Hertzbaugh, the Academy's stage door keeper. Behind him was a head of brassy, blonde hair that let out a loud scream and then collapsed into the ready arms of a tall, thin, dapper man sporting a pencil mustache and a shocked look. Interested others were behind them.

"Fuzzy, you'd better get the cops," I said to the geezer, who was leaning over and peering at the stiff. I wanted to let him know that I was not the perpetrator of the crime. Hertzbaugh hated me for any number of reasons that I will not go into now, and would have tried to pin it on me immediately.

The alley was getting crowded, and I wanted to separate myself from the dead body as quickly as I could. "Never mind, I'll find a cop." I began to guide Miss Darlington back to the street. I took her in tow, my arm circling her waist for support. She really didn't seem to need it, but I wasn't going let the opportunity pass.

Just as I was trying to think of something important or comforting to say, I looked up to see a large, dark, sinister figure blocking the head of the passageway. He was dressed in a long coat and wore a sort of high, rounded topper. The club he held in his hand kept finding its way into his other in a menacing, come-and-get-it sort of way.

When we stopped, he said, "Now, Frankie, what would you be doing in that dark alley with a woman at this time of the morning?"

Baltimore City Police Patrolman Chauncey Spittle was a mean-spirited, obnoxious, officious son of a bitch. There were probably a few other ways to describe the man, but they all would have been pretty close to that. The badge he wore on his chest was just license to annoy, frustrate, and anger. He played by most of the rules when it suited him, and even made up a few himself. Chauncey was a beat cop, and his beat was Baltimore's Theater District. On his turf, bums, panhandlers, or derelicts didn't stick around. Partying revelers didn't stay too long, and drunken college boys often found a throbbing lump on their skull that matched their morning hangovers. No stage door johnny, celebrity hound, photographer, newspaperman, or any other lowlife went unrousted in Spittle's patch.

The cop loved the theater as much as I disliked it, and he never missed an opera, a play, a variety show, or an individual act that was staged. Most wouldn't, when the tickets were free. Because of management's largesse, he was very protective of these purveyors of art, culture, music, and the occasional cheap laugh.

The Monumental and the Maryland Theaters, around the corner on Franklin, also received his good intentions. I'm sure that the many highbrow diversions the District offered were very soothing to such a sensitive soul. I'm just as sure that those Vaudeville acts featuring skin and innuendo were uplifting for him as well. I'm further convinced that his associations with the impresarios of these palaces of entertainment were as soothing to his wallet as they were to his spirit.

Unfortunately, Spittle's sensitivity was spent on the theaters, and there was little left for the other enterprises in the area, including my own tavern. If you weren't directly connected to one of the theaters, or you resided on what the cop thought was the "wrong side of Howard Street," you were no better than Shanty Irish, and they were not to be tolerated by anyone. It was some solace to us non-artsy types, however, that he reserved a special brand of hostility for Johns Hopkins and its snotty students just up the block. These Baltimore inhabitants he held in his lowest regard.

When Muggsy, Uncle Robbie, and I first moved into the café in the middle of the 500 block, it came as a real surprise that we weren't welcome. We thought that we'd be hailed as part of the ongoing party amid the bright lights and stuffed shirts. But it turned out that the theaters didn't want us there. It seemed we were of an inferior class of entertainment. This was a judgment of some cheek, given that the very week we arrived, the Academy of Music staged "The Lilliputians," an abysmal and disturbing act featuring a troupe of damnable German midgets.

Whether it was the Diamond, another bar, one of the many hash houses along the street, or even McGinnity's shooting gallery, it got the cold shoulder from theater management. Once we got our feet on the ground, this situation thawed a little, though. The theaters began to realize that we helped put fannies in their seats.

The Orioles were enormously popular, local heroes who offered the most coveted of assets—championship bragging rights. The team and its Big Four spent a lot of hours bending their elbows in the Diamond. So, the chance to hobnob with the likes of McGraw, Robinson, Willie Keeler, Hughie Jennings, and other stars may have brought more Baltimoreans to Howard Street than the theaters themselves did. It didn't take the proverbial two-by-four upside the head for the stuffy managing directors to swallow a little pride. Money has a way of doing that.

But Officer Chauncey Spittle was different. He maintained a higher standard. As a result, I would have liked to lay a little non-proverbial wood upside the cop's skull myself, preferably a Louisville Slugger. The dolt persisted in maintaining a strict class structure on Howard Street, and we show business outsiders were definitely on the wrong side of the trolley tracks.

I remember one afternoon, John McGraw, in a highly unusual interlude from his usual flying frenzy, tried to reason with Spittle. We were standing on the sidewalk with Wilbert Robinson, outside of the Diamond. The policeman had just given us an earful for trash in the alley behind the bar.

"Now, Chauncey, I know you're a big fan of entertainment," Muggsy started.

"That's Officer Spittle to you, McGraw," the cop cut in, pronouncing his name "Spy-tull."

"What's more entertaining than a baseball game?"

"I hate baseball," the man in blue said. "Low class. Stands full of drunks. Fights on the field."

"It's sport, Chauncey, sport. It entertains people, a lot of people. Just because the seats are wooden and its outside doesn't mean it isn't everything vaudeville or opera is."

"Not the same, McGraw," the big man growled.

"Sure it is. We're artists, too. It's not easy doing what we do. Takes skill. Practice. Call it rehearsal, if you like."

"Kid's stuff," Spittle answered eloquently.

"You think Wee Willie's magic with a bat is kid's stuff? He hit .384 last year!"

"Means nothing to me, McGraw. What's more, the way you and your team play, the language you use—you should be banned from the league. It's disgraceful."

"It certainly is not." The color began to rise on McGraw's neck. "It's scientific! Everything is done for a reason. That's the way skipper Hanlon wants it, and that's what we give him. We are scientists of the horsehide sphere. You might say the Birds are a team of goddamned ball-ologists!"

"Some fool might say that, but it wouldn't be me," was the reply.

"What did you call me?"

Muggsy could never hold it for long, even when talking to a cop.

"You heard me, punk. Now, clean up the alley behind your place or the fine will be bigger next time," the badge answered as he pulled out his citation book.

That's when Uncle Robbie, who had been standing quietly, rocking on his heels, waiting, grabbed McGraw around the middle and lifted him off the ground. It looked like he had just picked up an angry blue crab. Appendages were flailing, foam was bubbling from his mouth, and his eyes were bulging. Robinson simply turned around and walked back into the café with him. Spittle ignored the tantrum, stuck the ticket in the door, and sauntered away, swinging his billy and whistling Tom Turpin's "Harlem Rag."

"Officer Spittle," I said. "Good to see you this morning. I've got some business for you."

As we emerged from the alley, Spittle only ignored my mispronunciation because he immediately knew the beauty on my arm.

"I beg your pardon, Miss Darlington. I didn't recognize you at first." The policeman had actually removed his topper and gave the actress a little bow.

"No need to apologize, Chauncey. We were coming to look for you anyway," I said.

"I wasn't apologizing to you, Van Sant, and this is the last time I'm going to tell you to address me properly."

"If I did that, Chauncey, I'd be spending an overnight in the Pine Street lockup."

As the cop began to puff up like a blowfish, Fanny Darlington spoke. "Officer, there is a dead man in the alley." It sounded like a stage line.

"What? A dead man? In the alley?" The cop began to deflate. "Don't either of you move," he ordered and ran down the passageway.

Spittle found the body and Hertzbaugh going through its pockets. I watched as the cop began berating the doorman, sticking his club into the man's sunken chest. Finally, the old guy handed over a gold pocket watch and something else I couldn't see. Then, he pointed back up the alley, directly at me. The bastard.

The cop gave three loud blasts on his whistle. Then, with some harsh orders, he directed the group of people craning through the stage door back inside. He walked purposefully to us standing in the mouth of the alley.

"Van Sant, Fuzzy Hertzbaugh tells me he found you with the body. What's your story?" he asked, none too gently.

The still lovely Miss Darlington then spoke again. "Officer, I was the one who found the body. I thought he was overcome with drink. Mr. Van Sant was just helping me move the man so I could get to rehearsal."

"You moved the body, Frankie?" the cop accused.

"No, no, officer." The actress was leaping to my defense! "We thought he was inebriated, not—"

"Like I said, Ch—officer, we were coming to interrupt your breakfast."

"What time did you find the body, Miss Darlington?" With a daggered look at me, Spittle had started to do his job.

"I think it must have been about seven o'clock," she answered and looked at me for verification. I nodded encouragingly.

"Do you know the man or have you seen him before?"

This time, she was not put out by the question. "No, sir. I do not know the man and I cannot recall ever seeing him before." Once again, she looked at me, this time with an imploring look in her deep green eyes. I said nothing.

"Did you see anyone else around when you found him," the cop pressed.

As she was shaking her head, I said, "Miss Darlington has had quite a shock, Chauncey. Perhaps you can question her later. Right now, I think she should come with me to the Diamond for a small restorative."

"Fat chance of that, Van Sant," he growled. "Miss Darlington is staying with me at the moment. Why don't you beat it? But don't go anywhere. The Precinct will want to talk to you."

With that, he dismissed me, took charge of the angel, and together they stood on Howard Street and waited for the several other policemen now converging on the murder scene.

The opportunity to get away from him was too good, so I avoided protest and headed back across the street to the Diamond. As I did, Fanny Darlington graced me with a beatific smile of thanks that will be hard to forget.

The next time I saw her was under less than ideal circumstances.

Chapter 4

In the Diamond Café

"But why did she lie, Robbie?"

I was leaning on the bar and Robinson was behind it, dusting bottles—not that they ever got dusty in our place. Next to me sat Moss Tilghman, the Diamond's ace cook and resident source of all knowledge. He was half-listening, leaning on his elbows and perusing *The Baltimore Sun,* spread out before him.

The Orioles were about to leave for spring training in the next few weeks, and Uncle Robbie was getting in a little last-minute bartending. Wilbert thought being able to bartend on occasion was the best part of owning a bar. In truth, he was quite good at it. He could pull an Eagle tap with the best of them, of course, but he also could concoct punches, sours, slings, cobblers, shrubs, toddies, flips, and a variety of other mixed drinks. He even knew just the right amount of bitters to use to turn these wonders into "cocktails." Robbie's cocktails were so famous that they drew people from far-flung, foreign countries like New Jersey. It's hard to imagine how anyone could think the Diamond was not classy.

"Frank, people lie to you all of the time," the Orioles' catcher answered.

"But she didn't lie to me, she lied to Spittle. Wait, what do you mean people lie to me?"

"They do, Frank. Right, Moss?"

"Uh huh," the cook agreed.

"What the hell is that supposed to mean?" I whined.

"No big deal, Frank. You're just that kind of person," Robinson said. "Take the other day. You forced John to lie to you."

"What! I caught McGraw red handed, paying his bowling debts out of the bar's till," I squawked.

"You hurt his feelings," Robbie observed.

"Uh huh," Moss agreed again.

"Hurt his feelings! I saw him grab a fistful of paper and stuff it in his britches. Two or three dollars were hanging out of his pocket! Then, the crumb said he won the cash on the lanes, and we all know better than that. He can play third base, but he's no bowler. Those hustlers downstairs love to see him coming."

"Uh huh," Moss agreed once more with emphasis.

"Frank, cut Muggsy a break. A good chunk of that money is his. He needed it."

"What kind of business are we going to have, thinking like that? No business is what. A chunk of it's his—after we pay the bills! You know that."

"After you pay the bills, especially me," threw in the cook.

"Moss, you know you'll get paid," Robinson said. "We can't afford not to pay you."

Robinson was absolutely right. Moss is the Diamond. We fool ourselves thinking the team draws the crowd, when in truth it's Tilghman's terrapin stew, oysters Baltimore, crab fluffs, crispy duck, rockfish almandine, fried chicken, venison stew, hasenpfeffer, and lots more Chesapeake and Eastern Shore delights. That menu of his is a perfect blend of art and science.

"Anyway, I let it drop, didn't I?"

"After a big stink, you let it drop. Folk just find it easier to lie to you, that's all I'm saying," Robinson observed.

"Well, all that's beside the point. What I'm trying to tell you is that Fanny Darlington lied to the cops and I'd like to know why."

"It's easy to lie to the cops, too," Moss offered. This, too, was something the cook knew about. He had spent a good portion of his youth either dodging slave hunters or whatever else was being used as law enforcement a few years ago. "By the way, you boys been reading about the gold that's laying around on the ground in the Klondike?" he asked.

"What's a klondike?" Robinson asked.

"Where. The Klondike is in the Yukon Territory. In Canada. Seems the whole world is headed up there. Been thinking about it myself."

Now, this was a serious threat. We couldn't afford to lose Moss. The Diamond would suffer, even with all of its other attractions. The bar, the bowling alleys, the gymnasium, the card rooms, the billiards, the sports library, even the electric Orioles scoreboard were just window dressing compared to the food that came out of Moss's kitchen. I forgot about Fanny Darlington's lie.

"Moss, do you know how cold it is up there?"

I knew his Eastern Shore roots and I knew how much he hated the cold. Baltimore was as far north as he wanted to go and as far south as he would go. I also suspected that I was about to get hit up for a raise.

"That's true, Frank, but a few ounces of gold can buy a lot of firewood."

"You know it's not that easy. Plus, it'll take forever to get there. It's not even in the U.S. What is it, two thousand miles away?"

"Three thousand plus some," Moss answered.

"That's a long way to go to freeze to death." I was building my argument and thought I just might be able to fend off the possible touch I was about to receive. "In fact, with what we pay you now, it's like picking up gold right here on the floor."

Robinson rolled his eyes and Moss finally looked up from the newspaper.

"Frank, you and I are friends, but sometimes you put a lot of pressure on that," Tilghman said with a certain look in his eye.

I knew I had gone too far. Moss was taking my desperate attempt to dissuade him from leaving as if I were saying we paid him for doing nothing. I also knew that he normally gave me, and some of my lamer comments, the benefit of the doubt. That's when I realized he actually was working the edge for a raise—and I had just handed him the "I'm insulted" trump card!

Sensing defeat on the horizon, I shifted to an emotional tack, but it felt like I was throwing empty trashcans at a raging assailant as he backed me into a corner somewhere.

"Moss, you know we need you and your magical menu. Robbie, John, and I need you. The Diamond needs you. Baltimore needs you," I soft-soaped.

"How much?" he pounced.

I looked for Robbie, but he had moved down the bar to wipe off some clean glasses.

"How much?" I stalled.

"Yeah, how much do you need me? Let me guess. I'd say you needed me at least another thirty bucks a week." His opening bid was outrageous.

So, I was outraged. "What? Thirty dollars! No way I—we—can do that! Maybe five, and that's a lot." I began my roll over.

"I wonder how much a train ticket to San Francisco is?" Moss mused.

"Okay, seven and that's it."

"Make it twenty and I'll stay awhile longer. No promises."

"Cripes! Okay, ten, but you have to agree to stay for a period of time. Two years."

"Ten's not enough for that. I want Mondays off, too. The bar's closed in the morning anyway."

"What?" I yelped. "You already have Sunday off!"

"That's right. I want Monday too. I have a life to live. Things to do. It's fifteen more and Monday, or I'm getting me some mukluks."

"I don't want to know what you do on your days off."

"They're boots, Frank. The Chilkoots wear them in the Yukon."

"Chilkoots or galoots, I don't give a damn. It's not right, but okay. Twelve and you stay for two years at least. Monday mornings off."

"Whatever you say." Moss knew about escaping whenever he needed to do so. So, he extended his big hand with a grin just as big. I wasn't as happy.

In truth, I'd just as soon see some more cash find its way into Moss's pocket. Better than giving it to McGraw's creditors. Moss and I are close friends and have been ever since we opened the Diamond. Over the years, he's proven that time and again. I try to do the same whenever I can, but he always seems to be a step ahead when it comes to doing a good turn. Willie Keeler notwithstanding, Moss is the nicest person anyone could ever meet.

But, as good a man as Moss is, it's his brain that's most impressive. His knowledge of art and culture wrestle around in that big head of his with understanding of the latest scientific breakthrough and uses for the newest mechanical wonder. Where he got it all, I don't know. I know he's had some schooling, but how much, I'm not sure. I do know that he's always reading something, even in the middle of our busiest night. One time, I asked him about a book he was reading as he stirred something into a huge kettle of crab soup. He had the thing propped up between a tub of butter and a can of shucked oysters so that he could see it. He told me that it was the Hoosier Poet, Riley. When I cracked that there ain't no crab soup in Indiana, he told me that poetry teaches rhythm and good restaurants operate that way.

Invariably, he and I find each other after closing time. With a bottle of Mount Vernon rye or a pitcher of Eagle between us, we discuss whatever is on our minds before we decide whether it's worth going home. Neither of us is married nor has family anymore, but it's not unusual for him to talk about his kin and his days on Poplar Grove Plantation over in Queen Anne's County back in the '40s and '50s.

I remember one time Moss said that when Massa Emory wasn't beating him, he was teaching him to read. It seemed that the old bastard was going blind and needed someone to read to him. Books, newspapers, letters, documents, anything. Moss chuckled then, saying that the fool didn't know what he was creating. The sizable library the cook keeps in a storeroom back behind the pantry attests to that. His friends are always giving him something to read, sometimes to review. Those friends aren't me, however. I limit my reading to ledgers, balance sheets, detective novels, and box scores.

The body of acquaintances and cronies Moss spends time with is also amazing. I've seen him sitting at one of the tables late at night or early in the morning with an array of Baltimore's notables. He's introduced me to none other than James L. Kernan, the owner of three of Baltimore's theaters and the Kernan Hotel around the corner. Another time, I heard him explaining something to Professor Dan Gilman, president of Hopkins University, located just up the street. Still another time, he was talking diseases with that stuffed ham, Dr. Halsted of the hospital. How he met these guys, I don't know. But late one night in the kitchen, I watched him teach Walter Damrosch of the New York Symphony how to make a Maryland crabcake. I've seen him hold court with a gaggle of medical students and later the same day, discuss the merits of various Italian tenors with gray-templed men in tuxedos.

Don't get me wrong. On the other end of the scale, Moss counts musicians, bookies, grifters, gamblers, mollies, baseball players, and newspapermen as friends as well. You might say he spreads his personality and wisdom around.

Once, I made the mistake of referring to his friends as confederates, and the man made it abundantly plain that the term offended him with its inaccuracy and insensitivity. A Confederate would not want him as a friend and vice versa, he explained. A lot of folks are still fighting a war that ended over thirty years ago. So, in a hurried attempt to make up for my political gaff, I tried flattery, referring to Moss as a jack-of-all-trades. Again, I was corrected in no uncertain terms. He called himself instead, a Renaissance man, saying it was simply a matter of depth and interest. When I found out what a Renaissance man was, I couldn't argue. That's exactly what he is. And I will tell you this: not only is Moss Tilghman smart, he is the toughest, bravest man I ever met, black or white. True as that is, though, he told me once that he learned a long time ago that smart is a hell of a lot more useful than either tough or brave.

As Moss turned back to his newspaper, John McGraw and Willie Keeler arrived with some self-fanfare, McGraw's arm around his friend's shoulders.

"Hello, you sports cranks!" he bugled. "Mr. Keeler here was just telling me that this is the year we win our fourth pennant. With Stevie Brodie gone and Jake Stenzel on the team, 'The Genius' not only got us a better bat, but we got smarter, too. Willie thinks we're a lock. He's even got me ready to head to Macon next month."

McGraw's pronouncement was made as he climbed onto his favorite barstool —the one nearest the door. That man loves being seen. Robbie had returned to us and set a frothy mug of Eagle down in front of the third baseman and slid a bowl of hard pretzels alongside it. When he looked at Willie, the little man waved him off and took the stool next to me.

The Orioles were sitting atop the baseball world in the spring of 1897. The team had won three pennants in a row. Ned Hanlon, the managerial "genius" had held the team together. And it didn't look like the Cleveland Spiders, Baltimore's rivals over the last couple of years, could make a run at the championship this year. Keeler was right, the Birds looked invincible.

"Moss, what do you think? Time to tie the record for consecutive championships?" McGraw, like everyone else, respected the cook's opinion.

I knew Moss had a passing interest in baseball. How could he not, working at the Diamond? I remember him saying that he had even played some. But, I also knew that he was more amused by the players and their antics than he was a true crank of the team, or a follower of baseball in general, for that matter.

"John, I don't know what Moss thinks, but I'll tell you that it wouldn't be hard for Hanlon to make the team smarter than it is," I observed.

That snide joke got a soft push in the back from Willie, a laugh from Robbie, and a snort from Moss. McGraw, as usual, was offended.

"Frank, there you go again. Always with the negative," responded McGraw. "And you call yourself a baseball man."

In truth, I was crazy about the team. I loved everything about them. I was proud of their success and tickled for my hometown. I followed them religiously and would get belligerent when anyone ran them down. I was loyal to each and every one of the players—with the possible exception of Jack Doyle, who was very difficult to tolerate under any circumstances. I was the one who got them into bed after a night of heavy drinking and got them up before a game. I was the one who introduced them to their wives, even arranged McGraw's recent wedding. I was the one who managed a lot of their finances, bailed them out when they needed bailing out, and I was their big brother when they needed me. And I felt that all of that personal investment gave me a little leeway to point out the occasional wart.

"Frank's not negative," Moss said. "He just looks at the debits and the credits at the same time."

"Seems he sees more debits than credits, whatever they are," McGraw replied petulantly, taking a long pull from the mug.

"To answer your question, John," the cook said, "I think, on paper, you all look mighty strong this year."

"On paper and in the field," McGraw responded.

"What do you mean, Moss?" Willie asked.

"Well, I just think it's awfully hard to keep a team's spirit, their chemistry, at such a high level, year after year," Moss said.

"We've never had a stronger bunch than this year. Even the pitching is solid with Doc Pond healthy and Corbett past his rookie year. Barring injuries, no one will touch us," said the third baseman, missing the cook's point.

"Yeah, there's always injuries," said Robinson, the oldest member of the team.

Those who knew National League baseball, in fact, considered "Foxy" Ned Hanlon, the Orioles' manager and part owner, something of a genius. It was the term used by the nation's sports writers who, although well known for their normal concoction of hyperbole and outright lies, actually believed the tag.

In fact, Hanlon was about to take a team of superb ball players down to Macon, Georgia for spring training for the fourth year in a row. It was a team that could hit, run the bases, pitch, and field. In three years, they had won 266 ball games, thirty-four more than any other team. As skilled as they were, however, it was what Hanlon did with them on the field that really earned the accolades—and a lot of vitriol, as well.

New York, Boston, and Cleveland writers regularly referred to his team as "ruffians" who should be expelled from the game. But the handle-barred manager instructed and drilled his ruffians mercilessly in the science of "Orioles Baseball." As a result, they were truly a team, and they played fast and they played hard. The Birds may not have invented many of their unique on-field tactics, but undoubtedly, they were the most prolific practitioners of them. These included signals, bunting, single and double base stealing, the Baltimore Chop, sacrifice flies, hit-and-runs, pick-off plays, position shifts, and many other "scientific," legal manipulations.

There were also plenty of not-so-legal manipulations, facilitated by a league that hired a single umpire for most games. The Orioles were also reviled by rivals for shaved bats, hidden balls, use of slippery substances, cutting the base paths, impeding runners, soaping the mound, sharpening spikes, and anything else that would give them an edge. We passed the hat at the end of last season to give Tom Murphy, the Union Park groundskeeper, a little "thank you" present for the way he worked his bunt-loving grass magic along the first and third baselines.

When those tricks didn't work, the team would "kick" the umpire, a stratagem that included foul language, fist fighting, and other forms of intimidation. But while players, cranks, and sports writers from other cities howled, the City of Baltimore loved them for it all.

"I will leave you gentlemen to ponder the fate of the baseball world. I'd better get my kitchen ready for tonight. My help should be in by now," Moss said. He stood up, stretched, and folded the newspaper.

As he did, two grim men came through the Diamond's double doors. The first looked like a businessman whose stiff celluloid collar was fronted with a gray-patterned tie, pulled up tight. His gray wool suit and vest were not cheap, but they had seen a lot of use. His shoes were worn at the heels, but also well shined. When he removed his fedora, he revealed hair that was meticulously parted in the middle and oiled flat. The skin on his face was stretched so tight that it didn't look like skin at all, and his bulbous, purple-veined nose looked pasted on as an afterthought.

The second man through the door was even bigger and uglier. He wore blue and sported three stripes on each arm. Two rows of brass buttons ran from his collar down past his waist to the end of his long coat. The coat supported a shield-shaped badge with the word "Police" on the top, the Maryland seal in the middle, and the number 306 across the bottom. It was an impressive thing. The sergeant left his tall, rounded helmet on and it, too, held a badge. This one was a crescent of laurel, enclosing another number. A long billy hung from his hip and a telltale bulge could be seen at the waist of his coat.

McGraw knew a detective and his hammer when he saw them. So did Moss, who stood as still as the suddenly poisoned atmosphere in the bar.

The third baseman immediately assumed his greeter persona. "Welcome to the Diamond Café, officer. How can we help you? I'm John McGraw, and this here's Wilbert Robinson," he said, trying for a little Orioles leverage.

The police detective ignored the reference and the bully cop snorted in derision. McGraw dropped his act and I could see the red begin to rise at his collar.

"I am Detective Thomas P. O'Donnell of the Baltimore City Police Department, and this is Sergeant Enoch Gatch."

What a warm-sounding name, I thought.

"I'm looking for a Frank Van Sant."

"I'm Van Sant," I said.

"Mr. Van Sant, I understand that you have knowledge of a murder that took place in the alley across the street. I'd like a word with you, please."

His use of "please" was not particularly polite, nor did it indicate an option.

"Alone," Gatch added.

"I'm happy to answer your questions," I said pleasantly enough. "But I'd like to do it right here." Like Moss and McGraw, I had had some experience alone with cops. It was something to avoid, especially when the cops looked like Sergeant Gatch.

I noticed the man in blue giving Moss the fish-eye, and I watched our cook retreat inside of himself—smart over brave. The cop had a revolting habit of continually flaring his nostrils, like he was getting ready to charge.

"What're you doing in here, boy?" Gatch asked of Moss. "Why don't you get back in the kitchen."

At that, McGraw stood up and I saw the interview turning sour very fast. But the detective was astute and had a job to do.

"Sergeant Gatch, I can take this from here. Why don't you wait for me outside?"

As the cop glared at Moss, I saw McGraw's hand move to a heavy, leaded glass ashtray on the bar. The detective waited until Gatch shrugged, turned, and departed through the front door.

"Mr. Van Sant, I don't care where we talk," O'Donnell said, taking out a pad and pencil. "How did you happen upon the body, and what time of day was that?"

Robbie, Willie, and McGraw moved away, but not out of earshot. Moss turned and walked into the kitchen. I answered all of the detective's questions— at least, those that I wanted to.

Finally, the detective asked me, "How well do you know the actress Fanny Darlington?"

I felt like O'Donnell picked up immediately on my split-second hesitation.

"I—I don't know her well at all. In fact, I just met her this morning. I told you already that she walked in here looking for help."

"You never met her before?"

"No. Never."

"Then can you explain to me, Mr. Van Sant, why she is asking for you now?"

"Asking for me?" I echoed lamely.

"Yes, sir. She told us that you would help her. Now, why would that be, if you just met her?"

"Help her?" I had returned to my bewildered state of earlier that day, and the detective was getting a little exasperated with my rendition of an idiot.

"Mr. Van Sant, Ms. Fanny Darlington has been arrested on suspicion of the murder of one Alcott S. Worthy. At first, she claimed not to know him. But, come to find out, she knows—or knew—him quite well."

CHAPTER 5

1857
THE BEGINNING

As mentioned, Moss Tilghman and I are close, despite our obvious differences. When the Diamond is closed or in a lull, often we spend the time just gabbing. Because my friend has a lot to say, I mostly listen. I also listen because it's rare that he doesn't either surprise me or tell me something new about himself. Over time, in dribs and drabs, an incredible, sobering story has emerged. At least, it's sobering to me. It just seems to make Moss drink more. Sadly enough, though, as compelling as his life has been, early on, it may not have been all that unusual. America has its dark side.

Moss's people came to Maryland from the Gold Coast of West Africa in the 1700s. If I heard him correctly, he is from the Igbo tribe; or, as he put it, the Igbo "culture." He told me that they were very dark people who were brought over with families. His own family was sold out all over Maryland, Virginia, and the Carolinas as soon as they arrived. His grandfather spent most of his life as a field slave called Sam, working on the Poplar Grove Plantation over in Queen Anne's County. Moss spent his early days there, as well. When the Revolution broke out, the patriarch of the Emory family took Sam with him to join Colonel Smallwood's 1st Maryland Regiment. It seemed that Sam was a rather sturdy man, and Emory wanted both body servant and protector, so he was brought in from the fields and taught the basics of tending to his master. Sam soon saw hot action in the New York and New Jersey campaigns.

When Smallwood was promoted to brigadier general after the Battle of White Plains, Emory and his manservant stayed with the general, continuing to serve under General Washington in the Philadelphia campaign and fighting in the Battle of Germantown. After that, the pair returned to Poplar Grove, where Emory rewarded Sam's loyalty by bringing him in permanently from the tobacco fields and making him a houseman.

That was the life that Moss's father, Nathan, was born into. But the life of a slave, inside or out, was not for the man. When the British arrived in 1813 at Tangier Island in the Chesapeake, Nathan escaped and joined them. In fact, Moss told me that his father was wounded fighting in what he called "the Corps of Colonial Marines," a British guerilla group that consisted entirely of ex-slaves. Once the British left, however, Nathan was recaptured and returned to Poplar Grove. There he stayed, serving the Emory household, hampered in his dreams of freedom by a knee that carried an American musket ball.

Moss was born in 1837, and within the year was orphaned when his mother, a ladies' maid, died of typhoid fever. The boy grew up among the household slaves and by the time he was a teen, he was reading and writing for old Mr. Emory. But when Emory died, his son found the young houseman unnecessary and, to use Moss's word, "uppity." So, the former scribe found himself out in the fields, where his grandfather had started years before.

At the time, the tobacco economy was sagging and slavery in Maryland was losing its profitability. Cotton planters in the Deep South, however, were offering as much as $1,600 for healthy, young men. At first, Moss was judged unfit due to his lack of developed muscle. So, he was given work that either hardened a man or killed him. Eventually, his good genes and life of clearing fields, chopping and hauling wood, draining swamps, and loading and unloading the plantation's schooners on Baltimore docks made him a strapping, valuable piece of property. It was on one of the usual trips across the Chesapeake with a load of produce, just before the Emorys were going to sell him "down the river," that Moss made his break for it.

Baltimore in the 1850s was a unique place in America for a number of reasons. Not the least of these was that it held the largest population of freedmen in the country—nearly 50,000 lived here then. And because the city was situated just below the Mason-Dixon Line, it was one of the landmarks that escaped slaves sought out on the way north.

Maryland was a slave state at the time and rife with those who would return runaways to their masters for profit. Among the most active in this endeavor were the city's street gangs, those "social clubs" affiliated with the volunteer firehouses and one or the other of two vying political machines—the

Democratic Party or the American Party, better known as the Know Nothings. With ominous names such as the Plug Uglies, the Regulators, the Double Pumps, the Blood Tubs, and the Rip Raps, these groups controlled Baltimore's streets and most of what moved along them. Moss was unaware of these hoodlums when he decided to go.

The Poplar Grove slaves were unloading the pungy *Peggy Ann*, as they had done dozens of times in the past. The work crew used a line of men who tossed watermelons and boxes of tomatoes from one man to the next, then stacked them in market wagons hired for the purpose. That day, Moss told me, he and another Poplar Grove slave were working on one of the many piers that radiated from Baltimore's huge City Dock. The boat's captain and his mate, who held a shotgun lazily by his side, were overseeing the off-loading. The work was all very routine for the bored men and no trouble was expected.

As Moss watched the load of produce in the boat diminish, he also saw a neighboring skipper approach the *Peggy Ann's* captain and mate. A bottle was produced, and the three white men stepped behind a stack of empty barrels. That was when Moss launched his escape.

He vaulted up and over one of the melon wagons and took off at a sprint down the long pier. This break in the routine raised immediate attention and set off a chorus of howls and yells from surrounding boats. The noise was enough to get the attention of the *Peggy Ann's* mate and, stepping out from behind the barrels, he raised the shotgun. But the busy pier was no place to fire a gun of that sort without damaging either innocent people or market goods. Instead, the mate let go into the air, alerting everyone in the area that a runaway was on the loose.

Moss slammed into and ran over several who stood in his way. Shouts were going up all around him. Numerous times, he had to maneuver around the detritus found on one of the busiest piers in the world, but he was making good progress up the long approach that ran from the harbor to Pratt Street and the city beyond it. As he neared the head of the pier, he saw that his exit was blocked by three bullyboys with clubs. He didn't know it at the time, but Baltimore's East Harbor at City Dock was the turf of the Double Pumps street gang. The thugs had easy pickings running right at them.

Seeing the danger, Moss veered left, climbed a pile of cabbage crates, and jumped into the filthy water sloshing between piers. His move was desperate, but he was a strong swimmer, and the distance to the parallel dock was only about twenty or thirty yards. His pursuers would have to negotiate the unloading of the oyster fleet using the pier before they could reach him. Once across, he scrambled over the rail of a sloop, surprising the oystermen unloading the boat. He bulled his way past them, leapt up onto the pier, and then dove a second time into the water on the other side. This time, he went deep and swam unseen, surfacing between two old pungies in for repair and re-caulking on the far pier. He could see the *Peggy Ann's* mate and the three men looking for him on the pier he had just vacated. He also saw, with some relief, that they were getting no help from the oyster boat slaves or their white crews.

As he bobbed in the water, wondering where he was going from there, a voice from above said, "Take my hand, son."

Moss looked up to see the face of a stern god. The man was older and wore the long, gray beard of an Old Testament patriarch. He extended a sinewy arm that was covered in dried and cracked pitch.

The escapee took the hand and was immediately lifted up out of the water with seeming little effort. Wordlessly, he was pushed down into the hold of a pungy that had been dry docked. There, he found himself among a half-dozen black men, some holding caulking mallets or chisel-like irons, others twisting cotton into strands or stretching black strips of oakum and wedging them into seams between planks. Another man stood with a pot and a thick brush that was dripping pine tar. Moss immediately thought he had been caught and thrown in with a work crew of dock slaves.

"Get those pants off. Put these on." The old man drew a set of rough, filthy canvas overalls out of a locker and threw them at Moss. Then he said to the workman with the tar pot, "Make him look like he's been working all day."

With that, the man began to hit his face, arms and chest with his brush. Another threw a handful of oakum dust in his hair. Another sloshed his feet with the last of the black bilge remaining in the hull of the boat. A ratty cap was jammed down on his head. The old man handed Moss a brush, gave him a quick, silent lesson in paying the boat's seams, then disappeared out of the hold.

Before long, Moss heard voices out on the pier.

"Mister, I'm looking for a big, black runaway," a rough-sounding man said. "They say he came this way."

"Not that I've seen," the bearded man lied. "There was some commotion down the pier a bit, though."

"I don't believe you, old man. I want to see your slaves," another hard voice said.

"I don't much care what you believe, mister. I am a Quaker, and if you knew anything, you'd know the law says we can't keep slaves. This is my worksite and these are my men. They're not slaves; they're free with every right not to be troubled by the likes of you."

"Watch what you're sayin' to me, old man," the voice threatened.

"Now, Cuddy, you back off now. I'm in charge here and I say what goes. The man's right, he can't keep slaves." That voice sounded like the law.

"Officer, that runaway is my property and I want him." Moss recognized the mate's high pitch.

"Okay, okay, you men just step back a bit and we'll get these boys out here," the cop said. "Mister, what's your name?"

"The name's Stroup, Mordecai Stroup, and I've been working this dock with my men for near twenty-five years and I don't have to take this from street trash like these. The Friends Meeting House up on Lombard Street owns this caulking business. Check with the harbor master. I've got standing."

"You won't be standing for long, you keep talking to us like that. Now, get those boys out here."

"I said I'm in charge," the policeman re-emphasized. "Now, unless you want to spend the night in the lockup, back off!" After a moment, he said, "Mr. Stroup, sorry to interrupt the work, but I need to see your men."

Then Moss heard the old man say with some hesitation, "James, bring the men on up out of there."

With that, one by one, the work-stained, seven-man crew made their way onto the pier. Since they were large, well-built men and the pier was jammed with material, the space available to stand was limited. Just the same, they emerged, going chest to chest with those already there. The sudden presence of sweaty humanity made it very close, and one of the bullyboys backed away, almost falling into the water. The caulking crew was intimidating in its size, solidarity, and demeanor, so much so that the man hunters and the cop were put off their nob.

Moss stayed in the thick of the men with his head down. From under the bill of his cap, he could see the *Peggy Ann's* mate craning around the men, trying to see all of them, but also looking very anxious. Perhaps it was anxiety, or maybe it was Moss's disguise, or maybe it was just the mere fact that the mate never knew Moss's face because he had never really looked at it. Whichever it was, when his eyes ran over Moss, there was no recognition whatsoever.

"Is he here?" the cop asked the mate.

"I don't see him," the plantation man said with some hesitation.

"Christ, what a waste of time," one of the thugs swore. "He's got to be over on the next pier. Let's get away from here, these niggers stink."

With that, the searchers moved away from the caulking crew and continued their efforts back down the dock and out onto the adjacent pier.

For the rest of the day, Moss worked with the crew, nearly learning a new trade in the process. When dusk began to fall, the Quaker boss came to him.

"Son, we've got to get you out of here tonight. This ain't the first time I've done it, so here's how it will go. The men will carry the tools we normally stow in the box on the underside of the work wagon. It'll be tight, but you can fit in there if you ball up. Once I get it closed, we'll work our way up the pier, across Pratt Street and on over to Lombard to the meetinghouse. You'll be safe there for a night while we figure out what to do next. It's not too far, but we'll be going slowly. You can expect to be in there the better part of an hour. It'll get uncomfortable, but you have to stay in the box and you have to stay quiet. They'll be looking for you, sure enough. Those Double Pumps don't have much else to do. Do you understand?"

Moss nodded his head, but the bearded man wanted to be sure. "I need you to tell me you understand. I can't have you going rabbit on me, if and when we get stopped. That'd mean prison time for me and my crew will be forfeit. They'll be back in chains. Now, tell me you understand."

"I understand, Mr. Stroup. And I want to thank you for helping me," Moss said clearly. Then he nodded to the men of the caulking crew in recognition of the risk they would be taking.

"Don't thank me, son. My God would have it no other way, and I don't want him angry with me. Now, as soon as it's dark, we go."

The ride to the Friends Meeting House was long and painful for Moss, but without incident. So, in a couple of hours, he found himself clean, clothed, fed, lying on a straw mattress, and tucked safely away in a windowless, brick room in the basement of a building that could have been anywhere. As excited and fearful as he was, he told me, he was just as exhausted. So, it wasn't long before he fell dead asleep.

CHAPTER 6

FANNY'S STORY

Detective O'Donnell instructed me that Fanny would be spending the day and night answering questions. He then told me that he wanted to see me in the Northwestern Police Station first thing in the morning. At that time, I could talk to Miss Darlington. They might have some additional queries for me as well. I hated the building at Pennsylvania Avenue and Lanvale Street because it held some unhappy memories for me.

I was up early just the same, hopped the streetcar, and rode with the shop girls and factory workers up Howard Street. When I walked into the red brick pile with its tall clock tower, I was immediately claustrophobic and queasy. A clerk directed me to a cop named Boyle who wasted our time by reminding me of a few of my minor transgressions as he thumbed through a file that was thicker than I remembered it to be.

Boyle asked about this and that, occasionally looking up at me in a way that said he knew I was lying and had known problems like me his whole life. I knew cops like him, as well. In fact, I ran his precinct's streets as a boy, having grown up over a produce store operated by my mother over on Biddle Street. I blame any anti-social behavior to my credit (or debit) on the lack of a fatherly influence in my life. All I knew about my old man came from my ma, and that wasn't much. Reportedly, he was an Araber who, when sober, sold cantaloupe and tomatoes out of a horse and wagon over in East Baltimore somewhere. I don't really know, I never went looking for him.

I'm pretty sure my mother loved me, though. She would read to me and look up the words we didn't know. When I got older, she even wanted me to take over the store and taught me how to handle the books. That's when I fled home at a ripe sixteen, borrowing a small stake out of an Old Havana coffee can she had hidden under a floor board.

Even then, I stayed in the neighborhood for a few years, surviving through petty crime and the occasional errand for the ward boss. It was enough to stay alive and pay Ma back. But as my record will attest, I wasn't very good at either crime or politics. So, after a couple of short stints in lockup, I vowed to stay clear of cops, taking a job as a cigar roller at the Flor de Baltimore company, where I worked my way up to bookkeeper until the place went bust. I hadn't been back in the Northwestern Station since those days.

All of Boyle's shenanigans were routine bullshit, and he got bored not long after he started. So, he ended the harassment, stood, and walked me past a row of desks populated with other bored cops who were sweating other alleged perpetrators.

I was put in a small, windowless room that had a surprisingly modern convenience—a single, electric lightbulb, hanging from the ceiling and covered in a green metal shade. The cop assisted me into a heavy chair, drawn up to a scarred table. He then left the room, slammed the door, and threw the bolt with a decisive click. Sealing me in also sucked the air out of the room, causing the light to swing back and forth. So, I occupied myself by fighting down nausea and counting the times the weak beam walked across the table.

In time, Boyle ushered in Fanny Darlington and sat her across from me. She looked worn and only a little less beautiful. She did her usual thing with a few random strands of her hair, then rested her arms on the table, stretching them out toward me. She began to wring her hands. Boyle leaned against the wall behind her with his arms folded and his head down, waiting.

Fanny looked at me with gratitude. "Thank you for coming. I know we've just met, but I really don't know anyone else in Baltimore. You were so kind to me yesterday."

"Don't give it another thought," I said. "I'm glad you asked for me."

"Mr. Van Sant—"

"Frank," I persisted.

"Frank, they think I murdered that man. But I didn't. I hardly knew him."

She had changed her story in the face of the evidence. But whatever the truth was, I didn't think it such a good idea to be admitting or denying anything with the law standing behind her. She really didn't need me; she needed a lawyer. So, I took control of the conversation.

"Fanny…may I call you that?"

"Yes, yes, of course." She was desperate for some direction.

"You need some legal help right now. In an hour or so, I can get that arranged and we'll see if we can get you out of here. Meanwhile, I would suggest you say nothing more to anyone."

I looked at the cop, who was now staring at me with that particular look they reserve for all would-be jailhouse lawyers. At that point, the door to the room was pulled open and Detective O'Donnell entered with a man in a suit and an air of authority. I could see that sweetheart Sergeant Gatch behind them, swearing under his breath.

"Miss Darlington, you're free to go. You've made bail. Mr. Pocock here has paid the freight. I would advise you to stay where we can find you," O'Donnell said.

Fanny looked at me, lost.

I said, "That means they don't have enough on you to hold you."

"Miss Darlington, I'm an attorney, my name's Pocock," the suit said quickly. "Your managing director, Mr. Dean, has hired me to get you released. I'm to take you to him at the Academy of Music this morning." Then, looking at me, he asked unpleasantly, "And you are?"

I ignored the snot and said to Fanny, "Come on, let's get out of here. Dean can wait. I'll take you to your rooms. Then, when you're ready, we'll get something to eat. You must be tired and hungry."

I knew this guy, Dean. Tunis F. Dean was his full moniker. Despite the fact that his mother named him after a fish, he was one of the theatrical powers on Howard Street. Just the same, he could wait.

"Mr. Dean wants Miss Darlington for this afternoon's rehearsal. She's already missed one. She's to come with me," the attorney ordered.

"Tell him we'll be in touch," I said. I shouldered my way past the man. As I returned Gatch's glare, the sergeant snarled.

"We'll be in touch, too, Miss Darlington. Real soon."

Fanny and I moved quickly through the station house and out the front door. We caught a cab on Pennsylvania Avenue and rode the short distance down to Howard and Franklin Streets, where she had taken a room in the Kernan Hotel. I waited in the lobby the forty-five minutes it took her to clean up and change clothes. Then, we walked around the block to the Diamond.

It was still early and the place wasn't open, but I found Moss sitting at one of the tables with a well-dressed, distinguished man wearing a Van Dyke beard and mustache with some blond still in them. I recognized him immediately. As we came in, the two rose, shook hands, and the gentleman moved to the front door. As he passed us, he greeted me.

"Good morning, Frank. Nice to see you. You're up early."

"Mornin' Mr. Von Der Horst," I replied. "I could say the same about you."

"I hope you don't mind, I just made some arrangements with Moss. He said you'd be okay with it."

Harry Von Der Horst was the owner of the Eagle Brewery and the Baltimore Orioles, not necessarily in that order. He was yet another of Moss's occasional associates.

"Good morning to you as well, ma'am," the brewer said with a little bow. Then with a smile, he was out the door.

I settled Fanny at one of the tables. Moss rolled up something he and Von Der Horst had been studying and put it on the bar. Then, he came over.

"Fanny, I'd like you to meet, Moss Tilghman. Moss, this is Fanny Darlington."

"Miss Darlington, it's a pleasure to meet you. Welcome to Baltimore. Frank speaks very highly of you," he said, embarrassing me and surprising her.

Fanny took Moss's hand with some hesitation. I doubted that she had ever shaken the hand of a black man. She returned his smile with the same hesitation.

"Fanny, Moss is the heart and soul of this place and a good friend," I said. "Moss, the lady has had a pretty rough night. Think we could find some breakfast and maybe some coffee for her?"

"Of course," he said. "It won't be but a minute." He disappeared into the kitchen.

When Moss had gone, Fanny let out a sigh, slumped, and put her head down on her arms on the table. I sat down and put my arm over her shoulder in a fatherly way.

"I know you're tired, but do you think you're up to telling me what this is all about? Maybe I can help."

With that, her head came up and I could see that she was drained. Don't get me wrong, she was still a knockout, but the dark circles under her eyes spoke clearly about the night in Northwestern Station. She looked at me.

"Why are you being so nice to me?" she asked.

The question was full of the fears and suspicions that a single woman alone in an unknown city would have. She had sought me out, twice. But it was obvious that it wasn't a matter of choice for her. She desperately needed a stable place to stand, something or someone she could rely on. In her question was the hope that I was that someone.

"Fanny, I honestly don't know. You may be everything those cops suspect you are, but I don't think so. There's no logic to my feeling and that's disconcerting. I don't normally put much credence in sixth senses, but I just feel like you're the victim here, and I want to help you any way I can. Call it my male protection instinct." I winced as soon as I had said it.

She was not very convinced. And why should she be? Given her attraction, it's very likely that she dealt with all manner of stage-door johnnies. I needed to prove myself to her. But first, I reasoned, I needed to get the story.

"Why don't you tell me what happened," I suggested, moving back from her.

"Frank, I don't know what happened. At first, I told them I'd never met Alcott Worthy. Then, when they found out that I did, they accused me of murdering him."

"Why did you tell them you didn't know him? And who was he, anyway?"

"He was a very persistent man," she responded with a non-sequitur.

"Wait, we're not going to have this conversation like that." I stopped her gently. "I want you to start at the beginning, go through it step by step, logically." I was remembering my Arthur Conan Doyle. Holmes might have said the same thing.

Then Moss arrived with a plate of eggs and bacon with all of the extras. He carried a big tray that also held a pot of coffee and three mugs. It wouldn't have taken London's most famous detective to deduce that he wanted to hear the story, as well.

"Watson, why don't you join us?"

He gave me the look I was hoping for. "I want you to hear this, too."

A flash of dismay crossed Fanny's face. Whether it was the black man or just the man, she wasn't sure about my invitation. Moss took care of it, though.

"Miss Darlington, why don't you ignore Frank for a few minutes and eat this breakfast I made. Cream in your coffee?"

He put the plate and silverware down and poured her coffee. He then laid a white napkin across her lap. Smiling, he sat and filled his mug, not even offering to fill mine. I reached for the pot; I could pour my own coffee.

"Fanny, Moss can help us. He knows people. That man he was just talking to, for instance." Then I asked Moss, "What was Harry Von Der Horst doing here this morning?"

"Not much."

"Come on, what'd he want?"

"Why don't you just deduce what he was doing here?"

"Moss, just tell me. I like Harry, but he's not a man to waste his time. And he wouldn't normally risk coming in here on the off chance that he might have to talk to McGraw."

"True," Moss responded. "Harry just wants to reserve the bowling lanes in a couple of weeks."

"Right," I said at his dubious dodge.

"No, that's what he wanted. You know he's a big tenpins man. One of the best in the city. He's got the German Fellows Tournament in here next month and he wants the practice."

Baltimore was full of Germans. That meant it was full of beer-drinking bowlers. Harry Von Der Horst was not only an avid kegler, but also he made beer and sold kegs. He sponsored more tournaments than anyone else in town and made a profit on every one of them, thanks to the barrels of lager he pedaled in the process. He used the same business model that made the Orioles profitable. An educated businessman might have said he controlled the supply and was creating the demand.

In fact, the Diamond did have six very nice, modern bowling alleys with steel lanes and electric ball return. It was not unusual to hold a tournament here. We like to generate our own demand, as well.

The Diamond, despite its baseball pedigree, is just as famous for bowling. We're even known for inventing the game they are now calling "duckpins." I'm particularly proud of that because I invented it. Well, Robinson, McGraw, and I did, anyway. But that's a story for another time.

When Fanny had finished her breakfast and Moss had refilled her mug, she sat back, obviously feeling a little better. I got her started.

"Tell us from the beginning. How did you know this man? Worthy, was it?"

"Yes, Alcott S. Worthy. I first met him in New York when I was at the Union Square Theater doing *The Whirl of the Town*. He had a lot of money. I think he was friendly with the artistic director. He said he was from Baltimore and was somehow associated with the Academy of Music here. Anyway, he was always backstage, talking to the girls. One night, he asked me out to dinner after the show. I wasn't attracted to him, but he was nice enough, I was hungry, and a little lonely.

"Well, one dinner turned into three, and before I knew it, he was telling me he loved me. He wanted to marry me. He even offered me an expensive necklace as an engagement present. I didn't take it, of course, but he insisted. When I refused and demanded he take me home, he still didn't give up. All the way through the end of the run, he pestered me, pledging his troth."

My eyebrows shot up at her use of the ancient word and I snuck a peek at Moss. He ignored me, took a sip of his coffee, and leaned in closer to her.

"Mr. Worthy even followed me to Philadelphia when I was in *A Loan of a Lover.* He thought he was wearing me down, but he wasn't. I wished I had never met him by that time. But he wouldn't give up.

"When the Philadelphia show was about to end and I had no other prospects, he told me that he could get me a role here. It was too good to pass up, so I accepted. But when I arrived and checked into the Kernan, there he was in the lobby, waiting for me. He acted like I had made some sort of commitment to him, and it was clear he had certain expectations.

"When I went to see Mr. Dean for the first time at the theater, Mr. Worthy was there yet again. He continued to hang around backstage, even when we had begun rehearsals. Finally, I had enough. There were harsh words exchanged. I may have said I would do something drastic if he didn't leave me alone. I had no idea what that might be, but the words just came out. I guess the theater's backdoor keeper heard me. He must of told that Detective O'Donnell."

Old Man Hertzbaugh, again! That weasel would be just the one to blabber to the cops.

"When they asked me if I knew him, I lied. I wanted nothing to do with him, so I lied. Come to find out, I was one of the last people to see him alive, according to the police."

"How did he react when you threatened him?" I asked.

"He had been drinking and he just laughed. He said what he always said: that I would come to him in time."

"Where did he go after you were with him?"

"I have no idea. Backstage was chaotic. They were staging a three act comedy, *Miss Francis of Yale.* He just left, I guess."

"What time was that, Miss Darlington?" Moss asked.

"I'm not sure. It was late. I stayed after rehearsal because I wanted to meet Dorothea Baird, who played Cosette."

"Who?" I asked. But Moss just nodded.

"I swear, the next time I saw that man was yesterday morning in the alley, lying there, just as you saw him. The police came back about two hours after I talked to them. They searched my dressing room, then they accused me of murder and arrested me. You know the rest." She put her head in her hands.

Moss then asked, "More coffee?" When she refused, he asked, "Before you left him, do you recall seeing him with friends or anyone else that day?"

"Oh, he was always with someone. He was either chatting up the cast, talking to other theater people, or joking with other men who enjoy cluttering up the backstage."

"Is there anything else you can tell us about Worthy or the day before the murder that might help?" I asked.

She shook her head, and once again I could see how tired she was.

"I've got to explain things to Mr. Dean and get a couple hours of sleep before I'm any good," she said without her heart in it.

"Will he want you to rehearse today?"

"Probably not when he sees how tired I am," she admitted. "But we're opening with *The Prisoner of Zenda* in a couple of weeks, and there's a lot of work to do before then."

The play sounded awful—jail in a foreign country. I said, "Okay, I'll take you over to the Academy, then back to your hotel, if that's what you want to do."

We rose. Fanny thanked Moss for the breakfast and gave him a small smile. As we were leaving, Moss stopped us.

"Let me ask you something, Frank. Take a look at this—what do you see?"

He unrolled the long tube of paper that he had placed on the bar when the Orioles' owner had left. It was a pen, ink, and chalk drawing of a lecture hall. The students were captured with humor and clarity. Some sat, others sprawled, still others waved their arms or otherwise gave the drawing a great deal of animation. In the middle of it all sat a composed black man in a dark suit.

"That looks like you, Moss," I answered. Fanny waited, glancing at the scene with little interest.

"Yes, yes, of course it's me. What else do you see?"

"A bunch of obnoxious Hopkins students?" I offered.

"Sure, but what else?"

"Nothing else, Moss." I was impatient to get Fanny out of there. "It's done pretty well, I guess."

Moss looked at me in frustration. "The right side of your brain needs some exercise, Frank. How about you, Miss Darlington? What do you see?"

Fanny then looked at the drawing a little closer. "I see the same things, Frank did. But, wait, yes, there's something else there." She leaned over the picture. "I see two words. No, that's silly. Yes, yes, I see two words clearly. Spelled out in the boys' arms, legs, and the positions of their bodies is a phrase. It says...." She hesitated. "It says, 'Help me.'"

"Yes, that's what I see too," Moss said gravely.

Chapter 7

1857
Escape

Moss woke in confusion, sat up abruptly, and stared wide-eyed into pitch black. A weak shaft of light from under a door eventually softened the black and offered shapes and angles in a cell-like space. His immediate fear was that he was locked in. The events of the previous day came flooding back, and he knew he was in danger and on the run. At least, he thought he was on the run. When he swung his legs over the side of his bed, there was a rap on the door and the bearded Quaker entered with another man.

"Good morning, young man. I'm glad you got some rest. The women will be down with some breakfast shortly. I brought you a pair of old shoes to wear, so you don't have to break them in. You'll be needing them where you're going." The man handed Moss a well-used pair of roomy, leather brogans with laces that still had a fair amount sole.

"This gentleman is Mr. Thomas Garrett of Wilmington, Delaware. He's one of us, and he's had a lot of experience getting people like you out of Baltimore. I want you to listen to him."

Moss found his voice. "Mr. Stroup, you took a big risk for me, and I don't want to put you in any more danger. Maybe it's best I just say thanks and get out of here."

"It most certainly would not be best," the bearded man said. "I don't think you realize your situation. You are in the heart of a very cruel city, one that would sooner see you in chains or dead without caring which. You have no money, no friends other than us, and no plan. What do you think you can do?"

"Well, I don't know. Just run, I guess. At least I'm free. That's better off than I was yesterday," Moss said with some heat.

Then Garrett spoke. "I'm not going to say that I know how you feel. There's no way that I could. But I do have some experience with helping your people to greater safety. You're safe here in Mordecai's community for now, but you can't stay. You have to go. But if you run and you're caught, they're caught. So, our best chance to avoid that is to use our friends to get you out of the city. Do you understand?"

Moss understood, of course, and he was more than a little put off by the man's direct manner. But he also felt the truth of what he was saying. Garrett seemed a good man that wanted to help him. So, Moss just nodded.

"Son, I don't even know your name, and it's probably just as well that I don't," Garrett said. "But I have some ideas on how to get you further north. Let me tell you what I have in mind."

The two men pulled up chairs while Moss sat on the bed. A woman in a white linen bonnet came with a tray that held a mug of coffee and a bowl of some kind of grainy porridge with a wooden spoon in it. As he devoured the meal, he listened to the Quakers.

Their plan was to move him as soon as it got dark. They would go by the same wagon they used the night before and, once again, Moss would curl up in the toolbox. They warned that the trip would be longer because they had to go across town to the northwest part of the city. There, they'd hide him in a church on Orchard Street until the following night.

There were no orchards on Orchard Street. In fact, it was in the middle of one of the densest parts of the city. What was worse, it was in the heart of the neighborhood run by the Mount Vernon Hook and Ladder social club, the Plug Uglies, the most brutal of all of the street gangs. To add to the danger, the church was watched closely, since it was one of the few African-American built churches in Baltimore. It was a miracle that it was tolerated at all.

The pastor at Orchard Street would watch over him until the next night. Then, he would be helped aboard a train that ran by the church, a block away. The train was a freight that used the Susquehanna Railroad. Since the Susquehanna merged with the Northern Central Railway, with luck, Moss would get carried north, all the way to Harrisburg, Pennsylvania. There, he would take the Pennsylvania Railroad east to Philadelphia. Garrett had friends in that city who would help.

Moss's head spun. He had heard of these cities, of course, since old Mr. Emory had done business in both of them. But it all seemed like such a thin string to be staking his freedom on. When he said as much, Garrett responded, "Sadly, my son, you have assessed the situation correctly. It is very perilous, even if you make it out of Maryland. The Fugitive Slave Law is in effect, and that means whether you are in a Free or a Slave State, if you are captured, you must be returned to your former owner. Truly disgraceful!"

"Blasphemous!" Stroup thundered.

Moss shook his head, then said, "I guess when it gets down to it, I have little choice. I do have a choice in one thing, though. If I'm captured, I plan to take steps to be sure that I don't get returned to Poplar Grove Plantation or anywhere else. I will not go back."

The two white men could see that Moss's face was set.

After a moment, Stroup said, "There will be times when you will have to use all of the resolve you can muster. You will have to be alert and creative. You will have no friends once you leave Orchard Street, even among your own people, until you get to Philadelphia."

Moss had a lot of questions, but his first one was, "Once I leave the church, how do I find and board the train?"

"Reverend Lewis, the pastor, will help you," Garrett said. "There is an abandoned heating duct under the church. At the end of it, there is a panel that, once removed, opens to a long dirt tunnel dug a few years ago. The tunnel leads to the North Central Railway's tracks. The Reverend will tell you when it's time to go so that when you emerge, the train will be passing slowly as it makes its way out of the city."

"I don't know Harrisburg or Philadelphia. What do I do once I'm there?"

"Harrisburg's easy. They will transfer the freight cars to the Pennsylvania Railroad line. Just stay on the train, if you can. Once you are in Philadelphia, I will have my friends looking for you. Wear this and don't lose it."

The Quaker pinned an artificial, white carnation on the heavy cotton shirt Moss had been given the night before.

"Pastor Lewis will make sure you have what you need to travel, but it won't be much," Stroup offered. "Now, I suggest you rest and conserve your strength. You'll need it. We'll be leaving here around nine o'clock."

With that, the two men rose, extended their hands, wished him God's grace, and left Moss to his thoughts.

Moss told me one time that, even with all he had gone through, those last few hours alone were the longest he could ever remember. He laughed when he compared himself to a knight left to pray before the altar prior to setting out on a quest. Leave it to the man to picture himself a member of King Arthur's roundtable.

The time did pass, however, and he did cram himself back into that wagon. The dray managed, albeit slowly, to make its way across the city, despite twice running into bands of what sounded like drunken men. They pounded on the sides of the wagon and heated words were exchanged, but nothing came of them.

In time, they drove into the dark yard of a large, red brick church. The wagon was backed up to a door, and Moss was led quickly into the sanctuary off the main congregation. There, a short, rotund cleric wearing a cassock and white collar led him to a set of stairs in the back. They led down to a comfortably furnished room that must have been the pastor's personal sanctuary. Moss was given a glass of water, pointed to a tray of johnnycakes and cracklin' bread, and asked to wait while the man climbed the stairs again.

When he returned, he was not alone. Following him down was a thin, anxious black woman, maybe ten years or so older than Moss. She had a young boy by the hand. The skinny child could not have been any more than five or six.

"Alright," the beer barrel-like churchman began. He was no young man, but he had the energy of one. To burn some of it, he rubbed his hands vigorously, as if he were cold, even as hot as it was. The backs of his big paws were fleshy and covered in veins that ran around and through a series of dark age spots. His palms were dry, near white, and they made a rasping sound as their calluses grated against each other. The man had known hard work.

"Now that we're all together, we can relax a little bit. Hattie, I'm sure the child is starving. Please, help yourselves to the cakes and bread. There's a little butter there, too."

The woman looked at the pastor thankfully, but didn't move. The boy eyed the food, but disappeared behind his mother's threadbare skirt. At that, the churchman put his arm around the woman and his hand on the child's head and guided them to the table. The boy was shy at first, looking up at the woman, but the cracklin' bread quickly overcame his reticence and he began to eat hungrily. The woman selected a small johnnycake, wobbled over to a chair, and sat down with it in her lap. The minister brought her a glass of water.

"I'm Pastor Lewis, and you are now guests of the Metropolitan Methodist Episcopal Church. I'd like to make you as comfortable as possible this evening before your journey tomorrow."

Moss didn't like the sound of this. "Sir, you are not suggesting that the three of us travel together?"

"My boy…" Pastor Lewis began, then stopped. "I don't even know your name. What name did they give you?"

"You can call me Moss, Pastor. But if you are suggesting that I be responsible for those two, I believe you will have to rethink that."

"Moss? Just Moss?" he asked. "You are a free man now. You need a surname as well."

Moss was frustrated with the obvious avoidance of his point. But there was something about this man that kept him calm.

One late night in the Diamond, I asked my friend about his last name. He told me that it just popped into his head the night Pastor Lewis called him a free man.

"Tilghman. Moss Tilghman is my name," he answered. It was a family that was spread out all over Maryland's Eastern Shore, and he would be damned if he would take the Emory name.

"Well, Moss Tilghman, this here is Hattie McQuinn and her son, Joshua. Since you will be traveling as man and wife, she'll be going by Hattie Tilghman."

"Now, wait, Pastor, I need to move fast. These two can't hold me back. It wouldn't be safe for any of us."

"Moss, we do what we have to do," the man answered. "Hattie and Joshua have no chance whatsoever without you. They need your strength."

"But—"

The Pastor raised his hand. Then he reached out, grabbed Moss by both biceps, and leaned into him. "It's true that the chance for all of you is slim. There will be danger everywhere. That's precisely why we have to act as one. So, no arguments. You will be going with Hattie and Joshua."

There was steel in the man, and it was evident in his words and the strength of his grip. So, Moss just sat down in resignation and looked at the woman. She had some fire in her eyes, but she was homely and unhealthy looking. To prove his assessment, she began a wracking cough. This did not offer Moss any solace.

The pastor went to her, helped her with the water, and said something quietly to her. Her coughing eased. He then went over to the boy and brought him to Moss.

"Joshua, this is Mr. Tilghman. He's going to be your daddy for a while. That alright?"

The boy looked at Moss wide-eyed, then ran to his mother, who folded him into her. Moss put his head in his hands.

Over the next day, he learned that Hattie and Joshua had already come a long way. They had been in North Carolina, slaves of a detached owner who left their management to an overseer. The man, while not wantonly cruel, was calloused by the work he did. One day, about a month after her man died from sunstroke, Hattie just up and left, taking Joshua with her. The two had been walking for weeks across open fields, traveling mostly at night. River crossings had been particularly harrowing. Twice, they were chased, once by dogs. Another time, a goodhearted farmer let them sleep in his barn—at least until he got to town. Then, he returned with two slavers. A cornfield and a hailstorm saved them that time. When they had an opportunity, they stole to feed themselves—an egg here, a tomato there, raw corn if that's all there was. Their saga was hard for Moss to imagine, given the look of the pair. Maybe he wasn't the only one with resolve.

Moss also learned that they would have to crawl almost fifty yards through an unlit, dirt tunnel to get to the train. He wondered whether Hattie and the boy were capable of that, but he didn't have long to worry about it. Almost too soon, night came and the three of them were crouched in a brick-lined culvert under the church.

Pastor Lewis gave Moss an envelope of papers. They described the Tilghman family as freed, traveling to visit relatives in Philadelphia. The documents were not likely to fool someone who knew, but they were better than nothing. The churchman also gave Moss and Hattie each a cloth bag of basic provisions, including two thick candles and some Lucifer matches. He then squeezed past them and pried away a wooden board that was covering a hole in the wall.

"Now, understand, we haven't used this recently, but it should be fine. Just take it slow and steady. You have plenty of time before the train passes. At the other end, you will find a wire mesh grate. I checked it yesterday, and you'll be able to kick it out easily. Just wait until you see the railcars going by. The train will be moving slowly. Pick a car that's open, hop on, and hide yourselves as best you can. Avoid everyone, if possible. Any questions?"

Moss had questions, but he didn't ask them. He just wanted the crawl ahead of him to be over. He would lead, the boy would follow, and Hattie would be last to enter. He lit one of the candles and ducked into the tight, dark hole.

The tunnel was cold, but dry. He had no more than five or six inches on either side of his shoulders, but if it didn't narrow any further, he would be all right. If he could fit, then the woman and the boy would have no trouble.

They held their bindles in their teeth, with Moss extending the candle and moving forward in a sort of three-legged crawl. They stayed close as they left the church's heating duct behind. One of his first thoughts was that he hoped that there was nothing else in the tunnel with them. But it didn't take long before another fear surfaced. The smell of the earth and a sense of the crushing walls around them created a flash of panic that he had never felt before. For a moment, he let the thought of being buried alive overtake him. The idea that he would disappear forever beneath the streets of Baltimore was more than he could take. He began to sweat, and he felt a scream rise in his throat. Then, he heard Joshua whimper behind him.

The boy's small cry brought Moss back from the edge. He couldn't afford to lose his calm, he told himself. They were depending upon him. He needed to be stronger. So, he stopped and turned in the tunnel as best he could.

"Joshua, we're alright. I'm here and so is your mamma. We'll take care of you, don't worry. It won't be long. Just stay close to me. Hattie, tell him, we're fine." Moss reached back and touched the boy's head. He heard the woman, shaky at first, begin to comfort the boy as well.

They began their journey again, and after ten minutes Moss felt like they had been in the tunnel for hours. He knew, however, based upon what the pastor had told him, that they had almost half of the way yet to go. Joshua began to cry steadily and only stopped to call after Hattie, who had begun to lose touch with him. Moss had no way of knowing that the woman had become separated from them until he heard the boy. Then, he stopped to allow her to rejoin them.

He had to do this three times as they moved along the tight passageway, and three times he fought back the terrible feeling of burial. As he and Joshua waited the third time, Moss felt a slight tremor in the walls around him. Something heavy was moving above them. The panic flooded back. He heard a muffled "whoom," his face felt a rush of air, and his eyes and ears were immediately filled with dust and dirt. The candle blew out. His instinct told him to rush forward as fast as he could.

Something stopped him, however. He tried calling Joshua's name, but got no response. He relit the candle and managed to crawl a few feet back, only to feel a wall of dirt. He began in near panic to scrabble at the pile and was about to give up hope when he felt the boy's hand. He grabbed the child's wrist and slowly pulled until a small head emerged from the gloom. He then pulled the boy out of the pile.

Joshua emerged spitting, coughing, and frantically wiping dirt out of his eyes. "Mamma, mamma, where's my mamma!"

Moss didn't answer, and he didn't try to dig for Hattie, either. Instead, fearing that the cave-in was not over, he let the candle drop and clenched his cloth bag in his teeth. He grasped Joshua by the scruff of his neck and began to kick and crawl as fast as he could away from the blocked tunnel. The boy must have been frozen in the trauma of what just happened, because he was no longer crying.

It was certainly fear that was driving Moss now, but the fear did not make the rest of their passage any easier or faster. The hell that he was living seemed to go on forever. And then, suddenly, there was a dim light.

The pastor was right; the wire grate was easily removed, and Moss stuck his head out tentatively and gulped air. It was very dark, but after the tunnel, it was bright enough. At any rate, he could see no one, but he could make out the train coming steadily toward them.

The two emerged like bodies from a grave, shaking the dirt from their clothes and hair. Joshua seemed stunned. Moss carried the boy against his hip as he moved toward the tracks in front of him.

As the train came on, Moss realized that it was not moving as slowly as Pastor Lewis had suggested it would. In fact, as the engine and its tender passed, boxcars followed in a steady beat. He realized that he would have to begin running. As he did, he saw no cars with open doors. One after the other went by with no chance to hop on with the boy. He might have been able to grab a rail or a bar and hoist himself up on the side of a car, but with the boy on his hip, that was impossible.

He slowed his run to a stop and looked down the track at the passing train in desperation. About six cars away, there seemed to be a slatted cattle car coming at them. Maybe the two of them could jump that one instead of the closed boxcars.

Moss began his parallel run again, holding Joshua tightly. Looking over his shoulder, he could see that the cattle car was open. As it drew next to him, he heaved the boy aboard and onto the hay-strewn floor. Then he tossed the cloth bag in. The effort to throw the child forced him to lose pace, however, and he fell behind.

It was a mystery where he found the strength to pick up the run again enough to catch the moving car. But he did, grabbing one of the slats on the car's side and swinging himself up and into the bed of the uncompromising thing.

He had made it and he lay exhausted and relieved. But before he could locate Joshua, rough hands grabbed him and something very sharp was held against his throat.

"Well, it seems we have some unexpected visitors," said a deep, southern voice.

CHAPTER 8

DR. MUNSCH

Dr. Munsch sat in his private office on Howard Street and considered the situation. This was his sanctuary, where his thinking was clearest. Here, he was well removed from the reception area, the examination rooms, the lab, the surgery, and any of the other physicians' offices that shared the building.

At one time, his personal quarters might have been called spacious, but now the room was decidedly academic; which is to say, tight and overflowing with clutter. Dark oak paneled walls were nearly hidden by various plaques, certificates, photographs, mementos, and other bric-a-brac of university and hospital life. One wall held tiers of shelves overflowing with bound textbooks, reprinted articles, medical journals, and manila folders. Some were in English; most were in German. Another wall offered a half-blocked doorway, which led to a sleeping apartment that was in direct contradiction to the office, oddly Spartan.

Within the office, a massive oak desk and a matching sideboard were practically buried under piles of reference books, open files, handwritten notes, and other loose papers. A wide glass case in the corner held shelves crammed with ominous-looking diagnostic equipment arranged in no discernable order. A large, wooden clothes tree, bedecked with overcoat, scarf, and derby hat gave the impression of a hulking man waiting in the corner, listening. More spores of the physician's world covered several fan-back chairs placed around the room. One held a white lab coat with dark stains.

Green-shaded oil lamps, located off in the reaches of the room, were unlit, but an intense, focused beam from an electric gooseneck lamp carved a small radius on the desk. The doctor sat behind it, his face in shadow, his hunched silhouette suggesting desperation and menace. His posture and the atmosphere of the cluttered, cave-like room were reflective of the growing chaos in the doctor's mind.

He had to let William Johnson die. The man's right brain had deteriorated steadily, and that left nothing of use. Despite all of the doctor's efforts to stimulate and develop the right lobe, no procedure had worked. Even electroshock offered no improvement. Johnson had slipped deep into some place within his own mind—what was left of it. So, during his last surgical exploration, Dr. Munsch simply let the patient slip away completely. No one was surprised that the man had finally succumbed.

Why had Johnson been so fragile? Mrs. Flannigan survived and continued providing useful evidence in the proof of lateralization, but not his male patient. *Was that it? Was it because he was male? There are significant physiological differences in the brains of men and women. Perhaps a new direction—can I tie those differences to lateral preference or chance of survival? What about age? Or, maybe African heritage has something to do with it.* The doctor needed to know more. There were so many unanswered questions.

One thing he did know was that William Johnson had become of no value whatsoever to the continued pursuit of science. For that reason, he had to go; but now, the surgeon was forced to find another subject.

He had searched for weeks to find a replacement, even traveling to Mercy Hospital in Pittsburgh when he heard of a man who had fallen from scaffolding and injured the left side of his head. Unfortunately, the officious Sisters of Mercy were like all of the rest of his disbelievers and detractors, refusing to release the patient to his care. Then there was the debacle at the Pennsylvania Hospital for the Insane in Philadelphia. Despite the several promising candidates in residence, the hospital's administrators clearly cared more about individual "patient care" than making a major contribution to the future of medicine. Munsch's histrionics over the rejection of his request almost cost him his own freedom.

And, finally, the physicians at Bellevue in New York refused to even talk to him. They hinted that if he persisted in harassing their staff over his request for experimentation, certain damning letters would be sent to Drs. Halstead, Osler, Welch, and Kelly—the "Big Four" at Johns Hopkins. These were men who could and would snuff out his career within a half a moment's consideration. He could not afford to have those letters written, given his already shaky status at the hospital, so he left the small minds at Bellevue alone. But this final ignominy left him without a means of pursuing his life's work. As a result, he could feel himself sliding back once again into the depression that bedeviled him.

It seemed like depression had always been a part of Leopold Munsch's psychology, reaching as far back as his childhood in Bavaria. He experienced some relief once his imperious and disdainful father died, an event that was both uplifting and freeing for him. But his feelings of helplessness and self-loathing came back in a rush when the mother he worshipped took her own life a year later. This tragedy left the boy alone, impoverished, and without direction.

The young Leopold began to sink into an abyss that he barely survived. The combination of a kindly Austrian *oma*, an innate intelligence, and a battery of well-meaning therapists kept him from the suicide he regularly contemplated. Eventually, he managed to reach a functioning emotional plateau. Once there, the pendulum swung and he discovered an inner anger on some other side of himself. His fury at the world, and his place in it, fueled an arousing ambition and a hunger for academic excellence and the recognition that comes with it.

In 1862, his grandmother passed away, leaving her entire estate to him. The young man now had the financial wherewithal to pursue his passion for schooling. So, he enrolled in the University of Vienna the next year. Within the proscribed four years, young Leopold built an impressive academic resume and was thought of as something of a prodigy. His professors recognized his intellect and steered him toward medicine, using their connections to assure him a seat in the university's renowned medical school. Here, too, Munsch exceeded all expectations, earning the highest grades while demonstrating very innovative thought on the human brain. His published papers on lateralization and behavior even picked up research citations around the European neurological community. By the time he completed his graduate program, he sat at the top of the class of 1871.

Despite his skills and hunger for the work, Munsch was judged by colleagues to be reclusive, curt, and moody to the point of being antisocial. These general aspects of personality, however, are often overlooked by academe, especially when they are attached to talent. So, the young man was offered a position at the prestigious Vienna General Hospital just the same. The budding doctor accepted eagerly, interning and serving his residency at the hospital in the minimal three years. Once his training was at an end, he was asked to join the research staff of the institution in order to continue with his study of the brain. Dr. Munsch remained at Vienna General, advancing his work over the next twelve years.

As successful as he had been, however, his depression was never very far away. Only rapid and continuous accomplishment seemed to keep it at bay. He often felt like a man going blind—still able to see, but sensing the black growing at the edges. As a result, Dr. Munsch studied human depression almost as much as he did the physiognomy of the brain itself. In his research on the illness, it was inevitable that he would discover and be intrigued by the properties of a new drug called cocaine.

This derivative of coca leaves offered him a possible way to dispel his demons, or at least manage them. The doctor had heard and read of the properties of coca leaves for some time, of course. Both the American company Parke-Davis and its German rival, Merck, had been in heated competition to produce a coca drug in various forms for some years. All over Europe and the United States, makers of patent medicine had begun to infuse coca extract into innumerable products as far back as the 1860s. As a result, users on both sides of the Atlantic had succumbed to claims of treatment for everything from children's croup to the rheumatism of old age. One of the most popular wines in the world, Vin Mariani, was a Bordeaux wine treated with coca leaves. The drink claimed to be a tonic that restored health, strength, energy, and vitality. It was particularly reflective of the Victorian mindset that the substance's curative properties be emphasized rather than its euphoric side effects, although there could be no doubt that the latter was a huge part of what kept customers coming back.

As a highly trained physician, Dr. Munsch was rigidly skeptical of these restorative claims. It wasn't until 1884 that he began to think differently. In his regular scan of the academic journals, he read a monograph by one of the physicians on the hospital's staff, a young Viennese neurologist by the name of Sigmund Freud. Freud's paper, *Über Coca*, stated in no uncertain terms that an extract of the coca leaf, currently being used as an analgesic during ophthalmological procedures, produced the relief Dr. Munsch had been seeking. Freud's self-experimentation with cocaine moved him to claim at least seven separate benefits from its use. What's more, Freud's research showed no lasting side effects, physical addiction, or psychological dependence resulting from its intake.

This was an important departure from other drugs Dr. Munsch had tried, like opium or its offshoots, morphine and heroin. These treatments certainly relieved his depression temporarily, but they also left him drowsy, nauseous, and constipated. He also could name a number of acquaintances using opiates who showed all of the signs of dependence on the poppy extract. Finally, each time he used morphine, once the elation wore off, his melancholia seemed to return deeper still. He could easily see himself falling into the same destructive cycle of increasing use as his acquaintances had.

Of cocaine's supposed benefits, its ability to relieve depression—albeit short-term—was most important to Dr. Munsch. Yet, it was Freud's claim that the substance was a stimulant to mental abilities that eventually moved Munsch to experiment. In truth, his initial reluctance to try the drug had more to do with his animosity for Dr. Freud than it did any skepticism over its effectiveness. In short, Munsch loathed Freud. The man was younger and junior to him at the hospital, yet he enjoyed greater acclaim and recognition for his achievements than Munsch did for his own leading research. Freud's work in the new scientific field of psychoanalysis had caught both the attention of science and the interest of the public.

Perhaps his rival's insights and energy came from use of cocaine. Once Munsch made that connection, he resolved to do his own experimenting. When he did, the intense euphoria, the feelings of superiority, the clarity of thought, and the manic energy made him a believer. These advantages were so valuable to him and his brain lateralization work that the other side effects—loss of appetite, increased heartrate and breathing, occasional panic, and the inevitable return of depression—were eclipsed.

With his psychological troubles now being managed to some degree, Dr. Munsch's work increased and took new directions. For the next three years, he worked feverishly at his research and the experimentation it required. This resulted in a series of long, erudite academic papers that made the best journals. His latest work on the human brain began to be recognized and discussed. He was invited to lecture on his theories throughout Europe. But, at the same time, his use of cocaine steadily increased.

The neurologist began to exhibit another type of noticeable behavior. He often felt paranoiac, anxious. That made him angry and hostile. His relationships around Vienna General Hospital, tentative at best, began to deteriorate in serious ways. Hallway discussions turned into shouting matches. Accusations were hurled in all directions, and physical confrontation seemed like it was never far away. Finally, a disturbing incident that took place in one of the surgical suites forced both the administration and faculty to take action. They could no longer pander to the brilliant Dr. Munsch.

During a routine lobotomy, the surgeon lost self-control over a minor misstep by one of the attending nurses. Screaming that the assistant was trying to murder the patient, he stabbed the man's hand with a scalpel and may have killed the fellow had he not been restrained. Munsch continued to rant about murder even as they held him down, and it was clear that he was hallucinating. As soon as he had gained some semblance of calm, the doctor began to convulse and twitch, eyes rolling back in his head, feet flailing.

During the subsequent investigation, Dr. Munsch's addiction and dependence became obvious to the most casual observer. Despite the surgeon's claim that it was all due to the lack of sleep, it was clear that Vienna General Hospital had to distance itself from him. This revelation would also throw all of Munsch's research into question, leaving the hospital embarrassed and apologetic. So, in the spring of 1887, Leopold Munsch was directed to step down from his post and leave the hospital.

There followed two years spent in various Bavarian sanitaria. Munsch managed to separate himself from cocaine, but the desire to use the drug remained. His general depression returned, and he spent most of his time in various therapies. In time, however, he once again managed to find a sort of equilibrium that allowed him to function.

In 1889, he was appointed on a conditional basis to a post at the Royal London Hospital. The hospital was executing a major expansion into the fields of neurology and psychology and was seeking talent. Leopold Munsch was a well-known name with a robust body of work and his ideas had started to regain interest, despite the history of their genesis. So, if Dr. Munsch could demonstrate ability that was not drug-induced, he would be made welcome.

He worked hard under these conditions for six years and managed some modest contributions to the hospital's research. However, he never again flashed the brilliance of earlier days and his efforts around segmentation and lateralization of the brain never recaptured the interest it had at one time. He felt that this was due in large part to the cloud that hung over his earlier work and the circumstances of his departure from Vienna General. As a result, he became convinced that to succeed, he had to leave Europe.

Within two years, Dr. Munsch began a correspondence with Dr. William Stewart Halsted, a surgeon and founding member of the staff at the new Johns Hopkins Hospital in Baltimore, Maryland in the United States. His persistence in requesting a post at the hospital paid dividends when the institution finally accepted him into their growing neurology department in 1895.

The last two years at Hopkins had not been easy, although he was given everything he needed, whenever he needed it. He was compensated very handsomely as well, but money meant little to him. It was his work that was the problem. It was lack of respect for his work, and it was his critics on the faculty and staff. They just couldn't understand what he was doing and so they devalued, in a thousand little ways, everything he did. He blamed this on his read of the Hopkins culture and was convinced that his critics were fueled by professional jealousy. He thought them so focused on procedure and subservient to the strict rules of "scientific method" that they were ignoring the far-reaching implications of his research. He was alone once again, and once again he began using cocaine.

Munsch was convinced that his use was under control and that the benefits justified the risks. This reasoning was given greater impetuous when his most recent breakthrough occurred. What if he found someone with a pre-existing artistic intelligence? Would a lobotomy of the left hemisphere then produce even more amazing skills in the patient and more evidence of his theories?

With William Johnson now deceased, the search for a new "preprogrammed" right brain became an obsession. Unfortunately, finding an actor or artist who had damage to their left lobe would be next to impossible. That reality led him to take a risk.

At a hospital conference held in one of the Academy of Music's meeting rooms, he had been introduced to Tunis F. Dean, the theater's managing director. Munsch thought the man an ass, but Dean seemed to be oblivious to the doctor's poor manners and invited him for a drink. Over a couple of whiskeys, Munsch found Dean to be an attentive listener, even fawning in his interest. Eventually, the doctor got around to his idea regarding the right brain of an artistic person. Dean was fascinated, and even jokingly referred to a couple of actors whom he thought might be prime candidates for experimentation.

As the third whiskey was being consumed, the managing director finally revealed the reason for all of his attention and bonhomie. Dean wanted to put the arm on Munsch for financial support, and he wanted similar entree to others connected to Hopkins. The "touch" came in the form of a joke that Munsch didn't understand. What he did understand was that he was being presented with an opportunity for a quid pro quo.

"What the Academy needs is good, solid, sustainable support from Baltimore's top layer," the theater man began. "I've been trying to establish an elite group of charitable-minded donors that would assure the growth of culture in our fine city, and your ties to Johns Hopkins University and the hospital could be very helpful."

Munsch suffered through this blather and allowed his drinking partner to continue. The doctor sat smiling, awaiting his opening.

"It certainly is true that our contributing membership has been growing nicely, and we do have a few wealthy patrons, including the Garrett family. But I have not yet been able to build a rapport with anyone directly affiliated with the hospital. Someone like Dr. Kelly or Dr. Osler—you know, one of the institution's Big Four. Unfortunately, the only Big Four I see on Howard Street are those damned Orioles and their so-called baseball stars!" Dean laughed heartily.

The witticism was lost on Munsch. He didn't know the Garretts or have any idea what a "Big Four" was. He had heard, of course, of John Work Garrett, the builder of the B&O Railroad, and he knew what baseball was, since the people in this dismal city were constantly talking about their team. But the game had never really penetrated his consciousness. What he now knew, though, was that Dean wanted money and some introductions. Both were going to cost him.

"Yes, yes, I see how my colleagues could help. I myself am willing to support the theater," Dr. Munsch said. "I could certainly write a bank draft tomorrow and arrange for you to talk to my colleagues." The doctor watched the grin widen over Tunis F. Dean's face, and before the theater director could begin a genuflecting response, he said, "I was wondering, though, if you might consider helping me with a matter of my own."

"Of course, Dr. Munsch, just name it," the managing director answered, thinking a free ticket or two would be no problem at all.

"Well, you recall me mentioning the need for a person willing to further the science of neurology?"

Chapter 9

1857
The Railroad

The train rocked, but Moss kept as still as possible, the arm around his neck and the blade at his throat holding him rigid. With legs still dangling through the opening in the cattle car, he stared at dark shapes passing within increasing speed. The occasional spot of light showed the ratty backsides of North Baltimore houses and buildings. Trash-filled freight and storage yards slid by. Moss knew his attacker could just as easily slit his throat as throw him off the train. Or both.

Then Joshua began to cry, and a woman's voice said, "Joseph, don't you hurt that man! Remember what the Lord said to Moses: 'Thou shalt not kill.'"

In response to that, the man slid Moss further over the edge so that all he had to do was let go to rid himself of the interloper. The knife seemed to be convulsing in his hand with the swaying train's increasing speed. Blood trickled down Moss' chest.

The woman tried a different tack. "Joseph, he's got a child with him. You going to do that boy as well? No, you're not. You've never killed no one, never. And you're not gonna start now. Not with me, you're not. Now, leave him be." Her appeal was personal and desperate. Although it was made with force, there was no confidence in it.

Joshua now realized, at some basic level, that he was about to lose the only scrap of security he had. His cry became frantic.

The woman, too, was frightened by the situation and was no longer sure that she knew the man, Joseph, or what he was capable of doing. Just the same, she spoke to Joshua as gently as she could. "Now child, don't you be afraid. My man ain't gonna hurt your daddy." Then speaking as much to Joseph, "He's a good man and a daddy too. See, we have a child of our own."

That broke the silence of Moss's attacker. "Esther! What did I tell you? We can't trust nobody. It's too dangerous. What's more, we ain't got enough for ourselves. It's too many in here!"

The man's arm tightened, but the blade wavered. Joshua's cry became a desperate wail and he lunged at the shape hunched over Moss, nearly sending all three out into the night.

With that, the woman was up grasping at Joseph's shirt with one hand while the other held her baby against her chest. Moving with the train, she bent down close to her man's ear and whispered, "Joseph, leave him be. He's got a boy with him. He's just trying to get away, like us."

"Esther...."

"Joseph, you know this is wrong."

The moment hung for an eternity as Joseph made a decision. The knife moved away and he dragged Moss in from the lip of the railroad car.

Moss was on his feet immediately, pushing Joshua hard into the hay piled in the corner. He leapt at Joseph and took a wild swing that grazed the man's head. Then he bulled into him, and together they slammed against the slatted timber. The blade came up again and Moss bent double to avoid the weapon's swift, horizontal arc. The knife tore Moss's shirt and left a long burn across his stomach. The force of Joseph's sweep and the lurch of the train turned him enough for Moss to bear hug him from behind and drive him face-first into the bed of the car. The blade skittered away in the dark. Moss pressed his forearm hard into Joseph's neck, hoping to snap it.

"Stop! Stop right now! We can't have this! You'll kill each other. Mister, please don't hurt him. He spared your life. He could have done you easy!" The woman said this in a high-pitched, rat-a-tat way, full of fear and pleading.

At the same time, Joshua screamed, "Stop fighting. Stop fighting!"

Moss got up from his enemy and stepped back. Joseph rose quickly, but in pain. He crouched, facing Moss and holding his left arm. The last lights of the city bled through the slats of the speeding cattle car, becoming oscillating bars across the floor. The fight became slow motion as the pattern continually found the adversaries, pulsating with hate and fear.

"Joseph! Stop, please for the love of God, stop!" Esther begged.

But the battle was already over and the energy for the struggle began to drain away. A fierce staring match ended when Joseph backed away to sit in the corner with Esther and their baby.

"Joseph, what's wrong with your arm?" Esther asked in alarm, but a look from him silenced her.

Moss edged backward, checking his belly. The red line was not deep, but it oozed a little blood and stung mightily. He patted it with his shirttail and dabbed at the cut along his throat, then slid down into one of the corners, gathering Joshua under his arm. Their world was dark now that Baltimore was left behind, and he could see little but shapes in the far corner. They must have been traveling for some time, since he could smell their human mustiness even over the odor of the car's previous occupants. A family, running, just as he was. He recalled the Quaker's warning not to trust anyone, even if they were runaways.

After a long silence, Moss growled, "You have my bindle. I want it back."

"Come and get it, houseboy," the man answered.

When Moss stood, Joseph stood as well, despite Esther's attempt to hold him in place.

"Seeing that I let you join us, Mister, I think it's only fair that you pay your way."

"Joseph…" the woman began.

"I want the bindle and I will have it now," Moss said.

As the two men stalked each other again, Esther grabbed the bundle of supplies and flung it at Moss, hitting him in the chest.

"Esther!"

"Joseph, we'll manage without having to steal from folks who ain't got much. And I can't have you dead."

Defeated, Joseph sat back down and hung his head. "What are we gonna do for food now, Esther?"

Moss picked up the provisions Pastor Lewis had given him. He felt around in the bag and identified a few of the johnnycakes from the night before, a hunk of fatback, and two small apples. Hattie had been given a bindle as well, but that was now buried with her. He tucked the bag behind him.

Within a few minutes and as hard as Joshua tried to stay awake, the day's events and the rhythm of the train soon put him to sleep. Moss dozed too, unwillingly giving in to his own fatigue. Several times he awoke in a panic, only to hear the regular sounds of sleep coming from across the car. The starry sky wavered in width as an irregular line of inky trees passed steadily across the entranceway, rising and falling with the rocking of the train as it made its way north.

Sometime in the first gray of dawn, his fitful sleep was interrupted by a baby's cry and its mother's soothing tones. As the dim light began to transform the cattle car's contents, Moss feigned sleep and took inventory through hooded eyes.

It was obvious from the smell and the hay pushed up against the sides and into corners that the cattle car had been used for its intended purpose very recently. Iron stock rings swung against metal plates bolted to the car's main timbers, creating atonal music as the train lurched and swayed. There was nothing else in the space except for the shapes huddled in the opposite corner.

The woman held her baby to her breast, arms enfolding her precious charge, taking whatever little pleasure there may in such maternal duty. Next to her, Joseph hunched, his right arm held against his chest and his left around his knees, the knife in evidence.

Moss immediately reached behind him for the bindle and found it still there. When he looked across at Joseph again, the man was staring at him, eyes shining, alert and calculating. Moss knew he was building courage enough to try to get at the food.

Joshua stirred and came awake. The first thing he did was call for his mother, then when the memory of the previous night came flooding back, he began to let out small keening sounds of misery and loss. Moss sat up, reached for the boy, and pulled him tight against him.

"Joshua, I've got you. I've got you and I'm not going to leave you. Your momma loved you, boy, but she's with the Lord at present and is better for it. It's you and me from now on, and we'll be alright. No need to cry. You'll be safe before too long. Hush up now, or you'll wake the baby."

Moss comforted the child until the boy grew quiet, although he continued to shake. The man needed to take Joshua's mind off his mother.

"Are you hungry?" he asked in a whisper.

When the boy nodded through tears, Moss rummaged through the bundle of food behind him, careful not to bring it out into the open. When he looked, he saw that both the man and the woman across the car were locked on his hands and what they were going to produce.

Moss gave Joshua one of the apples. He had no water and knew a hoecake would be difficult to get down, regardless of hunger. The apple was gone quickly and the boy looked for more.

"Mister, you have any water over there?" Moss asked across the car.

When the man didn't answer, Esther said, "Yes, sir. We have some water. A canteen, nearly full."

"But keep your distance," Joseph warned.

"We have a couple of johnnycakes here that I'd be willing to trade for a cup of water, if you're willing."

"Those dry biscuits are no good to you without water, Mister. Why don't you just hand them over?"

"Joseph, the man's trying to share with us. Listen to him," Esther chided.

"I don't trust him."

"I don't trust you either," Moss answered. "I see you've found your blade."

With that, Esther handed her man the baby, stood, and came across the space holding a battered tin cup and a cavalry canteen with a wooden stopper. Balancing with the train, she knelt and poured out a cup of water. Moss handed her the hoecakes and, with the food cradled against her chest, she lurched back across the car and extended the meager sustenance to Joseph. He refused her offer and urged her to eat, his face torn with anger and relief.

The day began to break and the new sun struck the moving train. Bright yellow bars of light cut the interior of the cattle car into horizontal layers. These shafts were dense with hay dust, churning and blowing in the air with the train's movement. Moss pulled his shirt up over his mouth and nose and did the same for Joshua.

Soon, the scenery began to slow, the swaying became less, and the train stopped altogether with a clanging of its couplings.

Through the car's slats, Moss could see they sat on a gravel embankment that fell away to a patch of cleared land. There, well-tended apple trees straddled a small, winding brook. Beyond that, a thin wood gave way to a wide river about a quarter-mile distant. If they were anywhere close to Harrisburg, the river would be the Susquehanna.

The opening on the other side of the railcar revealed a dirt road and fenced farmland, cultivated with some low, green plant—beans or alfalfa, maybe. Not far beyond the field, a large white frame house and a grey stone barn sat at the foot of a long, soft-shouldered run of ancient mountains, just beginning to get the morning sun.

Joshua drank the water and chewed on a cake; Moss ate the last apple and surveyed his traveling companions. The little bit of food he had traded with them was quickly eaten and he watched as Esther fretted over her man's arm. He was sweating and holding the limb still and close. It was probably broken.

Moss pulled the slab of fatback from the bindle and stood. He put his hand on Joshua's head and told him he would be right here. He wasn't leaving. Joseph's head came up but he didn't move.

"I have some salt pork here that I can share," Moss said.

Joseph just stared with red-ringed eyes, but Esther said, "That's very kind, thank you."

"I can hand it to you if you want to cut a piece. Take half."

Esther looked at Joseph and reached for the knife. When she took it gently from his hand, he resisted weakly. He was feverish and in pain.

As she cut a slab of the fatback, she began to cry.

"Your man is in a bad way," Moss observed.

"Yes, he broke his arm," she answered as if she was describing a death sentence. Her voice revealed all the worry in her.

"I'm no doctor, understand," Moss said. "But I've set a few broken arms before."

"You?"

"Yes, your man was right. I was a houseboy. But I learned some valuable things in that house. Broken arms was one of them. Maybe if I see it, I can set and bind it. Might ease some of the pain and give it a chance to mend right."

"You won't hurt him, will you?"

"Oh, I'm going to hurt him alright. But it'll only be for a little bit, and he's in no shape to resist."

"I don't..." Esther started.

Moss cut her off and moved to Joseph, who had rolled over onto his side. "It has to be done, if he's going to have two arms tomorrow and be alive the next day. I need you to hold him. I'll let you know when the pain will come."

With that, Moss examined, then set Joseph's fracture and bound it to his chest with strips cut from the bindle. There was agony, but it was short-lived and afterward, the man lay flat in a fevered state, his head sharing Esther's lap with the baby.

Moss returned to Joshua, gave him some of the salt pork, and bit off a piece for himself. His plan was to stay on the train, as the Quakers had advised. If they were outside of Harrisburg, the railcars would be transferred to an engine headed east to Philadelphia. He guessed that it might take a couple of hours before the transfer would occur and anticipated some anxious wait time as the day started to take hold. The food was gone, and he knew that Joshua was still hungry and was likely to get hungrier on the way east.

"Joshua, would you help me pick some apples for the rest of the way?"

The boy said nothing and simply moved closer to Moss. He was afraid to leave the scant security of the cattle car and the man's side. But, before long, the idea of ripe apples and exploring the brook that he could see through the slats broke his resistance.

"Will you be there with me?" he asked.

"Right there," Moss answered. Then he spoke to Esther. "There's an orchard just down the embankment, and a mountain stream as well. If you give me your canteen, I'll fill it and bring you some apples."

"Thank you, mister. And thanks for everything else, too."

Esther handed him the container and watched as Moss and Joshua climbed down from the car, ducked under the train, and slid down the embankment to the orchard.

They filled the canteen and made three trips with apples cradled in shirttails. It only took one before Joshua lost interest and began forgetting the recent past by playing in the brook. Eventually, Moss joined the boy and sat on the bank in the shade, munching on an apple and waiting for signs that the train was going to move.

As the sun reached its peak, Moss was propped up under a tree, dozing. Joshua was already asleep. Suddenly, there were sounds of men and horses.

Moss scrambled up the rail embankment and lay on his stomach, peering under the train. He could see the legs of two horses riding slowly up the tracks on the other side. At each car, the men stopped and checked for open doors. When they reached the cattle car, Moss slid further down the incline, staying below eyesight.

"Whoa, Tyree, what do we have here?" one man yelled.

The horses merged on the other side of the car and the speaker dismounted. He was a big man, full black beard, wide brimmed hat, high leather boots with short spurs, long black duster. His pistol belt held a Colt and several sets of shackles that jangled as he walked.

"Looks like some payday in here, Curtis."

"Now why don't you freeloaders come on off of Mr. Thomson's train? Do it now!" the black beard shouted. "Don't make me use this shotgun."

Moss heard Esther rise with the baby and move to the door.

"My man. He's hurt," she said.

With that, the man on the horse grabbed her arm and jerked her out of the car. Esther fell hard on the roadbed, just barely able to protect the baby in her fall. The infant began to wail, but Esther lay still in the gravel, clutching her bundle to her chest.

"Nigger, I told you to get up and get out of there!" the man on foot barked. He climbed up into the car, grabbed Joseph by the boot, and dragged him to the edge. Once on the ground, in one muscled heave, the slaver hauled Joseph out onto the roadbed as well. The fall was hard and awkward.

Joseph groaned and stared with blurred eyes. In the process, the knife, which Esther had tucked into his belt, fell out, bounced, and came to rest against the slaver's boot.

"Did you see that, Curtis? The man tried to stab me!"

"He don't look so good, Tyree. Looks sick, and that's probably a broken arm."

"Not much use to us then, are you, boy? Come at me with a blade! We both saw it."

With that, the man drew his pistol and put two shots into Joseph's chest, killing him.

Esther let out a scream and Moss lay frozen.

"Shut up, woman, or I'll put you and that baby out of your misery as well." The pistol's hammer clicked back.

Moss sprang up from under the train, grabbed the dropped knife, and drove it deep through the man's beard and into his throat. The swiftness and violence of the surprise attack shocked both slavers. With the knife deep in his neck, the wounded man spun and, in panic, fired the Colt into the side of his partner's horse. The horse reared and threw the rider into the side of the train. Moss was on top of him immediately, banging his head against the wheel of the cattle car until he moved no longer. When he turned, the other slave hunter had pulled the knife from his neck, but was on the ground with both hands at his throat, trying to stop the pulsating rush of blood.

As if an understanding god were watching, there was a sudden screeching and banging of couplings. The train shivered as the engine began the effort to drag its load once again.

Moss picked up Esther and the baby and put them gently back into the car. Then he ducked under the train and found Joshua just making his way up the embankment from the brook. The two swung up into the train and disappeared into one of the corners.

Moss watched for signs of alarm up and down the road and from the nearby farm. He saw nothing moving except the field of alfalfa as the Pennsylvania Railroad began to pick up speed going east. Shortly, they were crossing the bridge that spanned the river between Lemoyne and Harrisburg, on their way to Philadelphia.

As late afternoon set in, Moss sat in the hay with Joshua under one arm and the woman and child under the other. No one spoke, which was okay, because he needed to think about what he had just done.

Chapter 10

A Woman of Substance

It wasn't that Mary Elizabeth Garrett hated men; after all, she had adored her father and had walked out on a few social and financial planks over the years to fulfill his last wishes. Rather, it was the damned arrogance of men in general and their conviction that women were not capable creatures. She never bothered to determine whether this was out of fear or plain stupidity or both. Yet, it was real, as real as a brick wall.

She found that pulling down that wall required a good deal of energy and resources. Fortunately, she had plenty of both. Her vast fortune was clearly her most powerful tool in the demolition, and she believed it always would be in a world dominated by the male of the species. But it was their very bigotry that gave her a second very useful way to pry apart bricks. Invariably, she was underestimated.

Her partner, Carey Thomas, often suggested that Mary Elizabeth chose her appearance just to add to that advantage. Her bespectacled, matronly face, soft, round figure, and demure dress was what the opposition saw when she joined them in various conference rooms. They soon found, however, they were negotiating with a woman focused and powerful, every bit their equal and then some. It was guaranteed that whether the talks went well or not, men left meetings muttering under their breath.

That was how the Hopkins Medical School got built. It was how she got women admitted on the same basis as men. It was how she propped up Bryn Mawr University in Pennsylvania and assured Carey its presidency. And, it was how she established a superior college preparatory school for girls in Baltimore. She accomplished it all when women were supposed to be about teas and husbands. Money was her bait, male bias the barb to her hook.

How Mary Elizabeth came to this place in her life wasn't entirely due to her control of the Garrett fortune. She was the dutiful daughter when she watched her father send her brothers, Harry and Robert, to Princeton with the intent of parsing out the affairs of the estate to them as heirs apparent. Yet her father refused to offer her the same opportunity, making it clear that she was meant to preside over the uncountable and often dreary social responsibilities of the family. Her genuine disappointment in his dictum was shrugged off by the men in the family, saying Mary Elizabeth's attitude was the result of her suffering from "the vapors."

The delicious irony of it all was that there was a much more valuable opportunity ahead of her. John Work Garrett was a nation builder and a confidante of presidents, but the role took its toll on his health. His symptoms could only be relieved by getting away, and that usually meant restful, European landscapes and an abundance of French cooking. Because he was alone, it was Mary Elizabeth whom he took with him on his vacations. She was to be nurse and companion.

To her, it was a welcome change from Baltimore society and an opportunity to explore. As it happened, because the press of business didn't always disappear with the change in scenery, she was inevitably asked to assist with the flow of work in addition to her other duties. As a result, within a matter of weeks, Mary Elizabeth became her father's trusted personal secretary and right hand.

Their working relationship continued upon returning to the States, and she went where he went, did what he did, listened, and learned. In the process, the elder Garrett discovered a quick, voracious mind—albeit female—that became indispensable to him. It wasn't an Ivy League degree she earned over those years, but rather hands-on training in the most competitive, rough-and-tumble business in America.

Mary Elizabeth learned railroads as the industry rebuilt the country after the war. It was rail that set the nation's direction for the future and created an economic power like none the world had ever seen. Of course, the industry was owned and overseen by alpha males, ruthless in both strategy and tactics, lions with names like Vanderbilt, Sanford, and Gould. For an essentially quiet person, her education was eye opening and life changing. It also formed a large part of her character.

When her exhausted father died in 1884, managing the Garrett estate and its finances fell to Mary Elizabeth. Her oldest brother, Robert, was often incapacitated by depression and chose to focus his energies on the operation of Robert Garrett and Sons, the family's investment banking firm. Her second brother, Harry, despite his business training and predestined path, seemed more interested in spending the family fortune than in managing it. When he drowned in a boating accident while sailing in the Chesapeake in 1888, Mary Elizabeth became the estate's administrator by default.

Now, with the responsibility and control, she was not reluctant to kick down doors when she had to do so. Once at the table, she was both strong and confident in her convictions.

Among her many opinions, there was nothing she was more sure of than the equality of women. It would infuriate her when she'd wade through the latest *Sun* op-ed piece debating "rights for women," as if a right like voting was a man's to give or withhold. Denying that right was tantamount to invalidating women as human beings.

Ten years after her successful battle with Dan Gilman and the others holding the reins at Hopkins, Mary Elizabeth enthusiastically took up the banner of women's suffrage. She became close friends with two venerable ladies building national reputations for women's issues, Susan Anthony and Elizabeth Cady Stanton. In Baltimore, she worked with and supported Emma Funck's efforts. These experienced toilers for suffrage saw a sister in Miss Garrett. They liked her mind, her organizational skills, and they liked her personally. Of course, the legitimacy that her financial and societal position could bring to the National American Woman Suffrage Association was also very appealing.

All of this passion and discontent with the status quo came with a price, however. Mary Elizabeth was often estranged from her family over business and real estate issues. Her politics were a lightning rod for a wide range of opposition, and both men and women saw her as disruptive and autocratic. Her established friendships narrowed as her acquaintances and petitioners grew. Her freedom of movement became limited as her activities became news.

It was in this environment that she agreed to organize a national convention of women, and to do it in Baltimore. Some leaders in the suffrage movement thought it unwise to flaunt the issue in a city that in recent years had become more and more conservatively Southern in its attitude. But Mary Elizabeth believed in the almost one-hundred-year-old advice of Admiral Lord Nelson: "Desperate affairs require desperate measures."

The Academy of Music on Howard Street was big enough and prestigious enough to hold the kind of national meeting Mary Elizabeth envisioned. She had been a contributor for some years, and her brother had sat on its Board. She was friendly with, if not close to, James Kernan, the theater's majority owner, although he was out of the country on an extended hiatus. Just the same, she was well known at the Academy, and her name was of national significance. She could expect at least a hearing on what she had planned.

Tunis Dean, the Academy's current managing director, was not someone with whom Mary Elizabeth wanted to spend a great deal of time discussing anything. But her plans were important to the NAWSA and their national objectives, so she approached him with the idea just the same.

Dean immediately and enthusiastically agreed to her proposal, pronouncing his convention facility to be the only venue in Baltimore worthy of holding such a large, prestigious gathering. His gushing acceptance and cloying deference to her made her uncomfortable. She had seen this kind of behavior before and it created distrust, making her wonder about his motives. She also knew that it would not be that easy. Unfortunately, with Kernan somewhere in South America, Dean was the primary conduit to the Board of Sponsors that would make the controversial decision whether to go forward.

Mary Elizabeth first insisted on speaking to the Board directly, and found the managing director more than willing to put it on the next agenda. Then, later, she got word from him that the Board's agenda was completely jammed. When she pressed for an ad-hoc meeting, she was told that they had declined to meet because of "the probable inability to raise a voting quorum."

Dean was personally very disappointed in that decision, of course, but then explained that he had convinced them to review a written proposal outlining her plans. This sounded like more dismissal to her, but she was willing to play the game, for now. So, the proposal was written and submitted with a codicil: acceptance could result in a sizable contribution to the Academy. She met with the managing director in the Garrett Mansion in Mount Vernon Square to get the Board's decision.

"Mrs. Garrett—"

"Miss Garrett."

"Yes, yes, of course. My apologies. Uh, thank you for meeting with me. Have you been well?"

"Mr. Dean, I appreciate your asking, but I'd like to get down to why you have come to see me."

"Of course." He gave a little bow with his fawning response. Then, drawing himself back up, he began, "Well, as you know, I provided each of the Board members with copies of your proposal. By the way, I must say it was quite well done."

"Mr. Dean...."

"Miss Garrett, I can assure you that the Board has reviewed your idea with all seriousness and has discussed it at length. I answered all of their questions, just as you explained your plans to me."

"I would have appreciated the opportunity to do that myself."

"Yes, well, then an open vote was taken on whether to accept the proposal, recommend some changes, or to reject the plan outright. As you must know, I myself do not have a vote unless a tiebreaker is needed."

Mary Elizabeth was reminded as to why she disliked this obsequious man.

"And, Mr. Dean, what was the vote?"

"I'm, sorry, Miss Garrett, the proposal was rejected."

"Rejected outright, or rejected with recommended changes?"

"Outright."

"Did you make clear my financial offer?"

"I did."

"Are they negotiating with me?"

"No, Miss Garrett, they are not. It was a unanimous vote against."

"You must have some very well-to-do supporters at the Academy. What were some of the arguments against?"

"Well, the arguments were varied, but many felt the controversy around giving women the vote—"

"Who led the discussion?"

"Miss Garrett, I cannot—"

"Mr. Dean, I know most of those men on your board. In fact, I spoke to several of them beforehand. So, I have a good sense of the opinions. What I want to know is who took the lead?"

"Miss Garrett—"

"Mr. Dean, do you want the Garrett family's contribution this year?"

After a long hesitation, Dean sighed, asked for confidentiality, then coughed up a name: Alcott S. Worthy.

Chapter 11

The Academy of Music

The Academy of Music's annual fundraising event was scheduled for the Saturday night before the Orioles were to leave for spring training in Georgia. Along with the standard corporate pats on the head and the blatant appeals for financial support, the theater was staging the Baltimore debut of a play that had gotten rave reviews in its New York opening. As a result, a large flock of Baltimore's nobility would be there in all of their finest plumage. It was to be Fanny Darlington's debut in my town, as well.

As mentioned, I hate the theater. But I don't hate Miss Fanny. In fact, I had already promised her that I would attend the opening. She was playing Princess Flavia, and I liked the sound of that, although I had no idea who Princess Flavia was.

Unfortunately, I didn't have a ticket, and all seats had been either reserved or sold out for days. So, I was very pleased to hear that Harry Von Der Horst had suggested to the prickly Ned Hanlon that he should purchase a block of seats for his players. Evidently, Von Der Horst had decided that a play was just the thing to keep his rambunctious employees out of trouble on the eve of getting back to the business of baseball. It also happened that his wife, Bernadette, was chairwoman for the fundraiser. The *Playbill* promised adventure, courage, loyalty, love, and a few swordfights to boot. Harry thought this just the ticket, so to speak.

Hanlon liked the idea of keeping his boys on the straight and narrow, but would have preferred locking them up in the jug for the night. Just the same, the manager bought the tickets, making sure that Von Der Horst knew he was doing it in protest.

Hanlon has never shown me much warmth, due to my association with the Diamond. Key ingredients of his team are my partners, but Foxy Ned choses to ignore that. He'd rather blame me for the occasional bonehead play after a night of carousing. I find this both annoying and unfair, since I am usually the guy who gets his charges on their feet and in some semblance of shape to walk onto the field in the first place. I've done his job more times than I can count while he was at home dreaming of successful squeeze plays.

Now, all I had to do was figure a way to cadge a ticket out of the man. My plan was to get the players to meet at the Diamond for a drink or two before walking across the street to the theater. Since none of them had been inside the Academy, I suggested we all go together. This wasn't too hard to pull off, since McGraw and Robinson were going to be in the café anyway and the rest would prefer to wash down the dose of art and culture with either a mug of Eagle or something stronger. I would simply join them when Hanlon was handing out the duckets. There were bound to be extras, since I knew that crumb, Doyle, would be a no-show and the second baseman, Heinie Reitz, would be kept at home by his distrusting wife who was bigger than he was.

As the time to go approached, I found myself with a problem. The team was settling in and showing no inclination to move from various barstools and tables. Wilbert Robinson, the Orioles' de facto leader and current bartender, seemed perfectly happy pulling the tap and chewing the fat. I knew I had to start with him.

"Robbie, it's time to go. Hanlon's going to be waiting. How do we get these guys out of here?" I asked with an edge of frustration.

"Frank, you sure you want this crew out of here? They're spending money," Uncle Robbie said.

"Why do we have to leave?" Joe Kelley asked, glued to his barstool.

The Orioles' glamour-boy leftfielder had earned inclusion in what Baltimore's sportswriters called the "Big Four," having hit .364 last year and .365 the year before. But there was nothing glamorous about him at that moment as he sat eating the Diamond's free hardboiled eggs and waving his empty beer glass at Robinson. Kelley was having trouble keeping the eggs to himself, spitting as he talked.

"What's this thing we've got to go to anyway? I never heard of it."

If it wasn't in *The Police Gazette* or *The Sporting News*, Joe never heard of it.

"Kelley, you're still in Hanlon's doghouse for that incident in Cleveland last year and you've yet to ink a new contract for this year. You really want to give Hanlon more leverage?"

"That Cleveland woman came on to me," Kelley replied. "I couldn't help it."

"I was referring to your fighting on the field with those Spiders cranks."

"Oh, that."

"Hey, Joe, I hear the women in Macon are something," chimed in Corbett, the young pitcher who had not yet been to spring training with the team.

McGraw didn't want to go to the play either, and was perfectly happy watching his teammates buy his beer. So, hearing a chance to derail my attempt to get everyone moving, he said, "That's where Georgia peaches come from, boy. Let me tell you what happened last year...."

"Oh, no, Muggsy, let's stick to the topic," I said, grabbing the conversation back. He hated that name.

"Frank, what's this we're seeing? And why are you interested? This isn't your normal cup of tea." Willie Keeler had joined the group.

"Frank is interested in the female lead," Robinson answered from behind the bar. "He thinks he has a shot."

"Speaking of shots, how about a little rye for everyone?" Kelley suggested.

"You payin'?" Robinson asked.

"Look you corncobs," I said. "This is going to be good. It's *The Prisoner of Zenda*. An adventure story. It has swashbuckling in it."

"There you go again, Frank, showing off your vocabulary," McGraw said. "You'd have more friends if you stopped that."

"Who's this guy, Zenda?" Kelley asked, spitting egg white on me.

"I have enough friends already, Muggsy," I said, "and you're the last one to be giving advice about making friends. Look, we've got to go. I saw Hanlon waiting outside the theater now."

I was telling the truth. Through the front window, I spotted the manager standing across the street, chewing his mustache. He was checking his watch and pacing up and down among the Academy's arriving crowd.

That got everyone's attention. Robinson said, "Okay, you fools are cut off. Let's get out of here."

With that, Robinson handed his bar towel to the night man, lifted the hinged part of the bar, stepped out, and began pulling the chairs out from under the rest of the team as they rushed to finish their drinks. Before long, there was a loud group of complaining men crossing the cobblestones and avoiding the bicycles and horse pods of Howard Street.

Hanlon was clearly put out. He was doing something he didn't want to do, and was now having to wait for his team, all the while feeling out of place in front of the gaudily lit theaters. There were two sets of pedestrians competing for the sidewalk space that Hanlon was occupying—those attending the Academy of Music's play and those patronizing the Auditorium's vaudeville acts next door.

The Auditorium was featuring Kate Davis, a popular character impersonator and Bert Coote, the ribald comedian. Hanlon noticed that the rival theater was doing a brisk business and its show was probably more to the taste of his team. But he had bought these damn play tickets and by God they were going to *The Prisoner of Zenda*!

It was surprisingly warm for a March evening, and I could almost see Hanlon sweating through his signature, brown, three-piece, wool suit. This was his standard uniform; he would wear it even in August, sitting on the Union Park players' bench. Watching him bob and weave to stay clear of the throng of people arriving in carriages and on foot, I suspected that I'd be in for a hard time.

In addition to those funneling into the comedy acts, the sidewalk was full of well-heeled playgoers, as expected. I found it amusing to watch the formally dressed gentlemen and ladies trying to avoid the semi-rowdy ballplayers milling around Hanlon. Many women wore high, broad-brimmed hats topped with a variety of feathers, lace, floral wreaths, birds, cameos, and other feminine doodads piled in fantastical arrangements. These fashion statements brought whistles, sly comments, and laughter from the Orioles. The jokers were answered, of course, with turned-up noses from the women and black glares from their men.

Hanlon began to hand out the passes when he was indecorously pushed aside by the footman of a huge barouche that had arrived. A smallish woman, dressed expensively in muted colors, was handed down from the carriage. She waited while a second passenger was assisted out of the conveyance. Emerging was a middle-aged woman of grand stature, imperious and disdainful of the plebeians that she had to wade through. She was both formal and conservative in her fashion.

"Watch your step, Miss Garrett," the footman said as he helped her onto the sidewalk.

The woman ignored the servant and immediately took the arm of her companion, who commented, "It looks like the theater will be well-attended tonight, Mary Elizabeth."

The two then glided past Hanlon, brushing him slightly and leaving behind the scent of arrogance and wealth. I watched, gauging the mood of the manager, and began to reconcile myself to the fact that I may not get to see Fanny that evening.

When McGraw and Robinson came up, Hanlon said, "Where the hell have you been? I've been standing here like an idiot for twenty minutes."

"We've been getting ready in the Diamond, Foxy," McGraw answered with an infuriating grin. "Do you have my front row seat?"

Ignoring his third baseman, Hanlon said, "Robbie, I thought I could depend on you."

"You can, Ned, you know you can," Robinson replied. "We're here now, and the boys are alright. They're just excited to see the show."

"Yeah, that's it," McGraw commented.

I stood with McGraw and Robinson, smiling affably.

"What's he doing here?" Hanlon asked, noticing me for the first time.

In earlier encounters with this crusty man, he had made it very clear to me that he believed the three of us should never have opened the café. Not only was he a teetotaler, but also the bar was a constant source of headache for him and his players—literally. There wasn't a thing he could do about it though, despite his attempts. McGraw was difficult enough to talk to on non-inflammatory subjects, much less one that he felt passionate about. And threats had no effect. Getting rid of the café was not a subject to broach with Uncle Robbie either, given what little he was paid by the club. The Diamond was Robbie's retirement plan. So that left me as the lightning rod for Hanlon's frustration.

"Foxy, you have extra tickets because Doyle said he wouldn't get caught dead with any of us outside the ballpark and Heinie's old lady doesn't trust him. How's about handing one over to good ole Frank here?" McGraw boomed.

Hanlon's snit got deeper when he looked at me. I just smiled at him sweetly and extended my hand for the ticket.

"Van Sant's not part of the team," Hanlon groused.

"Now, Ned, are you going to hold out on the guy that holds your team together off the field?" I asked with my most annoying smirk.

"C'mon, Ned, it's getting late," Willie Keeler said, reaching for his ticket.

"Yeah, Ned," came a chorus from the other players, now impatient to get to their seats.

Hanlon glared at me and grudgingly gave up the pass.

"Van Sant, I hate hangers on. I better not see you in Macon."

As mentioned, I thought his description of me patently unfair, given my unofficial, but important role on the team. I just continued my smug look and thanked him politely.

"C'mon you hangnail," Robinson said, putting his arm across my shoulders and leading us through the front arches of the ornate palace of entertainment.

The Academy of Music is an impressive structure, built of red brick with sandstone trim in Romanesque style. On my first visit to Howard Street, I thought it was the cathedral of some wealthy religion of mercantilism—as solid and trustworthy looking as a bank, yet somehow speaking of conspicuous consumption. The building is a wonderful comingling of those opposing fiscal philosophies and, as a result, the structure welcomed people of both persuasions, as long as they could afford a ticket.

The face of the building is broken with a series of soaring, triple-arched, windows that draw the eye upward to a second and third set of glassed openings before ending in a steep French roof of glossy, blue-black slate. There is no lack of ornamentation on each level, including dormer windows, finials, fancy ironwork cresting rails, and dentil cornices. In a way, its general layout reminds me of the Sphinx in Egypt—façade looking east, then stretching out behind in a long structure that provides seating for a grand concert hall, an opera house, a theater, and multiple lecture rooms.

A broad, green awning protects the entrance in case of rain and ushers patrons through three classic arches. These give way to a hall lined in Italian marble and furnished in large settees made of dark wood and covered in heavy, red brocade. Floor-to-ceiling, gold-framed mirrors hang on the walls every few paces and electric chandeliers reflect in the glass, throwing a rich, soft light throughout the wide passageway.

In case it seems odd that a tavern bookkeeper/bouncer can speak in such glowing architectural terms, I am quoting from a brochure I picked up in order to impress Fanny. Like the guys on the team, I had never been inside the Academy of Music.

The promotional pamphlet also spoke of two "exquisitely frescoed" and brilliantly lit cafés that serve cocktails and cigars. These fancy watering holes grace each side of the entrance hallway and cater to the kind of people who hold their drinks by the stem of the glass. In other words, these saloons did not compete for patronage with the Diamond.

As the team and I passed through the entrance hallway, we were stunned by the sheer opulence and grandeur of the place. I thought I'd never see it, but even McGraw was quiet, head swiveling like the other players, mouth open and staring. If they were like me—and they were—they had never been in such surroundings and were a little bit cowed by it all. Call me too self-conscious, but our ogling and the obviousness of our general "rubiosity" embarrassed me. Finely attired patrons moved past us with knowing little smiles on their well-powdered and well-trimmed faces.

At the end of the broad entrance, a pair of immense stairways flowed around a center display of flora and statuary. The way up was carpeted in red, at least fourteen feet wide and sporting gold banisters that wound their way to the second level. We followed the crowd to the set of stairs on the right and climbed together like a school of fish, tightly packed for protection. We were clearly out of our depth.

The stairway was decorated with painted panels that treated the eye to what they call "classical scenes"—pastoral landscapes with ruined Roman columns in the distance, frolicking cherubs fondling pan pipes, semi-nude maidens laughing as they ran from men with goats' legs and wide grins. I didn't know what it was all supposed to represent, but as subdued as they were up to this point, the team finally recognized something familiar and something they could appreciate—half-naked women.

"Now we're talking," Kelley said with a grin.

That broke the team's intimidated silence and they began to babble and laugh all at once, wisecracks abounding.

"Must be terrible to not catch one of those beauties forever like that."

"Look, Kelley. That goat-man must be your great-grandfather."

"Where?"

"Nah. Couldn't be, the Kelleys have longer horns than that."

We stayed together in our phalanx, but began to relax and look forward to what was ahead as we climbed the stairs. At the top, another fantastical world unfolded. Open oak doors on either side allowed peeks into enormous, arcaded galleries, lecture rooms, a ballroom floor, and a concert hall that the brochure said could seat 1,200 people.

Beyond all of that, we finally reached our destination, the main feature of the Academy of Music—its Grand Opera House. The people milling around in its thickly carpeted and gilt-traced lobby began to melt through the entrance doors into the galleried auditorium as we arrived. So, we joined them, handing our tickets to men in white gloves and black, cut-away coats.

We followed these attendants up yet another set of stairs to a second-tier balcony where we were shown our seats. They were covered in rich maroon mohair and located in the center with an excellent view of the stage, the orchestra pit, and most of the audience below. Over our heads were more bucolic murals, two huge masks—one smiling, the other frowning—and above them, a soaring crystal dome. A dazzling chandelier, also of crystal, was suspended from the middle of the dome, its candle-shaped burners lit by electricity.

As we settled in, the team continued its chatter and I was surprised at their excitement. I began to think they just might enjoy the cultural sheep dipping. I was excited, too, anxious to see and hear Fanny. I wondered if she could spot me up in the balcony.

"That stage must be eighty feet long," an Oriole commented.

"How do you get those seats?" another asked, pointing to the orchestra pit.

"That's the band, you idiot. You don't get those seats unless you play the tuba."

"How about those seats?" asked yet another, indicating the loge boxes that practically overhung the stage on either side.

"You get to know that duchess sitting there."

"Fat chance of that, unless she can play short. Then you'd meet her comin' in, on your way back down to the beer league."

"I thought we already are in the beer league."

My attention was then drawn to the loge box as I heard Hanlon growl, "You mugs are on Mr. V's meal ticket tonight, remember that. Shut your yaps, you're in society now."

The woman and her companion in the privileged seats were the same ladies who had arrived in splendor as we entered the theater. I gawked as she coolly acknowledged several tuxedoed men below her in the orchestra seats. Actually, I knew who she was immediately when the name Mary Elizabeth Garrett was mentioned out on the sidewalk.

All of Baltimore knew about the B&O heiress and her fight with the Hopkins Board over its Medical School—and getting women admitted, of all things. I recalled from *The Sun* that the price of that had been her own contribution of the fantastical sum of three hundred thousand dollars. It was said that she learned the railroad business from her father and drove the same hard bargains as he did when he was building the Garrett's steel and grit empire.

I remember when Moss first mentioned the name to me. We were sitting in the Diamond afterhours and he was talking about the women's suffrage movement and how he felt about it.

"It won't be long now," he forecasted.

"I don't know, Moss, it seems to me that rights for women are a long way off."

"Listen to yourself, Frank. You're as arrogant as most men in this country."

"Hold on, Moss, you got me wrong. I think women should be given the vote."

"But you say it like it's something that should be granted by men, not something that is their unalienable right."

Moss had a point. That was the way I did think; but I really hadn't given it much thought at all. So, I shut up and let him expand.

"It doesn't make a lot of difference anyway," he said. "You're about to get steamrollered on the issue in the next few years. It's been slow, but ever since they passed the 15th Amendment, which was supposed to give us blacks the vote, but not women, their suffrage issue has picked up momentum."

At that point, he shook his head sadly and I knew why. He was thinking that it took blacks getting the vote for people, particularly white men, to realize that maybe their ladies should have it too. I knew as well how Moss felt about the 15th Amendment. "A sham," he had once called it. Then, he had begun to explain how subsequent state laws put up walls between people like him and the ability to vote, to go to school, to live where he wanted, to get a job, to join a union, to borrow money, to walk in parks, to ride public transportation, to enter restaurants, to go to the toilet, and to even get a drink of water. "Jim Crow law," he called it.

But Moss has long since put his resentment behind him, warranted or not. It isn't right, it isn't fair, and needs to change; but, he knows what he's capable of doing and he knows there are ways around almost any barrier. That's not to say he takes discrimination well—he doesn't—but he doesn't seem to let it stop him, either.

"Maybe if women win the vote, we men can institute a few Jane Crow laws," I cracked.

I received a slow, contemptuous head turn and a chilly look that indicated his disdain for my humor.

"I heard that some women just opened a suffrage club around the corner on Franklin Street," I said in hopes of bringing my friend back to our original topic.

"I read that in *The Sun* the other day," he confirmed. "Started by that Mrs. Funck. It's a part of the larger National American Woman Suffrage Association, the one founded by Miss Anthony."

Even I had heard of Susan B. Anthony, although I'm not sure everything I heard was good. So, I again attempted to inject a bit of humor into the conversation. "Is she the old lady who rode a mule through Yosemite National Park?"

"I can confirm that, Frank, I talked to her about it at Dan Gilman's house not too long ago. She was there with Mary Elizabeth Garrett," he answered with a smile. "That 'old lady' is as spry as they come, and sharp, too."

Once again Moss surprised me. I knew, of course, that he had a wide circle of friends in high places that he would visit from time to time. It was not unusual to see him sitting in the Diamond with Gilman and others like him, either. But the name Garrett was at the very top of society in Baltimore—in the world, for that matter. In addition to railroads, the Garrett family was known for banking, real estate, power politics, social reform, and philanthropy. At the time Moss met Miss Garrett, *The Sun* had reported that she was one of the richest and most powerful women in America.

"You run around in some pretty lofty circles, my friend," I observed.

"Yes," he said. "Some people don't care what I look like, just what I know. Miss Anthony was staying with Miss Garrett over in Mount Vernon. At Gilman's place, the conversation was about women enrolled in the Hopkins Medical School and how they were being treated."

"Sounds like money talks to me. What were you doing there?"

"You mean what was a poor negro doing with these persons of substance?"

"You know what I mean, Moss. What did you contribute to that conversation?"

Moss loved to do that to me. He knew the respect I had for him, but still relished making me a representative of the white, racist overclass.

"They were asking me about my own experience at Hopkins," he finally answered.

"I thought you said you went to Loyola College."

"I did, but I took some classes at Hopkins, as well. If it had been up to Dan, I would have enrolled there as soon as the school opened in '76, but the board wouldn't have it. So, between Dan and a few of his more tolerant faculty, I managed to sit in the back of some classes and meet outside of class with a few professors. No one wants to educate an ex-slave—at least, not so that it causes talk. Basically, separate but unequal.

"Miss Garrett described the female medical students' experience a little differently: 'included but unequal.' Since my experience was the same at St. Joe's in Philadelphia and only a little better at Loyola here in Baltimore in '71 when I came back from the Shore, they thought I might offer some perspective."

"What was Mary Elizabeth Garrett like?" I asked.

Moss hesitated a half of a beat, then said, "She's a little unsettling."

"Unsettling!" I almost laughed. "Nothing rocks your boat."

"She did. I was really uneasy around her. It's not her regal manner or her sharp mind. It's her singlemindedness, her forcefulness. She lets nothing stand in her way. No obstacle is too great."

"That sounds like someone I know," I pointed out.

"No, it's not the same. I've lived my life figuring ways around problems, doing things I'd rather not do in the short term for the long-term benefits. She hasn't that patience. Her money and her personality give her the opportunity and advantage to bully her way through to almost anything. I could see it in her relationship with Dan Gilman. The two of them have had some rough moments in the past. I'm not sure either of them have forgotten."

That conversation came back to me as I watched the Garrett party sitting in the loge box of the Grand Opera House. We were waiting with some impatience for the curtain to rise on *The Prisoner of Zenda* and tolerating various dedications and appeals from a parade of stiffs making their way on and off the stage.

An extraordinary scene unfolding in front of me ended my preoccupation with the Garrett woman, however. John McGraw sat one row in front of me. The two seats in front of him, initially unoccupied, were in the process of being filled by a very large woman and her husband, who looked like he made his living bending iron bars with his teeth. The woman was dressed to the nines and sporting one of those millinery fantasies that so amused the team out in front of the theater. As she wedged herself into the seat, her hat cut off a part of my view of the stage. McGraw's was blocked altogether.

"Pardon me, madam, but an ostrich has died on your head," was McGraw's welcome to the newcomers.

Since that was ignored, he continued, "Were you planning on eating that bird during the show?"

This reference to the woman's appetite also went disregarded by the couple, but not by McGraw's teammates.

"Maybe she'll share it with us," said Boileryard Clarke, the backup catcher.

"Not likely," someone else said.

"I could use some of those grapes she's got hanging on that hat," said a hungry Arlie Pond, one of our right-handers.

McGraw must have decided that the environment called for some tact, because he said in his most gentlemanly way, "Madam, your hat is blocking my view of the stage. Would you mind very much removing it?"

With that, the husband stood up and said, "How about I remove you over this balcony, smart guy?"

I watched McGraw's neck thermometer rise and I looked around for Hanlon and Uncle Robbie, the third sacker's usual handlers. Both the manager and Robinson were sitting too far away, however, evidently thinking Muggsy would behave himself in these surroundings. They were wrong.

After trying to be nice, being challenged in this way, by this lout, was too much for John McGraw. He launched himself up out of the seat, grabbed the woman's hat, balled it up, and threw the feathered thing as hard as he could over the balcony. Its momentum died in midair, then wafted down into the orchestra seats. I heard a shriek from some woman below.

The husband then grabbed McGraw by the lapels, dragged him across the seat, and shook him like a dog shakes a bone. The wife began clucking wildly. That got the entire team on their feet, yelling both insults and encouragement to McGraw. Much of the audience rose as well, everyone craning to see the altercation in the balcony.

Now, McGraw is a serious scrapper, but his adversary was huge and oblivious to the punches the third baseman was landing on the side of his head. I was convinced that the Orioles were going to lose their lead-off man over the balcony when a battery of ushers converged on the melee. Men in white gloves separated the combatants, dragged them out of the seats, and handed them over to several cops who had been quick to arrive on the scene. Among the men in blue was that jerk Chauncey Spittle, looking for a chance to use his nightstick. But he and his mates were too busy dealing with McGraw's flailing arms and legs and the husband's sheer bulk to get a clean shot. As the knot of bodies disappeared loudly down the stairs, I couldn't help but admire the efficiency of the theater's operation. Union Park could use that kind of security.

The team enjoyed the unexpected entertainment immensely, cheering Mc-Graw and hooting at the woman as she struggled over a row of theatergoers to make an ungracious escape. As the tumult subsided and the audience began to settle down again, I saw Hanlon leaving with a disgusted look on his face. I also checked the Garrett box and noticed that Miss Garrett was no longer there.

When the curtain finally rose on the play and the actors began to deliver their lines, the team became enthralled and respectful. They didn't hiss at the villainous Count Rupert of Hentzau or sigh loudly at the vision that was my beautiful, wonderful Fanny, Princess Flavia. Nor did they cheer the heroic Rudolf when he rescued the king. I did see, however, several hands wipe teary eyes and runny noses as cousin Rudolf left his love, Flavia, behind to her king and her kingdom. When the curtain fell, the Orioles stood as one, clapping and calling "Bravo!" long after the rest of the audience was reaching for their hats and coats. Myself, I could only think of Miss Fanny Darlington and how I could get her to think more of me.

Chapter 12

September 1857
Among the Jesuits

The train came to a full stop in the early evening and the lack of motion woke all four passengers in the cattle car out of a semi-sleep. When Moss peered through the slats, then through the open door, all he could see was other railcars along adjacent track. The area between was littered with the refuse of the rail industry. When he climbed down and was able to look down the lines of waiting freight cars, he could see in the distance the city that was probably Philadelphia.

He had made it—he had escaped.

But his exuberance was short-lived; he realized immediately that he was not out of danger just yet, at least not until he made contact with the Quakers' abolitionist friend. Moss had no idea how to do that, and just assumed someone would be waiting for him. No one was.

While that was his most immediate problem, he had others as well—Joshua, for instance. Moss didn't know what he was going to do with the boy, and he had made a promise.

The woman and her infant were another worry. Esther had been hurt badly when she was pulled from the train by the slaver. She had not spoken a word since Moss had put her back in the railcar, and at one point he noticed her nose was bleeding. Other than some nasty scrapes, he could see no apparent damage, but her eyes were glassy and she had difficulty sitting up. At one point on the way east, he had slept and was awakened by the baby wailing. Esther was holding the child, humming softly and rocking. But she was clutching the baby very tightly, too tightly. Moss was sure that she would suffocate or crush the poor thing. So, he spoke quietly to her and gently extracted the bundle from Esther's arms. She collapsed against him and began to weep.

Moss knew Esther needed help that he could not give her. He also knew that the baby needed to be fed. Joshua, too. He himself felt lightheaded from lack of food.

They could not stay on the train for long, so he had to find help that could be trusted. He knew of only one way to do that—make the planned contact. So, he climbed back into the cattle car and said, "Joshua, I need your help. You understand?"

When the boy nodded fearfully, Moss explained, "I need you to stay here for a few minutes and watch over Miss Esther and her baby. I have to find the folks who will help us." Before the boy's panic could rise, Moss hurried on, "I said I wouldn't leave you and I won't. But, I need you to be a big boy right now. Miss Esther is sick and I need you to watch over her. I will be back in no time. Okay? Can you do that?"

Giving Joshua some responsibility was probably a risk, but Moss needed the freedom to move quietly and to move fast. Maybe a job would offset some of the boy's fears, at least for a few minutes.

"Now, be sure they stay away from the door and they have plenty of hay to lie in. Gather it up from the corners. I'll be right back and I'll find us a safe place."

Moss didn't give Joshua a chance to react. He just smiled at him, patted him on the back, and jumped down from the train.

He could see no one up and down the line of cars, and looking beneath them was fruitless. Moss climbed the side ladder of a car on a parallel track and stuck his head up over its roof. About a hundred yards away, across the railyard, was a building—some sort of office. He could see a few people milling around the place. He could also see two men walking toward him, crossing tracks and stepping between the lines of waiting cars. They were looking for something, checking a manifest, and pointing to stenciled numbers on the trains they passed.

As they drew nearer, Moss dropped down and worked his way closer to them. He stayed out of sight and tried to hear what they were saying. From what he could make out, Moss knew that one man was clearly with the railroad. The other, taller man said nothing, but he wore the same broad black hat that the slavers had worn and the same long, dark duster.

When they reached the train that carried Moss, the railroad man said with some satisfaction, "Ah, the North Central up from Baltimore. Number 1202, just like I told you. Here she is!"

The man in the black hat still said nothing, but looked up and down the line of cars, then under them. They were about three cars away from Joshua and his charges.

"I don't know why you wanted to see this train, mister, and I don't care what your business is. But I could get in trouble pointing it out to you, and I need you to make it worth my risk."

"I've already paid you," the other man responded, speaking for the first time with an accent that wasn't American.

"My supervisor could show up at any minute," the yardman said. "I'm not sure what I could tell him if he saw me out here with you."

After a beat or two of silence, Moss heard the clinking of coins and the man in black say, "This is to help you think of something to say. It's also to help you forget we ever met. If you can't do those two things, I'll be back to get my money and more. Now, why don't you get back to the rail office before you're missed?" The taller man had no warmth in his voice.

Moss recognized the accent as French. One of the Emory's kitchen slaves was from Martinique, and she had taught him a little of the language and a few other things.

He watched the rail employee nod and shuffle away quickly in the direction of the office building.

The tall man again looked up and down the line of cars. Then, he began walking in the direction of the cattle car, checking for open doors.

Moss had to act. It wouldn't be long before Joshua and Esther were discovered. So, he looked for a weapon and dug a rusty rail spike out of a pile of scrap thrown along the tracks. He ducked down until the man, concentrating on the North Central cars, moved past him. Then, Moss stepped out from the parallel train, very close to the man in black. He grabbed his shoulder and jammed the blunt end of the spike into the middle of his back.

"You looking for something, mister?"

The man froze and raised his hands. "I'm not armed," he said.

"Sure. Just move real slow and get on your knees, if you want to live."

"Are you wearing a white carnation?"

"What?" Moss asked, surprised.

"A flower, a white flower. Are you wearing one?" the man pressed.

Moss had forgotten completely about the drooping white carnation that the Quaker, Mordecai Stroup, had given him. Somehow, it had remained pinned to his shirt.

"If you are, son, I'm the man you came to meet."

Moss stepped back and held the spike at the ready, allowing the man to turn.

"I'm Felix Barbelin from Saint Joseph's College. I've been looking for you," he said, noticing the carnation, then extending his hand.

"Mister, don't come any closer," Moss warned.

"Father," the man responded. "I'm a Jesuit priest."

Moss knew what a priest was, of course—the Emorys were Catholics. He had served a number of them at the plantation's dinner table. He had found them to be no different than any other white man—maybe a little worse, as far as he could tell.

"Who told you to look for me?" Moss asked cautiously.

"I'm a friend of Thomas Garrett" he said. "And I've been in touch with Brother Stroup in Baltimore. They sent you to me. Now, we don't have a lot of time. It's not safe here. I don't trust that yardman and the work crews are about to change shifts. Please, come with me. I have a carriage and driver waiting outside the yard."

The priest's duster flapped open and Moss could see the high, black, buttoned collar of the cassock underneath. Relief washed over him and his emotions rose in his throat. He tried to speak, but he was overwhelmed and words wouldn't come.

Seeing this, the cleric gently patted Moss's arm and said, "Looks like you've had some time of it. Once we get out of here, you'll be fine. You're with us now."

When he found his voice, Moss simply said, "Thank you." Then, when the priest began to move off, Moss stopped him. "I'm not alone."

The priest just stared, so Moss led him to the cattle car. When they looked in, Joshua jumped up and ran to Moss, who reached for him and lifted him down from the train.

"Mister, there's also a woman and her newborn in there. I think she's in pretty bad shape." On cue, the baby began to cry.

"Without comment, the priest climbed into the cattle car and returned quickly with the baby, handing it to Moss. Then he went back for Esther.

A long minute passed. Finally, the priest pulled a small vial out of his pocket, wet his thumb with it, and made signs on Esther's forehead.

When he jumped down from the cattle car, he said, "I'm afraid the woman is with Jesus now. She's at peace." Then he looked at the boy, as if to say he was sorry.

"She wasn't his mother," Moss said. "Only this baby, here. The boy's with me."

"Son, we have to move now, or all of your suffering will have been for nothing," the priest urged.

He took the baby from Moss and began to hustle up the line of cars. Moss followed, holding Joshua's hand.

※※※※※※

Moss had escaped into a world he had no idea existed. Even his exposure to the outside world through Old Mister Emory had offered no inkling of it. He was living among a group of men that called themselves the Society of Jesus. Catholics, but like no Catholics he had ever known. They were priests, but unlike any priests he'd ever known either.

Back at Poplar Grove, a priest sat at the table with the family most Saturday nights, then again on Sunday afternoon. And not always the same man. Most were middle-aged or older, but each and every one of them had been sleek, fat, satisfied men—men who played up to the Emory family and didn't mind a little ham gravy dripped on their tunics. They lamented over the difficulty of writing a sermon every week, or they asked for help in making repairs to the church roof, or they passed judgment on the quality of that year's oysters, or they bragged of their familiarity with Archbishop Spalding in Baltimore.

Moss remembered well the young Mister Emory easily getting bored with these people. When he did, he would begin haranguing the family's clerical dinner guests over the issue of slavery. Not that freedom should be granted or that laws against cruelty should be passed; rather, he was trying to convince the churchmen that they should instruct the slaves that the surest way to reach heaven was to obey their masters. The priests would nod and agree but say that blacks were not permitted in the church unless they were accompanied. At that, the master would suggest with no little heat or sarcasm that the priests might consider visiting the negroes' shacks every now and again. Despite this diatribe being aimed at most every priest who came to Poplar Grove, Moss couldn't remember ever having seen one outside of the main house.

His first conversation with this Jesuit kind of priest, however, was one he would recall periodically over the years. As they were putting distance between themselves and the railyard, the man who said his name was Felix introduced himself formally as Father Felix Barbelin, born in the Loire Valley of France. He mentioned again that he was a Jesuit priest. When Moss asked what "Jesuit" meant, the man laughed and said he'd been trying to answer that question for nearly thirty years.

Then he explained, "We are an order of Catholic priests dedicated to the honor and glory of our Lord, Jesus Christ. These days, we focus on teaching people, all people. Jesus was a teacher. Our founder, Ignatius, was one too. So, that's what we do. We teach.

"But our mission goes far beyond sermons on Sunday and filling stuffy classrooms with privileged young men. The world demands more. Sometimes those demands involve us in politics. Off and on, that means we are forced to follow our conscience in matters of the law, like helping you and the boy, and this little one."

He held the baby, patting and rocking him like someone experienced in doing so. Then he continued, "We Jesuits are historians, scientists, writers, mathematicians, and many other things. And that's what we teach all over the world, including at Saint Joseph's. We're going there now."

When Moss showed little reaction to this, Father Barbelin fell silent. After a moment, he laughed again. "You know, the word 'Jesuit' was first used in France as an insult—a way of describing fanatical acts and the people who commit them. It was an accurate name for some of us. And we all paid for it. That was a bad time. But most of us were humble. We also were obedient and we worked hard. In the process, we built something good. Today, Jesuits serve both God and his people."

When Moss still didn't react, the priest tried one more time. "Simply put, by helping people, and by educating them, we honor God. It's not always easy work, but that's not important. Do you see?"

Moss understood very well the sermon just delivered—hard work and obedience equals happiness. It was a familiar story he had been told most of his life. But his life hadn't gotten better from the results of his toil, and the idea of obedience to a white master just made him angry. What's more, the little education he had picked up had done nothing to prevent him from being sent out to the fields. He was certain that he would have continued to live a hard life had he not escaped. Well, now he was no longer a slave, but the more he thought about it, the more his freedom seemed hollow. Ever since he dove into the water of Baltimore Harbor, his burdens had gotten heavier. Now, this man was telling him once again that hard work and obedience were the future.

"Father," Moss started, with some hesitation in using the word. "I know what it is to work hard. I've done it all my life. My grandfather died a slave; my father died a slave; and, if I had been obedient, I would have died a slave. Now, if I work hard for you, what do I get for it? Will you pay me? Will you teach me, as well?"

With these questions, Felix Barbelin got his first real glimpse of Moss. The young man had managed to escape across the Mason-Dixon and bring three others with him, so he certainly seemed a capable sort. He had said little up to this point, so the priest had no way of judging the young man's intellect. But now, he could sense depth, in his words and in his eyes.

"May I ask your name, son?"

"Moss, Moss Tilghman."

"Well, Moss, first, you decide whether you want to stay with us at St. Joseph's or not. It's up to you. If you choose to stay, we will certainly put you to work. God knows there is enough to be done. If you choose to stay, you'll get an opportunity to learn. That is how we will pay you. But, understand this: we will teach you, but learning is your responsibility. You reap what you sow. You may work harder than you ever have before, but every seed you plant will come back to you tenfold."

For the next six years, Moss was as happy as he'd ever been, despite the fact that he found the Jesuit life very structured and hard. The Order had taken a vow of poverty, and their lives and their finances showed it. When Moss first arrived at Saint Joseph's, the college resided on Filbert Street in a well-to-do area. By 1860, the Jesuit fathers were forced to move back to their original, hardscrabble location in Willing's Alley, a block from Independence Hall. Life in Philadelphia, it seemed, was no more forgiving than it was in Baltimore. Regardless, no one at the school ever seemed to complain about what was lacking.

But as spare and rigid as his life was, it was of his own choosing. He chose to live at St. Joseph's, he chose to work for these men, and he chose to study. And in his choosing, he found the freedom he had been seeking.

Joshua had stayed with Moss and the priests for several weeks before it became plain that the boy's needs could not be filled at St. Joseph's. Like Esther's baby, a caring home was found for the boy nearby, and there was a time that he and Moss remained close. But because of Moss's responsibilities within the school and the boy's own activities, the relationship slipped away over time, as each found their place within their new lives.

The end of each day at the college found Moss as tired as he had ever been, pulling stumps out of Queen Anne's County swampland. But once he got used to it, he fell easily into a pattern that melted away the days and even the years.

In the first year, for safety, the work was limited to domestic tasks within the confines of the college's community. He dug foundations, built walls, planted and tended gardens, chopped firewood, shoveled coal, cleaned chimneys, tarred roofs, raked leaves, shoveled snow, and did a hundred other jobs that helped to maintain the college.

In his second year, he was often asked to accompany Fr. Arneaux, Fr. Schumann, or one of the other priests when they went on their regular rounds of Philadelphia's slums, mostly negro or Irish. They would feed families, tend to street kids, or find shelter for those crammed into alleys. Sometimes, they would render basic medical help, ease the suffering of the sick, or help bury the dead.

Moss liked the work around the school and became adept at the manual chores. In the process, he learned basic carpentry, plumbing, electrical work, and even cooking. But, once he got outside of the walls of the college, he began to see dire need all around him. His outside work with the priests became more important but less satisfying. He understood the value of what they were doing, but he couldn't say that he enjoyed it. There was too much pain, too many helpless people, and the job never ended.

He had seen this back in Maryland—people so beaten down that they wouldn't or couldn't help themselves, retreating into liquor or worse. Moss wasn't proud of it, but he couldn't avoid feelings of disgust. He had been no better off than these folks, maybe worse in some ways, and he had survived. He found that he had little patience for people who would not help themselves.

He recognized this as arrogance, and it troubled him to the degree that he and Father Barbelin discussed it often. The priest, come to find out, was the president of St. Joseph's; yet he, too, was frequently occupied outside the school's gates. Many times, he and Moss found themselves together doing the Order's work. These were often good times to talk.

The Jesuit became both a temporal and a spiritual advisor to the young man, guiding his education and helping him to a better understanding of the world and his place in it. He would frequently talk to Moss about God and Jesus, but never attempted to convert him to Catholicism. He preferred to let Moss make his own decision about those things.

In fact, as Moss explained to me during one of our late-night sessions, there was a time in the first couple of years that the two men explored the possibility of Moss entering the priesthood. It was never pushed, and Moss never felt the calling that was supposed to accompany such a decision. In short, his education made him less interested in heaven and more curious about how things worked here on earth.

Father Barbelin also kept his promise to teach Moss. As a result, the young man received a strong, classic, liberal arts education, albeit informal due to certain social restrictions demanded by the school's creditors. The priest, however, made the most of the forced informality of Moss's curriculum, exploring ideas, methods, and processes with him in ways that he never could in a classroom. All learning was integrated and offered within the context of normal daily activity.

There were no set hours to Moss's training. A mathematical principle might be explained on the way to a hospital. Practical economics was demonstrated when Fr. Barbelin paid the bills. Organization and planning might be on the menu when it was Moss's turn to prepare an evening meal for the faculty.

But it was the student's problem to manage his day efficiently enough to get work done, to attend necessary lectures from the back row, and to have time to study the notes and texts that were regularly given to him by the priests. Testing might come at any time, from any direction. Just the same, Moss thrived in this environment, became quick-witted, and developed a command of the language that served him well, and still does today.

On summer Sundays, after the last Mass was said, Moss even learned to play the American game they were calling "baseball." Rounders and Town Ball had, of course, been around for some time. But this game had an addicting balance of precision and chaos to it that appealed to him.

Organized initially by privileged young men with a sense of fair play, the game took on certain physical aspects as the contest gained popularity in the nation's cities. St. Joseph students fielded a team against other amateur nines in the Philadelphia area and played with some skill. But, as bigger, faster, and stronger teams began to have their way with the Hawks, as they called themselves, the team recruited Moss, whose athletic build was unmistakable. They found him in the collegiate boxing ring, where he would regularly spar with Fr. Barbelin.

As it turned out, the Maryland man threw an intimidating fastball, and could field as well. But his desire to watch a batted ball soar out over the heads of outfielders made him an all-or-nothing kind of hitter. He didn't really care, though, because he had never had the chance to play a game before, except maybe mumblety-peg or crack-the-whip.

It was a good time for the man from the Eastern Shore. His world was broken wide open to possibilities and concepts that he might never have known existed. Beyond that, he had been given the means of understanding those ideas, the skill to sort through them, and the ability to put them into action.

As an example, during a particularly slow night in the Diamond, I was reading sports results from the newspaper and telling Moss about a football team called "The Fighting Irish" that beat a team called Chicago Dentistry by a score of 62–0.

"That's getting it in the teeth," he mumbled.

"Yeah, those are some tough Catholic boys. They really drilled them." I parried just as halfheartedly.

"I don't know about those boys, but I do know that the Jesuits have some tough guys among them. Tough and disciplined."

Moss is very familiar with Catholics, having lived with and around them for most of his life. But he is particularly versed in what the Jesuits refer to as "Ignatian Spirituality." This is a kind of goal for these guys. It's all about finding the ideal balance between service to their God and service to man. As honorable as that is, Moss said that he never fully bought into the philosophy. But there is a very practical aspect of it that he accepts wholeheartedly.

As a part of this spirituality, Jesuits practice what they call "Examin," twice each day. It is their way of praying, prescribed by their founder long ago. The purpose, they say, is to assist each man in seeing God's hand in his life and to help determine direction. It's a solitary activity, designed to temporarily shut out the world in order to better reflect upon experience. Moss was immediately attracted to this meditative practice, not because he felt the need to talk to a god, but because he found it a powerful tool in understanding the new ideas to which he was constantly being exposed.

When Moss first came to the Diamond, I found him a couple of times after-hours closeted in his pantry. When I asked him what he was doing in there, he simply said that he was "reflecting." I have since come to learn that Moss does this every day, somewhere, by himself. He started it at St. Joseph's as a way of better understanding his studies, and he is still doing it today, after all these years.

Reflection, he says, helps to make connections and helps to surface new ideas from those connections. He believes that connecting our experiences is how we learn. He regarded this understanding as the most valuable thing the Jesuits taught him.

He has another theory that goes along with this reflection business. Moss contends that reflection works because the human brain often labors independently of any conscious will. When you get away by yourself and it's quiet, or even when you are sleeping, he said, the brain has less stimuli to process and it starts to do other work, like trying to make sense of what happened to you that day. The brain makes unconscious connections among those events and things you already know, and those links become understanding. That's why, he explained, problems of the night before often become solutions in the morning.

He further believes reflection is a skill that can be practiced in order to get better at it, like balancing the books or turning a double play.

One time we were talking about how to solve problems in general and I remember arguing that information was critical and working it through logically was the best way to come up with solutions.

"If you can gather good information," I said, "and apply the rules of logic to it, you get answers to problems. Mathematics is evidence of this. You gather the right numbers, apply the step-by-step, logical rules of mathematics, and you get your answer. It works in running a business and it works in running a baseball team."

"What if you don't have the right information, or you are missing some information?" Moss asked innocently.

"The right information is always there, you just have to look for it and be able to recognize it. Look at Sherlock Holmes—"

"Frank, the detective is a figment of Arthur Conan Doyle's imagination."

"Yes, of course, but Sherlock's processes are being adopted by the law all over the world."

"Maybe, but without the right information, what you do with it makes no difference."

"Well, you have to have the right information."

"Okay, maybe Holmes can identify clues, then apply logic to solve a crime. But what about you and me? We don't have that detective's special powers of observation. Often, we have to live with incorrect or insufficient information. How do we solve problems then?"

"We don't," I answered.

"Of course we do, Frank. We do it all of the time. Haven't you ever just had a feeling about something that turned out to be right? There's no logic there. How does that happen?"

"If you are talking about intuition, I don't buy it," I said. "Humans use conscious, logical thought to solve problems. Everything else is guesswork and chance."

"Chance?" Moss laughed. "You mean luck? Then how did Ned Hanlon decide to add John McGraw to the Orioles, much less play him at third base when he first came up?"

"Well...." I paused.

"John was a utility man out of the New York bush leagues. He was a less-than-mediocre fielder and a Punch and Judy hitter with statistics that impressed nobody. To use your words, there was no information to be had that would have led Hanlon to the logical conclusion that John was going to be a star in the major leagues."

"Yes, but—"

"So, do you think Ned could afford to just try his luck with a young nobody?"

"No."

"Frank, Ned Hanlon saw something in John that could not be defended with logic. He had a feeling about the player—an intuition, if you want. It wasn't a logical choice because if Hanlon had been logical, he would have traded for an established third sacker."

I had nothing to say to this, so Moss continued to press his point. "We humans have abilities we haven't discovered yet. That doesn't mean they don't exist. Maybe, it's simply a matter of developing the abilities through use. Logic isn't the only tool in the toolbox."

Chapter 13

The Investigation

The Diamond was packed for a Tuesday night, despite the fact that McGraw, Robinson, and the rest of the Orioles had migrated south to Georgia for spring training. The tavern was not only crowded, it was loud and raucous. The swearing that rang throughout the bar and the good-natured insults flung back and forth between tables had a distinct Teutonic flavor to them. The 1897 German Fellows Bowling Tournament was in full swing, and its contestants were taking full advantage of the availability of two Eagle lagers for the price of one. I had made sure that the bargain was fully underwritten by the event's sponsor and current pins leader, Harry Von Der Horst. So, I was happy.

This was the big one for the season, and any bowler worth his salt was here. Keglers of German heritage from as far away as St. Louis had arrived, drawn by the prize of a pair of wild, honey-colored, ironwood bowling balls of two-hole design—the latest and most expensive equipment available. More important, of course, was the chance to earn bragging rights for a year.

It was not my imagination that quite a few of these contestants were large, mustachioed men, straining the buttons of their vested suits and puffing on stogies of varying quality. This, too, was a welcome circumstance, since Moss's cooking and Oriole Brand cigars were both house specialties. The books would balance nicely this month.

On a night like this, I wouldn't see Moss at all, just a steady flow of waiters with dishes in and out of the kitchen. My job was to maintain the flow out front, keep my eye on the receipts, and restore order when necessary. But this bunch seemed too happy and pleased with each other to be of much trouble. So, I was standing alone at the end of the bar, thinking about Fanny as Princess Flavia and regretting that I couldn't be with her at that moment.

"Frank, your place is jumping tonight," Harry Von Der Horst said, walking up with a big smile and reaching for the large glass of water the bartender had put on the bar. He was in his suspenders, sleeves rolled up and sporting large sweat stains around his armpits.

"Thanks to you, Harry. Thanks to you. With your team out of town, the Diamond would normally be a lot quieter on a weeknight. Say, does that smile mean you are doing well downstairs?"

"That I am, Frank, my man," he said. "I could take this damn thing."

"Well, your strategy of rolling against tipsy, fat men while you drink water and stay away from the meat and potatoes seems to be working then."

Harry just grinned, downed the water, squeezed the excess out of his Van Dyke, and rejoined the tournament downstairs.

While the games downstairs were of the standard tenpin variety, as mentioned earlier, the Diamond was also known for offering an exciting new version with smaller pins. We called this game "duckpins," and it was my very own brainchild. How this came about was through a simple application of logic to a problem.

The problem was that, due to a stretch of bad Baltimore weather, we were experiencing a temporary shortage of cash to pay bills at month's end. It also happened that I had a lot of cracked, chipped, and otherwise unusable tenpins piling up downstairs in a storage room. Putting the two concerns together, I had the carpenter up the block whittle the pins down to about the size of fat milk bottles. For decoration, he painted them white and put a little, red stripe around their necks.

Initially, I wanted to play a little joke on Muggsy. So, one night, when he was three sheets to the wind, I replaced the tenpins in one of the lanes with the smaller pins. Then Robinson, Moss, and I made a bet with the third sacker that the first one to roll a strike would win a pool of five bucks each. We even let him go first.

We barely held it together when he stood in front of those pins, ball in hand. Muggsy peered at them as he normally would, eying the target and straightening his hips. Then he dropped his hands and turned his head like a curious dog. One hand went up to rub his eyes. He looked again, shrugged, and then rolled a perfect strike.

Tenpins disappear fast when they are struck properly, but the movement on these smaller targets was electric. In a blur of action and a sharp crack—the pins were gone. A very satisfying result for the bowler. McGraw turned to us with a big grin on his face and his hand out.

It was precisely the pin action that gave the game its name—"duckpins." Muggsy and Uncle Robbie came up with it one cold morning on the Eastern Shore, sitting in a duck blind, passing a bottle. It seemed that the action of ducks coming off the water at the sound of a shotgun reminded them of the pins when struck. The name stuck after Robbie put it in the ear of a reporter from *The Herald*.

The fleeting memory added to my fine mood, but I quickly went back to thinking about Fanny. The success of *The Prisoner of Zenda* in its Baltimore debut resulted in it being held over for another three weeks, two performances a week, Friday and Saturday. Fanny was the current "darling of the stage who enchants and enthralls," according to *The Baltimore American's* entertainment writer. She was also Tunis Dean's darling, since between the play's action and her final, heart-wrenching scene with Rupert, the Academy was sold out for all performances.

While one play a year was enough for me, the longer run meant Fanny would be around for a few more weeks at least. That meant I would get to see more of her—I hoped. To Fanny, I'm afraid, all it meant was gainful employment and no more traveling for a while.

Regardless, I managed to spend a fair amount of time with her in the weeks following the day Alcott Worthy's body was discovered. O'Donnell and his thug, Gatch, had continued their official investigation, but they must not have been making much progress. They seemed to keep coming back to Fanny, asking the same questions a little differently each time, but always full of innuendo and menace.

I could see this was wearing on her, and I wanted to help. So, even before the opening of the show, I suggested that she and I institute our own investigation of the murder.

At first, she flat-out said no. She was preoccupied with rehearsals and needed to concentrate on the role of the princess. After one particular visit from Sergeant Gatch, I suggested it again and she began to consider my idea. Fanny didn't really understand what I had in mind, so it was natural that she was fearful. When I explained a little further, she was immediately skeptical.

But then she realized that there might be no other way to put an end to the police harassment, so the idea started to grow on her.

I wish I could believe that what finally convinced her was the fact that we'd be working closely together. But, as I said, I have no idea of how I stand with Miss Darlington. At times, she is as sweet to me as the day is long; at other times, she is distant and can be very curt when displeased. My offer of doing some joint sleuthing is a good example of what I mean.

"Fanny, we'd be perfect together," I said with probably too much enthusiasm. "My powers of observation and logic, your connections to the theater and your feeling for the dead man—"

"I have no feelings for that man and never have. I told you that. I thought you believed me!" she charged.

I hurried to clarify. "No, no, that's not what I meant. I mean you have a good sense of how he behaved, how he thought, who he saw, what he liked or didn't like. From all of that, you may have a feeling for why the murder might have been committed."

"I have no idea why the murder was committed! You sound like that awful Detective O'Donnell. You think I had something to do with it!"

"Now, Fanny, you know that's not true. I'm on your side. I'm just trying to help."

"Accusing me of murder isn't helping."

"I wasn't…. Okay, forget what I said about you knowing the murder victim. Let's just see if we can work together to get to the bottom of things. You want to put this behind you don't you? I don't trust O'Donnell or Gatch to consider your best interests. Do you?"

"No, I guess not," she conceded with reluctance.

"Maybe together we can think of something they have not."

After a bit more stroking on my part, she agreed. So, we began to meet when the Diamond was closed on Sunday or in the morning over coffee, or later, after a rehearsal or performance. We discussed the results of various investigative tasks that we had divvied up, and I recorded everything. What emerged was a partial timeline of events occurring the night before the body was found. This produced a few threads of interest that warranted further pulling.

First, Fanny said she talked to one of the Academy's stage hands who told her that Tunis Dean, the managing director, had asked him to deliver a note to Mr. Alcott Worthy in his rooms on Cathedral Street. This was sometime around midafternoon of the day before his body was found in the alley. I learned from the bartender in one of the theater's lounges that Worthy had had drinks with an unknown man at around six o'clock that evening. Apparently, there had been a heated exchange before Worthy walked out. We needed to know who that man was.

Fanny also said that Alcott Worthy attended the eight o'clock presentation of *Miss Francis of Yale,* as a guest of Tunis Dean. It turns out that Dean knew Worthy quite well, since the victim was an influential and active member of the Board of Sponsors. We further learned from several people that the sponsor had stormed into Dean's office right after the show around 10:00 p.m. What passed between the two men or why Worthy was agitated was unknown.

It is a fact that Fanny, who was waiting to meet the show's star, Dorothea Baird, was accosted backstage by Alcott Worthy around 11:00 p.m. that evening. Her assessment that he had been drinking was supported by the doorman, Fuzzy Hertzbaugh, who described the victim as "stinking drunk." While Hertzbaugh admitted to seeing Worthy backstage, he claimed that he did not see the man again until the next morning, when he found me outside, bending over the body. The doorman couldn't or wouldn't say when the victim left the theater.

Finally, no one Fanny asked remembered seeing the murdered man after eleven that night. We had no idea how much or how little of all of that the cops knew.

I myself went back to the alley between the theaters where we had found the dead man. Sherlock Holmes would certainly have noted that the crime scene had been compromised by the police and by the hoard of theater people who had used the passage since then. But, I wanted to see what I could remember from that morning.

The debris I kicked through had grown since the last time I was there and I found nothing of help. I recalled an empty bottle of rye and looked for it, but found only broken glass that might have once been an empty half-pint bottle of Pikesville Rye.

I recalled seeing some busted crates and a couple of empty rain barrels. The crates were still there, but there was only one barrel now, and it was empty. I wondered what the barrels were doing there in the first place. Normally, they were used to gather water from downspouts, but there were no downspouts running into the alley.

I sensed that there was something else missing, but I just couldn't bring it back.

"What the hell are you doing out here, Van Sant?"

Old Man Hertzbaugh had opened the theater door and discovered me milling around. "Aren't you in trouble enough?" he prodded.

"Fuzzy, I'm in no trouble," I shot back. "But if you keep telling lies to the coppers, you're going to have more trouble than you can handle."

"Lies? I've told no lies!"

"That's not what Detective O'Donnell said," I lied.

"What did O'Donnell say?" Hertzbaugh asked, suspicious.

"You'd better ask him. By the way, what happened to the other barrel that was out here? And there was something else...."

"Why ask me?" he responded. "How would I know? Probably was used as a prop or something. Why do you care, anyway?" When I didn't answer, he said, "Look, I'm not talking to you. You're nothing but trouble. Get the hell out of here, before I call Officer Spittle."

"Why don't you just do that, Fuzzy. Give the badges an excuse to come see you again."

I turned and walked out of the alley, leaving the old coot muttering. He was a pain in the ass, but his appearance jogged my memory about something. What was it that the doorman had lifted off the dead man? There was the watch and chain, but Spittle took that. The cop took something else away from Fuzzy, too. What was it? That was a good question, but, for the moment, I wasn't going to get an answer.

"Let's go over this one more time."

Baltimore City Police Detective Thomas O'Donnell was frustrated. All he had were a lot of loose ends in the Worthy murder, and he couldn't tie enough of them together to come up with a plausible suspect, much less a reasonable explanation for the killing. What's more, the Northwestern Commander was getting heat from Mayor Hooper's office, demanding progress. Hooper was coasting through the last months of his term, and his record was plenty of assurance that this would be his last public office. So, he had designs on several board seats in the business and arts communities around town that paid well and asked for little other than a name. But that meant he couldn't afford to annoy certain powerful people. In this case, it was one James Lawrence Kernan, millionaire entrepreneur and the unquestioned authority in Howard Street's Theater District. Kernan, Hooper reasoned, would not abide unexplained bodies lying across the entrances to his palaces of entertainment.

To make matters worse, O'Donnell had been saddled with that ape Gatch to aid in the investigation. The sergeant had been taken off the street until his most recent battery of a citizen blew over. The detective was basically babysitting a psychopath with a badge and a bad attitude.

And now, O'Donnell was seated behind a battered desk in a small, hot office in the Lanvale Street lockup with Gatch and that idiot beat cop Spittle. He was trying to make sense of what the investigation had turned up so far and making no apparent headway. The room's one window had been painted shut, there was no fan, and its occupants had been recycling the same stale air for the last hour. As a result, O'Donnell was getting the same stale responses he had since they started.

"Detective, how many times do we have to hear this?" Gatch whined. "Chauncey here has been over the events of that morning five times."

"Yeah, and every time we do, I learn a little more. So, we'll go over this as many times as it takes for Officer Spittle to remember everything he knows. Sit there and shut up."

"I'm getting something to drink," the big man said sullenly.

The sergeant rose, pulled his shorts out of his butt, and left the room, slamming the door behind him. Nothing was said, but the two left in the room felt the air lift considerably when he was gone.

"Officer Spittle, you say you found the body a little after eight o'clock in the morning on the eighteenth?"

The cop let out a sigh of exasperation and said, "Yeah, that's right. Eight o'clock in the morning, February eighteenth."

Spittle was slumped in a chair in front of the desk and was in the process of putting his feet up on it when O'Donnell grabbed a nightstick lying there and swung it hard against the sole of the beat cop's foot. The blow stung mightily and almost spun the man out of the chair and onto the floor.

"Look, Spittle, you're not my favorite cop for a lot of reasons we won't go into right now. And I understand it's hot and we're both tired. But the next time you disrespect me, this billy is going to do some real damage. You understand?"

Chauncey Spittle hated Detective O'Donnell; in fact, he hated everyone in the Police Department he referred to as "brass"—anyone he had to answer to, really. Out on the street, he was the unquestioned authority. Down in the Theater District, the citizens answered to him. In here, he would play the bosses' game, but he didn't have to like it. So, he sat back upright in the chair and gave O'Donnell a wounded, submissive look that gave the impression that he was chastened. He was not.

"You say you found the body. But I have it from the Academy's doorman that he found the body about that same time. Were you together?"

"Well, no. Actually, it was the actress Fanny Darlington and that lowlife from the Diamond, Van Sant, who found the dead man first."

"So, it was those two who were first on the scene?"

"That's right, I found them coming out of the alley and I stopped them. Van Sant claimed he was coming to find me to tell me."

"You didn't believe him?"

"I wouldn't believe anything that bum said."

"Why is that?"

"Because he's one of those baseball players and everyone knows they're scum."

"Frank Van Sant plays for the Orioles?" O'Donnell asked, leading Spittle on.

"No. No, but he's real tight with them. Always hanging around."

"He manages and owns a part of the Diamond, doesn't he?"

"I guess so, but he's a problem. Likely mixed up in this somehow."

"In what way?" the detective asked.

"I don't know, he just is. A real smart aleck."

"I would suggest that unless you have something more concrete—"

"Look, Detective, I know my beat. I know everyone on it. I've watched them all, and Van Sant can't be trusted. He's got a record. You can check it. He's also linked somehow to Miss Darlington, and she lied to you, didn't she?"

"How do you know that, Officer?"

"Well, Sergeant Gatch told me."

"Sergeant Gatch needs to keep his mouth shut. I don't want either of you talking about this to anyone. You hear?"

Again, the beat cop said nothing, taking the tongue lashing, but thinking that if he was ever given the chance, he would give it to O'Donnell good.

"Now, there's something else I want to know from you," the detective said. "I know you took the dead man's watch from the doorman, Hertzbaugh."

"I was going to turn that in—"

"You're damn right you're going to turn that in! It'll mean your badge if you don't. What kind of cop steals from a dead man?"

"I—"

"Spittle, you've been walking a pretty fine line in your district, and you've stepped over it too many times."

"Detective, I don't have to take these accusations from you or anyone else. I run a tight beat and the people who count appreciate it."

"And they show their appreciation regularly, don't they, Spittle?"

"What do you mean? What are you saying?" The cop turned red.

"I don't have the time or patience for this right now," the investigator snapped. "What I want to know from you is what else you took from the body that morning."

"What else?"

"Spittle, you have about two seconds to tell me what it was that you took back from Fuzzy Hertzbaugh, besides the watch." O'Donnell glared at Spittle and watched him squirm.

"There was nothing—"

"Be very careful how you answer, Officer. I know you took something else."

Chauncey Spittle wasn't all that sharp a tool, but he quickly weighed the pros and cons of a lie. O'Donnell looked like a cat ready to pounce, almost as if he were just waiting for this opportunity to rid himself and the police force of a headache. The beat cop decided he could best control the damage by telling a partial truth. Maybe his theater friends would provide some cover.

"Okay, okay. I'll tell you the truth."

This preamble immediately made O'Donnell skeptical. He ducked his head and stared at Spittle like he was looking over reading glasses. Spittle's words then came out in a rush.

"It was just a couple of bucks. Nothing more than lunch money. That's all. No big deal."

"Spittle, I'm going to give you one more chance, then I'm going to step on you like a cockroach."

Sergeant Gatch reentered the room in enough time to hear this last exchange, but said nothing. O'Donnell watched a fleeting look pass between the Sergeant and Spittle; then, the beat cop came clean.

"There was also a note in with the bills."

"A note. Who from? What did it say? Spittle, don't make me drag this out of you."

"Yeah, a note. I mean, yes. It was from Mr. Dean, the Director of the Academy of Music."

He hesitated but continued quickly after looking up at O'Donnell's face. "It said that Mr. Dean had someone he wanted Worthy to meet and could they get together in one of the Academy's cafes before the play that evening. That's all."

"That's all!" O'Donnell was nearly shouting. "You didn't think that it might have some bearing on the case? You withheld evidence! Where is the note? Give it to me."

"I don't have it. I tossed it away."

As Sergeant Gatch quietly left the room again, O'Donnell lit into Officer Spittle.

"You didn't say a word about this, then you destroyed evidence! Why? Why would a Baltimore City policeman do that? Do you have any idea of the consequences of your actions?"

"I didn't think it was important. And since Mr. Dean couldn't have anything to do with this, I just thought he might appreciate my watching out for him."

"What!" O'Donnell exploded, standing and reaching for his coat. "He might appreciate it? I can guess just how much he might appreciate it! Spittle, you are in deep trouble. I've got to talk to this Mr. Dean right now. But understand, this is not over. It has just begun for you. Stay where I can find you."

With that, the detective bolted out of the door. On his way out of the station, he passed the sergeant.

"Gatch, you stay here. I'll be back, and maybe then you can tell me what you and Spittle have going on."

✖✖✖✖✖✖✖

Gatch returned to the room where Spittle sat worrying over the threat from O'Donnell and what Tunis Dean would think once the detective questioned him. There were other things on his mind, as well.

"You are about the dumbest beast in the barn," Gatch started, filling the space behind the desk O'Donnell just vacated. He picked up the billy club laying there, leaned forward on the scarred desk, and began tapping out some imagined, dark rhythm with it.

"Sergeant, look, I just wanted to keep my working relationship with Mr. Dean!" Spittle brayed.

"I don't care about that, asshole. If you want to end your working life bent over the rail of an oyster boat, it's not my concern. Unless...." Gatch eyed the beat cop.

"Unless what, Sergeant?"

"Unless you start to think that maybe you can lighten that cart of shit that you're about to be hauling by putting some of it in my cart." The rhythm increased.

"Hey, I would never do that to you. You think I'm crazy?"

"No, I think you're stupid."

"Maybe you shouldn't have clubbed that guy so hard."

"You are stupid," Gatch observed, as if he had just won a bet with himself.

The big man stood quickly, but Spittle was faster. The beat cop bolted for the door and the security of the crowded precinct processing room.

CHAPTER 14

1863
AT WAR

By the spring, there were no more illusions about the war, anywhere. There were no more farm boys looking for adventure, no street punks joining up to escape local authorities, no college men seeking glory and honor. The moneyed were lined up to write bank drafts for three hundred dollars to buy theirs out of the draft. And any man who had already "seen the elephant" knew what this new Industrial Age war was—blood, guts, fear, hunger, disease, stupidity, cowardice, and, sometimes, astonishing heroism.

Even the noble causes that allowed the choosing of sides in the early years were now made superfluous by the boundless carnage and suffering that touched everyone. Daily reality overwhelmed any thought of a higher purpose. Some still fought for an ideal, but most were just fighting to survive.

The high-hats in Washington and Richmond still spoke of principle, of course, but they were whistling into the wind. For those cowering among the dead piled in trenches and for those left standing in some corn field, stunned that they were still alive, there were no ideals. For the families who had given up hope of ever seeing again the man or boy who had marched away, there were no principles. They just wanted it all to end—one way or the other.

Moss was an exception. He believed in the war's purpose—at least the one he cared about. Maybe it was because he had not experienced comrades all around him wrenched off their feet in splashes of red. He didn't know what the impact of a lead ball felt like. He was not witness to scorched fields and burning barns, destroyed cities, or families left to starve by soldiers just as hungry. His experience with the war was limited to waiting with Father Barbelin among crowds of wives and mothers in front of the *Philadelphia Inquirer* as they anticipated the posting of the long lists of war dead. He was well acquainted with the rising screams of anguish and despair when the lists appeared. But, as painful a reality as that was, for him and a growing number of other black men, the war had become an opportunity. To them, the purpose was just as real as battlefield death.

When President Lincoln made his proclamation in January, it became harder and harder for Moss to continue his life with the Jesuits. At the same time that the worst draft riots in American history raged in New York, the Union Army was enlisting more and more negroes into its ranks. The president could not have been clearer: "The colored population is the great available and yet unveiled force for restoring the Union." Saving the Union was important, Moss supposed. But, the country had a disease that was going to kill it, if it wasn't stopped soon. And here was a desperate chance, but the first real chance, the country had to end the evil of human slavery. This thought grew until he knew he could not stay in Philadelphia much longer.

By February, Moss was aware that Governor Andrew of Massachusetts was recruiting for an all-black regiment and was taking enlistees from all around the country. The 54th Regiment was paying thirteen dollars a month, providing food and clothing and offering a one-hundred-dollar bounty, to be paid at the end of service. This information made any life at St. Joseph's untenable. Fr. Barbelin offered arguments against Moss enlisting, but only for so long. The priest detested war and loved Moss, but he also knew the young man would not be held back from what he felt compelled to do.

Moss couldn't help but feel proud as he marched smartly through the city of Boston in the uniform of the 54th Massachusetts Volunteer Regiment. The Prussian blue, high-collared, thigh-length, wool coat with brass buttons hung well on his sturdy frame. He liked the contrasting sky-blue pants, and even the shapeless forage cap felt good. His thick, black leather belt and its shiny, oval buckle, stamped with a bold "U.S.," was a manly thing and served to tell the world that he was a part of something important. It was a feeling he had never had before.

Even marching in formation had changed for him since his early days of drill. At first, he hated the surprising physical strain and the toll that endless miles took on newly shod feet. He resented the insults leveled at him by bawling drill instructors, fixated on sameness, constantly prodding him to get in line.

At some point, Moss felt the training start to erode whoever he thought he was. Fr. Barbelin used to say that self-reliance and independence were two topics he never had to teach Moss. But now, the army was remaking him into a very small part of bigger mass.

It wasn't long, though, before those feelings were replaced with a different sense. Now, as he marched with his Springfield on his shoulder, he was satisfied with himself as a part of a large, powerful machine. He found dignity when he realized what could be accomplished if everyone worked together. Pride came once they were able to work together repeatedly. And now, they had a proud name—the 54th Massachusetts Regiment. Soon, this new cog would be integrated into Lincoln's war machine and have a chance to accomplish something.

The rhythm and tramp of hobnails on cobblestones, the beat of the boys' drums, the cadence called by the sergeants, and the unified response from the ranks was both hypnotic and addicting. Inside the machine, secure, one can lose himself.

The crowds lining the streets on this perfect May day cheered the thousand men of the 54th as it executed a perfect column-left march. They had left Camp Meigs behind that morning for the first time and were headed to Boston Harbor and the transport *De Molay*. The rumor was that they were being deployed to South Carolina, where it all started back in 1861. Moss found it hard to imagine any rebel force standing against his regiment, much less the other regiments of the endless ranks of Union blue.

The truth, however, was sobering. Over the last three years, the Union's forces had seen one major defeat and replacement of one commanding general after another. Last summer, McClellan had managed to block a Southern invasion at Sharpsburg, Maryland, but at terrible cost. Any advantage Little Mac gained in blunting the advances of the men in gray and butternut had been allowed to slip away due to delay and indecision. It was said that Lincoln was so angry and disappointed in the missed opportunity to end the bloodshed that he immediately replaced the general. What followed was a series of like disappointments—Joe Hooker, John Pope, Ambrose Burnside. None were the tactician the president needed to defeat the Confederate forces in the East. In the meantime, the Army of Northern Virginia was being led by the best West Point had to offer—Robert E. Lee.

The month of May, 1863 had not started well for the Union, either. During the first week, the Army of the Potomac left 17,000 men either dead or wounded in the fields around Chancellorsville in Virginia. Now, Lee's forces massed across the river from Washington while he decided whether to brave that city's defenses or attempt yet another march north. The only good news that Moss had heard was that Thomas Jackson, Bobby Lee's right-hand man and the devil incarnate, had been shot accidentally and had died from complications.

On July 18, 624 men of the 54th Regiment squatted on a spit of sand, scratching fleas. Just as the sun began to set on Morris Island, South Carolina, they could feel the earth shake in response to the rumble of big guns,. The men had seen their first sharp action two days earlier and they were waiting for "what came next." The rumor was that General Strong wanted to take Battery Wagner because it guarded Fort Sumter and the defenses of Charleston Harbor.

The soldiers were exhausted, hungry, and anxious. As a result, they were even more fractious than they usually were.

"We lost fifty men two days ago on that little island. Now, we sit in this sand and wait. The least they could do is feed us."

"Feed us? They don't feed us. They don't pay us. They don't care about us."

"That's because you're contraband, stupid. When are you going to get wise?"

"I may be contraband, but they don't hesitate to use us when they need bodies to run at those gray boys' guns."

"Exactly, son. Now you're getting it. They use us because we're brave and good at dying."

"I hear they don't take prisoners. They say it was a cold-blooded massacre at Fort Pillow. Lot of hate behind those guns."

"I don't plan on taking any damn prisoners tonight either."

"Those boys don't think about all of this like it's a war. They think it's a slave rebellion."

"Can't put a slave back in the fields once he's come at you with a bayonet."

"Man, the skeeters were bad in 'Bama, but these fleas are just as big, and a lot meaner. Look at my legs," said a man drawing blood from his vigorous scratching.

"Stop whining, Meathead. Just pray you have legs to itch after tonight."

Moss sat with Sergeant William Carney and listened to the men gripe at the soldiers' lot. The sergeant knew that it was little enough release for what his men had given and what they were about to give. The Marylander and the NCO had formed a friendship back at Camp Meigs because they found that they could rely on each other. It wasn't long before they found they could talk to each other as well. The entire Regiment was bonded by the reason they all had joined the 54th, but that didn't mean everyone was the same. There were men in his unit that Moss couldn't stand to be around, yet he was around them constantly. He thought Carney felt the same way.

"You think we're taking Wagner tonight?" Moss asked him quietly.

"I do," the sergeant answered. "Otherwise Colonel Shaw wouldn't have us just sitting here with no water and no vittles."

"That's probably right. The colonel tries to look out for us, mostly."

"Maybe. The word is that he volunteered the 54th to lead the attack. Wanted to show them what we could do."

"Volunteered?"

"That's what I heard, but I don't know. Even if it's true, the colonel doesn't always get what he wants."

Moss stared out over the water and after a minute asked, "Bill, what do you know about our pay? Watts and Goosberry were saying that we'd only get ten dollars instead of the thirteen they promised, and they were taking another two dollars for uniforms and such."

"Lots of people mad about that," Carney answered. "We're getting it in the neck on pay for certain, but that's not why most of us joined the 54th."

"I don't know about that, man. Cutting our pay seems like more of the same old shit to me. Is that the kind of freedom we can expect, once we win this thing?"

The sergeant shook his head and said nothing. Moss's point was painful to think about, mainly because it was likely the truth. Finally, he said, "Right now, all I care about is that Watts, Goosberry and the rest do what I tell them, when I tell them."

With that, the order to form up came, just as the sun was disappearing into the ocean.

Off and on over the years, some minor thing would trigger hazy memories in Moss of that horrific evening when the 54th Regiment stormed Battery Wagner. They weren't memories, really. Not now. They were more like old tintypes kept in the bottom of a drawer. Forgotten until they leapt up at him while he was looking for something else. Stilted portraits. Flashes. Almost posed. Single points in time, capturing men in extraordinary situations, doing extraordinary things. Mostly faces, fighting, and dying.

He would see Private Goosberry, determined, head down, hunched against what could have been driving sleet, but was actually lead. Abraham Brown, bewildered, staring down at his arm on the ground, still holding his musket. Colonel Shaw at the top of the parapet, bent backwards in surprise and agony, sword high in the air. A bloody-faced Sergeant Carney with a look of pleading as he scrabbled up that sandy incline to recover the fallen Stars and Stripes.

Half of the men died that day, and most of the rest were slaughtered in the Crater a year later at Petersburg. There was a time that Moss wondered not how he survived, but *why* he survived. Repeatedly, he searched for the logic of his deliverance and found none. The best he could muster was an evolving sense that maybe he was meant to do more with his life.

This wasn't a particularly spiritual thought. He didn't believe that a god, like the one Fr. Barbelin worshipped, had plans for him. It was more like he was meant to play some role in some future event, or maybe just be a part of a larger pattern of human endeavor. It certainly wasn't a sense of destiny, either. That idea was far too egotistical for him.

He couldn't explain or justify this idea that his life had some future value, yet it kept recurring. Maybe there actually was some larger force driving the fate of men. Some would call it "God," others something else. He didn't know. What he did know, however, was that the world was chaotic and uncontrollable, and human beings needed a stable place to stand in a churning world, even if it meant believing in a deity that was often pitiless.

His struggle with the idea of a higher controlling power left him without the compass that gods were for so many. Yet, his need for direction was no less. In the end, he determined that principle was all that was left. He would be guided by his idea of right and wrong, based on principle. Fairness and integrity would control his decisions. In simple, concrete terms, the promises he made to himself, he would stick to. The promises he made to others would be few and cautious, but he would stick to those as well.

Moss also knew of folks who felt guilty over surviving the war—almost as if they felt undeserving of their fortune. But he didn't feel any guilt over his survival at all. Maybe it was this mysterious sense of purpose looming in the future that allowed him to avoid this particular malady. Or, maybe it was simply an inheritance from his days as a slave, separated from society, that created a detached perspective on his place in the world.

Survival, purpose, perspective—these things remained intellectual puzzles for him over the years, ones that he would reflect upon whenever his battlefield experiences emerged. Like all experience, they were a part of who he was. But Moss also had the capacity to put the war and its personal consequences behind him. It was not repression; he was not afraid to look experience in the eye. He accepted that his experience formed his view of things, but he managed to keep balanced, not to dwell on the pain. He fully expected his war tintypes to fade away completely one day.

Whether the images disappeared or not, Moss would take one crystal-clear lesson from it all: he would never again lose himself inside of a machine.

So, like a determined Private Goosberry at Battery Wagner, he marched toward something in the future. The difference between him and his comrade of the 54th, however, was that Moss would not just put his head down as he marched.

CHAPTER 15

THE NIGHT OF THE MURDER

Around 6:00 p.m.

"So, you see, Mr. Worthy, I am on the cusp of a great discovery, one that will change our understanding of human capabilities. Potentially, my work could go far beyond understanding. In fact, it could open the door to enhancing human capacity itself."

Alcott Worthy had no idea what the man was talking about. He was only half-listening, but he was fully enjoying the crackpot's offer of a whiskey. It was Tunis Dean who had asked him to have a drink with Dr. Munsch of Hopkins Hospital. Dean had said there might be a sizable check in it for the Academy and it was a free drink. What could it hurt? All he had to do was listen to the man, no commitments and he could just walk away afterwards and forget about it.

"I have already proven that an ordinary person, one that has no training or inclination toward the artistic, has no ability to imagine what could be, or is limited in intuitive power, can be made to exhibit all of these skills. In other words, we have the opportunity to alter the prospect of man and, in turn, change the world!"

The doctor's voice rose shrilly, and his eyes had an intensity that was unnatural. Both revealed a passion that bordered on the imbalanced and this made the theatrical sponsor decidedly uncomfortable.

"Doctor, I can appreciate your fervid interest in your work. Your intensity for it is impressive. But, why are you talking to me about it? I assume that when you referred to 'we,' you were speaking universally."

"I was not, Mr. Worthy. I was referring to you specifically," responded Munsch, happy to have been given the chance to get to the point of the meeting.

"Me? Why me?"

Munsch nodded to the bartender who poured a second double shot of rye into Worthy's empty glass.

"You, Mr. Worthy, offer a unique opportunity to science. You are an artistic person. You love the theater. You have spent your life following it. You have invested in it. Mr. Dean told me you play the piano and have even written an operetta. It would be hard to imagine that there was much of that world that you do not either participate in directly or understand and appreciate."

"That's true, of course," answered Worthy with immodest pride, ignoring the fact that he had not touched a piano since childhood and Dean had lied about the operetta. With a theatric flourish, he reached for the refilled glass.

"That is exactly what makes you special. It makes you ideal for what I'd like to propose."

"And, what's that, Dr. Munsch?"

"To summarize it, Mr. Worthy, I'd like you to be a test subject."

"A what?" asked a stunned Worthy, splashing a drop if rye in his nose.

"That's right. I have a way that we could take advantage of your natural proclivities while causing you no harm whatsoever."

Drink or no drink, Worthy was now looking for a way to rid himself of this lunatic. There was no way in hell he was going to be anyone's test subject. Tunis Dean and his hope for a contribution be damned.

Munsch immediately saw this in his companion's face and hurried on.

"You see, I have a safe way of numbing the left side of your brain, freeing the right side to achieve its full capability. Since you already have a highly developed artistic bent, I postulate that you may be able to demonstrate some extraordinary talents, far beyond the norm."

Worthy simply stared at the man. The doctor really was mad. It was time to leave and he rose to do so. But, Munsch reached out to prevent his rapid departure, seizing his wrist with surprising strength.

"Sir, unhand me!"

"But wait, you haven't let me explain fully."

"I have heard all I am going to listen to, sir," shot back the theater man, standing and ripping his arm away from his captor.

"But ... "

"In fact, Dr. Munsch, I am deeply offended by your proposal and your offense shall not go unanswered! I happen to have a few contacts at your hospital and they shall hear of this absurd conversation forthwith."

Worthy was now on his high-horse, aided undoubtedly by the whiskey. It was now Munsch's turn to stare. He remained on the bar stool, speechless, as he watched Worthy finish his drink, then stalk away.

Over his shoulder, the outraged man took one last shot: "Be assured, Doctor, I shall stop this insane idea of yours."

Worthy was determined to carry out his threat to Dr. Munsch. He had replayed his conversation with the doctor several times on his way home, and every time he did, he got angrier.

The gall of that Austrian maniac to think that he could experiment on a man of his standing! It was crazy! Criminal! And how dare Tunis Dean put the two of us together? What was in that little weasel's mind? It could only be money. Dean was all about lining his pockets. He must be getting something out of this, and at my expense!

Worthy had intended to nap for an hour before he had to return to the theater for the play at eight o'clock. But outrage and alcoholism drove him to the silver tray of bottles in his study, rather than to his bed.

He stood looking out of the bay window watching Cathedral Street's evening carriage traffic over the rim of a crystal glass of Baker's Pure. He lived just on the edge of the prestigious Mount Vernon Square neighborhood and his address never failed to impress. But he knew Baltimore's real money and power ringed the park around the Washington Monument and someone such as he could never penetrate that tight circle. He hated them all for that. But, he held a special animosity for the two branches of the Garrett family who dominated, not just the Square, but the City's entire social and business elite.

Even tonight, as he reached his own door, he could see activity at the huge, illuminated mansion built by John Garrett, just a couple of blocks up Cathedral Street, at the head of the Square. The Garretts were receiving well turned-out guests who were being disgorged from a line of big, black carriages. Something was going on there tonight, another dinner to which he would never be invited.

Again, he thought of Mary Elizabeth Garrett and her attempt to bully the Board of Sponsors with her obscene bribe. He made short work of that by Jove.

The whiskey fed his hostility toward the Garretts; but, it also helped him to stoke his resentment of Dr. Munsch and Tunis Dean. As he nurtured these irritations, his thoughts gravitated to what was really bothering him—that bitch, Fanny Darlington. She owed him. She had something of his and he would have it back.

Around 10:00 p.m.

Worthy had dozed through the play, not quite sleeping off the alcohol he had been pouring into himself since early in the evening. He roused occasionally, as the audience laughed at the lines in the comedy, but quickly settled back into a nodding state. When the people around him stood to applaud at the end of the show, he pried himself out of the seat and went to find Tunis Dean. He would straighten the man out over this Hopkins doctor.

"Listen, Tunis, do you know what you got me into tonight? That man was not well. He wanted to experiment on me!" Worthy had caught the managing director in his backstage office, preparing to leave for the night.

"What? Experiment on you? I had no idea," Dean lied. "I'm so sorry, Alcott, he told me he wanted to contribute to the Academy's fund, and that he wanted to meet you to discuss the possibility of partnering with you on some project of his."

"Yeah, some project!" Worthy found the bottle that he knew Dean kept in an oak sideboard. The two had opened the cabinet on many occasions. Now, he stood in front of the director, waving his glass around in his pique, sloshing the liquid onto the carpet.

"Tunis you're a slimey toad, aren't you? What else were you hoping to get out of it?"

"Nothing. Nothing at all. Just what I told you!"

"Tunis, you're a liar. What were you trying to do?"

"Look, the doctor was going to make a contribution. That's all. It was for the Academy."

"I don't believe you. There's something else."

"No, Alcott. That was it. He might also be able to bring in some additional Hopkins money."

"It's always about money with you, isn't it?"

"Well, maybe if you hadn't killed Miss Garrett's proposal—"

"Like I said, Tunis, it's always the money."

"Look, that's why the Board and Mr. Kernan pay me. It's my job. I just try to do it the best I can."

"Yeah, often at the expense of someone else."

"Alcott...."

"Forget it, Tunis. Never ask me to do anything again. I don't trust you." Worthy poured another half-glass, downed it, and for the second time that evening, left a conversation with some angry last words. This time, however, he was staggering as he turned to stalk out of the door.

He was tired, and probably had too much to drink. He would go home to sleep, but first he'd see what parties were still going on backstage.

Around 11:00 p.m.

Fanny was still fuming. She had told herself not to wear the necklace when there was a possibility of Worthy being around. But she wanted to impress Dorothea Baird. Now, after harsh words and his surprisingly quick hands, he had it back.

She watched the drunken pig try to weave his way through the backstage crowd to the alleyway exit. He caromed off several people and fought with a rack of costumes before he reached his destination. Fuzzy Hertzbaugh had been rocked back on two legs of his chair, arms crossed, watching her and Worthy. He spilled over in a heap of bones and profanity as Worthy landed two convulsive body slams against the door before he managed to disappear through it.

Fanny, wanting to avoid Hertzbaugh, pulled her wool wrap around her, threw up its hood, put her head down, and followed a late group of backstage partiers exiting through the front entrance before they locked all of the doors.

Once outside and on the sidewalk, she left the revelers as they waited for carriages. She turned south and began a fast walk down Howard Street toward Franklin and the Kernan Hotel, a long block away. She should have been alright by herself for that distance; besides, she had her pistol in her bag. Within a few steps, however, she had stopped dead, and then moved to the side of the building. There, she found a deep shadow between two marble columns and sunk into it.

At the top of the passageway that ran between the Academy and the Auditorium Theater, Fanny saw three figures. Two of them were big and seemed to be manhandling the third person. Maybe it was a street robbery. The victim was being jerked around and shaken violently. Then, she watched the larger of the two swing a club down on the head of the wretch they were bracing.

The men rocked on their heels as they watched their prey struggle to his hands and knees and begin to crawl back down the alley. One of the muggers started after the victim, but there was a sudden burst of shrill female laughter from the Academy's departing partiers. The larger of the two men stopped his confederate with a grab of the shoulder. He turned, peered at the knot of people departing, then searched into Fanny's shadow. After a long moment, he pulled his partner down Howard Street and quickly away.

Fanny waited until Sergeant Gatch and Officer Spittle were out of sight. She had recognized them immediately. She also knew who their victim was.

The actress walked to the mouth of the alley and watched Alcott Worthy drag himself through the trash. He was no longer on all fours, but nearly prone, dragging himself along, fingers prying into the cobblestones ahead of him. He had almost reached the theater door.

Fanny watched dispassionately, considering Worthy's plight. Then, checking over her shoulder for Howard Street pedestrians, she walked down the passageway toward him.

CHAPTER 16

1865

IN BALTIMORE

Moss was to be discharged from the Army in September, nearly five months after General Johnston surrendered to General Sherman in Durham, North Carolina. He and the remains of the 54th Regiment were to travel by train to Camp Meigs near Boston, back where they started two years earlier. There, they would be paid and processed out. The battle of words over paying black soldiers three dollars a month less than white soldiers and charging them another two for their uniforms left Moss disgusted, but not any more disillusioned than he already was. Experience told him not to expect fair treatment any time soon; and though he could certainly use the money owed him, when the train stopped in Baltimore, he jumped off.

Moss walked north until he found the Lexington Market, six blocks away. There, he bought working man's clothes, a slouch hat, and enough food to last until the next day. In the vendor's stall, he stripped off the worn, blue uniform and changed into the civilian attire. As he left the market, he found a trash barrel, wadded up the costume he once wore with pride, and threw it in. Now, as far as he was concerned, he was processed out of the Union army, regardless of the required formal demobilization process.

Moss was starting fresh in a city he didn't know. He had spent time on its docks unloading vegetables and had traveled through its streets crammed into the toolbox of Mordecai Stroup's wagon. That was about it. His most vivid memory of the place was on a train, watching the dark, dirty shapes of buildings pass as he struggled for his life.

He could connect with the Jesuits again, he knew. When at St. Joe's, he had met Fr. John Early, who lived here in Baltimore. In fact, at the time Moss had spoken with him, Early had just stepped down from the presidency of Loyola College, a school he had founded. The priest and the ex-slave had struck up a quick friendship, and the result was a standing invitation to work at Loyola and possibly take classes when and if the desire to come to Baltimore ever arose.

But Moss was looking for something new. He had liked his life with the Jesuits, but further schooling would have to wait, and working in city slums was not his calling. It was clear that he needed a job and a place to live. What was not clear was how he would find those things. Who was going to hire an itinerant, black, Yank veteran in a Southern city? He had heard that Baltimore's docks were some of the busiest in the world, and he guessed he could hire on to one of the schooners in the oyster fleet working the beds in the Chesapeake. But he also recalled talk of backbreaking work, bitter weather, brutal captains, and bad pay. There were also rumors that once some dredgers had their season, rather than paying them, they threw black men overboard. Moss could swim, but if he found himself knocked overboard in the middle of the icy bay, swimming would do him little good.

He did have one errand to perform. He wanted to shake Mordecai Stroup's hand and thank him for his kindness eight years earlier. It seemed like a lifetime ago, but maybe he was still running the caulking business. Maybe he could repay the Quaker in some way. So, Moss found Pratt Street and headed for City Dock by walking in the opposite direction of a steady flow of drays loaded with all manner of goods from all over the world.

✳✳✳✳✳✳✳

The smell of pitch and oakum led Moss to the same pier and eventually to the same refitting company owned by the Lombard Street Friends. As he walked, he became immersed in the tumult of commerce and the wealth it created. He also had to negotiate a labyrinth of appalling clutter and filth, further byproducts of trade.

Moss had been cautious in his search and very careful about who he spoke to. He avoided quieter doorways and alleys, staying where there was legitimate activity. He ignored the hostile stares and occasional provocation from white watermen and dock workers. City Dock was full of hard people doing hard work, and those idlers who were not laboring evoked in Moss the memory of the street gangs that held sway in Baltimore before the war.

"Pardon me, friend, I'm looking for a man named Stroup." Moss had approached a black man, spotted with pitch, directing a crew of caulkers swarming around a weathered pungy.

The man reluctantly looked up from the hold and said, "I ain't your friend. And there's nothing here for you. Why don't you take off before you get chased off."

Moss was a little surprised at the sour reception, but not much. The docks were not for the sensitive or those looking for a pal.

"Mister, there's nothing I want from you. I'm just trying to find Mordecai Stroup. The Quakers used to own this business, right?"

"I already told you, there's no work here. Hard enough with all the whites coming back."

"I'm not looking for a job. Not here, anyway. I owe Stroup and I want to repay him."

"Stroup's dead."

"Dead?"

"A couple of years ago now. Beaten to death on the street."

The caulker must have read the look on Moss's face. He softened somewhat. "The Meeting House is still up there on Lombard Street. If you owe the Quakers something, they can work it out with you."

"Thanks. Mr. Stroup helped me get away a few years ago."

That information seemed to break down a little more of the man's animosity.

"Mordecai helped a lot of people in them days. He's with the Lord now, you can be sure of that."

"Lombard Street, you say?"

"That's right, two blocks north and four blocks west on Lombard."

"Thanks, I appreciate it."

"You in the war?" the man asked, looking at Moss' boots.

"Yeah, 54th Massachusetts."

The drydocker's eyebrows raised a tick. "You looking for work?"

"I am, but caulking's not for me. Turns the hands black," Moss said, trying for a little joke.

The man managed a small smile. "Look, I know of a kindred soul named Isaac Myers. Been a freedman since before the war. He's started his own business, the Chesapeake Marine Railway and Dry Dock Company. Shipbuilding and repair. He hires people like you...and me. You should go see him. Kennard's Wharf, at the end of Philpot Street."

※※※※※※※

The Chesapeake Marine Railway and Dry Dock Company was exactly what Moss was seeking. Isaac Myers and his partner, John Locks, were hiring, and they were hiring black men. Baltimore's port had always been multiracial, employing all colors. But since the war ended, most around the harbor were filling their work rosters with returning white veterans. That left men like Moss, veteran or not, in a tough spot, even when competing for hard, dangerous jobs like oystering.

Underlying the hiring issue, however, was good news. Postwar Baltimore was exploding. The city had begun to flex its economic muscles by leveraging two key assets—the port and the B&O Railroad. The harbor was full of ships from all over the globe and its docks were loaded with produce, seafood, building materials, textiles, household goods, coal, iron ore, and anything else that could be floated up or down the bay. These things didn't stay long on the piers, either, as they were quickly transferred to Mr. Garrett's railroad and distributed throughout the rebuilding and burgeoning country.

The two entrepreneurs, Myers and Locks, were native Marylanders, born free and raised in the shipbuilding and repair industry. They were also adept businessmen and immediately recognized the value of a ready and willing work force in both the city's native black population and the steady flow of emancipated slaves pouring into the city.

It wasn't long after he walked onto the site that Moss was put to work. He quickly found himself fully engaged in repairing and refitting a wide range of Chesapeake watercraft, including pilot-schooners, pungies, bugeyes, sloops, and other working boats. There was certainly caulking work at first. But the company was interested in developing skilled labor, so he also served an apprenticeship in carpentry. His talent and his enthusiasm were rapidly recognized and within a year, he found himself coming to the attention of Mr. Myers.

"It's Moss, isn't it? Moss Tilghman?" the businessman asked. He had gotten the name from a list of promising employees, put together by one of his crew bosses.

"Yes, sir, that's right."

"Of the Eastern Shore Tilghmans?" Myers asked with a smile.

"Well, sort of, sir. There are a lot of Tilghmans over there. I grew up on the Poplar Grove Plantation in Queen Anne's County."

"Ah, the Emorys," the owner observed with an ulcerous look.

"Yes, sir," Moss replied, a little surprised that the name was known here on the western shore of the bay.

"Well, Moss, I hear that you have a talent for carpentry."

"Maybe, sir, but I have a lot to learn yet."

"The foreman says you came to him with some skill already."

"A little. I learned some things in Philadelphia."

"You were in Philadelphia?"

"Yes, sir, the Jesuits at St. Joseph's College took me in when I managed to get away from Poplar Grove."

"The Jesuits, huh? Interesting men. I hear that when they're not helping kings to take over countries, they're pretty good teachers."

"That they are, sir."

"Did they teach you anything else?"

"They did. I can read, write, keep books, and some other things, as well."

Myers leaned forward in his chair. "Moss, it just so happens that I could use someone like you working here in the office with me. Someone I can trust. Someone who knows figures and the work."

"Mr. Myers, thank you for thinking so highly of me, but keeping ledgers is something I already know. I really like working on boats, and I'm interested in learning new things."

The owner regarded Moss for a few moments without saying anything. Then, he seemed to come to a decision. "You realize I could simply say that your job is now in the office?"

"Yes, sir." Moss could see that forcing him to take the position was not the man's preferred approach to solving his problem, so he said no more and waited.

"We probably could work out a little raise in pay." It was said as if the offer were more of a question to see if it would change Moss's mind, but he remained silent. "I think that if I made you work in the office, I wouldn't be getting what I wanted. So, I won't do that." Myers paused again. "Unless you have something else to say, I guess I'll just be satisfied with employing a damned good marine carpenter."

"Mr. Myers, if you don't mind, I have a suggestion that might satisfy both of us."

Myers sat back and looked again at Moss with mild surprise. It wouldn't be the first or the last time that someone had underestimated the man standing in front of him. The owner was about to see Moss' depth.

"I'd be happy to help you in here with whatever you wanted me to do. And a pay raise would be most welcome. But, there is something I don't know that I would like to learn. If we could do that during off-hours, then I would take the inside job."

"What is it you want, Moss?" Myers was now guarded in his question.

"I'd like to learn sailing and navigation, sir."

Over the next two years, Moss learned more than he had anticipated and Myers got more of an employee than he ever imagined. Once the ex-slave understood the basic arithmetic of business, he began to understand business itself. That opened the door for frequent conversations with both Myers and Locks, and Moss became not just trustworthy, but a regular sounding board for decisions. The rudimentary management skills he picked up at St. Joseph's began to take concrete shape and meaning. It was clear that Moss got it and could apply it.

In the meantime, Myers was good to his word and introduced Moss to various sailing captains and sailing masters who had ties to Chesapeake Marine. The time was mined out to turn Moss into a fair sailor, and he soon found himself not in the office, but plying the waters of the bay. Sometimes, he would represent Myers and Locks in business dealings. Other times, he would be asked to return a sloop or a schooner to a client once it was repaired. Off and on, he would just knock about the harbor, testing his skill against the port's proven pilots. In this way, Moss learned sailing, he learned Baltimore from the water, and he learned the Chesapeake Bay. He also began to further grasp what true freedom was. Those times that he was alone—just him, the water and the boat—he was free to reflect, free to dream, and free to pursue those dreams.

Reflection continued to be a regular part of his daily routine. When he wasn't on the water, Moss made it a habit of thinking about the experiences of his workday each evening. One October night, as he walked the four blocks from Philpot Street to his room in Apple Alley, he was recalling Isaac Myers's comments about the history of the point in the harbor that now held the business. The owner had shaken his head sadly over the irony that Kennard's Wharf had been the center of Baltimore's slave trade at one time. He described traders, like the Tennessean Austin Woolfolk, shackling "goods" together and marching them under armed guard west on Pratt Street to a pen near Cove Street. There, the slaves would await sale and eventually be shipped south on one of the innumerable packet boats that lined the harbor's inner basin.

Myers mentioned that the famous writer and orator, Frederick Douglass, had spent time on Kennard's Wharf and had written about the things he saw there. The owner spoke with some reverence in explaining that Douglass himself had been some man's slave over in Talbot County on the Shore. It was back in '38 when he made his run, escaping north to Philadelphia. He had hopped a train out of Canton, just a few blocks farther east around the harbor. Now, he had the ear of President Lincoln.

This, of course, resonated loudly with Moss, and he was turning over in his mind the choices that Douglass's story seemed to make possible for someone like him. As he approached Thames Street, he slowly became aware of dark figures close behind him. When he turned, he felt the blow of a heavy club. The night went white, then there was nothing.

Chapter 17

The Suspects

The Diamond seemed to be holding its breath, just like the rest of Baltimore, in anticipation of April and the return of the Orioles from Macon. Business had been slower over the last few weeks, but the weather had been raw and not even the working girls were out on the streets. The sleet made it hard to even find a hack.

One night, around nine or ten o'clock, Moss and I sat at a table in the near empty taproom, lamenting the news of the day and halfheartedly sharing a pitcher of Eagle. If the truth be known, I was doing the lamenting and Moss was explaining where I was going wrong. In other words, we were having our typical conversation. I was also killing time until Fanny got out of rehearsal.

"I can't believe this country elected William McKinley."

"Elected him with the largest majority of the popular vote in twenty-five years, Frank."

"Yeah, by spending a lot of East Coast Republican money."

"Maybe, but Bryan's ideas on silver and gold also scared a lot of folks. We just came out of a fiscal crisis. Switching from gold to silver would risk serious inflation."

"Yeah, and those who already have theirs wouldn't want that. It's the have nots who got it in the neck."

"Think about it, Frank. A dollar that's only worth seventy-five cents is good for nobody."

I was over my head already, so I moved on quickly to the latest from Arthur Conan Doyle. "Hey, I hear there's a new Holmes out. I wonder if Izzy Tatter's got it in yet."

"He's got it. *The Adventure of Abbey Grange*. I tried to get you a copy, but he wouldn't sell me one. Said he only had a few. When I asked him if he was a bookseller or a collector, he screamed at me and told me to get out of his shop. I might have been offended, if I thought a Jew could be a bigot with all the crap that those people have been through."

"Oh, he's a bigot, alright. When I first went in there, he asked me what kind of name Van Sant was. Evidently, he doesn't like the Dutch, either. At least he spreads his warmth around."

"Speaking of heat, what do you hear from the cops? Had any dealings with Sergeant Gatch lately?"

Gatch hadn't gone away. He was still harassing Fanny, and I had seen him with Spittle a few times now. They were somehow connected, and not just through the police force. Fanny mentioned that the Sergeant was one of the things she wanted to talk about tonight. But I didn't know what she had in mind, and I didn't want to discuss our side investigation with Moss—not yet, anyway. I needed a few more answers before I brought in the big gun.

"Yeah, he's still around. I see him more than I do O'Donnell. I'm not sure what his story is."

"Does he know you're looking into the murder?"

"How did you know that we—I was looking into the murder?"

"Frank, you're not always as slick as you think you are."

"Yeah, well, neither are you."

My rejoinder was weak and Moss just gave me a sad smile. So, I let the topic go and changed the subject again. "I read that the Cleveland Spiders just signed a full-blooded Indian. Chief Sockahooey, or something."

"Louis Sockalexis. He's a Penobscot. Outfielder. Pitches some, too. Pretty good, I hear."

"Probably learned to throw by pegging rocks at grizzlies."

Moss looked at me with disgust. "Now your bigotry is showing. He's from Maine—no grizzlies there. Only black bears. Sockalexis went to Holy Cross, then Notre Dame. What school did you go to, Frank?"

With that embarrassing question, the door opened and Fanny's arrival spared me further skewering by Moss. The woman, as always, was breathtaking. Tonight, she wore a camel-colored coat with some kind of fur collar that not only kept out the Baltimore cold, but framed her face in a way that would have entranced John Singer Sargent. It certainly entranced me.

I stood, took her coat, gave Moss a little smile over her shoulder, and led her to a table away from where my friend and I had been sitting. That move didn't faze him a bit. He stood and joined us with the pitcher of beer.

"Miss Darlington, it's always nice to see you," Moss said, sitting down.

"Mr. Tilghman, nice to see you too," she responded, nodding at his latest request of her to call him Moss. Then, with a sideways glance, she looked at me as if to ask if I thought it a good idea that he join us.

I don't think Fanny was ever comfortable with Moss. She'd been in his company several times since that first morning, of course. But, as amicable as he was to her each time, she seemed to have difficulty warming to him for reasons she never explained. Maybe it was his color, but I don't think so.

Moss obviously was determined to hear our conversation. That meant he was interested, and maybe even had something to offer. At any rate, a determined Moss is not someone easily deterred, so I let him be.

"Are you hungry? Do you want something to drink?" I started.

"No, I'm not hungry but a glass of water would be welcome," she answered.

I looked at Moss, but he gave me a blank stare and made no move to get up. So, I rose and walked behind the bar to get Fanny her drink.

"Did rehearsal go well?" Moss asked her.

"Yes, of course. It's not so new anymore," Fanny replied with little enthusiasm.

"As I'm sure you know, the play has gotten wonderful reviews, thanks in no small part to your performances."

"Yes, it has been well received," she said modestly, offering no more. She acknowledged Moss's compliment with a small smile and a shy duck of her head.

"How much longer do you think they'll stage *Zenda?*"

"April 3 is our last performance."

"Then what will you do?" he asked her.

I arrived back at the table to hear his question. I was more interested in the answer than he was, but Fanny chose to ignore it.

"Thank you, Frank." She focused on the glass of water, taking a sip. Then she asked me, "Did you manage to find out who Alcott Worthy met with before he was shot?"

"Well, we know he met with Tunis Dean after the show."

"No, I mean before that, in the Academy's bar. The man he argued with."

"Worthy seemed to be arguing with everyone that night—the man in the bar, Dean, you...."

"Frank, we have to find this man. We need to know what they talked about. It might give us a possible reason for the murder."

"I might have something," I said, "but it's not much. It cost me ten bucks to pry it out of Fuzzy Hertzbaugh. The geezer saw a note from Tunis Dean to the dead man. But he said Spittle took it away from him."

"Spittle?" The mention of the beat cop jarred Fanny.

"What did the note say?" Moss asked.

"Fuzzy didn't get it all, but he did see a name that he can't remember. Even for another five he couldn't remember."

"Nothing at all?" Fanny asked.

"Well, he did say that the name was German, it could have begun with an 'M,' and that there was a title of some sort. Professor, doctor, something like that."

This news meant nothing to Fanny, and she expressed her frustration with a sigh. Moss, though, sat up and leaned on the table and gave me that "I've got an idea" look of his.

"A German professor or doctor, you say?"

"That's what he said."

"Name begins with an 'M'?"

"Maybe."

"You might want to track down a Hopkins doctor by the name of Munsch," he offered.

"Munch?" Fanny and I asked at the same time.

Moss spelled the name for us and explained, "I heard a lecture at Hopkins from an Austrian doctor named H. Leopold Munsch. He seemed a bit questionable to me. It's just a gut feel, but there was something not right about him."

"Something that made him capable of murder? How would he be tied to Alcott Worthy?"

"I think this man could be capable of some things worse than murder. Do you remember that sketch of me and the students that I showed you the morning Harry Von Der Horst was in here?"

"The one that spelled out 'Help me,'" Fanny recalled.

"That's the one. It was from a lecture I heard from this Hopkins neurologist, Dr. Munsch. The artist, Munsch's patient, died not long after he did that drawing."

"Wait a minute. That's a pretty thin connection, Moss. What logic puts your crazy doctor together with a theater promoter? How does a patient dying make this Dr. Munsch a murderer?"

"I didn't say he was a murderer. I'm just saying that he seemed capable of some real antisocial behavior."

"Seemed?" I accused.

"Yes, seemed, Frank. How many times do we have to have this conversation? It's a sense. You were talking about murder. You mentioned a German doctor or professor whose name began with an 'M.' I remembered an oddball with a German or Austrian accent who may have caused his patient to reach out for help in desperation. No logic, just intuition."

"Ah," I said knowingly, exasperating Moss.

"Frank, we have nothing else to go on. What would it hurt to look into this Dr. Munsch?" Fanny was losing patience with me.

"What you might want to do," Moss suggested, "is to see if you can make a connection between Munsch and Dean or Munsch and Worthy."

They were right. We had nothing else. I still thought Moss was reaching, but a lead was a lead. I also wondered if O'Donnell was aware of this Hopkins neurologist and whether the police had linked the three men.

"Fanny, have you seen Detective O'Donnell or Sergeant Gatch recently?"

"If you mean did I see them when they turned my hotel room upside down again the other day, then yes, I've seen them."

"What were they looking for, did they tell you?"

Once again, a question I asked seemed to annoy her. Was it me or was it the situation?

"They didn't deign to tell me, but it doesn't take a genius to guess that they were looking for something to tie me to Alcott Worthy," she replied.

"Maybe the murder weapon. Maybe a pistol," Moss suggested, watching Fanny closely.

"I've told you—"

"Moss, I think we should wrap this up for tonight. I'm beat, and I'm sure Fanny would like to get back to her room."

The already thin relationship between Fanny and Moss was about to get tested and I didn't want that. Truth be known, she was testier now than when I first met her. Despite that, she remained a beautiful woman and I was starting to have serious feelings for her. So, I ended the conversation and walked her back to her hotel, promising on the way to look into this Dr. Munsch.

As it turned out, it was a much later night than I had anticipated. Fanny had put her arm in mine and leaned into me to ward off the cold. I could feel her warmth as she swayed gently against me. Her glorious hair smelled wonderful—rich and feminine. As we walked, I stole glances at her delicate profile and they made my heart ache. Once again, I could sense her vulnerability and I realized that she had a lot on her mind—the play, the murder, her future. I began to understand better why she had been a little out of sorts.

When we arrived at the Kernan, she asked if maybe we could have a drink before she went to bed. I'm not sure I touched my whiskey, but it wasn't long after the cubes in her empty glass were bumping her perfect red lips that she asked if I wanted to come up to her room. I did.

Tunis Dean was sweating on one of the colder days of the year. Thomas O'Donnell was supplying the heat. Dean had avoided the detective's first attempts to reach him, so Sergeant Gatch was sent after the Academy's managing director.

The pent-up violence emanating from the sergeant was enough for the theater man to stop demanding to know why he was being hauled in. It seemed wisest to keep his mouth shut until he found someone in charge. He was right about that. Gatch was just looking for an excuse to rumple the citizen's starched shirt. Now, as they sat in one of the precinct's ugly offices, O'Donnell was getting some answers.

"Mr. Dean, one would think you didn't want to talk to me. It's enough to hurt my feelings."

"No, sir. That's not true," Dean replied, sounding as cooperative as possible.

When he was first ushered in to see the detective, he tried his normal bluster, railing about the indignity and the mistreatment of someone of his stature. He dropped the act quickly enough, though, when he realized that O'Donnell found it all quite amusing. The cop laughed, knowing that Ole Tunis was in for a few more serious dents in his dignity.

"I was surprised that a man of your...what did you call it? Oh yeah, 'stature.' A man of your stature didn't come clean with me when we first talked back in

February. When I found out you withheld information, it made me curious about why someone of your stature would do such a thing."

"What? Withhold information? I...."

Like a buzzard on a branch eyeing its next meal, O'Donnell peered at Dean. "Mr. Dean. You didn't tell me that you and the victim were so close."

"We were acquainted, but we weren't close."

"You were close enough to meet with him the night of the murder."

"Yes, yes, I did. But it was about business. It was about the Academy of Music. Mr. Worthy is, uh, was a member of our Board of Sponsors."

"What kind of business would have made him so angry with you?"

"Angry with me?"

"Mr. Dean, why do I get the feeling that you're still not ready to tell me the truth—all of the truth?"

"I am telling you the truth!"

"You are making me pull teeth, Mr. Dean. Now, understand, we are fully prepared to do just that, and Sergeant Gatch would relish the opportunity."

"You are threatening me. I demand that I be allowed legal counsel."

"Do you feel like you need a lawyer, Mr. Dean? What is it that you don't want us to know?"

"Nothing, nothing. But you are bullying me. I have nothing to hide."

"Then explain to me why I have three witnesses who say Alcott Worthy was in your office shouting at you around ten o'clock the night he was killed."

"I don't know, Mr. Worthy was very inebriated."

"What was he shouting about?"

"It was a business thing. We disagreed on a vote that was taken by the Board," Dean lied.

"Uh-huh. What vote?"

"It was all about scheduling a women's suffrage convention. I wanted to book it and he didn't. It would have been very good for the Academy."

"And that was occasion for shouting?"

"Yes, sir. Mr. Worthy disagreed and, as I said, he'd been drinking."

O'Donnell knew the man was not telling the whole story, but he was willing to let it pass for now. He knew who the members of the Academy Board were and was sure he could get them to comment—maybe even get meeting minutes if he pressed it.

"Okay, Mr. Dean, I'll let that go for the time being. But I have something else I want to ask you about."

The detective paused and his eyes bore into Tunis Dean's. He watched a salty bead run down the man's face and puddle at the top of his celluloid collar. Dean fumbled after a white handkerchief, then mopped his neck and forehead.

"What was in the note that you sent to Alcott Worthy earlier that afternoon?"

This question produced a gobsmacked look on the managing director's face. Dismay quickly replaced it. Then, his eyes drifted up and to the left as he struggled to arrive at a plausible explanation. He failed, and the hankie was put back to work.

"I'm waiting for an answer, Mr. Dean."

"I—I wanted Mr. Worthy to meet someone," he finally said.

"And who was that, Mr. Dean?"

"Just a possible contributor. Occasionally I ask Board members to speak to potential supporters of the theater."

"Who was that, sir?"

"I am pledged to confidentiality in these matters, detective."

"Mr. Dean, I'm pledged to finding a murderer and, goddamnit, if you don't play straight with me right now, I pledge that I'll turn this interview over to Sergeant Gatch."

O'Donnell stood, walked to the door, and barked for the sergeant.

"Okay, Detective O'Donnell. It was a doctor from over at Johns Hopkins Hospital—a man with money and connections, a man who would be good for the Academy."

"Name?"

Dean still hesitated, but when Sergeant Gatch entered the room, he said, "Munsch. Dr. Leopold Munsch."

"Okay, now, that wasn't so hard, was it?" O'Donnell asked as he watched Dean swab his decks yet again. "Now, what did they talk about?"

"A contribution is all I know. Dr. Munsch had indicated he might be willing to write a draft for a large sum."

"That's all?"

"I don't know what else they may have discussed." Dean was whining now.

"Where did this conversation take place?"

"I'm not sure. In one of the Academy's bars, I think."

The detective looked at Gatch and gave him a nod. The sergeant understood that he needed to have a talk with the bartenders and he left the room.

"Okay, Mr. Dean. You can go now. Stay around town where I can find you. And if you're still holding out on me, if there's something else you're not telling me, I swear I'll find you a nice barred room over on Gay Street."

Tunis Dean was now a worried man. Somehow, they were connecting him to this damned murder. God knows Worthy deserved what he got. The man made enemies wherever he went. But he couldn't tell the cop about Munsch's crazy idea to experiment on Worthy. Not only did it sound insane, but it would embarrass the Academy's Hopkins financial support, and kill any opportunity to expand it.

But this is about murder. Why should he protect a murderer? No, he had to let the police do their own work. If it turned out that Alcott Worthy was shot by Dr. Munsch, he wouldn't be the one that pointed the finger.

But there was something else worrying him as well. The night *The Prisoner of Zenda* opened, he had received an unexpected visit from Mary Elizabeth Garrett. She had attended the play, but had left her loge box and had come to his office. She was aware of Worthy's death, and now was interested in revisiting the Board vote on her planned convention. She had been as arrogant as ever and cared little about the murder, other than it presented another opportunity to get what she wanted. She had even upped the ante if the Board would meet again on her proposal. What's more, there would be a sizable bonus in it for Dean—if he secured approval. Miss Garrett had been forceful to the degree that there was also an implied threat to him personally if the Board rejected her again. It wasn't clear whether the threat extended beyond the loss of his position.

But he wouldn't put anything past that woman, including the active removal of any roadblocks that stood in her way—any roadblocks. Given all of that, he certainly wasn't going to mention his thoughts on the matter to Detective O'Donnell. He was not going to take on the Garretts, cops or no cops.

Thomas P. O'Donnell lay in his bed, staring at the pressed-tin ceiling. A shaft of light from the street below intersected it, having found a crack between the shade and the window frame. He listened to his wife sleeping, making those little noises that dreams produce. He wished he was asleep as well, but his day was not yet ready to let go.

He was feeling much better now that he had another possible suspect—a doctor named Munsch. Once they got the guy in for questioning, maybe a motive would surface, if there was one. If there wasn't, there was always Fanny Darlington. Unfortunately, the woman had proven to be a harder nut to crack than he first imagined. Was her bad relationship with Worthy enough of a motive? Maybe. Now, the investigation was picking up some traction and he was relieved.

Then his mind switched to his other problem, Gatch and Spittle. A real pair. He would see that the beat cop was sent up on theft charges, withholding evidence, and obstructing an investigation. Any internal hearing was bound to bring out his "special" relationship with various businesses along Howard Street, as well. And when it's all added up, it should be enough to get Spittle moved out of the District, maybe off the force completely.

Gatch was a bigger issue. He and Spittle had been seen together on the street the night of the murder. Plus, O'Donnell didn't like the look Gatch gave Spittle when he asked about the dead body. They knew something. Or, they had done something. Regardless, they weren't talking—yet.

The pathologist at the Fleet Street morgue told the detective that the cause of death was most likely a bullet to the brain. But he also mentioned that it was just as possible that Worthy died from whatever blunt object put the dent in his skull. A blow to the head fit Gatch's modus operandi. The sergeant liked hitting drunks, and Worthy certainly was one. Gatch was also in the area at the right time and he had the opportunity. It wasn't hard to figure a motive, either—meanness and psychosis would do, a pattern the sergeant had already established.

Maybe he now had three viable suspects. As the detective mulled it over, he realized that, of the three, Gatch was the one he wanted gone the most. The man was a menace. He also sensed that the best way to get what he wanted was to work that dunce Spittle. The beat cop would provide the evidence he needed.

Just before O'Donnell nodded off, the detective had one more thought. How was Tunis Dean involved? He certainly wasn't spilling everything. What would he gain from Worthy's murder? Was convention money enough of a motive for murder? Four suspects? This was getting interesting.

CHAPTER 18

OPENING DAY

It was fair weather for Opening Day of the 1897 baseball season, and the streets were jammed with cheering cranks, lined six deep along the two-and-a-half-mile parade route. A mounted police escort led the 5th Regiment Band and Drum Corps who, in turn, heralded a long train of carriages of all sizes and shapes, decorated in orange and black bunting. The open transports overflowed with top-hatted dignitaries, city officials, bankers, merchants, clergymen, and party bosses. In the middle of all of that, five huge, four-horse victoria rigs carried Harry Von Der Horst, Ned Hanlon, and his horse-hide heroes, the three-time World Champion Baltimore Orioles. At the rear of the entourage, municipal firemen, social clubs, unions, and assorted artisans' guilds carried their banners, waved pennants, and marched in ragged formation as they tried to avoid the droppings left by the equine-powered caravan preceding them.

The exuberant celebration started at the Eutaw House Hotel, worked its way east along Baltimore Street, then up Charles to the Washington Monument. There, the spectacle did one pirouette around the great man, then continued its momentum, spinning off north to Huntington Avenue and the green field of Union Park. The Birds would begin their title defense against the Boston Beaneaters, a team they considered pansified.

In the second victoria, the Big Four sat together. With them were catcher Wilbert Robinson and second baseman Heine Reitz. The four stars were in one carriage at the request of Harry Von Der Horst, who also had asked them to wear their uniforms. The brewer clearly understood the magnified power of his luminaries when they were together. The publicity garnered during their triumphal European tour last fall was proof enough of that.

But the men seemed jaded by all of the attention. In years past, they would have been hollering and whooping back at their adoring public. Instead, they sat with frozen smiles, halfheartedly waving at the throng and complaining about the long ride. It didn't help that their new wool vestments, trimmed in orange and black, itched like hell.

If the truth be known, not all was well between McGraw, Keeler, Kelley, and Jennings. What's more, the rest of the team seemed just as fractured. Spring training in Macon had been a disaster due to an overabundance of both rain and short tempers. Hanlon's constant drills and nightly meetings focused on improving individual players' weaknesses. But his training strategy seemed to backfire. The emphasis on individuals contradicted what had made them so successful over three exhausting seasons in a row—the Orioles had always been about teamwork. Now, it seemed more about individual stats. It felt like the old gang was breaking up.

But it wasn't just that. During the time in Georgia, and in the Carolinas on the way home, they really hadn't played enough games. When they did play, it was often against inferior competition. That meant little challenge and no opportunity to practice those special tactics that were so feared and hated around the league. The plain fact was that the Oriole baseball machine could not build to its normal efficiency because their time together had been fragmented.

Distractions also abounded, some small and niggling, others of more serious concern. The team's general malaise mirrored Georgia's rainfall and often caused the smallest irritation to mutate in importance, creating sparks even between close friends.

Some of the Birds' discontent came from the outside. In the off-season, the League made three crucial rule changes that many of the Orioles believed were aimed directly at dethroning them. The first was new foul-language guidelines that seemed to have been written by Baptist ladies. In many places, baseball was not played on Sundays for a number of reasons, but at least one of them had to be the colorful way players normally converse with each other. Taking the Lord's name in vain was one of the Orioles' specialties. One Catholic umpire was heard to suggest that Jack Doyle had singlehandedly upgraded cursing from a venial sin to a mortal sin.

The second rule change was the restriction that only the on-field team captain could dispute an umpire's call, and everyone else had to stand at least ten feet away. This was outrageous because it hit so close to home. "Kicking" the umpire was one of the Orioles' most effective dodges, and they were the best in the business at it. Games were often won or lost based upon umpire intimidation, and every team understood this. As a result, the League struggled to keep umps who were both tough and worth a damn. This affected Baltimore mightily because their on-field captain was Uncle Robbie, the least combative and least profane (other than Willie Keeler, of course) of all of the Orioles.

Now, violators of the language and dispute rules risked immediate ejection, something that the Birds already led the league in over the last couple of years.

The third injustice was the news that the League would be paying for an additional umpire on the field for certain games and certain teams. Of course, the Orioles knew "certain teams" meant them. Hanlon had always told them, when running the bases, to keep one eye on the ball and the other on the umpire. When he heard the news, McGraw's sarcastic observation was, "We all gotta grow a third eye now."

Unfortunately, these were not the only adjustments the League decided to make. The word was that players all around the majors were fuming about how the game was changing. Some new rules were particularly noxious to pitchers, like the emphasis on calling balks. Others made hitters like Keeler and McGraw grind their teeth. Foul balls, deliberate or not, would now be called strikes. There would be a cost to fouling off pitches until a fat one came in there. No more protecting a slow base stealer by spoiling a pitch. Bunting, a major weapon for many teams, would be reduced, since any foul bunt would be called a strike, as well. While hitters whined that averages would plummet, Bill Hoffer and Doc Pond, the Orioles' best two righties, swore that averages would soar.

To Baltimore, the baseball world at large seemed to be ganging up on them. Not a day went by without some sports writer extolling the "purity" of the game while lambasting the Birds' "cutthroat style of ball." Writers like John Morrill of the *Boston Morning Journal*, Joe Villa of New York's *Morning Sun*, and Ren Mulford, correspondent for the *Sporting News*, were writing the same sorts of things about the team, calling them "corrupt," "godless," and "blackguards from a wharf city." It was enough to hurt one's feelings.

Trade and sale rumors involving Baltimore players were constant. No one seemed immune. One day it was Kelley, another it was Robinson or Reitz. Newspapers reminded readers and the players that Hanlon once said, "Everything I have, except my family, is for sale at a price."

The hated Reserve Clause gave teams the right to hold on to their players while renewing contracts at the same salary for as long as the club wished. When League Owners voted to continue the $2,400 annual salary cap on all players, there was angry buzzing and murmuring within the team and all around baseball. It was indentured servitude. Talk of unionizing resurfaced. So, at the beginning of the new season, salary and security were on everyone's mind.

Ned Hanlon was a rock through it all though. He ignored the talk of a League conspiracy against his team, saying that the Orioles played "baseball as she is played." Instead of wasting time worrying about rule changes, he trotted out brand-new scientific stratagems, like the pitcher covering first base on ground balls to the first baseman in the hole, and situational hitting based upon the positioning of outfielders. At the start of the season, he assured Albert Mott, *Sporting Life's* Baltimore man, that the team was "in fine condition" and primed to win their fourth straight pennant.

But even if the outside world was conniving to bring the team down, cracks in the plaster had already begun to show early on in Macon. No one was happy that Hughie Jennings had hardly been in spring training at all, claiming arm soreness, then hiring out to coach the University of Georgia team instead. John McGraw brought his wife, Minnie, with him. As sweet as she was, her presence and Muggsy's vigilance in maintaining everyone's propriety when she was around changed the normal manly atmosphere of social gatherings. Joe Corbett, the righty the Birds thought of as their rising star, wasn't in spring training at all, agreeing instead to help prepare his brother, Jim, for a boxing title defense against Bob Fitzsimmons.

Joe Kelley stayed in a different hotel from the team with some doxy he met in the Pig 'n Poke Roadhouse and only showed for practice. Reitz missed his family, and Jerry Nops complained of homesickness. Uncle Robbie spent most of his time trying to lose weight, talked ad nauseum about his "mud runs," then became sullen when he couldn't get anyone to join him. Keeler and McGraw had been sniping at each other the whole spring, each accusing the other of a combination of personal offenses and sloppy ball playing. Once, their jibes devolved into a locker room fistfight with Willie as the surprise victor when Muggsy slipped on the wet floor.

And then there was Jack Doyle, who had come to the Orioles the year before from the New York Giants. A pearl on the field, Doyle was also the classic grit in the oyster, an irritant to everyone. While he hit .339 in '96 and played a fine first base, he was just as skilled in delivering foul-mouthed assessments of his teammates. On top of that, it was clear that he thought only of himself, an attitude that was becoming infectious within the team. Umpires hated Doyle, and no Oriole had forgiven him—or ever would—for stiffing Wee Willie for two hundred dollars on the Temple Cup split in 1895. Put bluntly, he was an abscess on the team's rear parts.

Robinson, normally the peacemaker, had all he could do to keep a lid on things. No amount of threatening from Manager Hanlon had an effect on his team's temperament, either. In the off-season, the Oriole chemistry had undergone a not-so-subtle change.

When the team finally arrived back in Baltimore, a week of exhibition games against amateur clubs did nothing to sharpen or solidify the champions. Yet now they found themselves pressed together in carriages, staring out at an unsuspecting crowd of cheering zealots and about to start the new baseball season.

"Robbie, you're sure Frank has the keg count correct? What about oysters? Primes only, no selects! What about steak? We'll have a lot of meat eaters tonight. The Diamond's gonna be jammed," McGraw shouted over the noise.

"John, stop worrying. Frank's on board, he knows what he's doing, and he's got Moss. The two of them know a hell of a lot better than you and me," Robinson answered. Then, Robbie yelled something to someone in the crowd and laughed, waving and giving the thumbs up.

"They'd better know what they're doing," was the surly reply.

"I hope you know what you're doing today," Keeler said, just loud enough for the third baseman to hear him.

"What's that, Willie? You have something to say to me?" McGraw yelled.

This got everyone's attention. "Hey, this is a celebration, act like it," Kelley suggested to both men.

"Yeah," Jennings and Reitz echoed.

"Does he know he's got a ballgame today? No, he does not! He's thinking about his damned saloon. Get your head into it, McGraw." Keeler was upset; normally, he never swore.

As John McGraw rose with the color in his face, two things happened. First, Robbie grabbed his arm to yank him back down. Second, as he stood, the crowd went crazy. The conflict of emotions that crossed his face would have been a topic of merriment among friends in another time, but now it was a matter of tension.

Returning Willie's stink-eye, Muggsy wavered, but finally gave in to the twin forces of his love of public admiration and Uncle Robbie's upper body strength. He sat back in the coach and glared across at the man who was an usher at his wedding at St. Vincent's just a few months earlier.

Unfazed by the black look, Keeler's last words on it were, "Play ball, Mc-Graw!"

Despite the strain, the Orioles, in front of a full house of 13,000 cranks, won the game that day by five runs. The beating started with the Beaneaters ahead 5–4 with one on and one out in the sixth. Hughie Jennings leaned into a fastball, turned slightly, and took it on the shoulder. The rule was that a player would not be awarded first base if he intentionally got hit. But Jennings was a master at this and was given the base. It would be the first of forty-seven times he was hit that year.

Umpire Tom Lynch, as tough as any ball player and tougher than most prizefighters, stood his ground as the Bostons howled about cheap play. Kelley was then walked on four pitches by an upset Beaneater pitcher, loading the bases. Next, Doyle lined a shot over the centerfielder's head for a double, scoring two runs and cracking the nut that fell open completely in the seventh and eighth innings as the Birds took advantage of some sore-armed pitchers.

There would have been smiles all around that day with the victory except for the fact that McGraw incurred a bad ankle sprain in the first inning. Not thought too serious at first, the injury nagged on for several weeks after that, keeping the star out of the lineup, just as the team was trying to get its feet under itself. No one knew at the time that this was the start of many such injuries that would keep most of Baltimore's starting lineup on the bench at one time or another during the long, grueling season.

CHAPTER 19

OCTOBER 1868
OYSTER PIRATES

Moss woke in blackness to the smells of oysters, bilge, and human filth. His head hurt and he was disoriented. He was in a boat—the motion was unmistakable. He was queasy, but it could have been his head or the sea. He vomited. Then, he heard something very close to him move and he threw up his arms in defense. That's when he realized he was in chains.

"Looks like the new one's come to," a negro voice said.

There was no response to the observation, but another body shifted in the blindness, on Moss's right this time.

"Mister, near as I can tell, you're a big man. Little Lou and I ain't going to hurt you. But it gets real crowded in here with you thrashing around and all."

Moss started to process the precious little feedback he was getting from the environment. He had been shanghaied! The realization made him angry. Angry that he knew the practice was rife on Baltimore's docks. Angry that he wasn't paying better attention when he got hit. Angry that he was once again in chains.

"What day is this?" Moss demanded of the voice.

"I believe it's Tuesday. Don't rightly know the date."

Moss estimated that he had been unconscious for several hours. The feel of the boat also told him that the time had been spent making way out into the Chesapeake.

"What boat is this and where are we going?"

The same man answered, "This here's the pungy *Mary Kate,* out of Crisfield. And you're not going anywhere except this rotting hold and a place at the dredge winch on its deck."

"Mister, I would not advise you to annoy me, chains or no chains. Where is she sailing?"

"It might surprise you to know that Captain Emory doesn't keep me too well informed. But if I were to guess, I'd say we'd be going back to where we been scraping for the last two months—the Pocomoke Sound."

The captain's name was all too familiar to Moss, and he couldn't help but wonder at the cruel joke of circumstance. He also knew of the Pocomoke Sound and had sailed there himself. Oysters. Black Gold. The numbers of shellfish taken out of there were huge at one time, but dredgers had been taking a toll on the deep-water beds for years. It was likely that the *Mary Kate* had moved on to the Sound's creeks and tributaries—territory reserved for tongers by state law. That meant the work would be illegal and under the cover of night.

"How many aboard?"

"There's six, all told. The three of us; Captain Emory; his boy, Caleb; and Mr. Workman. But you might just as well put those thoughts out of your head right now. Not with Snake and Winnie around."

"Don't try to guess what I'm thinking, boy." Moss used the pejorative term with a snarl. "Who's Snake and Winnie?"

"Mister, when we're out in the daylight, you won't be calling me 'boy.'"

"Who's Snake and Winnie?"

Moss had offended the man; so, he got no answer right away. Except for the sound of water flowing under the hull, a long silence ensued in the dark. Eventually, the voice spoke. "Snake is Mr. Workman's bullwhip and Winnie is his Henry rifle. He's very proud of both."

"Does the *Mary Kate* put in anywhere?"

"Mister, you ask a lot of questions for someone whose name I don't know."

Now it was Moss's turn to hesitate. He didn't know these men. And he didn't know whether giving them his name would help or hurt. But it would be safer to lie.

"Jim. Jim's the name. I work on the City Dock."

"Not no more you don't, Jim. You're oystering now. I'm Achilles, and the quiet one next to you is Little Lou."

"Where does the captain put in?"

"He don't. Not very often, anyway. Lou and I ain't seen shore in weeks."

"He has to offload his catch sometime, or buy supplies" Moss said.

"Oh, he does that. But he doesn't put in to do it. He meets one of those Yankee buyboats. He works out the money, unloads, resupplies, then turns right around, back to the beds."

"You were just in Baltimore," Moss pressed.

"Couldn't tell it by Lou and me," Achilles answered. "We spent the two days right here, chained up. My guess is they needed to replace Johnnie."

"Johnnie?"

"Yeah, he fell overboard. You're sitting in his place."

At the mention of Johnnie's accident, there was a sound out of Little Lou that was a cross between a snort and a chuckle.

"Ain't nothing to laugh about, Lou. It could happen to any of us. Knowing Captain Emory, it probably will."

"What are you saying?" Moss asked.

"You ever heard of getting paid by the boom?"

Moss, of course, had heard of the insidious practice. If a boat was using forced labor, then that labor was easily disposed of at the end of a season, or if someone was trouble, or if someone was worn out. At the right moment, an unexpected change in the wind or an intentional turn of the rudder would cause either one of the schooner's two booms to swing without warning, sweeping the unfortunate target over the rail and into the icy water of the Bay. It was some captains' way of keeping expenses low and evidence hidden.

"Jim, you'd better try to get some sleep. We'll be getting a few hours' work in tonight before dawn comes."

"We'll work tonight?"

Again there was a snort from Little Lou.

"Oh yeah, every chance we get. Can't work the creeks during the day—too dangerous."

"Cops?"

"Cops, hell. The tongers come after us dredgers with rifles from the shore. Depending upon where we go, it might be Virginians shooting at us from boats. Ain't no dredging in that state at all. The state line runs right through the Pocomoke."

"Aren't there police around? I heard the state created an Oyster Navy to stop this kind of thing."

Little Lou made his noise again.

"Jim, the Chesapeake's long and wide. I'd guess there are at least 600 pungies just like this one, doing what we're doing. Not only that, the money so good it's worth risking the fine."

"What about shanghaies?"

"The police don't care, and most men are too scared to say anything."

"You too scared?" Moss asked with a challenge in his tone.

"Mister, I try to be smarter than brave, and it's kept me alive this long."

Once more, the man was insulted and the conversation died again. Moss's head was pounding and he needed to bite back on his anger. So, he leaned back, closed his eyes and waited for the next thing to happen.

It wasn't long before the hatch was thrown open and a harsh voice ordered the three men to make room. An oil lamp showed a black-bearded oysterman with a rifle looking down at them. A teenage boy climbed into the hold, complaining about the smell of puke. He struggled through a wracking, rheumy cough, then used a set of keys on a big iron ring to unlock the shackles. Moss was rapped on the back of the head with the key ring and prodded first up a short ladder to the deck.

He emerged into a night that held a pale winter moon half-hidden in cloud. It was cold, and an intermittent breeze blew off the water. The man who must have been Mr. Workman stood back, levered a round into his Henry's chamber, and watched Moss with a red eye. He knew that if ever there was a time a new man was going to give him trouble, it would be now, upon first freedom.

Moss kept his look down and the boy, Caleb, threw a pair of stained overalls at his feet. Then, he slammed him in the chest with a smelly, oiled jacket, a knit cap, and pair of leather gloves with holes in them.

Little Lou surfaced next. He was a short white man, blockish, not fat, but thick. Finally, Achilles came up on deck and Moss could see why he had said what he did. The man was enormous and muscled.

The *Mary Kate* was making her way toward a dark shoreline when the captain spoke from behind the wheel. He was not loud, but his words were very clear.

"Nobody talks," he started. "I want quiet and no lights. I don't give a damn if you three get shot, but Caleb, Mr. Workman, and I don't want to be stopping any lead."

He pointed at Moss. "Boy, I want no trouble from you. You're here now, and you make the best of it. If you don't, I'll call on Snake. If that's not enough for you, then there are other ways to bring you around that are less pleasant. You work the dredge and the winch with the other nigger. Follow his lead and you'll get the hang of it soon enough. We'll be coming around shortly, so go to it. Move!"

The teenager grabbed Moss's arm and shoved him toward the boat's winch. The push did little other than to move an arm. Moss looked at the young man.

"Mr. Workman, did you see the look this boy just gave me? Lots of attitude. I think Snake might need some exercise." He then began his consumptive cough again which, after seeing the scowl on his father's face, the boy suppressed as best he could.

His comment about attitude got both the captain's and Workman's attention. But Moss just climbed to the rail of the schooner with Achilles and took the other side of a large, iron mesh basket. It was made of chains and open at one end, where a heavy, iron-toothed scoop would scrape across an oyster bed.

They labored on the boat's tilted deck as its sails maintained the schooner's steady progress. The work was brutal. The dredge was weighty and winching it back in was backbreaking. Then they lifted the dripping, muddy mess, shook out some of the mud, and dumped the contents onto the deck. Over and over they did this. But as taxing as the work was, it kept them from freezing. Moss was a strong man, and he was used to both hard work and the roll of the deck beneath his feet. It was the cold that made the night hell.

As the weather began to take its toll, the work got dangerous. Dropped baskets, fouled lines, snagged lines, snapped lines—all could happen at any time. The handle of the winch could slip out of a numb hand and spin hard enough to break bone. When the dredge basket was lifted aboard, its edges could slice a man good. Then, there were the normal dangers to the crew of sailing a boat at night through considerable chop. Pungies, like the *Mary Kate*, were shallow draft, but even then, the shifting bottoms of Maryland's tributaries could claim a boat without warning.

Three times shots rang out from the shore and Moss heard one of them thump into the foremast, but no one was hit. Shadowy boats moved past them twice and Emory peered at each cautiously, but no hostility occurred. Regardless, Workman's rifle always seemed at the ready.

As the sky started to show gray over the Pocomoke, the *Mary Kate* secured the basket and winch, came about one more time and sailed for the deeper and wider waters of Maryland's Tangier Sound. The deck was piled with the fruit of their labor. Mud, oysters, widgeon grass and eel grass, rocks, broken shells, the occasional clam, crab, spot, or blue fish, and some debris that was unidentifiable made up the heap.

At night, while Achilles and Moss were working the dredge, Little Lou rinsed the pile of its mud, sorted the catch, and shoveled whatever was left overboard. Once dawn had arrived, and they were well away from shore, the work of sizing, busheling, weighing, and stowing began.

Moss was exhausted, his back hurt, and while his calluses and the gloves saved his hands from the equipment, they could not save them from the elements. He had not even worked a full night and he was spent. The parallel with his days at Poplar Grove Plantation could not be missed, and again he felt the anger well up.

Moss and Achilles were stowing the bushels of oysters brought up that night when Caleb sidled up to the hatch and stood watching the men work. His pimply face was framed with greasy, lank hair. He wore his leather cap in a way that was intended to spit at the world. Caleb was caught in that age somewhere between man and boy when the development of reason had not quite caught up to the development of his frame. He eyed the workers, standing with his hands on his hips and straddling a long-handled shovel left on the deck by Little Lou.

Addressing Moss, he said, "Boy, did you leave this tool on the deck?"

Moss said nothing and continued to lift the baskets of oysters down to Achilles in the hold.

Lou, who was below deck arranging the heavy baskets in the tight space, popped his head out and raised his arm to Caleb, as if to say, "It was me."

"I'm not talking to you, white trash," Caleb snapped. "I'm talking to the new nigger." When Moss continued to ignore the captain's son, the boy's voice cracked as he screamed at him, "I'm talking to you, dumb shit! You got mud in those big ears of yours? I said come pick this up or you'll be using your hands to shovel bay muck tonight." The bullying was meant to impress his father.

Moss straightened and took the two steps necessary to get to the shovel. Then, with no warning, he stomped on the blade part of the tool. The handle rose fast and hard directly between the boy's legs, connecting with the soft tissue resident there. Caleb let out a yowl of pain and doubled over. The coughing began again. That's when Moss heard and felt the business end of Workman's bullwhip as it snaked across his back and shoulder. The next blow came immediately and caught him across the face and chest. The third revisited Moss's back as he turned to try to protect himself. The pain was severe, but he reached for the shovel and, as his frozen hands gripped its handle, he heard the sound of a round being levered into the chamber of the Henry.

"Mr. Workman, stop!" Captain Emory bellowed. "Don't shoot him yet. We still have a week to work before the buyboat meets us. You'll get your chance. We're done for today. Just chain him and the other two in the hold for now and keep an eye on him. Caleb, come here!"

Caleb had now recovered sufficiently to pick up the shovel and swing it at Moss's head. Moss ducked and the tool clanged off the foremast, snapping the handle and sending its blade twirling away into the water.

"Goddamnit, boy. I said that was enough! Now you'll be paying for that shovel out of your wages."

The teenager was beside himself. Injustice and insult quivered in him as he brandished the splintered handle. He hovered between obeying his father and attempting to stab Moss with it.

"Move away, now, boy," Workman said quietly but forcefully. "You'll get your time with this one."

As Caleb's eyes glittered with hate, Workman shoved the rifle barrel between Moss's ribs and steered him down into the aft hold. There, in the shrinking space, he was shackled again to wait in the dark for the night's work.

※※※※※※※

The day wore on to evening and no one in the hold had spoken. Achilles and Little Lou seemed to want to distance themselves from Moss and his rebellion. That was fine with Moss. He just tried to stay as warm as possible and not focus on the pain coming from the welts across his face, back, and chest. Instead, he tried to live in his head, exercising his normal practice of reflection. The escape didn't last very long, however, because his fury made concentration difficult. Each time it surfaced, he fought it back, until he finally gave in to it and let it reign. He knew what he would do, given half of a chance.

As the *Mary Kate* begin to pick up speed heading back to the Pocomoke Sound, Achilles spoke. "Jim, you okay? I mean, you gonna be able to work tonight?" When Moss said nothing, the big man continued, "If you don't work, they'll hurt you some more, and if that doesn't get you up, well—"

"They'll pay you by the boom." It was the first time Little Lou spoke, and it came out in a cackle.

This seemed to surprise even Achilles. "See, you even got Lou to say something. It's been a month since I've heard him say anything."

"I'll work. You two just worry about yourselves," Moss answered.

"We've got to work together, and if you're not—"

Moss cut Achilles off. "I said just worry about yourselves. And stay out of my way. When they take these chains off, there'll be an opportunity. Just stay back if you know what's good for you."

"You can't—"

"Don't tell me what I can't do. Just don't get in my way."

With that, they heard a board creak above them. Nothing else was said, and they sunk back into the blackness, waiting.

Caleb rose from the hatch where he had been lying with his ear pressed hard against the wood. He stood as quietly as he could and made his way to his father at the wheel.

The *Mary Kate* slowed and once again the hold was opened. Workman hovered as Caleb roughly undid the iron bracelets. The overseer stood well back and the three men emerged and moved to their work. The weather was still cold, but the clouds had cleared and the moon offered a little more light than the night before. Moss wondered if the snipers along the shore would improve their aim with better vision.

The men fell into a mindless rhythm that numbed their bodies and blurred time. The dredging routine went on all night long as Emory made lick after lick across the bed lying in a dark, nameless creek. Gunfire was heard at a distance, but no one seemed to be firing at them. Silhouettes of other schooners could be seen against the moonlit night sky but none came close. At one point, Captain Emory thought he detected the engine of a steam launch and called for complete silence. But the sound did not repeat itself, and he wrote it off as being overly cautious.

Eventually, the horizon suggested the coming of dawn and the *Mary Kate* came about for the last time and headed out of the creek toward deeper water. The sky was now gray and the wind had picked up considerably as the men began to sort through the piles on the deck.

The pungy was under good sail, heeled over, and moving quickly past the dark shoreline when Workman came to Moss and told him that Captain Emory wanted a word with him. Moss stood away from the heap of shellfish and made his way carefully up the side of the tilting schooner. The overseer was a step behind him, rifle at the ready. Moss turned his head in a quick glance and just caught Workman nod to the captain, then duck down. Suddenly, the cant of the deck flipped and the fore boom swung hard and fast across it.

Moss had been expecting something, but he misjudged the power and swiftness of the heavy beam. He managed to avoid the full force of the boom, but it grazed him and knocked him off balance on the pitched deck. He was going overboard but, at the last moment, he reached out and grabbed the barrel of the Henry rifle with one hand while sinking his other deep into Workman's beard. In his surprise, the overseer fired off a wild shot while trying to yank back the rifle. Moss's grasp was firm, though, and Workman slipped and hit the short rail of the schooner. The men tumbled together into the biting-cold water of the Chesapeake.

Chapter 20

Closing In

Wilbert Robinson, Moss, and I sat in the Diamond's second-floor lounge—or as Uncle Robbie likes to call it, the Sportsman's Reading Room. We were perusing the morning papers and enjoying the latest editions of *Sporting News* and *Sporting Life*. The café was closed, and it was just us, enjoying a leisurely second cup of jamoke. The Orioles don't play on the Day of Rest, and it was raining anyway. So, we were wallowing in the comfort and contentment that is often unique to Sunday mornings.

Our conversation was rambling, with no expectation of concluding anything except maybe who was right and who was wrong about some obscure fact. We chewed over the news of the day and judged the people on the social page as if we knew what we were talking about. Well, Moss might have. But Wilbert and I were enjoying trading unfounded opinions about everything from the Spanish in Cuba to the meteorite spotted over West Virginia. We were giving more serious topics a good working over, of course, like whether ladies should wear hats in theaters and how Bob Fitzsimmons managed to knock out Jim Corbett in fourteen for the title.

Uncle Robbie was convalescing and using a crutch for support. His absence from the team was due to a long, ugly gash he received in a collision at home plate in Cincinnati. But, so far, he had spent the time off very usefully, hobbling around, redecorating the Reading Room, the bowling alley, and the taproom downstairs.

In their years together, between them, Robinson and McGraw had amassed a pile of sports memorabilia from what seemed like the entire Western world. I heard they pilfer whatever they can each time they visit a locker room in a

National League park. And I know for a fact that they scour souvenir shops whenever they find them. They even send away for autographed pictures and use my name when they do it. That's why so many have "To Frank" written on them—it just wouldn't do to have someone like Cy Young know that a man facing him at the plate had requested his picture.

A couple of years ago, the two of them developed a collecting racket of sorts. In the cities they traveled to, they would often make an offer to a bartender or owner for something stuck on a tavern wall. It wasn't long before the word got out in those places that Robinson and McGraw had cash and they were buying. In this way, the pair had amassed hundreds of images, mementos, and assorted sports relics. Whatever form this "art" took, Robinson hung it on the Diamond's walls. The fact is that I, for one, love looking at all of it.

Hanging prominently in the bar are framed photographs of the three Orioles' championship teams, of course. But there are also photos of the great ball players from the '80s and '90s, like Cap Anson, King Kelley, and Dan Brouthers. There are sketches and cartoons of tennis, boxing, swimming, and cycling stars, men and women. There are autographs, pennants, scorecards, racing programs, and magazine covers. Signed bats, bases really stolen from most of the League's parks, old uniforms and caps, ball gloves, worn track shoes, and colorful saddle clothes are strategically displayed for the pleasure of Baltimore's sports addicts. It isn't the kind of stuff you'd find in a museum but, in a hundred years, who knows?

Uncle Robbie has even hung a large photograph of Ned Hanlon right over the bar, much to McGraw's howling displeasure. The mustachioed manager glares out at you disapprovingly while you're having an innocent drink and Muggsy swears that it hurts sales. I don't care, I like it. But my favorite of all is the life-sized portrait of John L. Sullivan. Taking the classic stance, with fists extended and biceps bulging, he looks for all the world like what he is—the greatest bare knuckler ever to grace a ring.

Facing John L. on the wall is the fight bill for the Joe Gans/George Siddons fight in '95 held over in the Eureka Athletic Club. Gans KO'd Siddons in seven in a lightweight bout that night. Joe is a Baltimore man and one of Moss's more regular cronies.

We all have our favorites, including our intrepid cook. His is the painting of last year's Kentucky Derby winner, Ben Brush. That was the first year they ran the race at a mile and a quarter, and the colt did it in such blistering time that many believe his record will never be broken. I think Moss likes the portrait not so much for the horse, but because of the jockey perched proudly on top of the horse. Willie Simms is certainly a great rider, but he also happens to be the first black man to win the Derby.

So, the three of us laid around among all of these heroes, extending the morning as long as possible. We even considered making a third pot of joe. Mass would be over soon, and McGraw and several other practicing Catholics on the team would be wandering in for a little liquid benediction to take the sheen off their recently scrubbed souls.

It isn't that those guys aren't always welcome; it's just that a lot of the friction that arose during spring training hadn't quite dissipated, even after the Birds got more of a chance to play together.

Last year, any hard feelings or wounded egos that might have built up would have been washed away in a flurry of wisecracks and a pitcher of beer. That was not happening this year. Willie Keeler wasn't even coming into the Diamond anymore, and Hughie Jennings had seemed like a different person ever since he grew that big red mustache of his. His recent beaning might have had something to do with it as well, as I think of it. Regardless, just as Moss had predicted, the Orioles' chemistry had changed. It even showed in their play—errors were going through the roof.

But we put these worries aside and continued our self-indulgence, awaiting the disturbance of our peace.

"Robbie, did you see where Ford's Theater down on Baltimore Street is staging Orioles' games?" Moss asked.

"Huh? You mean they have actors running around bases on stage?"

"No, they use the wire to track the action, just like we do on the electric scoreboard. Then, instead of using a picture of a ball diamond with colored lights for players, they have marionettes running the bases."

"What? Puppets!" I squawked. Can they do that? Does Harry Von Der Horst know?"

"They're doing it. And I hear it's pretty good. The paper says they're starting to draw a crowd."

"Damn! Robbie, we ought to go see that. It could be hurting business," I fretted.

"I have more things to worry about than dolls dressed up like ball players," Robinson said. "No serious crank is going to trade a cold mug of Eagle for that. We'll be fine."

Then, as we heard McGraw and the others coming in, the catcher rose and limped to the door. "I'd better do some bartending," he said and slowly made his way downstairs.

"Frank, where's Fanny today?" Moss asked.

"I guess she's back in her room. She said she wasn't feeling well and wanted to spend the day just resting."

"Good that she got a part over at the Auditorium," he commented.

"Yep," I answered simply.

I knew Moss was interested in whatever progress we had made in our investigations and was fishing for information. It wasn't that I was shutting him out; it was just that things hadn't been going as planned. Not with our digging into the murder, not with Fanny.

I'm not a teenager. I really hadn't formed any serious expectations from that one glorious, fantastic night together. But since then, Fanny had acted as if it never even happened. One likes to think that he leaves at least a small impression. And, in all humility, I know it wasn't my execution. I can tell when things go well, and that night, things went spectacularly. I think it surprised her. Hell, I surprised myself. But, regardless, it seemed that was that.

I know she was worried about what she would do after the *Prisoner of Zenda* run was over. But that was all resolved when she was offered a good part in a comedy called *The Hoosier Doctor* to be staged at the Auditorium. She would appear opposite the renowned Mr. Digby Bell, whoever he was.

This didn't make Tunis Dean of the Academy of Music very happy. He had finagled a part for her in a major cast for something they were putting on after *Zenda*. But, as he tried to negotiate lesser compensation for the new role, she passed on the offer. He had hoped to milk her popularity as long as he could, but he lost her to the Auditorium in his parsimony.

Fanny Darlington had become what they call a "hot property." I had always thought of her as such, but now her career was taking off. Oddly enough though, she didn't seem very pleased about it. It was as if she didn't want to spend any more time in Baltimore. On occasion, Fanny had mentioned her dislike of our weather, and she never said she would stay here forever. But, if I were to speculate, I'd say it was something else making her unhappy. Namely, she had been told in no uncertain terms by Detective O'Donnell that she was still a prime suspect in Alcott Worthy's murder. It was also made clear that leaving town would not be a wise thing to do until the cops said she could go.

What depressed me was my growing realization that she was only staying because she was forced to stay, and that I was not a serious part of the consideration.

Once again, I knew my terse response was not going to put Moss off. It was obvious that he wanted to talk about the murder case.

"So, what's going on with your investigation? Weren't you going to track down this Dr. Munsch?"

I wasn't going to be able to dodge his questions either, so I filled him in. "There is an H. Leopold Munsch employed by Johns Hopkins and working as a neurologist, just as you said. But he has been in Europe for the last few weeks. They expect him back shortly. Interestingly, the people I spoke to said that the police had been around asking about Dr. Munsch as well."

"O'Donnell?"

"Sounds like it."

"What about any connection with Worthy? Or Tunis Dean, for that matter?"

"Well, I went back to the Academy's lounge to talk to the bartender, the one who told me that he saw Worthy arguing with a man the evening of the murder. I gave him a description of Dr. Munsch, just as you described him to me."

"Good," Moss said. "What did he say?"

"He didn't say anything. He would tell me nothing one way or the other. I tried cash—no go. When I pressed, he clammed up completely and told me to beat it."

"What do you think that means?"

"I don't know, but I'll tell you, he was sporting some ugly bruises."

"Somebody beat him up?"

"But good. Maybe the somebody didn't want him talking?"

"Maybe. But that doesn't sound like something the man I saw would do. In fact, why would he leave the bartender alive at all, if the barkeep could incriminate him in a murder?"

"He hired someone?"

"Possibly, but it still doesn't seem that the doctor I saw would have those kinds of connections."

We both were silent for a time.

Then Moss asked, "What about any ties between Munsch and Tunis Dean?"

"I got nowhere talking to various staff at the Academy. Dean's a tough man to see unless you have some money to give him, and I'm not talking about a ten spot, either. Besides, other than asking point blank whether he knew the doctor or not, I'm not sure what I would say. And why would he speak to me anyway, even if he knew the man?"

"You're probably right," Moss said. Then, after a hesitation, he continued, "Look, I don't want you to think I'm horning in on your inquiries, but...."

"What is it, Moss?" I said, like Holmes might have to Watson.

"Well, I happened to bump into Fuzzy Hertzbaugh, and...."

Now, there was no way in hell that Hertzbaugh and Moss would ever bump into each other, but I let that pass.

"...He told me something I found curious." Then, after more hesitation, he said, "It's about Fanny."

"What about Fanny?"

"The doorman told me that the night Worthy was murdered, he saw Fanny and the victim arguing."

"We know that. He was harassing her about their nonexistent relationship."

"Yes, maybe, but there was something else. Hertzbaugh told me that Worthy took some expensive-looking jewelry from Fanny, and took it in a rather rough manner. A necklace."

"Necklace?" I was back to my one-word-idiot mode.

Tunis Dean had given O'Donnell the name, Leopold Munsch, and it had born a little fruit. The policeman traced it to a neurologist working on the Hopkins staff, but then he was told that the doctor was traveling and wouldn't return for several weeks. He was expected back by the end of April. And, yes, they would be sure to give him the message to contact the detective as soon as he returned. So, the lead was a dead end for the time being, but he could be patient.

In the meantime, Sergeant Gatch had spoken to the bartender who served Alcott Worthy and this Dr. Munsch the evening Worthy was murdered. Gatch confirmed that the two had argued, but the subject of the disagreement was less clear. In fact, if the information was correct, it was downright odd. Evidently, Worthy was incensed over some sort of human experimentation that Munsch was doing.

O'Donnell felt some level of confidence that what Gatch had gathered was accurate for reasons that made the detective wince. It turned out that the bartender took some convincing to speak up, and the sergeant only knew one way to convince someone of something. As a result, O'Donnell had heard from his superiors in the department that a complaint had been filed by the management of the Academy because the bartender had missed a couple of days of work after Gatch's visit.

The detective knew he had to get to the bottom of whatever Gatch and Spittle were hiding. He already had the patrolman in his pocket. Now, he would use what he had on Spittle to get to Gatch. The sooner he did that, the sooner he could get the ape off the streets. So, he had summoned the beat cop and, as he arrived, O'Donnell gave him no quarter.

"Officer Spittle, sit down. Do you know how deep in the shit you are?"

"Detective—"

"I'll tell you. First, you withheld a very important piece of evidence, then you destroyed that evidence—that's obstruction of justice on two counts. Second, you took Alcott Worthy's watch and gold chain—that's theft. The fact that you stole from a murder victim may not add weight to the crime, but it sure says something about your character and the pride you have in that uniform."

"I was going to—"

"Spittle, shut up. I'm doing the talking here. I also have all the proof I need that you've been collecting "favors" from businesses all over your district. Now, I haven't decided whether that's extortion, bribery, or both. But I will decide, and when I do, you can bet some of your friends will be taking the fall with you."

"Look, O'Donnell..." Spittle began, sitting on the edge of his chair.

The detective stood, leaned forward on his desk and craned into the cop's face.

"I said keep your trap shut! And if you address me like that again, I'll add insubordination to your list of sins."

Spittle sat back and scowled at his superior.

"You know how this works," O'Donnell said. "I write a report and recommendation on you. Because of the extent and nature of your crimes, I submit my report to both the Internal Review Board and the State's Attorney. When that happens, who knows what might come of it. Jail time? Expulsion from the force? Financial penalties? Maybe all of those things."

O'Donnell gave the cop a sweet smile, but his eyes were hard. Then, the smile faded into a snarl. "Your time has come, Spittle. Time to pay up."

The patrolman's arms were crossed and his face set defiantly. He said nothing, but the longer O'Donnell let his words perk, the harder it was for the officer to fight the fear that was lurking behind his mask. If the detective couldn't see it, he sure as hell could smell it.

"Now, this report can be written in a lot of ways. And depending upon how I choose to write it, your penance might be greater or lesser. Get it?"

Spittle didn't get it at first, but he slowly realized what O'Donnell was saying. "What do you want from me, detective?"

O'Donnell was glad he didn't have to spell it out any more than he did. So, he sat back down and took a more reasonable tone. "I want Enoch Gatch."

"Gatch? But I—"

"Let me put it another way. I want you to give me Enoch Gatch."

"What? You think I have something on Sergeant Gatch?"

"We both know you do," O'Donnell stated flatly, running his bluff.

Spittle was not feeling so mutinous now. Several emotions played across his face before he returned to trying to maintain his façade. "I don't know what you're talking about, detective. I don't even know the man that well."

Switching tactics, O'Donnell said, "Look, Spittle, I'm not doing this anymore. You're lying, and I want to know what Gatch has on you."

"Wait a minute! It's not me, he—" He stopped, realizing he was about to say too much.

But he had already said too much, and O'Donnell pounced on it. "Let's cut the horseshit. You tell me about Gatch and I help you. Simple as that."

"How will you help me?"

"I can downplay your offenses, and I can tell the State's Attorney that you aided my investigation."

"Immunity?"

"Fat chance. You're a sure thing for the State's Attorney. He likes that. Good for his coming election. Gatch is a wild card. Plus, the Internal boys have been looking at you for longer than I realized. They like you, too. Makes the Mayor look good."

"I give you Gatch, and all I get a nice word from you?"

"Look, Spittle, you're crashing in a big ball of fire. It's just a matter of how hot the fire is. I can help reduce the sentence."

"Sentence?" Now it was beginning to sink in to the beat cop. He began to process a little quicker. *I can't go to prison. Why should I protect Gatch? He brained that guy, not me.*

It was satisfying for O'Donnell to watch Spittle come around. All he had to do now was wait.

"What guarantees do I have?" Spittle asked.

"Zero," the detective answered. "But you've got less than that now. You also only have about a half a minute to decide what to do."

"Can you protect me from him?" was Spittle's reply.

CHAPTER 21

1869
CRISFIELD, MARYLAND

The look on Workman's face as he hit the water was the fear and panic of someone who can't swim. Moss had let go, and now the overseer kicked and flailed at anything that might be solid. With one hand, he managed to grab Moss's collar; the other still clasped the Henry rifle. Moss was in danger of getting hit by the weapon as it dragged them both down into the frigid depths.

Once again, Moss grabbed the gun's barrel and in one violent blow, he smashed the thing against the side of Workman's head. The oysterman went slack. Moss pushed him away and watched him drift down, wide-eyed and still clutching his precious rifle.

Tumbled around, Moss couldn't tell the direction of the surface, and he felt a surge of his own hysteria. The moment transported him back to the tunnel cave-in under the Baltimore street. He fought down the horror, then followed what air bubbles he could see rising. As he rose to the lighter shade of murk, the extreme cold hit him for the first time and the fear returned. He knew that he only had a few minutes before he lost control of his arms and legs and joined Workman in hell.

When he broke the surface, his first gasping sight was of the *Mary Kate*, moving away rapidly in the growing light. He could see Caleb, Achilles, and Little Lou peering over the boat's rail. Moss gauged the possibility of swimming to shore, but soon realized it was no good. The biting cold left him no time.

Yet again, panic rose in him as he felt his end near. In desperation, he prepared to swim as long as he could. Suddenly, he heard behind him the mechanical sound of a steam launch coming fast out of the silhouette of the land. Turning in the water, he saw a big boat, belching black smoke and headed right at him. A loud, amplified voice called out to the disappearing schooner, ordering it to stop and come about.

Moss began shouting and waving his arms. He dipped below the surface briefly, rose once more, and cried out for help again and again. The vessel was almost on top of him when a man in the fore spotted him in the dim light and raised the alarm, yelling, "Man overboard!"

Elation and relief swept over Moss as he bobbed in the water.

A different voice roared from the launch, "Engine, full stop! Get a boathook over the side!"

As Moss reached for the saving pole, the command voice spoke again. "Fire!"

There was an ear-shattering boom. A fiery flash shot out from the vessel and the scream of a projectile from a large gun ripped over Moss's head toward the fleeing *Mary Kate*.

"Son, my name is Commander Hunter Davidson. I am appointed by the State of Maryland to police these waters. You are aboard the steam launch *Leila*, and you just cost me an arrest. Do you mind telling me what you were doing floating around out there by yourself?"

Moss sat in the launch's cabin, out of the wind. He had been given some dry clothes and was wrapped in a blanket. He held a cup of hot coffee in two hands and nodded at the skipper as he spoke. Davidson was not a big man, but he carried himself like one. It was also obvious that he was used to command and the *Leila* was run in a military fashion. The commander spoke with the accent of Maryland's Eastern Shore. When he listened, it was with the same intensity that he brought to his responsibilities.

"I was being paid by the boom, Commander."

Davidson looked at Moss, attempting to detect a lie, but only saw a man who was glad to be alive. "Can you tell me the name of the schooner and its captain?"

"Gladly, sir. It was the pungy *Mary Kate* out of Crisfield. Captain Emory piloted her."

"I knew Emory was out here somewhere. Who else was aboard?"

"Emory's boy, Caleb, and a bastard named Workman."

"I know Workman, too. Hired for his muscle, usually."

"That's right, sir. I took him overboard with me."

Davidson looked at Moss again, closer. "You took him overboard?"

"Yes, sir. I just grabbed his beard and yanked him along with me."

Moss tried to keep the satisfaction out of his voice, but it came through clearly.

"What a shame," Davidson said with a smile, stroking his own long, black beard and undoubtedly imagining what it would be like to be jerked over the rail by the hair on his chin. "Any more like you aboard?"

"Two others, shanghaied like me. Been there a while, and still on the *Mary Kate* when I left."

The two men looked at each other for a moment, then laughed out loud at Moss's casual description of being knocked overboard.

"You seem to be taking it all pretty calmly, Mr. Tilghman," the Bay policeman observed.

"I can now, sir. I wasn't too calm an hour ago."

"Still, it sounds like you've been through a pretty tough time. Another man might not be taking it so well."

"Well, sir, I've seen a lot of bad in my time."

"I bet you have. You in the war?"

"I was. I was with the 54th Massachusetts."

"I saw the elephant myself, Mr. Tilghman. But I'm afraid I was on the other side."

"Commander, I try not to think about it very much. Best that way."

"I guess you're right. In war, right and wrong tend to get blurry."

"It isn't too hard to determine what's right here. You've got some people sailing the Chesapeake that are both vicious and greedy. I'm glad somebody's chasing them."

"Oh, we're chasing them, alright. But most of the time, that's all we're doing. We've had some success, and maybe my new howitzer will help. But it hasn't been nearly enough, and the Chesapeake is a big place."

Then Moss said, "Well, I don't know about the rest of these pirates, but I'm not through with Captain Emory. He's got to come back to Crisfield sometime, and when he does, I'll be waiting for him."

It was two weeks before the *Leila* could complete its patrol and put in to Swan Point, its Potomac River base in Charles County. It was another week before they could resupply and head across the bay to Crisfield on the Eastern Shore. During that time, Moss served as a deckhand and was deputized by Davidson to support their night operations. They were very active and managed to catch and stop a number of baycraft, checking licenses, making arrests, and levying fines. Twice, they used the cannon to sink boats, fishing the oystermen out of the water, then turning them over to local authorities. Their most successful tactic—the one Davidson was using when he rescued Moss—was to lie in wait in one of the smaller tributaries at night, then pounce on the dredgers as they sailed back out of various oyster creeks, loaded with poached shellfish. But the Mosquito Fleet, as the commander called the pirates, were just too numerous and too spread out. It became obvious that Maryland's Oyster Navy had been given the responsibility, but not the resources to fulfill it.

During the three weeks together, the two men became friendly and spent a fair amount of time talking. Davidson was struck by the anomaly that was an educated, skilled ex-slave and listened intently to Moss's stories of his experiences. At the same time, Moss could not get enough of Davidson's recounting of his days at the U.S. Naval Academy and in the Confederate Navy. They discovered that they both grew up not too far from each other, albeit in very different circumstances.

In hopes of recruiting Moss, Davidson recounted his skirmishes with his watery adversaries with a tinge of heroism and a lot of satisfaction in his limited success. He described the communities that gave rise to the oyster dredgers as "isolated, poor, tribal, and full of refugees and outcasts." He called the pirates lawless, reflecting the free and roving habits of their lives, normally removed from the restraints of society and considering themselves the masters of the oyster industry. Their clannishness created conspiracy, safeguarding their methods and trade secrets in order to control the markets, and thus, profits. Even with all of that, Commander Davidson couldn't hide some level of admiration for their toughness, their seamanship, and their ability to function in the most brutal of conditions.

Moss learned that the Mosquito Fleet was centered in Somerset County, particularly in Crisfield. Once John Crisfield built the railroad spur, the town transformed overnight from a collection of dilapidated shacks on piles over the water to a boomtown, much like a frontier mining camp. The first residents advanced toward the river and deeper water by filling in the swampland with an untold number of crushed and compacted oyster shells. This allowed the construction and operation of numerous shucking and packing houses, crammed along the shoreline and employing hundreds of former slaves. What was created was a sewer of honkytonks, full of brawling, swaggering watermen, gamblers, prostitutes, and drunks. Money was made quickly, and it changed hands just as fast.

At one point, Moss asked Donaldson about how it all worked in dollars and cents. The commander's explanation made it obvious why violence, including murder, was accepted as a normal business practice. It seems that the captain of a dredger could earn as much as two thousand dollars a year at a time when most Marylanders earned less than five hundred.

What's more, he said, oystering had done a deal with the devil in tying its growth to another exploding industry—the railroads. As the B&O began to open the way over the Appalachians and into western states, it carried with it the bounty of eastern ports, including canned Maryland and Virginia oysters. Demand for the delicious and abundant food soared, and with the demand came those who would exploit it, both legally and illegally. To hammer the point home for Moss, Davidson quoted the 2,500-year-old Chinese philosopher Lao Tzu: "There is no greater disaster than greed."

✕✕✕✕✕✕

As the *Leila* steamed into Daugherty Creek and the docks of Crisfield came into view, Moss was reminded of the frenetic activity on City Dock in Baltimore. Baycraft of all shapes and sizes were crammed together, creating a forest of masts. Men swarmed over them and their moorings. Many boats were pilot schooners or pungies, as they were commonly known, but also there were coastal schooners, coffee schooners, brigs, barques, packet boats, log canoes, a host of little skiffs, and even a sizable yacht anchored just outside the tight harbor.

Moss studied his new destination from the rail, trying to spot the *Mary Kate*, when Hunter Davidson walked up.

"Moss, we'll not be here long. I've got two prisoners to pick up, some supplies and fuel to load, then we'll be gone. I want to try one more time to convince you to stay with us. You're a damn good man, and I can just about guarantee I could get you the command of one of our armed schooners. It may be a way to get your hands on Captain Emory."

"Thanks, Commander, but I don't think I'm going to take your offer. I'm no cop, and the chance that I would run into Emory is a lot greater right here in Crisfield than it is out on the Bay."

But Davidson was not one to give up so easily on a potential resource. "Well, how about if you work for us in an unofficial capacity?"

"What's that mean?"

"What if you just keep your eyes and ears open for us? If you become aware of something you think will interest the Oyster Navy, you contact me. I'm in and out of here quite often, and we can work out a way for you to reach me."

"Like I said, I'm no cop." Moss was not sure he wanted to be tied to law enforcement. Other than his recent recue, it had done him few favors in the past.

"You would have no formal obligation to us, no expectations, just adjunct status. It might even be of use to you, if and when you ever find Emory."

"Commander, I don't know—"

"I could even advance you a small stipend. I know you're probably broke. Isn't that so?"

It was so. All Moss had was the clothes on his back, and they belonged to Davidson. He hadn't thought very much as to how he was going to get along in Crisfield, and the commander's offer brought the problem front and center. It was also true that Moss felt an obligation to the man for his life and for the friendship he had offered over the last few weeks.

"Okay, I'll do what you ask—as long as it remains unofficial. I'm not signing anything, and I'm not wearing any badge," Moss said with a smile.

This seemed to make the commander happy. With a grin, he stuck out his hand to seal the agreement.

"Thank you," Moss said sincerely. "And thanks for all you have done for me. Pulling me from the water was just the start."

The men shook hands once more, and Davidson turned to go, but then he turned back.

"You be careful in there, Moss. Watch your back."

"Yeah, I guess I do stand out a little."

"It's not that. You'll blend in fine. Almost half of the watermen in there are ex-slaves, and a lot of your folk work in the plants. It's the whites looking for the main chance you have to be ready for, and their opportunity might come in an office, a barroom, an alley, or a cathouse." With that, he reached into his coat and produced a Liege pinfire revolver and handed it to Moss.

"I picked this up on the Choptank River. Six shots. Its owner won't be needing it anymore. Any experience with handguns?"

"Not yet," Moss answered, taking the weapon.

Davidson was correct when he described Crisfield as bawdy and corrupt. But it wasn't just that. It was full of people hustling, trying to take advantage of the opportunity that was there. Trying to build lives, trying to find their place in America. The war had opened everyone's eyes to the fact that life was not a given. It had to be fought for. Most city dwellers learned this quickly; but, now, rural towns like Crisfield were coming to realize it. The country folk, watermen, and former slaves that filled the place had lived hard lives, certainly. But those lives had also been predictable and familiar. Now, there was freedom and choice that didn't exist previously, and the two liberties were open to more people than ever before. So, Crisfield hummed during the day and throbbed at night with the ebb and flow of humanity seeking the opportunity that comes with freedom.

This suited Moss just fine. Despite the trials he had suffered, he had managed to open a few doors, as well. He could read and write, he had business experience, he knew boats and how to sail them, he had acquired planning skills and the manual skills to execute those plans. He realized the importance of education, and he appreciated philosophy and the perspective it afforded. He also knew Crisfield was a place he could thrive with a little luck and a lot of caution.

There was work to be had in the shucking and packing houses, but the pay was poor, the days long, and the work disabling. There was also work for him in shipbuilding and repair, or on the water itself. But Moss had had enough of boats and the Bay for the time being. He knew he could convince a business to hire him as a clerk, and he knew he could build that into something bigger, just as he had done with Chesapeake Marine Railway and Dry Dock. He had muscle, but he knew there were better ways to go. So, with Davidson's advance in his pocket, he took his time looking around and settling in.

One afternoon, a few days after his arrival, Moss was walking down Main Street toward Broadway, headed for the docks. He had it in his mind that maybe working for a chandlery would allow him to do some things he understood and, at the same time, afford him access to the watermen that were constantly coming and going. Maybe there was a chance to do more than just work there. In a boomtown built on boats and what you could do with them, the business had to be lucrative, and maybe in time he could find a way to make some real cash.

He stopped to let a carriage splash by on the muddy street, and from behind him he heard a man curse.

"Goddamn! Is it you? I thought you were dead for sure!"

Moss turned and found the imposing figure of Achilles, his former winch mate. The man stood straight and tall, making him seem even bigger than Moss remembered. He was dressed decently and wore an expression of content that never showed on the *Mary Kate*.

"Achilles!"

The oysterman grabbed Moss and hugged him. When Moss recovered, the man held him at arm's length and said, "Boy, I saw you go overboard with Mr. Workman. How is it that you're here?"

"I was very lucky," Moss answered.

"You must have been. Do you know that you saved my life? What're you doing right now? Let me buy you a drink. I wanna know what became of you."

"Well, I was about to—"

"Whatever it is, it can wait. I owe you. C'mon."

With that, Achilles pulled Moss into a nearby saloon called the Pearl and, before he knew it, they were sitting in the corner of a very loud, very busy barroom with two mugs of beer and two shots of whiskey in front of them.

Moss had never been in a saloon before. In fact, he had never in his life tasted whiskey. The Emorys used to keep it under lock and key in the big house, and they kept close watch over their slaves. He had not even tried the wine that the St. Joe's Jesuits drank in great quantity. He watched Achilles down the shot in one gulp, then take a long pull on the beer, ending with a satisfied "ahhh!"

Moss looked at his two glasses, then looked around. No one was paying them any attention.

"What's the matter, Jim? Don't like Eagle? It's from Baltimore. German. Everyone up there drinks it. I'll get you something else."

When Achilles stood to yell for the waiter, Moss pulled him back down and said, "No, no this is fine. Sit down. It's just that...."

Then, without finishing his comment, Moss picked up the whiskey and followed the same procedure that Achilles did, downing the shot, then gulping the beer. The rye hit him like a fist, first his mouth, then his stomach. His eyes watered and he shook his head violently.

Achilles laughed and said: "Good stuff, huh?"

Moss wasn't so sure and didn't quite get the liquor's appeal—at least, not until the liquid's warm glow began to spread. Achilles signaled for another round.

"Jim, it's great to see you. Tell me what happened. I was shocked when you grabbed Workman's beard. That was really something!"

Moss managed to smile as he remembered that moment, and he wondered himself how he had done it.

"Some things, you just do," he replied. "I was picked up by the Oyster Navy. They were chasing the *Mary Kate*."

"Someone or something must be watching over you," the big man observed.

Maybe it was the whiskey, but Moss found he liked the oysterman, now that they weren't locked up in a hold.

"Achilles, I want to tell you, my name's not Jim. It's Moss. Moss Tilghman."

"Moss, huh? I'm Achilles Swann. Good to meet you again." The men shook hands formally. "Well, sir, you saved me whether you know it or not."

"What happened?" Moss asked.

The oysterman paid for the second round, sipped at the whiskey, and said, "When you and Workman went into the water, we tried to spot you, but there wasn't much hope. Captain Emory wasn't stopping for anything. The next thing I know, a steam launch is ordering us to come about. When the captain ignored the order, they fired some big cannon at us. Scared the bejesus out of me. Tore out a big hunk of the transom, but missed the rudder."

"That was a howitzer."

"I'll say it was! But there were no more shots, the launch was falling back, and we kept on. It wasn't but a minute or two before Lou and I realized that Workman's Henry rifle was gone. Lou grabbed that weasel Caleb and put an oyster knife right up under his chin."

"Must have been one hell of a temptation." Moss finished his first beer and made another face.

"It was, but the captain pulled a big Colt from somewhere and aimed it at us. I jumped behind Lou and Caleb. Then the boy began screaming, 'Don't shoot,

Pa! Don't shoot!' We stood there frozen for a few seconds. Then, I told Captain Emory that if he put into shore and let us go, we'd spare his boy."

"And?"

"Well, he thought about it, then guided the *Mary Kate* into reasonable swimming distance. Little Lou held onto Caleb and jumped with him into the water. I went right with them. Emory fired but missed. When Lou came up and began to swim, the captain was at the rail and shot him with that hog's leg he had. Seeing that I was next, I dove down, swam a ways, and got scot free."

"Little Lou's dead?'

"Dead as dead can be," Achilles said, shaking his head sadly.

Moss left the second whiskey alone and took a drink of the beer. After a pause, he asked, "How'd you come to be walking the streets of Crisfield? You know there's a chance Emory will be here—if not now, then someday."

"I hope he does come back," Achilles answered seriously. "But he's not why I'm here. I was on my way when they jumped me. My family's here. They run a small restaurant just off the main pier. I'm the cook—well, me and my grandma anyway."

"You're in the restaurant business?" Moss asked, surprised.

"Oh, yeah. Best food in town. Fresh. Good. I'm really just learning. You going to drink that whiskey?"

When Moss shook his head, Achilles snatched it up and made the amber liquid disappear. Their conversation continued about this and that, with Moss explaining that he was looking for work and wasn't sure how long he'd stay. The big man was not stupid, and realized that the length of stay probably depended upon how long it took for Moss to find Captain Emory. As they rose to leave, Moss accepted an invitation to dinner that night at the restaurant.

The big man had been right. The food at the Dockside was special. It wasn't Moss's first introduction to Eastern Shore cooking, since he grew up in Queen Anne's County. But this was extraordinary. He thought it both delicious and fascinating in its preparation. The multiple crab dishes, oysters prepared in ways that enhanced their delicate taste, the freshest fish and fowl from the tidewater area, wild game sausage, and seasoned vegetables were all prepared in ways Moss never knew possible. The restaurant was doing a brisk business, and its clientele was of all shapes, sizes, colors, and creeds. Those who knew found their way to the Dockside.

As jammed as the place was, the Swann family made him feel welcome and treated him like an honored guest, ensconcing him at the family table near the kitchen. Achilles's people were a hardworking clan that included his mother, Althea, his grandmother, his sister, and her husband. Althea managed the receipts, worked the door, and otherwise kept the whole enterprise running. The married couple was tasked with the dining room, and Achilles was content to assist his grandmother in the kitchen. There, Moss saw a very different Achilles than the one that had worked on the *Mary Kate.*

Once the crowd fell off, the family gathered at Moss's table to meet and talk to the man who "brought Achilles back to them." They were a close group, bound together by blood, experience, and the force of the mother's personality. Achilles's father had passed some years before, and it was clear Althea was in charge. She was very proud of her boy, but in the ways of mothers and sons, she made sure Achilles stayed humble.

They asked about Moss, where he'd been, what he'd seen, and how he came to Crisfield. He was circumspect in his answers, not knowing how much Achilles had told them. So, he gave them enough to satisfy their curiosity, ending with the fact that he was looking for work there in town.

As the evening wore on and talk slipped into the business of the restaurant, Moss listened and realized that the place was, in fact, having a few difficulties. Mostly, they had to do with things he understood—inventory, accounting, and supply. So, at an appropriate moment, he made an offer.

"Mrs. Swann, I may be of some help. I used to run the back office for a good-sized shipbuilding and repair company. I might be able to give you some suggestions that would help you to cut a few costs."

"Well, thank you, Moss," she answered. "But I'm afraid I can't afford you. This is a little place."

"Ma'am, you wouldn't have to pay me," Moss said, smiling. "As good as your menu is, I'd be tempted to take it out in trade. But I have another idea."

"An idea?"

"Yes, ma'am. You see, ever since my days in Philadelphia, the thought of learning to cook has been of interest to me. If I could just watch how you prepare your dishes, maybe pick up a few things in the process, then we could call it even."

This surprised everyone at the table. They all started talking at once. No one thought Moss's offer a bad idea. Although, Achilles's grandmother wasn't saying very much. Finally, Mrs. Swann smiled and extended her hand.

"Mr. Tilghman, you are now the Dockside's new assistant apprentice chef."

Chapter 22

The Rooftop Garden

It was May before Dr. Munsch arrived back in Baltimore, but I knew exactly what day it was and when. In my first inquiries at the hospital, I noticed that the secretary I was chatting up was an Orioles crank—all of the baseball tchotchkes decorating her desk were a dead giveaway. I told her that I was a personal friend of Willie Keeler's and asked if she would like his autograph. This put me in solid with her and allowed me to be bold enough to ask if she'd let me know when the doctor returned. It was a private, family matter, I explained in a pathetic way that discouraged questions. She hesitated, then said she'd be glad to do it. It helped that the woman detested Dr. Munsch as much as she loved the little right fielder.

One morning, I received a message telling me that the neurologist was arriving that same day on the SS *Albano* from Hamburg to New York. He was then taking the train to Baltimore and would reach the Mount Royal Station around six o'clock that evening. The message also recalled my promise to provide Willie's signature.

I suspected that Detective O'Donnell was also very interested in Dr. Munsch's whereabouts, and I wanted to get to him first before the cops did. When I told Moss what I was going to do, he asked a good question: what was I going to say to him? In truth, I didn't know, exactly. I wanted to confront him with why he argued with Alcott Worthy. I was hoping to identify a possible motive for murder. I also thought it was suspicious that he left the country just when people here were looking for him. When I explained this to Moss, he was concerned about the possible danger, and even suggested that maybe it was better left to the police.

Since I'm not much of a hero, I could certainly see his point. But I wanted to put an end to this, and I didn't trust O'Donnell or his thugs to do it for me. I wanted Fanny off the hook and in a position to make a decision about us. Would she stay, or would she go without this murder hanging over her head? I needed answers.

So, I made my way up Howard Street to Mount Royal Avenue and the fashionable Bolton Hill neighborhood. There stood the granite and limestone train station built by the B&O a year ago to serve its New York passengers. I was almost as impressed with this building as I was with the Academy of Music. Its soaring clock tower told me that I was a half-hour early.

Double checking the arrival time of the Royal Blue Line coming from the north, I picked up the station's descriptive brochure for something to read while I waited. I then looked for a place to sit that allowed me to monitor the exits from the platform. I figured that Dr. Munsch would be fairly easy to spot, given Moss's description and as long as there weren't a lot of Van Dyke beards arriving that evening.

Across a sweeping, mosaic marble floor and next to an enormous unlit fireplace, I found a comfortable rocking chair, something new to train stations. The leaflet taught me that the station's architect, Francis Baldwin, was the chief designer of many of the B&O's buildings, including the massive passenger car shop and roundhouse downtown. He also designed a lot of the churches whose spires grace the Baltimore skyline. Evidently, a very busy man of granite conviction.

As I was having that deep thought, the arrival of Munsch's train was announced. In a few minutes, passengers began to pour from the platform area. I got up, moved closer to the exit, and eyeballed the fast-moving crowd. Unfortunately, none of the people arriving were wearing pointy little chin whiskers. It was then that I got lucky.

I heard a redcap who was pushing a cart speak to a passenger walking behind him. "Doctor, would you like me to get a carriage for all of your luggage?"

When the two came even with me, I noted that the man the porter had spoken to was not wearing a beard, but he did reply in a distinct Germanic accent.

"Yes, of course. Do you expect me to carry it all myself?" Then, indicating a particular bag on the cart, the accented man said, "This one needs to be delivered to my office at the Johns Hopkins Hospital."

Sherlock Holmes might have shouted "Elementary!" or "Eureka!" or something. But, I said nothing. In fact, seeing my target right in front of me, was a bit unnerving. So, I followed closely behind the man who had to be the elusive Dr. Munsch. Evidently, they have razors in Europe, too.

As the porter loaded the bags into a carriage, I heard the doctor issue orders to the driver, directing him to an address on Howard Street, not two blocks from the Diamond. I hurried to hail my own cab and urged it to follow.

I pursued the neurologist back down Howard Street until he stopped in front of a building housing doctors' offices and other professional enterprises. He walked into the place as the cabbie was unloading. I entered the building and checked the directory for H. Leopold Munsch, MD and found it on the second floor. Once I had it, I repaired to a small beanery across the street to watch the building's entrance. The man's manner unsettled me, and I was not sure what to do next. I wanted time to think.

But I didn't get the time. I was just stirring my coffee when Dr. Munsch reemerged from the office building. He walked quickly down its marble steps and went south, toward Franklin Street. I hopped out of the café, dodged carriages, buggies, and bicycles while navigating the cobblestones, and fell in behind him.

His pace was brisk, but it didn't last long. When he reached the corner, he walked into a large drug store. According to the display in the front window, the place was having a sale on dyspepsia powder, cocaine toothache drops, and Listerine. I glanced in, and when I saw that there were about ten people milling around in there, I joined them.

Dr. Munsch was oblivious to anyone else in the store and busied himself impatiently looking around the three people in line waiting to talk to the druggist. I casually walked over to a glass display table and acted interested in an array of pint bottles of brown elixir, lined up right next to a stack of boxes of some sort of balm.

As soon as I picked up one of the bottles, a pretty young girl arrived and asked if she could be of assistance. Then she said, "That is the best worm syrup on the market, sir. Guaranteed to purge you within twelve hours."

I quickly put down the bottle and picked up one of the boxes. Again, she attempted to be helpful.

"Sir, are you interested in that for your wife?"

"No, it's for me." I said coolly. "Why?"

The young thing blushed. "Well, sir, I don't mean to be impudent, but Pinkham's Female Salve is for, uh, females."

I put that down rapidly as well. "Oh, so it is. Thanks, maybe I'll just have a Hire's."

Her eyes followed me as I walked over to the fountain, sat down on one of the stools, and stared at the back of a soda jerk who was ignoring me while stirring something with a glass swizzle. Munsch was next in line to see the druggist, so I got up and slyly moved closer so that I might hear his conversation. I read the directions on a tin of Spratt's Dog Soap and hoped the sales girl would leave me alone.

The doctor arrived at his objective with a prescription in hand, which he slapped down on the counter and stabbed with his finger. I heard the words "precisely" and "immediately." The pharmacist nodded, stepped into the back, and returned quickly enough. He handed Munsch a vial, which the doctor held up to one of the overhead gas lights, squinting at its label. Satisfied, he paid the druggist, turned on his heel, and was out of the door as rapidly as he entered. I returned the can to its pyramid and followed.

My quarry was easy to track because I knew what he was going to do. He was going back to his office and make use of his recent purchase. The prescription that the druggist filled was for an drug called cocaine.

I had some familiarity with cocaine. Everyone does, these days. In varying doses, it was being used for everything from baby's coughs to kidney ailments. They were putting it in cola drinks and in altar wine. I know what the drug does to you, and what more it can do in strong doses. The prescription told me that Dr. Munsch was not taking it for a cough. It also told me that there was a good chance that I would see the doctor emerge again before the night was out.

It was as dark as it gets on Howard Street with the lights from the Auditorium Music Hall and the Academy of Music shining brightly just a block away. I didn't want be spotted and I was hungry, so I ducked back into the small café across the street, ordered a fried oyster sandwich, and waited.

An hour passed. I was about to pack it in and admit that my latest piece of logic was a bust when the doctor reemerged from his office. He looked both ways before descending to the sidewalk, timing the passage of an oncoming streetcar, then quickly crossing to my side of Howard Street. He turned north toward the theaters, striding past my window without noticing me. To my surprise, the doctor stopped in front of the Auditorium, looked around, and checked his pocket watch.

I hung back out of the light of the marquee, anticipating that the neurologist was meeting someone. If he was going in, he was attending a cheesy Vaudeville review that didn't seem to be the kind of thing he would appreciate. The headliners on the bill that night were a boy soprano, a comedian with his "funny coon," a pair of female double-talkers, midget acrobats, Helmut the Strongman, the Kasbah Harem Dancers, and a dog act called *Sparky and His Master*.

At a little before eight o'clock, a young man who was not much more than twenty, if that, joined Dr. Munsch. They walked to the music hall's box office, the older man bought tickets and the two entered through the building's ornate, carved limestone arch.

I wasn't happy that I had to spend fifty cents for the cheapest seats in the place, but I trailed the two inside. There, I watched my targets turn away from the main hall and climb the set of wide stairs leading to the balcony. I followed, but the pair passed the entrance to the balcony seats and continued up two more flights to the roof.

The Auditorium had just opened its rooftop garden and concert pavilion within the last year or so. I had been there to see that billiard master I mentioned, and I know Uncle Robbie had attended its grand opening, featuring none other than John Phillip Sousa. A big poster in the hallway said there would be a concert tonight, free to all attending the show downstairs.

The place was actually quite stunning. Entirely enclosed in glass and lit by electricity using small incandescent bulbs, the room itself seemed like a big light bulb. On one end was a large, white, octagonal bandstand decorated with gingerbread carving, just like you would see in Patterson Park. The opposite side of the room held a long, gleaming, copper bar and matching French mirror that served to reflect the room's lights and double the density of the roof garden's varied foliage, growing in painted, cast iron planters.

There were white folding chairs in rows around the bandstand and wrought iron tables and chairs tucked in the innumerable corners created by the greenery. But, as inviting as all of that was, the feature that caught the eye immediately was the large, multicolored glass dome rising out of the center of the floor. Because it was actually the ceiling of the theater below, the thing was lit from within and radiated its colors in an entrancing way.

When I walked in, the place was not yet crowded. The clutch of idle waiters standing in the corner told me that the place was just waiting for the end of the Vaudeville show. There were a few people at the bar, maybe a half-dozen scattered in the concert seats and only a few seated at the private tables. That's where I spotted Dr. Munsch and his young friend.

I made my way to the bar, ordered a rum sling, and sat at an angle so I could keep an eye on my prey. A single violinist sat by himself on the bandstand among the waiting instruments. He was playing something Viennese and syrupy, creating a well-matched musical ambiance. Occasionally, through the glass dome, I could hear muted laughter and applause, rising and falling as the various acts down below entertained their audience.

Munsch and his friend seemed to be absorbed in whatever they were talking about and paid no attention to anyone else in the room. I wouldn't say they were looking into each other's eyes; rather, Munsch was working hard to either explain or sell something to his guest. I could see that the young man was no stranger to the clear liquid on ice he was drinking. Long about his third drink in less than a half-hour, he sat back in his chair and crossed his arms. Whatever the doctor had said to him, all of a sudden, it was not being taken very well.

A roar of laughter from the theater audience told me that someone's routine was going over big. It seemed to coincide with a burst of laughter from Munsch's young man, as well. I could see that the doctor, however, was not amused. His companion's mirth became more mocking, and it was obvious that he was making the doctor angry. Finally, he stood, pointed at Munsch, and said something with a sneer.

I rose from the bar and sidled closer to try to catch the gist of the argument— a move that was now becoming second nature. When his friend made motions to leave, Dr. Munsch stood and grabbed his sleeve. The young man shrugged him off and, as he passed me, I heard him say in a voice that betrayed how much he had to drink, "Absurd! Imagine! They'll love this in the conservatory. You'll be famous!"

The doctor caught up with him then, and the two scuffled just as they reached the glass dome.

"Get off of me, you freak!" the young man yelled, shoving Munsch away. Furious, the doctor then pushed back hard and his companion staggered, tripped, and fell onto the glass bubble. For a split second, he lay there wide-eyed. Then, with a startling crack, the glass shattered and the young man disappeared in a rain of colored shards.

The argument had drawn the attention of most of those in the garden concert hall and the fall shocked them to the point of immobility. As I ran to the opening and looked down, screams had replaced the audience's laughter. The young man lay askew among scattered instruments and strewn bodies in the orchestra pit. From the angle of his neck, he looked quite dead.

As others began to flock to the hole in the dome, I turned to find Munsch fleeing through the door. I chased him down three flights of stairs and watched him bull his way through a knot of panicky people fleeing the tragedy in the theater.

In the open, Munsch flew diagonally over the roadway to his building. In the process, he threw a bicyclist off his balance. The unlucky soul wobbled across the cobbles and smashed into a nearby lamppost. I was only a few leaps behind as the fugitive climbed the stairs to his office. What I was intending to do, I wasn't sure, but that had been the situation all night. I was just reacting.

As I reached the second floor, I found the doctor fumbling with keys at the end of the hallway. I yelled, "Munsch!"

The neurologist turned as I took a few steps toward him. He reached into his coat, produced a pocket pistol, and pointed it at me. I froze under the light of a hall lamp. He hesitated, trying to identify his pursuer, but I knew I was about to get shot. Ridiculously, I went into a kind of protective crouch. Then I heard a hard, urgent voice bark.

"Dr. Munsch! Drop the gun. Now!"

The doctor still hesitated, looking past me. Then I watched him put the pistol in his mouth and pull the trigger, splattering the wall with pieces from the back of his head.

Chapter 23

Mid-Season Gut Check

Ned Hanlon sat in his Union Park office, staring at the lineup card for the next day. The little pine board room that Harry Von Der Horst thought sufficient for the club's minority owner and team manager seemed nailed to the backside of the far right bleachers as an afterthought. Its furniture—a battered desk, a file cabinet salvaged from some fire, and a couple of rickety chairs—was utilitarian at best, lacking any degree of comfort. But Hanlon didn't care. When he called a player in to see him, he didn't want them to feel comfortable anyway. Besides, he wasn't there much. Most of the time, when he wasn't in the ballpark or on the road, he was at home on Guilford Avenue, two blocks away. Red brick. White marble stoop. Plumbing. McGraw, Jennings, Keeler, and Reitz lived on the same street, and most team meetings were held in Hanlon's front room. Very convenient.

The last game of the weekend series against the Pirates was next, but the manager wasn't really thinking about that. He had already set the lineup. Rather, he was staring at the list of names that was the Baltimore Orioles—just letting them sink into his subconscious. He wasn't focusing; he was waiting for his mind to do what it did pretty well. He was waiting for an idea to emerge.

A long time ago, he had learned the logic of baseball—what it should look like when it's played correctly. He understood better than most the proper cause and effect. It was simple. When this happens, you do that. It was the standard that he used with the team, the one he had drilled into them, the one he held them to. It was precise and, as the writers were fond of saying, "scientific." It was also a means to finding better ways to play. The pitcher-covers-first thing, for instance. He got credit for the idea, but he knew it was just the logical thing to do when a ground ball was hit in the hole between first and second. Hell, it wasn't wireless science, it was baseball.

But he also knew that the toughest problems aren't always solved by logic. Sometimes, solutions just come to you or you have a feeling about things. You learn what you have to learn, clear your mind, relax or get a good night's sleep, and then wait for an idea to surface. Sometimes, answers woke you up at night. It was amazing how often it worked. He built this team doing that.

Hanlon would laugh to himself and shake his head each time he'd read some sports scribbler calling him a "genius." He knew it wasn't true. All he knew was that, sometimes, if you let your mind do what God intended it to do, the ideas and solutions came all by themselves. He thought of this automatic process as simply the way things worked, and he was trying to get it to work now.

But he couldn't relax. As he stared at the names, he worried about what had happened to his team. Too full of themselves. Too much cheering by outsiders. Spoiled by success. How was he going to pull them back together? There were cracks everywhere. Imagine—Keeler and McGraw, good friends, fighting in the shower. Naked, even. He was glad he wasn't there to see that. The mere idea made him cringe.

Maybe the problem was injuries. Hanlon hadn't even had a chance to field his best nine since opening day. Or maybe it was the schedule. The recent twenty-five-game road trip had taken a brutal toll. Some of the players' lost time was due to plain bad luck, but other injuries had nothing to do with luck. After three championships in a row, the Orioles were targets. Doyle had been beaned in Louisville, and Hughie Jennings almost died when the Giants' Amos Rusie hit him in the head with a fastball.

And there was more. McGraw was now out with a sore arm, his second injury this season already. The way he was going he'd lose more time than in '95 when he had malaria. Stenzel had bronchitis and coughed while at bat. Quinn and Bowerman were dinged up, and Keeler was playing through a groin injury. Twice, in Chicago, Kelley disappeared under the stands to deal with diarrhea. Hanlon hoped that was all it was, but he didn't want to know. Now, Uncle Robbie was going to be out for an extended period. Spiked. The man almost bled to death! With Robinson out, how the hell would Boileryard Clarke be able to catch with that split thumb of his?

Hanlon took a deep breath and sat back. He was focusing on the negatives when, in truth, the team had won a lot of games already. Thirty-three wins against only ten losses—not bad at all for the middle of June. The pitching had been great, especially Hoffer. And young Joe Corbett was turning into the pitching star Hanlon hoped he would be. Kelley was hitting .445 and Keeler .446. Willie had even set a record, stringing together forty-four straight games with a hit.

But even with the thought of their strong first half, the manager's mind was re-invaded by nagging concerns. The Orioles were only atop the league by a single game over the damn Beaneaters, who looked like they were in it for the long haul. And it was the long haul that Hanlon was most worried about. There wasn't supposed to be any serious competition this year!

The team was winning games, but not really playing all that well. Not playing together. Getting lazy. Committing errors, lots of them. And, this year, because of the new rules, ejections were happening almost every game. His gut told him that they were headed for a fall, and only so much of it could be blamed on injuries, the schedule, or that goddamn Georgia rain.

Hanlon sensed the core problem was none of those things. What started to crystalize for him was the idea that his amazing team of the previous three years was no longer a team. It had become instead an assortment of big cheeses.

By the time July 4 arrived, the Orioles had tumbled to third place behind Boston and Cincinnati, five and a half games back. Then, typical of the long arc of a punishing baseball season, the Birds went on a mild winning streak, thanks to the therapeutic St. Louis Browns and the woeful Chicago Colts. The run was no indication of a resurgence, however. After that, they immediately began to sputter and stall, playing poor .500 ball in Cleveland and Pittsburgh. The wheel turned one more time when the Washington Senators handed the Champs three games and the Philadelphia Phillies chipped in two more. When July had finally run its course, the team was three games behind the Beaneaters and holding down second place. Baltimore was operating like an expensive motor car with dirt in its fuel line.

That "dirt" was just what Hanlon had feared—discord. On top of that, he was dealing with a new wave of physical problems. The injuries had gone from bad to epidemic. Robinson was still in Baltimore, turning into a fulltime bar owner. Stenzel had to go home to tend a sick wife and got the flu himself.

The pitcher, Nops, was flattened by sunstroke. Neither Doyle nor Jennings were quite right after their respective beanings. McGraw's arm was making the throw from third to first an adventure. Clarke's thumb was not healing. And none of that was counting the assorted groin pulls, pitching hand blisters, and alcohol-induced "migraine" headaches that were distributed across the bench.

But at the heart of the Birds' problems was the clear disharmony among the players. Not only did it erode the teamwork that had made the Orioles what they were, but it also created a lack of focus on the task at hand. In a close one against the Phillies, Joe Corbett was not at his best, having already given up ten runs and walking the lead-off batter in the eighth inning. The situation called for a mound conference in which Doyle and Jennings demanded that Corbett be replaced. Hanlon refused, telling the infielders that the game wouldn't have gotten away from them if they hadn't already committed five errors.

In another incident, Doyle's foul mouth caused Umpire Tom Lynch to throw down with the first baseman. And while Doyle managed to head-butt and give the ump a black eye, Lynch knocked Dirty Jack on his back with a hard left to the neck. It said a lot to Hanlon that Doyle's teammates just stood and watched him lie there, gasping for air. That was until they had to defend themselves as Boston rooters started to pour onto the field.

As for focus, in a three-game series that saw the Orioles commit fifteen errors, Umpire Bob Carpenter found it necessary to call in the police to assist ejecting half of the Orioles' bench. After the Reds took a three-game series from the Birds, *The Cincinnati Enquirer* reported that four or five of the Champs had careened through the city's red-light district, engaged in a "drunken orgy."

Of course, the players frequently blamed the umpire for their woes rather than their own performance. In fact, umpiring bias became an obsession. Every marginal call that went against them was proof of the conspiracy to knock them out of the race. The press in opposing cities picked up on this and did their part to further the anti-Oriole sentiment in the sporting world. Their editorial drumbeat was: "Anyone but Baltimore!"

Even the national writers following the Orioles and their star players had begun to turn, pointing out fissures in the monolithic team that made for juicy reading.

The manager's response to all of this was to defend his team. Just the same, he initiated a series of early morning practices, taking the opportunity to call out the Birds on their selfish play and lack of concentration. Once the message was delivered, he drilled them rigorously on running, fielding, and hitting fundamentals, hoping to remind them of what it takes to win championships.

One Friday afternoon, I talked Moss into joining me at Union Park to watch the Orioles play their rivals from the last two years, the Cleveland Spiders. Cleveland seemed destined to be a fifth-place club this year. But, they represented an opportunity for the Birds to move up on first place Boston. It was not going to be easy, though. The team was shut out the day before by the Spiders' Cy Young. So, we needed to take the next two to win the series.

Moss was content to sit in his pantry with a book and wait for his guys to come in to help prepare for the evening crowd. He said he was reading a novel, *The Invisible Man*, by somebody named Wells. The story, the cook explained, was about the need to carefully consider the consequences of any plan executed. He also suggested that it would do me good to read it.

I didn't need a book to find out how to disappear; I was on my way to Union Park. I suggested that he let me show him how to do it. I was cracking wise, but he was probably right about consequences, given my history.

I only managed to pry him out of there by agreeing to buy the tickets and a couple of beers. Even at that, he hesitated until I told him I would spring for a cab ride as well. Frankly, I thought the streetcar was a fine way to travel. But Moss countered by reminding me of the Supreme Court's recent *Plessy v. Ferguson* ruling: he was equal but separate, and that included Baltimore's trollies.

So, we took a covered carriage and I soon stopped griping about not taking the cheaper streetcar. It was a typical August day in my city—hot and muggy. Being out of the direct sun was a blessing; just the same, the air stuck to us like a gauzy shroud smelling of horses.

Speaking of horses, as we crossed Barclay Street to the ticket window, I had the misfortune of stepping in a mound that could have been left by something the size of the Trojan Horse. Whatever beast it belonged to, it certainly had been well fed.

As I scraped my shoe against the curb, I got up on a high horse of my own. "Something's got to be done about this! In another ten years, the stuff will be up around our necks!"

"Frank, you have very little faith in mankind," Moss observed.

"What d'ya mean? You think somebody's going shovel that up?"

"Maybe not. But something tells me we'll solve the problem."

"Oh, no. Here we go again," I groaned.

"Frank, motor cars don't eat hay."

Now, for me, that is quite a leap of faith. Our dependence on the horse may go away, but that won't be any day soon. I struggle with the logic that leads to automobiles as their replacements. As loud, dirty, and expensive as those things are, they won't be used to deliver ice or Arab cantaloupes in the neighborhoods or do a thousand other things that horses do.

"Yeah, but they drink gasoline by the gallon, and it's a lot easier to shoe a horse than it is to change a tire."

I was very pleased with my analogy. Plus, I made Moss laugh—although, I'm not always sure what he's laughing about.

We entered the gates of Union Park and climbed to the second deck of the brick and boards stadium. Once there, we found a couple of seats between the owner's box and the press box in the very last row at the top, just to the left of home plate. I had learned in years past that these seats were out of the sun all afternoon long. What's more, that high up, the back of the stadium was open and the location afforded whatever faint breeze decided to show up.

The place was full and noisy despite the heat. I guess the cranks felt they needed to help the Orioles win. The league-leading Beaneaters were about to launch a thirty-game home stand.

We settled in to survey the crowd and watch our boys toss the ball around. The infielders looked loose, and their pegs over to first were crisp and right to Doyle's glove. Other guys were playing pepper, creating that sweet, summertime syncopation that is the pop of leather and the crack of the bat.

Willie Keeler in right was playing long-toss with Stenzel in center, and Joe Kelley was signing autographs for some kids along the wall in the leftfield stands. The pitcher, Joe Corbett, was throwing along the sideline. The beanstalk unfurled himself in one fluid, effortless rhythm as he warmed up with the catcher, Clarke.

The Spiders milled around the grass along the first base line. Some were burning off pre-game nerves by stretching, running in place or whirling their arms to warm them. Others were rubbing down bats or just white-knuckling their handles for grip. One Spider sat on the bench with his head down, hands clasped in supplication, praying. The man next to him was cleaning dirt from his spikes.

The crowd in the upper deck was fairly docile at the moment. Its buzz was low and content, just making themselves at home. Many were preoccupied with lighting cigars, flagging down the Eagle vendor, and buying those tasteless, dachshund-like sausages that some were calling "weckers."

From our seats, we could see down into a good portion of the owners' box. I didn't spot Harry Von Der Horst, but I did see a stylish woman wearing a straw boater with a daisy in its band. She was laughing hard at something said by an elderly man sitting with her.

"Looks like Jamie and Bernadette are here today," Moss said. "I think I'll go say hello."

With that, my friend made his way down and over to the rail of the box and leaned in over orange and black bunting to give Bernadette Von Der Horst a hug. She held on to his arms after and grinned at him. The older man stood and shook Moss's hand warmly, then said something with a scowl that made Moss laugh out loud.

When he returned, I saw he was eating a wecker with mustard on it. The thing smelled terrible and I turned up my nose. At the same time, I was offended because he hadn't bought me one. After all, didn't I pay for the tickets? Then he produced a second sausage and offered it to me, asking, "Don't you want this? I'll eat it."

I grabbed the thing and took a bite like I was doing him a favor. This time, he laughed because he loved to annoy me. But, I have to admit, the thing was quite tasty. As I wiped mustard off the corner of my mouth, the cranks in the lower deck started to get fired up. The game was still a few minutes away and we could hear rhythmic chanting coming from beneath us. Once it infected the crowd in the upper deck, the rallying call of Baltimore supporters came from everywhere. "Get at 'em!"

Over the noise, I commented to Moss, "You three seemed pretty chummy. I recognized Mrs. Von Der Horst, but who was her friend?"

"Bernadette is one of the funniest people I know. We like each other," he said innocently with a shrug. "That was Jamie Morgan, her father. A friend of mine with an interesting history."

My attention was drawn to the conversation that was taking place around home plate. Manager Hanlon stood there with the Spiders' player-manager,

Patsy Tebeau, and Umpire Jack Sheradin. At first, there was a lot of point-ing at various baselines and outfield fences. Then Tebeau started pointing at Hanlon, and Hanlon responded by sticking his finger in the Spider manager's chest. That's when Sheradin started pointing his finger at both managers. Their response was to return the favor by yelling in unison at the ump.

The players ignored this animated tableau as business as usual, but the crowd did not. Leather-lunged epithets began to ring out, attacking both Tebeau and Sheradin, and soon all of Union Park was screaming something or other. Once the managers and the ump realized that they had stirred up the animals, they jawed another second or two, shook hands, then broke up the home plate confab.

Moss and I stood with the rest of Union Park as a uniformed brass band, sitting in the sun, churned out an uninspired, oompah version of "The Star-Spangled Banner." Harry must have had connections in the German Musicians Union, because those boys were sweating like faucets while blowing into all of that hot brass.

We sat back down and I joined a good part of the crowd clapping in antici-pation of the gong that signals the start of the game.

"I read that some folks in Washington are trying to get that song designated as the national anthem," Moss commented.

"I'm all for it," I said. "It was written right here in Baltimore."

"That's not exactly true, Frank."

"Of course it is," I said. "Francis Scott Key—"

"He wrote a poem called 'The Defense of Fort McHenry,' not a song."

"Poem. Song. What difference does it make?"

"Probably none. But I think it's a little ironic that the music comes from an old British drinking song."

"What? That can't be right!"

"I'll bet you another wecker I'm right," Moss said with that infuriating know-it-all look of his. I knew from experience that probably meant he'd be eating another sausage.

"Damn. I liked that song," I said, giving in to Moss' annoying aptitude. "I guess we'll have to switch to 'My Country 'Tis of Thee.'"

"You mean the song whose melody is identical to 'God Save the Queen'?"

It's not easy having Moss for a best friend. I was glad that the gong sounded at that moment.

Truthfully, and I've probably said this before, I'm very fortunate to have Moss as a friend. Very fortunate. Each time I think back to that hallway outside of Dr. Munsch's office, I thank whatever god you want to name that he was there.

As I found out later, when we sorted things out with Detective O'Donnell, Moss had never trusted the neurologist from the first time he encountered him. It was just a bad feeling, of course. But when he spotted me through the Diamond's front window following Munsch into the Auditorium, he decided to trail us up to the rooftop garden. His sense of danger had been so strong that he also tucked some old pistol in his pocket. He stood invisibly among the waiters and watched events unfold, staying with us as I pursued the doctor. The rest you know.

He and I don't talk about it much, but every now and again, he will remind me that I should look before I leap, as they say. I don't mind, though; I'll take whatever advice he wants to give me. Anytime.

We sat comfortably through the sultry day and watched a terrible game. Moss dozed off around the fourth inning, like half of Union Park's attendance. The heat certainly played a role in creating the torpid crowd, but the Orioles' play was the main culprit. The Spiders' pitcher, Jack Powell, was sharp, and the only real excitement came in the sixth when one of the Cleveland players fouled a ball off and up into the press box.

Normally, the cranks will throw the ball back onto the field, and by league rule, the umpire decides whether to continue to use the ball. In this instance, Sheradin ruled that the ball was to be thrown out. This decision infuriated the Birds' pitcher, Corbett, who was already down three runs and unhappy that the Spiders would have a chance to hit a brand-new baseball. Evidently, the young pitcher had just about gotten the original ball soft and scuffed up just the way he liked it. It didn't help that earlier, Sheradin had decided to continue to use a ball the Orioles had fouled off into the stands. So, when the ump threw Corbett a brand-new ball, the righty fired it into the upper deck and stalked off the field.

In the ensuing argument, in addition to Corbett, the Orioles' Clarke, Kelley, and O'Brien got ejected. A grim Hanlon replaced his pouting hurler with Bill Hoffer who, pitching on two days' rest, promptly gave up two more runs. The Orioles eventually lost the game 6–0, suffering their second shutout in a row.

Moss woke up in the top of the ninth, and we decided to leave the mostly empty park before the game concluded. I was clammy and irritable as we climbed into the carriage that would take us back to Howard Street. Moss, on the other hand, seemed unaffected by either the weather or the game. I also suspect he was mildly amused by my emotional investment in the Orioles' fortunes. Just the same, he left me alone.

The only thing he said was, "Thanks, Frank. I really enjoyed that. Let's go find some ice cream."

Chapter 24

1869

Bare-Knuckle Justice

Moss had been in Crisfield for nearly three years and had seen four prime oyster seasons come and go. He watched the Eastern Shore's raw winters become soft, spring rains and its warm summers produce the unique beauty of marshland in the fall. By the time the wetland's reeds turned gold, the oysters had grown fat and the unforgiving Chesapeake winter had arrived, completing the cycle once again.

He noticed each change in the weather bring change to the rhythms of Crisfield's watermen, as well. Their lives shifted from oystering to crabbing, fishing, trapping, and hunting before coming full circle, back to the valuable resource waiting in beds beneath the Bay's waters.

Moss saw as well that, when each winter phased into the wet spring and the oyster season wound down, the bars and honkytonks seemed to get more crowded as men sought to keep their heads dry and their throats wet. Then, there was money to be made and money to be spent.

As it happened, in his time at the Dockside, Moss managed to provide the Swanns some real help. The first thing he did was set up a workable system with the books and make sure everyone understood it. He found a number of ways to cut costs; he made suggestions to avoid certain suppliers and patronize others who wouldn't cheat the family. When the Swanns decided to redo some of the little restaurant, Moss used a saw and swung a hammer while listening to Achilles's dreams of growing even larger. Finally, he and the big man found ways to promote the restaurant, making sure that anyone who set foot in Crisfield knew about the Dockside.

While all of this was unfolding, Moss served his apprenticeship with distinction. He and Achilles worked hard in the kitchen, allowing the eldest Swann to focus on transitioning the role she had held for so long. At first, the old lady was not quite sold on sharing her secrets with someone outside of the family. But Moss's interest turned into a passion, and she recognized potential when she saw it. As a result, she took him under her wing and not only taught him the standards, but challenged him to be creative in the process. In these ways, the Swanns became the family he never had.

Moss also found out how tightknit certain parts of Crisfield were, especially among the operators of its small businesses. When word got out about Moss, he readily found additional bookkeeping work that filled his time and put money in his pocket.

During those years, Moss hadn't forgotten his arrangement with Hunter Davidson, but he didn't exert himself gathering information, either. While the two met off and on, Moss had little to offer, reflecting his lack of interest in the task. Watching for Captain Emory, however, remained paramount.

One evening, after the restaurant closed, Achilles talked Moss into having a drink. He had not acquired much of a taste for rye whiskey, but he didn't mind an occasional beer or two. On the way, as they dodged mud holes, prostitutes, and peddlers, Achilles told him something that surprised him.

"This is an important night for me, my friend," Achilles said.

"Why's that, big man?"

"You know I've been doing some prize fighting around town?"

"Fists? Bare-knuckle?"

"You bet."

"You know, most civilized places require the use of gloves now. Marques of Queensbury rules and all that."

"How long you been in Crisfield, son?"

"I thought you told your mother that you had stopped that."

"Well, I did. But I didn't. I've been doing pretty well, though," Achilles bragged. "So well that I've earned a shot at the champ, and that's tonight in about an hour. One hundred dollars' prize money!"

Boxing was not new to Moss. He had found a small degree of success sparring with wrapped hands and five-ounce gloves at St. Joseph's. But this was different. This was bare-knuckle. Someone usually got hurt badly.

"Three-minute rounds," Achilles explained, "continuing indefinitely until one of the combatants is knocked out or can't get up."

"No set rounds? That's brutal!"

"Hell, it wasn't so long ago that rounds ended only when someone got knocked down."

The fight had been billed as a championship bout, and it was to be held in a huge beer hall at the end of Broadway. The place was owned and operated by a consortium of waterman from Smith Island, a hardscrabble place that had been steadily disappearing into the Bay for years. It was about ten miles across the Tangier Sound from Crisfield. Smith Islanders were both primitive and proud. Their champion, a brawler named Haynie Bradshaw, had worn the local crown for two years running and was happy to take on all comers. Tonight, it was Achilles Swann he would fight.

The two friends found the beer hall packed with shouting, drunken men itching for the mayhem to start and expecting results for the dollar they spent to get in. Tonight, they were promised two preliminary bouts, the main event and a finale that would see two women going at it in the ring. A raised, canvas-covered platform, ringed with what looked like mooring line, rose from the middle of the room. Around it were tightly packed tables and chairs that a battery of waiters negotiated, balancing trays with pitchers of beer and shots of local hooch.

Moss and Achilles stood at the entrance until one of the proprietors spotted them. He led them to a table near the ring. It was already occupied by three raggedy looking men who might have been there all afternoon. The owner yelled, kicked, and punched them out of the seats until they melted into the milling crowd. Then with a flourish, he waved Moss and Achilles into the seats.

"This your corner man?" he bellowed at Achilles.

"Yeah. He's going to need some water, a dipper, a sponge, and a few towels."

"He's going to need more than that," the man said ominously. "You want a couple of drinks, too?"

"You bet," Achilles said. "Bring us a pitcher and a couple of whiskeys.

When the man went away, a bewildered Moss asked, "I'm your corner man?"

"Yeah, it's no big deal. Just pick me up when I fall down and sponge me off when I'm bloody."

"What? I don't want any part of this!"

"I need you, my friend. You're in it now. Don't worry. This is going to be great. I'm going to murder this guy."

With that, the crowd got louder and began to clap and chant. The champion had arrived and his admirers seemed to fill the place. The same man that seated the challenger now was fawning over the crowd favorite, pulling a chair out at a large table that had been reserved for him and his party.

Moss looked at the group. Bradshaw was every bit as tall as Achilles, but he was built differently. The word "rawboned" came to mind. So did the word "mean." His wide shoulders were those of a distance swimmer. His chest, while not as broad as Achilles's, was generous enough and powerful looking. The man's hands were enormous and hung apelike at the end of long, ropey arms. His knuckles had been forged into lumps of pig iron from his many bouts, and he cracked them as he looked over at his challenger with an evil smile.

Achilles stared back with a bored look, then looked away to the men entering the ring for one of the early fights.

Moss tore his eyes away from Bradshaw and surveyed the men sitting with him. They looked more like a gang than an entourage, punching and kicking at any drunk that tried to get near enough to pat the champ on the back. Among them was a big, bald, black man with a handlebar mustache that quivered with energy. When Moss's eyes fell on the man, he realized that the tough was staring back at him. In fact, he spoke to Moss, but whatever he said was lost in the crowd noise, so Moss simply looked away. When he looked back, the man was standing over him.

"I said, ain't you a pretty houseboy! You fighting one of the girls tonight?"

It wasn't the first time someone hurled that insult at him, so Moss calmly stood and put his nose right in the man's face. Ignoring the smell of fish and mustache wax, he said, "Mister, anytime you want to see what I'm capable of, you just let me know."

Then Achilles rose and separated the two, saying, "Corny, save your bullshit for that pack of dogs you lay down with."

"Corny?" Moss asked with a sneer.

That seemed to incense the man, and he shuffled closer to Moss until Achilles shoved him away toward Bradshaw and his group. On the way back, he pointed at Moss and again said something that was swallowed up by the noise of the raucous fight fans.

"That man's dangerous," Achilles said when they had settled back into their seats. "He's fighting just before me."

They turned to the fight that had begun with the tap of a bell. Two lighter weights immediately began pummeling each other in vicious flurries of punches thrown from all angles. They were both likely to tire quickly the way they were going. Achilles took a sip of beer, but Moss downed his whiskey in one gulp. He no sooner winced at the burn than the crowd screamed its approval of a knockdown. When the fallen man was halfway up, his opponent ran from his corner and threw a haymaker that flattened the boxer and put him out cold. He was not going to get up. The winner threw his arm in the air in victory, but pulled it back down quickly to hold it close to his body. It looked like a broken hand.

There was a lot of booing, shouting, and swearing as losers complained about a fix and money changed hands. Then the ring announcer bawled for the next two combatants. The bald man from Bradshaw's table stood, removed his shirt, stretched, tensed an enormous bicep, then climbed into the ring. He danced and jabbed at the air as he moved smoothly around the canvas, flexing more muscles and glaring at the crowd.

When the announcer climbed into the ring, he called the boxer over to a corner and spoke to him and his manager. The crowd learned what was going on when the announcer shouted that one of the scheduled fighters for the second bout had not appeared. He was greeted with another chorus of boos until, waving his arms, he called for quiet.

"We have no fighter for this second match," he bellowed, then paused. "Unless there's a man among you brave enough to step in here with Mr. Cornish!"

Through the din of insults and invective, the ringman roared, "The winner gets twenty-five dollars, and you get five dollars when you lose!"

The crowd erupted again, until Cornish threw up his hands and demanded silence. When he got it, he pointed directly at Moss and shouted, "How about now, houseboy?"

The crowd exploded one more time and hands began prodding and poking at Moss. Finally, Moss stood to sodden cheering.

"You don't have to do this!" Achilles yelled.

"Yes, I do," Moss said simply.

Amid howls of encouragement and blasphemy, he shouldered his way through the crowd to the ring, receiving numerous thumps on the back as he went.

Moss removed his shirt and tossed it to Achilles, who had joined him in one of the canvas's corners. His friend began giving him advice in a rat-a-tat fashion, none of which Moss understood. Achilles continued to shout with increasing concern until the ring announcer called the fighters to the center. There, Cornish went chest to chest with his opponent, sticking his chin in Moss's face in a fierce glare. Returning the stare, Moss made a fist, dropped it to the level of Cornish's crotch, and pressed forward. This moved the aggressor away, outraged him, and elicited invective that made use of the word "kill" several times.

Ignoring the posturing, the referee gave them the basic rules in a flat voice and stepped away. To Moss, there didn't seemed to be a whole lot of rules.

The bell sounded almost immediately, and before Moss could even get his hands up, a left jab to his forehead drove him back, staggering to the rope. Hands pushed him back upright and he got hit again, this time with a right to the side of his head. He pitched to his left and Cornish moved with him, hitting him hard for the third time, knocking him down. The place went riot.

Moss looked up from the canvas. His opponent stood over him, left foot forward, arms extended, fists balled in the classic boxing stance. Moss stood quickly and shuffled back as a left missed. But, cat-like, his opponent pursued him and connected with a right, knocking Moss down again.

He looked across the ring to his corner. Achilles stood screaming something through cupped hands. He couldn't hear him; in fact, he couldn't hear anything but a roar in his ears. Nor could he see anything but the shuffling Cornish in front of him. For Moss, the world was reduced to a ten-foot bubble that held only him and the big, mustachioed man.

Moss knew that unless he did something soon, he was going to get killed. He began to recall a few things Fr. Barbelin had taught him. He rose slowly to a crouch and covered his face and stomach with his hands in a defensive stance. The crowd screamed its displeasure and Cornish at first looked surprised, then grinned and moved in.

The bald man began to pound Moss's protective arms. It hurt and it drove him around the ring, but the tactic allowed him to get his feet under him and to think. When he saw an opening, he landed a hard, straight right on Cornish's chin. This shocked and angered the fighter who wasn't expecting even that much from an amateur.

Cornish stalked the reeling Moss around the ring. He began to throw punches in combination, some of which were taking their toll. The blows were painful and Moss's arms already felt like lead. His antagonist was now deliberate, confidently stepping toward Moss, landing punches and expecting to end it. Moss went down for a third time, but then the bell sounded.

Once Moss was on his feet, the two men stood still, eyeing each other warily. But the referee stepped between them and forced the boxers to repair to opposite corners.

Achilles dumped water over his charge's head, probed at a right eye that was swelling dangerously, sponged away the blood from a split lip, and patted a right ear that hurt like hell. Moss still couldn't hear the instructions Achilles was spewing at him. Too soon, the bell sounded again.

Moss rose like an old man and moved out of the corner, but Cornish had sprinted across the ring and immediately closed on him, murder in his eye.

Moss managed to get his sore arms up and even stuck out a left, which Cornish ran into almost by accident. The punch stunned the bald man briefly and Moss used the split second to land a solid right to the side of his foe's head. Enraged, Cornish charged, again intent on total destruction. Moss slid away, generating more boos and sneering comments from the bloodthirsty onlookers.

Cornish rained blows on the top of his adversary's head, which did little damage and just served to increase frustration in the fighter. He was moving in consistently, sliding forward with his left foot and leveraging on the ball of his right to get power behind the punches. Moss timed the pattern and suddenly stomped down on his enemy's extended foot, pinning him to the canvas. That's when he landed a devastating overhand right that crushed the man's nose. When he followed with a left to the side of the head, Moss had his full weight behind it. Cornish's skull whipped to the side, sending a spray of blood from his nose into the howling crowd around the ring. Moss's right then came back and his foe's head flipped in the other direction, anointing another portion of the now frenetic mob. Cornish went down, stayed down, and the fight was over just like that. Someone grabbed Moss's arm and held it in the air.

Achilles was jubilant as he guided the wobbly winner back to his corner. As his friend again dumped cold water over his head, Moss could now see the cheering spectators and feel the congratulatory slaps on his back. He remained however in a foggy cocoon of sorts that only began to dissipate when he and Achilles had to swap roles.

"You were terrific, my friend. A natural!"

"Never again," Moss croaked. "Never again."

Moss was still dazed as he watched his friend move into the center of the ring with the champ, Bradshaw. After that, he performed his corner duties mechanically for eighteen grueling rounds as the two huge combatants battered each other, neither gaining the advantage each were seeking. It was an atavistically fierce battle between two accomplished boxers and looked nothing like Moss's fight. There were numerous knockdowns and a copious amount of blood drawn, but the men kept at it until they both began to tire. It would be stamina that won this fight, not some lucky punch.

Before Achilles went out for the nineteenth, as Moss was working the sponge, he could see that his friend had withdrawn into himself in a way that he hadn't before then. It was in his eyes. Something was wrong.

"Achilles!" Moss tried to get the boxer's attention. "You okay?"

"Yeah," the big man said. He rose with the bell and moved stiffly back to the fight.

As soon as the boxers came together, Achilles suffered a series of quick jabs, then a roundhouse punch that seemed to be thrown from Bradshaw's shoe tops. The black man went down, straight backward, as if he had been run over by a team of horses. His head bounced hard on the thin canvas floor and he lay still.

When Moss reached him, Achilles was unconscious and not responding. Amid the roaring noise of the crowd and the dancing of the champion, other hands grabbed the fallen boxer and helped Moss get him out of the ring and into a back hallway that held a long, wooden bench. They laid the beaten man there.

"This place have a doctor?" Moss asked.

"I ain't never seen one, mister" and "I don't know" were the responses.

Moss knew Achilles needed help badly.

"I've got to find a doctor. Can you stay with him that long?" Moss asked of one of the ring assistants. He got a noncommittal shrug and he knew they were all anxious to watch the female finale. But he didn't have a choice, so he sprinted down the hall and out a side door to the street. He seemed to recall seeing a doctor's office somewhere off of Main Street.

It wasn't but five minutes or so until Moss returned, having found the office shuttered and no response to his banging. When he pulled open the same door he had used to exit the beer hall and took a few steps into the hallway, he noticed a man standing over Achilles. Moss was relieved that one of the attendants had actually stayed with his stricken friend.

Moss began to offer his thanks when Captain Emory turned with a bloody club in his hand.

"I was surprised to see you two deserters together tonight," the captain said. Then he swung the cudgel, missing Moss's head but catching his shoulder and knocking him against the wall. As he raised the weapon again, the door to the hall opened and two drunks entered, telling each other how badly they had to urinate.

"Hey!" one yelled. "What's going on here?"

With that, Emory ran for the outside door.

"What'd you do to him?" one of the men demanded, pointing to Achilles, then grabbing Moss and hanging on him.

By the time Moss shrugged off the sot, Emory was through the exit, out onto the street, and absorbed by the Crisfield night.

Moss knew that Achilles was dead and there was nothing he could do for him. The anger in him rose in a rush and detonated in his head. He knew he had to act fast. So, he ran to his rooms, dug out the revolver given to him by Hunter Davidson, and headed for the docks. He wasn't doing a lot of reasoning, but he figured Emory would make for the *Mary Kate* and try to sail away once more.

He reached the waterfront and scanned the rows of piers, dimly lit by a few gas lamps. It was going to be impossible to find anything in the poor light. Then, he heard an angry voice and some scuffling down on one of the piers.

Someone distinctly yelled, "Emory, you're not getting away without paying me this time!"

Moss sprinted toward the voice and spotted a man picking himself up off the dock. A second figure was climbing over the rail of a pungy.

"Emory!" Moss roared, running toward the boat.

Captain Emory turned and when he did, Moss shot him. The dredger fell onto the schooner's deck, then rolled onto his side. Moss leaned over the rail, aimed, and emptied the revolver into the captain.

"Good Christ!" the dock attendant swore, stumbling and skittering away further up the dock.

Moss said nothing, but turned and strode back toward the street. The noise had drawn watermen to the base of the pier and a voice said, "The nigger shot Captain Emory."

A second man said, "Good riddance!"

A third, with anger in his tone said, "Emory was a Crisfield man!"

Then a voice Moss recognized said, "Son, you have to get out of here."

The small crowd began to mutter about murder, but began to back away when Commander Davidson pulled a large Navy Colt and announced, "I'm in charge here. Step aside! This man is coming with me."

Davidson hauled Moss off the pier, then hustled him down to another wharf, where the *Leila* was moored. Nothing was said until they were on board and below deck.

"Commander, I've got to go back. Achilles—"

"Moss, you're not going anywhere. You go back there and they'll lynch you. Whatever you left stays. Have you been in a fight?" Davidson asked when he got a look at Moss's face.

"But, my friend's family—"

"I'll take care of it. Whatever it is. But we have to leave now."

Davidson left Moss then, giving the order to cast off. When he found his friend again, the man was leaning on the rail, staring out over the black water. The *Leila* was under a full head of steam and the lights of the oyster town were fading into the dark Eastern Shore landscape. For the first time in his life, Moss felt the power of despair and grief.

CHAPTER 25

THE MESSY CASE

On my way into the Diamond on a fine, crisp fall morning, I bought *The Sun*, as I usually did, tossing it on the bar while I made a pot of coffee. When he heard me come in, Moss emerged from the kitchen and pantry, yawning and scratching his rear. He plunked down on a stool and opened the paper, as he usually did.

"The eye-opener ready yet?" he asked.

"In a minute. You just sit there and enjoy my newspaper. It only cost me twelve cents."

"That's twelve cents for a week, Frank, you can afford it." As I put a mug down in front of him and sat down, he said, "The Brits are fighting in Afghanistan. They think it'll be easy."

"Won't it? Nothing but backward tribes there. How about giving me page six? I want to read what happened to the Orioles."

"You know what happened. The whole city is in mourning."

"Yeah, but I want to know who to blame."

Despite its issues, the team had played well enough in August and early September to claw its way past Boston into first place and build a small lead. But then, they began to sputter again and the Birds watched the Beaneaters steadily close on them to gain a virtual tie for first by the end of September. The two teams were now engaged in an all-important, three-game series in Baltimore that would decide the 1897 championship. The first game had gone to the Bostons 6–4, and the panic in the streets of my town was only matched in intensity by the joy in New England.

As Moss handed me a part of the paper, he couldn't resist a sly comment. "You're worried about a baseball game when there's a typhoid epidemic in Europe, bubonic plague in India, assassinations in Mexico, and race riots in New Orleans?"

"No Europeans, Indians, Mexicans, or Cajuns are going to walk into my bar and buy a beer."

"Oh, so it's only about business, then?"

"Moss, stop being a shit. You know how much the Orioles mean to the city. And you know we can't lose to those arrogant jerks from Boston. Do you know that hundreds of them have invaded the Eutaw House and are taking seats at Union Park that should be filled by Baltimore cranks? They call themselves the Royal Rooters, shouting, waving pennants, and carrying bean pots and little, sissy replicas of bats."

"With fanatics like you all around them, maybe they should be carrying the real thing."

"If they win another game here, it's all over. The Rooters better be carrying guns, if they want to leave Baltimore alive."

As I watched Moss make a curdled face, we heard another voice.

"Was that a death threat I just heard?"

Standing in our entrance was Detective O'Donnell with a semi-serious look on his ugly puss.

Moss smiled and said, "Tom, good morning. Ignore Frank. You know how he likes to bloviate."

Now, I had no idea what that meant and it didn't sound flattering. But what really caught my attention was Moss's pleasantries and his use of the name the detective's mother gave him. Under my breath, I asked Moss, "What, now he's your best friend?"

Moss ignored my question and suggested that O'Donnell have a seat. He then went behind the bar to get a mug of coffee for the cop.

"How do you like it, Tom?"

"Black. Tell me again who you're going to murder, Mr. Van Sant?"

"Detective, I said nothing about murdering anyone. What I said was, 'The Orioles need to win the next one to stay alive.'"

"Uh-huh," he grunted.

"What brings you in here so early?" Moss asked.

"Well, the Alcott Worthy murder doesn't seem to want to go away. I still have a few questions nagging at me—just a couple of loose ends that I thought maybe your friend here might be able to help me to clear up." O'Donnell indicated me with his coffee mug.

"I thought you charged Sergeant Gatch with the murder. He clubbed the man to death, the last time I talked to you."

Moss and I had spent a lot of time with O'Donnell back in May explaining what had happened with Dr. Munsch.

"We did, and he's finally been arraigned after we fought our way through the Police Union and the politicians. He's now awaiting trial. Chauncey Spittle has been very helpful."

"Spittle? I haven't seen him around lately," I said.

"And you won't," the detective replied. "After he's testified against Gatch, he'll move on to a new career, somewhere down south."

"Thank God."

Obviously, whatever relationship Gatch and Spittle had, it didn't work out. I was glad to hear that the beat cop would now just be a bad memory. Howard Street would be better off without the weasel. But if O'Donnell had Gatch for the murder, what was he doing talking to us? And what about Dr. Munsch?

"Tom, I thought Worthy was shot in the forehead. You said Gatch had beaten him to death." How's that going to play in a trial?" Moss asked.

The detective nodded. "It's a problem. We know for sure that Gatch clubbed him, and that could have easily been the cause of death. What we don't know is who shot him and why."

"It doesn't make sense that someone would shoot him after he was dead, or that Gatch would slug him when he was already gone," I observed. "So, doesn't it follow that he got hit first and was still alive when he was shot?"

"Moss, your Mr. Van Sant here fancies himself a detective."

"Yes, I know," Moss said in a less supportive way than I would have liked.

"You make a good point, though, and that's why I'm here. A good attorney will make the same observation, and I need to strengthen the case against Gatch."

"Were you able to tie Dr. Munsch's gun to the gun that was used on Worthy?" Moss asked.

"No. Could have been the same gun, but the most we can say is that they were both small caliber pistols."

"But Munsch had a motive," I threw in. "According to the bartender, Worthy was going to expose Munsch's crazy experiments. You saw what he did to that poor Peabody student."

"Maybe, and that's what we'll say," the cop said. "But there are enough witnesses to that incident to make an argument that it was an accident."

"It didn't look like an accident to me. And if it was, why did he run? Better yet, why did he shoot himself?"

"He may have done those two things for any number of reasons," O'Donnell responded.

"It looks like what you have is a pretty messy case," Moss said. "You have two good suspects for killing the same man. You know Gatch is guilty of the beating that could have killed him—if not right away, then before long. And you could make a strong argument that Dr. Munsch was certainly capable of killing someone and was motivated to keep the victim quiet. I think Frank's logic holds up—it makes sense that it was the shot that killed a dying Worthy. But having two perpetrators could mean you have none, if reasonable doubt can be raised.."

"That's it," O'Donnell said with a resigned air.

"Okay, then why don't you prosecute Gatch for the beating and pin the murder on Dr. Munsch, who is dead. Neat and clean," I said, wiping my hands in demonstration.

"That may be exactly what we do, despite the fact that I'd rather pin the death squarely on Gatch. In the meantime, I still have a few things nagging at me."

I knew that O'Donnell was thinking about Fanny, and I knew why he came looking for me in the Diamond. After Gatch had been arrested and right after Munsch's suicide, Fanny had come to me. She seemed much relieved that the pressure was off, now that the police seemed to have their man—or men. It was of little concern to her whether the murderer was Gatch or Munsch. She was just happy that she was no longer under suspicion.

Fanny's runs at both the Academy of Music and the Auditorium had been over for several weeks and she was just treading water, waiting for the murder investigation to be completed. So, she wanted me to go with her to see Detective O'Donnell to secure permission to leave Baltimore. She seemed oblivious to the fact that leaving the city would mean leaving me. Her only concern was getting away.

O'Donnell was reluctant. But in the wake of his seeming success in closing the Worthy murder, he released her to do whatever she wanted to do. I think he realized he couldn't hold onto her any longer anyway. So, a happy Fanny Darlington and I returned to Howard Street and to the Kernan Hotel. There, I hinted that maybe the two of us should find a way to celebrate her vindication. But it was clear that my insinuation was going to be ignored. In fact, rather abruptly, she stuck out her hand, thanked me for all I had done, turned on her heel, and walked up to her room.

With my hands stuck in my pockets, I walked out of the hotel, feeling a bit trampled on. Then I stopped and got angry. I really didn't expect anything from Fanny except maybe a bit of sincerity in her thanks. I am a big boy and know how these things work sometimes. But she was treating me rather shabbily.

I was still working out what I would say to her when I knocked on her door and heard her call, "Come in." When I entered, she was standing in front of a mirror, adjusting what looked like a diamond necklace.

"Oh, I thought you were the bellman," she stammered, quickly buttoning her collar to cover the jewelry.

"Fanny, look...."

Then I noticed her bags were packed and ready, except for a small valise that was open on the bed. On the top of some dainties was a small caliber pistol. She moved to the bed and calmly closed the bag.

"You have a gun," I observed stupidly.

"Frank, you know you can't be too careful in this town," she said, offering a weak explanation. "I hope you're not going to make this difficult. You were nice and kind of fun, but we never had anything serious between us, and I've got to get on with my life. So...."

She stood there and looked at me guilelessly. Then, she walked to the door and opened it.

I was back to the state of mind I was in the day I first met her. But this time it wasn't her relentless beauty. Like a lamb, I let her take my arm and steer me out of the door. She closed the door quietly, leaving me standing in the hallway.

"Mr. Van Sant, have you seen Miss Darlington recently?" Detective O'Donnell asked.

I hesitated, trying to release the memory of that painful experience and my feeling of helplessness and loss.

Finally, I said, "Not recently. The last time I was with her was the day we came to see you."

"Did she say where she was going? She's checked out of the Kernan."

"No, she didn't. But she may have gone to New York. She was always talking about the theater up there."

"Uh-huh," he said. "Did she ever say anything to you about a diamond necklace? Ever seen her wearing one?"

I looked at Moss over the detective's shoulder and lied, "No. Not that I can recall. Why?"

"Oh, nothing. Just something someone said to me. Okay, let me know if you hear from her, will you?" he asked, finishing his coffee, rising, and walking to the door. At the entrance, he turned back, started to say something to me, and thought better of it. Instead, he said to Moss, "Take care, and thanks again for your help. Things have worked out fine."

When the cop had gone, we sat staring at the bottom of our coffee mugs. I had, of course, told Moss everything.

"What did O'Donnell mean by things working out fine?" I asked.

"Oh, nothing," Moss said with a wave of his hand. "I just put in a good word for his daughter with Dan Gilman."

We were quiet for a couple of more beats, then he said, "I think you did the right thing."

"Do you? But you think she did it, don't you?

"I do. I did from the beginning," Moss said without a hint of ego.

CHAPTER 26

1871–1880
THE ENGINEER

When Moss arrived back in Baltimore, after spending almost seven years away, the first place he went was the Chesapeake Marine Railway and Dry Dock Company to see his former employer, Isaac Myers. The old man was surprised, but glad to see that Moss was still alive, an assumption he had not made up to that point. During a very congenial dinner at Myers's home, Moss related most of his story, including the two years he spent with the Oyster Navy after his three in Crisfield. At the end of the meal, he told Myers that he now planned to stay in Baltimore. The businessman was pleased to hear it and offered Moss an opportunity to rejoin the company. But Moss politely declined, saying that he had had enough of the water for now and that he had developed some other interests, namely food and its preparation. Myers then offered to introduce him to Robert Fowler, a friend who just the year before had purchased the famous Barnum's City Hotel on the southwest corner of Calvert and Fayette Streets. Barnum's, Myers explained, was world famous for its cuisine, albeit decidedly French in its menu and selection of wines.

Once again, Moss found himself in the city, nearly broke. Commander Davidson had paid him fair enough as a hand on the *Leila*, but Moss had not bothered to save much. Most of what he managed to hang onto went for a carved stone back in Crisfield. He wasn't going to starve in the next couple of weeks, but he needed to find work. As a result, he made his way over to Barnum's hotel, once Myers had set up the introduction with his friend, Fowler.

The gentleman was very friendly, but ultimately unhelpful. There were no openings in his kitchen for anyone, even if they had the training expected for such a position. The hotelier kindly offered to break in Moss as a waiter, but that was the most he could offer. So, Moss began canvassing Baltimore's respectable inns, taverns, and restaurants. He found it easy enough to get a job washing dishes and busing tables, but it was nearly impossible for an unknown black man to secure a good position in a reputable kitchen. Nevertheless, he worked his way around to most of the city's hotels and eateries, unfortunately without any success.

As Moss was coming out of the Mount Vernon Hotel after his latest rejection, he was thinking that he'd have to take a job somewhere as a short order cook. Out on the sidewalk, he happened to exchange a flick of the eye with an older gentleman walking past. A step away, each man stopped and turned. Moss recognized Fr. Barbelin and the priest knew Moss immediately. It was a warm reunion between them and for the second time in two weeks, Moss heard someone say they thought he was dead. The Jesuit quickly added, however, that he was very glad to see that it was not the case.

Fr. Barbelin had a thousand questions, and when he heard what Moss had been doing over the last few weeks, he commandeered him and took him home. Home was the rectory of Loyola College on North Calvert Street, another Jesuit school like St. Joseph's. There, as a guest of the priests, Moss and his mentor renewed their friendship and brought each other up-to-date since their days together in Philadelphia.

It was a comfortable place for Moss. He liked the erudition of the community, and they knew a student when they saw one. So, he stayed on for a while and used it as a base for his exploration of Baltimore's dining establishments. It wasn't long, however, before the savvy clerics discovered Moss's latest talent—Eastern Shore cuisine. Soon after that, a job offer was made.

Moss, however, saw another opportunity and once again negotiated a trade. He would prepare the meals for the fifteen members of the administration and faculty in return for room, board, and a furthering of his education. Once the priests experienced Grandmother Swann's recipes, the deal was done. And once again, Moss would get the education, but no formal degree.

At the time Moss and Fr. Barbelin chanced upon each other, the priest was actually in transition. He had stepped down from the presidency of St. Joseph's and was on his way back to France to visit his family. First, however, he was asked to spend a year at Loyola filling an open slot teaching in the school's science department.

Fr. Barbelin immediately began to lobby Loyola's new president, Fr. Kelly, to convince him that Moss's education at St. Joseph's qualified the ex-slave for graduate studies. Since the school had no formal graduate program, the Frenchman would take over his protégé's education personally. He would design and execute the same type of practical program he had at St. Joe's.

Moss appreciated Fr. Barbelin's interest in his education and he knew that if he once again came under the priest's tutelage, he would be the better for it. The man was a natural teacher who knew how to get the best from those interested in learning. But Moss had been thinking about his days at St. Joseph's and his years spent out in the world. His experiences taught him all too well the disadvantages that came with the color of his skin. While the war may have put an end to slavery, it had done little to change men's hearts. And while he could appreciate the idea of learning for its own sake, Moss also knew that recognition of academic accomplishment in the form of a diploma could open some doors that otherwise stayed shut for people like him. Things were tough enough, even with a document attesting to his knowledge.

The priest was an astute reader of Moss's temperament and he knew that something was bothering him about the offer. So, the Jesuit went right at it.

"Moss, we both know you are ready for this and I'm sure you see the value in the opportunity. But there's something off, isn't there?" the Jesuit asked.

"Father, believe me, I understand what you are offering me. It's unusual and, unfortunately, unprecedented."

"But?"

"I don't want you to think I don't appreciate what you are doing."

"Of course you appreciate it. But?"

"Well, it's this business of my education as 'informal.' Why must it be that way? It separates me and says that my education is somehow not worthy of recognition."

Fr. Barbelin nodded and replied, "What you learned at St. Joe's and the way you learned it was in many ways far superior to that of our other students with degrees. But I understand that's not the point. Not granting you a diploma because you are a black man is clear discrimination."

"I'm resigned to that painful fact, but why does it have to continue?"

"As you well know, there was a war in this country that split it in two. Preserving the Union was only one reason why President Lincoln was willing to pay the blood price, and the emotional price as well. What drove him ultimately was the eradication of slavery in this country, and it took five years and a lot of lives to do it. Unfortunately, that was only the beginning. Changing the culture is going to take longer."

"Father, I know what is. But the difficulty of change is no excuse for not changing. We would be doing exactly what we did at St. Joseph's, and I find it insulting and just wrong. I'm not sure I want to repeat that here, despite your extraordinary offer. Why can't the change begin right here, right now, at Loyola?"

"Of course you are right, Moss. I could claim that I am only one man and that I'm limited by the forces around me, but that's only true to a point. I still have an individual responsibility, especially as a Catholic priest, to do what I can, whenever I can."

The two men sat without speaking for a few moments. Moss expected honesty from his friend and got it. Fr. Barbelin was facing a problem he had wrestled with many times without coming to a conclusion and a course of action. Now, the priest realized, he had a means of putting his principles into play.

"Moss, I will do my best to make the change you're suggesting. If it's all the same to you, I'd like to continue your training much as we have done in the past—most of it in the field. At the same time, we'll do what is necessary to enroll you formally and fight the battles as they arise. My goal is that you will be awarded a Loyola diploma, clear proof of your achievement."

"I don't expect any guarantees from you, Father, given what I know. But we, you and I, have to start somewhere."

The priest's promise to strive to change the status quo was what Moss was looking for and what he needed to make his own commitment.

Fr. Barbelin's degrees were in engineering, and so the college's new cook was again launched into a world of which he knew little. But, once again, Moss's sponsor outdid himself in finding practical ways to teach the science of engineering. While there was no immediate resolution on formal enrollment from the administration, Moss was granted access to the core liberal arts classes and the school's available academic resources.

In 1876, despite the country's financial woes, America was in a head-down, dead run. It was pushing and shoving into new lands in the west and, at the same time, its eastern cities were becoming swollen with immigrants. The nation was transforming itself, driven by the muscle of industry and the innovation coming out of labs like those of Bell, Edison, and Tesla. And it was, of course, engineers who were converting those innovations into reality.

Baltimore's city fathers and the industrialists pushing them were not about to be left behind in this great race. So, its decision makers and planners, through both evolution and revolution, drew on all available resources in the public and private sectors, including the academic world.

Because of his expertise, Fr. Barbelin had been asked to serve on several project advisory panels whose responsibility it was to coordinate the efforts across sectors. As a result, the Jesuit engineer found himself involved with the construction of municipal facilities, the expansion of transportation projects, the erection of new buildings, and many other ventures, both large and small.

Moss was the direct beneficiary of Fr. Barbelin's civic contributions and the man's overall approach to teaching. The protégé would earn his graduate degree in civil engineering by getting his hands dirty in a wide range of enterprises. Acting as the priest's on-site eyes and ears, Moss was immersed in these projects, allowing him to translate classroom concepts into mechanical reality. The construction of steam engines, the design of sewers and roads, the properties and use of stone, iron, and steel in building construction, the stresses associated with bridge building, the management of water and waste, and the properties of electricity were all chapters in Moss's personal textbook. He even worked with drawings and measurements in the massive construction of the earthworks that held Baltimore's new reservoir in Druid Hill Park.

The one area that Moss resolved to avoid was politics. Because of Fr. Barbelin's civic role, Moss was a familiar figure in the offices of the new City Hall. But he had no interest in engaging in the give and take that was required by that life, despite the fact that an increasing number of black men were finding politics and government to be an opportunity. The law was of some interest to Moss, but he also agreed heartily with the old joke that there were two things no one should ever see being made—law and sausage.

Eventually, the man from the Eastern Shore became a familiar face among those who called the shots and among those who knew how to get things done. In the process, in addition to getting an education, he built respect, trust, and a few important relationships in the city.

Another year passed, and then two more after that. Fr. Barbelin had postponed his visit home and extended his stay at Loyola, teaching, working with Moss, and becoming a part of his now adopted city. At the same time, the onetime slave's connections allowed him into certain academic circles where, at first, he was thought of as a curiosity. It wasn't long, however, before the curious found his views fresh and valuable. This opened doors to Baltimore's libraries, including the Peabody Institute, the Athenaeum and the Maryland Institute. A connection to Daniel Gilman, president of the new Johns Hopkins University, even granted him access to particular faculty and the occasional class that was germane to what he and Fr. Barbelin were doing for the city.

As Baltimore grew, so did Moss. His work and study introduced him to a wide array of people, black and white. His interactions were not always comfortable, and he regularly met with bald racial bias. When he did, his intelligence and lack of guile managed to break down many barriers. Whenever the fear and hatred he encountered was too deeply rooted and good sense broke down, his anger would rise to the point of exploding. These incidences forced him to become reasoned enough to weigh the temporary satisfaction of physical confrontation against the larger objectives he had set for himself. As a result, he developed an array of emotional calluses that allowed him to rise above most of the pettiness and hostility. At least, this is what he strove for. In truth, there were times when physical force had been a more effective means of resolving a situation.

It wasn't all study and work for Moss, either. One open door seemed to lead to another, and he was exposed to things many people were not. He had been invited into both public and private art collections, music concerts, dance recitals, and stage presentations from opera to slapstick comedy. He could be seen at Ford's Grand Opera House, the Academy of Music, and other less-sophisticated venues throughout the city. He had become "a man about town."

Moss, now approaching forty years old, saw himself as a lifelong bachelor, although he certainly was no stranger to women. With clear societal boundaries in place, women seemed to enjoy his company, and he theirs. When the boundaries were lowered, he was more than willing to indulge in that sort of play. But he never met anyone who had a sufficient enough impact to break him out of what had now become a comfortable pattern as a single man. That had been true, at least until he met Beatrice Anne Rhodes one evening at a dinner party thrown by his friend Isaac Myers.

In Annie, he had found the woman with whom he wanted to spend a lifetime. The feeling was obviously mutual, and the two found as much time as possible to be together. To the chagrin of Fr. Barbelin, Moss would easily sacrifice time from his studies or his work to be with her. The priest, who struggled with this particular emotional need and gave very little thought to women in general, expressed his concern that his protégé was letting all of his hard work go. But Moss got his mentor over yet another change and eventually, appealing to the Jesuit's French heritage, reconciled the priest to the fact that very soon Annie would be a permanent part of the equation.

When she died suddenly of smallpox during one of the city's recurring epidemics, Moss was reminded once again of the depth of misery that comes with the loss of someone loved. He only managed to emerge from his grief with the help of his friend who served simply to listen and encourage. In the years after, Moss had numerous relationships with other women he'd meet. Some were more serious than others, but none ever reached the same heights as the one he had lost.

With the help of Annie, Moss discovered himself to be a man of passions who could enjoy whatever endeavor absorbed him at the time. Even with that, food and the unlimited way it could be prepared and presented remained his first passion. The Loyola community had grown fat and content with their chef, guarding their find as if Moss were the *Pieta*. But as much as he enjoyed cooking for the Loyola community, he had set himself a goal of demonstrating his skill in one of Baltimore's premier kitchens.

By 1880, according to one Baltimore journalist, the Chesapeake Bay had become the most productive protein factory in the world. It's not surprising, then, that the city's chefs took full advantage of its proximity. Baltimore was already known for its hotels and the meals that emerged from their galleys. Epicures from all over the world were finding their way into the dining rooms of Barnum's City Hotel, the Rennert House, the Carrollton Hotel, Buck's Hotel, the Maltby House, Eutaw House, Guy's Hotel, and others. At one point or another, Moss had been with friends or business contacts in the private rooms of all of these enterprises. But what he really wanted was access to the pots, pans, ovens, and stoves of the hotels. The master chefs were all highly accomplished servants of the Chesapeake's bounty, of course, but most were adherents to European preparation. As a result, Moss knew there was an opportunity to do something unique—bring Maryland's Eastern Shore cooking to the world. When his studies were finished and his work complete, at the end of the day, this is what he thought about. But Moss's dream was not to be—at least, not yet.

✖✖✖✖✖✖✖

In the spring of 1880, Loyola College awarded its first graduate degree in engineering. That was remarkable enough, but the fact that it went to a man of color was extraordinary. The degree, a Master of Science in Civil Engineering and the document attesting to it, was very satisfying to both Moss and Fr. Barbelin.

Their pride in the accomplishment, however, was dampened by the refusal of the administration to allow Moss to join the school's other students in their graduation ceremony. The two had put a dent in the prejudice that was so deeply entrenched, but by no means had they dispelled it. As painful and disheartening as the rebuff was, Moss managed to temper his indignation with the realization that he had broken ground that now could be seeded by others.

Fr. Barbelin, however, was not as forgiving. After a loud and contentious argument with the Board of Trustees, he resolved to sever ties with Loyola, return to France to visit his family, and to seek another position there within the Jesuit community. No amount of reflection would allow him to release his anger at the folly and intolerance of men who claimed to exist for the benefit of others.

Once the decision was made, the priest sought out his friend and student.

"So, you're going," Moss said sadly after Fr. Barbelin had explained his plans.

"Yes, I am. I can't stay here now. Things have changed for me at Loyola."

"What will you do?"

"First, I'll spend some time with my sisters. I haven't seen them since I left for the United States. In another month, I will be seventy-two years old, and I want to go while I can still travel and still be useful."

Moss dismissed the idea that his friend would lose his usefulness, but he was surprised at his age. The man constantly seemed to radiate energy. But Moss didn't comment and instead asked, "And after that?"

"I will speak to my superiors. Perhaps they'll have something for me to do. Maybe there in France, but more likely the need is in Africa or Asia."

Once more, the two men sat in silence for a few moments, a comfortable state for them after so many years together.

Finally, the priest said, "You could come with me, if you like. I'm sure there's a need for qualified engineers in France as well."

"Father, you know the last few years here in Baltimore have been wonderful for me. I have grown to love the city, even with all of its problems."

"Yes, I know."

"And our projects together have become important to me, to who I am."

"Yes," the priest said again, waiting for Moss to say what he wanted to say.

"But you also know that engineering is not what I want to do, as rewarding as it is."

"Yes, I know that too. You want to be a chef. Correct?"

"It's hard for me to tell you that, Father, after all you have invested in me over the years."

"I hope I have been building a man, not just an engineer."

Fr. Barbelin's remark meant a great deal to Moss. It said that, even with all the education his friend had given him—especially during these recent three years—Moss was free to choose his own life, free to do what made him happy. The priest simply had been preparing him for the choice.

Again they sat in silence, thinking about the future.

"Moss, I fully understand and can appreciate your love for food. After all, I am French."

"Why do you say that, Father?"

"My boy, don't you know that France has the best culinary schools in the world?"

"Yes, but I don't want to cook like that."

The older man smiled and shook his head. "Do you remember the time we visited William and Henry Walters at their home in Mount Vernon?"

"Yes, of course, the father and son art collectors."

"Exactly. Do you remember the artist you found so remarkable? Edouard Manet?"

"His work is astounding. Maybe even revolutionary."

"Yes, but if I recall, it wasn't his early realism that excited you, rather it was his later work, his moody, atmospheric pieces."

"That's right. It was almost as if he were painting from his mind's eye rather than an actual model or scene."

"Well, I mention it because it took him some time to evolve to the point you so aptly describe. Before then, he went to school, learned the greats that went before him. Copied them. Then, and only then, with a platform firmly in place, was he prepared to play variations on understood themes. It was his foundation that allowed him to recognize the new, to create something different—something, as you say, revolutionary."

"And you think it's important to do the same with cooking?"

"The preparation of food is an art form, isn't it?"

"So, it's back to school for me? This time in France?"

"If you so choose."

"Where and how would I start?"

"Paris. Where my sisters live. We'll figure out the how once we're there."

CHAPTER 27

THE CHAMPIONSHIP

Friday, September 24

Baltimore was in an uproar and worried sick over the Orioles' loss of the first game of the crucial three game series with Boston. Whichever team took two of the three games in their last series against each other would be the Champions for 1897. The world could have been hit by a giant meteor and readers of *The Sun* still would have turned first to the sports section. There, the minutest details of the struggle between the Birds and the Beaneaters were chronicled.

The first game saw 13,000 cranks cram themselves into Union Park. Another 10,000 sat on top of the park's fences, climbed the utility poles ringing the place, and filled the neighborhood's rooftops overlooking the field. An untold number of baseball fanatics across the country stood near telegraph wires in theaters, bars, and music halls to hear the play by play tapped out. Not since the Sullivan-Corbett fight was there such a fire lit under the rumps of American sports enthusiasts.

But Baltimoreans were now on the brink of the abyss, looking down. And it was a shock. Confidence was sky-high before the first game because Hanlon was able to put his best nine in the lineup. Even Wilbert Robinson was back behind the plate. The manager had also sent out his ace, Joe Corbett, to pitch against the number one hurler for the Beaneaters, Kid Nichols. Admittedly, Nichols was the best righty in the league; he had already won twenty-nine games and thirty the year before. But Corbett was also damn good, and the Orioles had taken five of the nine games the two teams had played during the season.

The two hurlers dueled heroically over seven innings, but in the end, *The Sun's* headline said it all the next morning: "Outplayed By Boston." The secondary banners explained, "Brilliant Fielding Does It," and, "Orioles Nervous

And Erratic At Critical Times." Another paper was even more pointed: "Corbett Tires; Keeler Only One Hit In Four Tries." The result was a 6–4 Beaneater victory, and the Orioles were down to their last gasp.

Game two meant either win, or spend the winter thinking about what could have been. A loss would mean championship bragging rights were gone. The only thing left would be the residue of the taunts and cheers of the Royal Rooters planted firmly in the collective memory of the Star-Spangled City.

Baltimore's cranks were outraged by the invasion of Boston supporters who went by that appalling and pompous name. Royal Rooters, indeed! More like Royal Patooters! How they secured tickets was galling, but no mystery—the scalpers buzzing around Union Park were as thick as gnats in Pittsburgh. The ballpark rang with Beaneaters from the centerfield flagstaff to the last row in the upper deck.

The vocal war in the stands was often more heated than the play on the field. Each time the chant of "Hit 'er up again, Boston!" was howled, the Oriole faithfuls' ululations would build until the Beaneater loyalists were drowned out. Each time their paper megaphones spoke and their cowbells rang, the home crowd would answer. It went on all afternoon long, and it was exhausting. After the final out and the loss had begun to sink in, one raspy Orioles crank identified the only silver lining: "At least the bastards will be too hoarse to yell tomorrow!"

Of course, the Boston press was hysterical in its description of the game, calling it a "classic" and likening it to the Battle of Thermopylae. Its team was made up of demigods, capable of astounding athletic feats beyond mortal man. The city's scribbling oracles foretold with confidence the ousting of the blackguards of Baltimore from their tyrannical three-year reign at the top of baseball. Meanwhile, *The Sun* simply echoed the refrain of the bent but not bowed: "He who laughs last, laughs best."

Saturday, September 25

The second game of the series fell on a Saturday. How Harry Von Der Horst squeezed another thousand into his park was a feat of magic and greed. One Boston writer swore the owner made everyone stand sideways. The Royal Rooters were there again in force, and must have gargled all night because they were just as vociferous as the previous day. From their behavior, some must have been mixing gin with their Listerine. Evidently, Von Der Horst had heard some stories, because he hired fifty cops for the occasion, most of whom seemed to hover around the seats occupied by concentrations of the enemy. It was a question, however, whether they were there to control them or protect them.

It would be Duke Klobedanz, a lefty and twenty-game winner, going for Boston versus Bill Hoffer, the Orioles' stylish right hander who had also won more than twenty games. By the third inning, the Orioles had built a three-run lead and Hughie Jennings's slick fielding at shortstop had helped to hold the Beaneaters in check. The game was marked by Hanlon's scientific baseball, featuring double steals, advancing runners with bunts, and smart positioning of infielders.

The contest also had its share of insane baying at the two umpires, Tim Hurst and Bob Emslie, the best arbiters President Nick Young has. The Orioles, of course, had seen more than their share of two-man crews all season, and believed they were there just to police the team's "aggressive" play.

By the seventh, Hoffer was showing some fatigue and he yielded Boston's first two runs, bringing the visitors to within one with two men on and two outs. But, when Uncle Robbie used his bulk to block the plate and apply the tag to Billy Hamilton, who was trying to steal home, the rally ended.

In the bottom of the seventh, a single by Keeler and a double by Jennings put two men on for Kelley, who promptly lined a shot into right field, sending both of his teammates home. Runs were scored by both teams in the eighth, but that was all of the scoring, and the Birds flew out of Union Park with a 6–3 win and new life.

The next day, the hysteria continued in the Boston press. This time, instead of laurel wreathes, many were wearing sack-cloth and ashes. Instead of jubilation, there was a beanpot full of breast-beating, caterwauling, and general lamentation. Blame was laid to the poor fielding of Jimmy Collins, arguably baseball's best third sacker. Neck and neck with the Birds' own John McGraw, anyway. Billy Hamilton also came in for his share of brickbats for poor base running. "The competitive spark was gone," other observers said. And the *Boston Journal's* Walter Barnes went so far as to suggest that the party at the Eutaw House after game one had taken its toll. In point of fact, by the end of the game, even the Royal Rooters seemed to have run out of steam.

Baltimore's writers were just as excited about the victory as Boston's were the day before. Their prose was peppered with adjectives like brilliant, desperate, wonderful, nervy, and splendid. The city itself now could breathe a bit easier, but not much. The cockiness was gone, replaced by guarded optimism. The realization that the title was now down to one more game against Boston tempered emotions and made Baltimore supporters almost philosophical about the chase that had gone on all season. The Orioles were back at the top of the standings by the eyelash of one percentage point, and many people were affording their rival grudging respect. The third and deciding game was going to be the best against the best. Or, as they say in Mexico, *mano y mano*.

Sunday, September 26

Sunday might have been called a day of restlessness. No baseball is played in Baltimore on the seventh day of the week, but it sure is talked about and anticipated. That's what was going on in the Diamond Café that afternoon, as McGraw and Robinson held their normal benediction. A number of the players were in, and Moss and I just sat and listened. The impression was that of gladiators waiting to be released out onto the floor of the Colosseum. Any animosities that may have existed among the Orioles were suspended, at least for this final game. Call it artificial, but Hanlon could not have asked for more. Jokes were funnier, stories more interesting, and no one argued over whose turn it was to buy a round. And no one pulled apart the play of teammates, as they might have after a game in the middle of the season. All of that was put on hold as the players awaited the coming of Monday, a day *The Sun* called, "The Great Day."

Moss and I were sitting together, leaving the team to themselves. We already had argued ad nauseum the season, the series, the completed two games, and the coming final nine innings. So, we were voicing no further analysis or predictions.

My friend suggested that we simply absorb and relish the experience, because it may never come again. Back in the spring, I might have argued that the Oriole championships would go on forever because of Hanlon and the talent he had amassed. But Moss's preseason prediction had come true and he was right now, too. It may never happen again. The season had been an odd one, although the Birds had won eighty-eight games to this point and still had a hold—albeit tenuous—on first place. I thought their record was something of a surprise, because I didn't feel like they had played championship baseball all year. The team's execution had been as up and down as the roller coaster at Electric Park out on Belvedere Avenue. Yet, here they were, playing one more game for all the beans. It made me glad, certainly, but nervous as hell.

"Moss, I guess you were right about the Birds," I commented. "It's tough to hold a team together year after year."

He nodded and said, "I have to give all of the credit in the world to Ned Hanlon. The Orioles could have imploded at any time during the season with all that they were dealing with."

"Yeah, the injuries...."

"Well, every team deals with injuries. The great teams live through them by relying on intangibles. Team spirit, friendships, encouraging the discouraged, setting and maintaining expectations of success, not just for the team, but for individuals as well. Things like that become critically important. They allow the best teams to find ways to win that aren't always reflected in batting averages or win-loss records. Bench players step up, journeymen hit in the clutch, sore arms are suffered, and the truly gifted make great plays."

"I guess it's not always logical," I said.

"Of course not, nothing is. You've heard that before from me. I think it's exactly that understanding that has allowed Hanlon to accomplish as much as he has this year."

"Let's hope he has one more game in his right brain," I said, knowing Moss would understand me completely.

With that, the café's glass doors were swung wide and in walked Jimmy Collins, Fred Tenney, and a few other Boston Beaneaters. A cheer went up from the Orioles present and Muggsy went into his magnanimous host mode. There was no friction whatsoever, and the rivals seemed truly glad to see each other. It was much more than professional courtesy; their bonds had been forged over the season in such a way that true respect for each other was obvious. It was a moment in time that I sincerely wished I was a member of the team.

The afternoon wore down with everyone wishing everyone else good luck and McGraw proclaiming Collins and Tenney to be "the greatest players that ever covered third and first base." At the same time, the Oriole lead-off man couldn't resist lamenting over how difficult it was to bunt on the two Boston stars—a true compliment, coming from one of the best at using the small-ball tactic.

Monday, September 27

Finally, the wait was over for both the players and their cranks. The late afternoon game would see the largest crowd ever to watch a baseball game. Foul ground was roped off and tickets sold for its standing room. In addition, those outside of the Union Park walls looking in swelled the estimate of attendance to near thirty thousand. At one point, a wagon gate in the outfield was kicked down and another 700 or so poured in before the additional police hired for the game could plug the breach. Baltimore was at a standstill, just as Boston was, as thousands gathered around any source of news available.

With everything at stake, both managers, in controversial decisions, chose to go with experience. Boston's Frank Selee had rested arms on the bench, but he let them languish, sending out Kid Nichols once more, this time on only two days' rest. Ned Hanlon, too, had strong arms ready in Jerry Nops and Arlie Pond, but chose instead to come back with Joe Corbett. It was his gut that told him to give Corbett a chance to avenge his Friday loss.

The game began with all in attendance in full throat, including the Royal Rooters, whose ranks had swollen by another fifty voices. The omens were not good for the Orioles when, in the first inning, Corbett took a line drive off his pitching hand, jamming several fingers. The injury knocked him out of the game and Nops was brought in. But Hanlon quickly pulled him after an inning in which he gave up three runs. By the time the second frame was complete, Boston had a 4–2 lead.

With Hoffer now pitching on one day's rest, the Birds came back to make it 5–5 after three innings. It was obvious that both teams were tight and feeling the pressure. Errors were playing a huge role in the scoring, and the mistakes would continue throughout the day with eight official miscues incurred between the teams.

The roaring crowd also was a factor, especially those standing in foul territory. Foul pops that normally would be caught were lost in the throng and batters were given new life again and again. Once, Collins had to fight off cranks along the third base line as he muscled his way through them to snag a pop fly.

Boston hammered out a lead in the fourth to reach 8–5, but was held down by Hoffer until the seventh inning. Now having thrown fourteen innings in three days, Baltimore's most reliable pitcher began to show real fatigue and the Beaneaters exploded for three more runs. Hoffer was clearly through, and he signaled to Hanlon that he needed to be relieved, something that was just never done. For reasons known only to him, the manager refused to pull his righty and, as a result, he paid for it. By the end of the inning, Hoffer had faced thirteen batters in a row, giving up eleven hits and nine runs for a 17–5 deficit.

For all intents, that was the game and the championship. The Orioles battled back to score nine runs, but it was over by then and the Beaneaters won going away with a final score of 19–9, the most runs Baltimore had given up since 1894.

A dark cloud settled over the city that would hover for days as Baltimore's cranks choked down the bad oyster that was an embarrassing defeat at home in the biggest game of the year. Ned Hanlon was pilloried by the press and supporters alike for his illogical selection of pitchers during the game. It was a particularly cruel flogging for the manager, whose intuition failed him on the most important day of the season.

CHAPTER 28

1880
THE CHEF DE CUISINE

Just as his war years triggered major shifts in Moss, his first year in Europe changed him. The experience of his travels stretched him and gave him some much-needed perspective. The center of his world had been Baltimore, Maryland in the United States; now, he discovered that he was living on a much larger planet. One that was strange, diverse, and contradictory in so many ways. He was frequently exhilarated by what he saw and heard, yet sometimes, he just wanted to curl up into something familiar in order to halt the bombardment of the new for a while. Any pride in what he had accomplished in his life to that point began to fall away as he realized the magnitude of what he didn't know.

Moss endured an additional contradiction, as well. While Fr. Barbelin reveled in what he called their "footloose freedom to roam and explore," in truth, Moss felt restricted. In most places they visited, the American was isolated by language, color, and culture. The irony that he was actually confined within all of Fr. Barbelin's freedom was not lost on him. In those times, Moss found himself staring into mirrors.

The priest read this feeling from the outset and had been expecting it, of course. It was the culmination of his very selfish plan. Not only did the Jesuit have the best traveling companion he could ever want, he also had another opportunity to do what he liked to do best. So, the teacher took on and relished the task of teaching his favorite student one more time.

When he and Fr. Barbelin arrived in Paris, the priest spent the first few weeks visiting his sisters and meeting with his order's superiors. When the Jesuits urged him to take a sabbatical before accepting another assignment, Fr.

Barbelin used the time to introduce Moss to the old world. They would come back to France to stay for a while, so they began their tour in Brussels and Amsterdam, then crossed the North Sea to London. Back on the continent, they trained to Vienna, Prague, and Berlin, eventually making it all of the way to St. Petersburg. Then, traveling south through the Caucasus and the Carpathian Mountains, they reached Bucharest, Istanbul, and Athens. Finally, they crossed the Adriatic and came to rest for a month in Rome. Seville would be their last stop before returning to Paris. But first, the priest wanted to spend as much time as possible in what he called the Eternal City and the center of his world, the Vatican. There was a sense that the priest was seeking a sort of closure to his very full life.

Moss had collected many things in his exploration, though very few of them were souvenirs. He gathered ideas and honed his ability to judge them. He tasted a wide range of foods; he learned to appreciate fine wine; and with his friend's guidance, he devoured architecture, art, and music. And all of this experience served to spur creativity in his own thinking, as new experience always has.

Not all of it was a lark. In fact, he was often put off by what he saw. On the East Coast of the United States, the people he knew were either white or black. Here, they were white, black, brown, yellow, red, olive, and uncountable shades in between. But color wasn't necessarily the issue; rather, it was more the fact that culture and thinking could change dramatically on the other side of a river or just over a mountain. Unlike Americans, most people seemed fixed in their societies, and had been for hundreds of years. The rich would always be rich and the poor would always be poor. Their cities were not growing outwardly, and the growth inside of them seemed muted by the overwhelming dominance of history.

This was not the feeling Moss got in the States. Certainly, there were huge gulfs between blacks and whites, the haves and the have-nots. But, underlying that, there was always a feeling that things could change. There was a belief that a man could make those changes. This was the primary reason that he resolved to return to Maryland when the time was right.

As overwhelmed as Moss was at times, by the end of his travels, his experiences had managed to bring him full circle. He would never have described himself as a man of the world, but he was clearly much more at ease within it. The practical side of that was he now had a broader platform for decisions he would make. Perspective also allowed him to identify his greatest strengths—an appreciation for the unfamiliar and the facility to adapt to it.

Once back in France, Moss settled into a life in Paris that put him back in school, gave him a chance to explore the culture in depth and to learn the language. With Fr. Barbelin's contacts, he was enrolled in a progressive culinary institute of growing renown, called La Main Légère. He was singled out immediately, not only because of his dark skin and his age, but because he was an American. What learning he brought from Grandmother Swann's kitchen also marked him as distinctly different. These things set him apart, but certainly did not make life easier for him. Acceptance was not forthcoming, despite his aptitude and progress. After all, he was not French.

Regardless, in the four years he spent at La Main Légère, Moss's eyes were opened far beyond the Dockside's little kitchen in Crisfield. His learning went well past the understanding of food, the ingredients used in its preparation, and the construction of a meal. He was also taught manual skills, teamwork, preservation of food, presentation, and kitchen management.

His management instruction focused on a recently developed system to organize and operate a professional kitchen. This approach allocated the major elements of a meal's preparation to individuals specializing in a particular facet. For instance, an expert in the preparation of fish would have responsibility for all fish dishes, a sauce expert would focus on sauces, a pastry chef would concentrate on baking. The result was that expertise was inserted at every step and the time required to prepare a dish was reduced, making kitchens more efficient.

It also happened that all of Paris was buzzing about a revolution going on in French cuisine at the time. A master chef by the name of Georges Auguste Escoffier was changing this world by changing its emphasis. His philosophy was that the focus should no longer be on the abundance of a meal, but rather on the ingredients that went into its preparation. Simplicity, a lighter and precise touch with spices and the use of fonds, or base sauces, to enhance without overwhelming were his hallmarks. If it were painting, rather than cooking, his approach might be described as using a finer brush.

As exciting as all of this was to Moss, he missed America. His training in France would be his last foray into formal education. For some time, even with all of his experiences, he had begun to feel like he was late to the party. He wanted to get started on something, stay with it, and put down roots. It was now 1885 and he was forty-seven years old.

Fr. Barbelin never did receive a new assignment. When the two returned from their travels, the elderly priest brought with him a cough that would later be diagnosed as tuberculosis. It was not long after that he became fully incapacitated and was placed in a sanatorium maintained by his order. It was not easy on Moss, but the priest seemed happy and at peace. The man who saw the potential in Moss, believed in him, and mentored him through a significant portion of his varied life, died in the winter of 1884 at the age of seventy-six. One more time, Moss felt the acute agony of grief over the loss of someone close. He had loved Felix Barbelin.

Once back in the States, Moss immediately returned to Baltimore and Barnum's City Hotel. He was not the same rustic cook who had applied for work in the kitchen five years earlier, but Barnum's wasn't what it once was, either. Robert Fowler was still part owner, but he was now retired and the facility was now run by partners. In fact, the famous old hotel had been allowed to go to seed, and its reputation for Maryland cooking had faded.

Moss realized that he needed to do some work to understand the evolution of the culinary environment in the Monument City. He also needed a plan to secure a job that was both a solid start and a chance to build a reputation. Finally, he knew that he could not simply walk in and apply for the position he was seeking; he needed to renew a few old contacts that were in a position to make introductions and put in a good word for him.

As Moss rebuilt friendships, he also learned that dining in Baltimore had changed since he left for Europe. All fine dining and the best of Maryland cooking was still being done in the better hotels, but several standalone restaurants and even a few taverns were gaining popularity. He focused first on the hotel dining rooms and made a list that was ranked from good to very good to excellent. This gave him an idea of where he might be able to start, and it also allowed him to set a few goals. When he was finished, the Rennert House was at the top of the heap and, while he knew he couldn't start there, that was where he set his sights.

The most useful thing Moss ever did to prepare himself for a career in Baltimore's kitchens was storming Battery Wagner when he was with the 54th Massachusetts Volunteers. The fact that he was not a white man was just the beginning. Given his experience and training, there was no real apprenticeship, and he flew through the initial hoops that were established for new hires. This immediately caused jealousy and discord among those whose onion-chopping techniques were still developing. When he began to show his skills and training and left those who were still learning sauces behind, he generated real dislike. When his ideas on kitchen management were recognized, he began to experience sabotage. As he continued to rise and his menu suggestions gained acceptance, hatred was not too strong a word to describe the way his competition felt. When regular customers began to request his creativity in constructing and presenting a dish, hatred got quiet and dangerous. He could swear, but never prove, that someone had actually shot at him as he was leaving after one night's work. Who or why was never determined.

It was a very good thing for him that, as his reputation grew, he was able to leave certain situations behind, moving up the ranks not only within the kitchen, but also within the hierarchy of restaurants on his list.

Moss had gotten quite adept at negotiating the shoals of his world, building a following among those who counted, and avoiding the fear and loathing of those who didn't. As a result, within ten years, he found himself in the position of having accomplished almost all of the goals he had set. What's more, he still loved the work. It was an additional boon that it also happened to be very lucrative, creating a financial independence he never anticipated. In fact, Moss had moved along so quickly that he was about to leave a very prestigious position at the Carrollton for an offer at the Rennert House.

The former slave and engineer had been asked to have lunch with the executive chef of the esteemed hotel and, because he knew from friends that there was about to be an opening, he was sure he was going to be offered the position of Chef de Cuisine. If so, the staff would be his responsibility, directing all activity and assuring proper timing. It would be his job to correct small inconsistencies in dishes, test new recipes, ordering ingredients and assure their quality, and track the cost of all goods. In other words, he was about to achieve what he had set out to do.

Moss had been in the presence of August Williams on several occasions, but he had never had the opportunity to meet the great man. The word within culinary circles, however, was that the master chef was something of a prickly pear, rigid in his procedures and sensitive to the merest slight. As a result, Moss walked into the Rennert at the corner of Liberty and Saratoga Streets not knowing quite what to expect. He was a few minutes early for the meeting, which was in the hotel's dining room. So, he decided to check the state of his tie and collar, given that it was highly unusual for a black man to be seen dining in such a reputable place. The thought made him smile with no little sense of vindication.

Looking around for the men's lounge, Moss watched a young man, obviously looking for the same thing, find the correct door on the other side of the lobby. He followed, stepped into the lounge, and was about to enter the lavatory when he noticed a placard mounted on an ornate brass easel. Its message read: "Colored Gentlemen, two doors down, please."

Moss hesitated, thinking dark thoughts. He snatched the placard off the stand, tore it in two, and threw it in a corner. He considered the option of turning around and walking out of the Rennert. But after a moment's pause, he decided to hear Chef Williams out. It wasn't the chef's idea to discriminate in such an insulting way; after all, he was about to offer him a job. So, with a set jaw, he walked the extra few yards down the hall and yanked open the offending door and went in. For now, he would stomach one more time the reality that was freedom in America.

The soon-to-be Chef de Cuisine was not in the lavatory very long when he heard a loud bang come from the other men's room. Then there were two distinct pops, one right after the other. Moss recognized gunshots when he heard them. He rushed out, following three other men just entering the restroom. He noticed immediately one of the stall doors ajar and a pair of legs, askew and protruding from under the wooden cubicle. He watched a horrifying scene unfold as the three wrestled with the frenetic gunman, a scruffy tramp dressed in overalls. Another shot was fired wildly, but eventually, the men had the shooter pinned to the floor and his revolver in hand without any further injury. It seemed that, other than the victim, no one else had been using the lavatory.

Moss was recruited to find a policeman and to seek emergency help, but he ran into the hotel security man in the lobby, already on his way as a result of the noise. The private cop had sent for the police. The Rennert's manager was also quick to the incident and had ordered a staff member to summon a doctor and an ambulance. By the time Moss returned to the lounge, he could no longer get into the room. Between law enforcement and hotel personnel, the situation was now under control and all Moss could do was stand in the lobby.

He was joined shortly by Chef Williams who had also been drawn by the disturbance. Together, they watched the police drag the gunman out and the medical people wheel the victim past them. The young man had been shot twice, wasn't moving at all, and looked very dead.

Moss had never seen the victim before; but he certainly recognized the assassin. He had not seen Caleb Emory since the *Mary Kate*, but there was no mistaking the captain's son.

The recognition jarred him and his companion noticed. The chef asked if he had known either of the men. Shaking his head, Moss simply said that he didn't feel well and wondered if the chef would consider postponing their meeting.

Chef Williams was clearly unhappy with the request. He asked if Moss was normally like this under pressure and pompously commented that the Rennert's kitchen waited for no man. He looked long at Moss, giving him a moment to reconsider the request. When the would-be Chef de Cuisine just returned the stare, Williams turned on his heel and left Moss in the lobby with a final comment.

"To be a part of the Rennert, one must forget himself."

❈❈❈❈❈❈

When Moss spoke to the investigators, he had little to say. No, he didn't know either of the men. No, he didn't see anything because he was in the adjacent lavatory. No, he knew nothing about the ripped-up Coloreds sign on the floor. Yes, he was in the hotel to meet with August Williams, a fact that made them skeptical and one they would be certain to check. After that, he was treated as if he were invisible, so he managed to loiter a bit. In doing so, he learned a few things. The victim had been in the Rennert to apply for a bookkeeper's job. He had been shot both in the chest and in his right arm, probably trying to protect himself. He had been taken to Baltimore City Hospital over on Calvert Street.

Moss also heard a few snippets about the shooter. The assassin fought with such a frenzy that he must have been on some kind of drug. He was ranting something about his father's murderer. He had been dressed like a farmer or a fisherman, and no identification was found on his person.

Moss thought about what he should do, if anything. It would be crazy of him to walk into the police precinct and try to explain that their perpetrator shot the wrong man. That he, Moss, was the real target because he had killed the shooter's father. He was not going to do that. There was no guilt in ending Captain Emory's miserable life, and he'd do it again.

In truth, Moss wasn't particularly fond of Emory's son, either. But one way or the other, regardless of motive, Caleb was going to get his neck stretched for the crime and Moss would lose no sleep over that, either.

The victim was a different story, however. As a result, sleep would not come easily for Moss, nor was he able to engage in his ritual of reflection. The young man could be dead because of him. *The Emory boy must have thought he was following me into the lavatory. Then, when he saw no one else in there, he just threw open the occupied stall door and started firing.*

Moss was rocked by the threat to his very carefully constructed set of principles. An innocent person was a victim because of him. He owed something and he must make amends. These thoughts stole from Moss any joy in the irony that it was, in fact, racial prejudice that had saved his life.

Days passed, and finally Moss made a decision. He would help the man whose name he didn't even know. But he would do it anonymously.

In the meantime, he attempted to speak to Chef Williams at the Rennert, but the chef refused to see him. So, it seemed very clear that the offer to take the Chef de Cuisine role would not be forthcoming.

The position had represented a fulfillment of all of his plans, the thing he felt he had been born to do. But now that it was no longer a possibility, Moss was oddly at peace with the fact. He had made a choice in that one moment, standing in the hotel lobby. Initially, his decision and its result was a bitter pill to swallow. But then, Moss realized that something inside of him had worked automatically. The situation went to how he thought of himself.

Fr. Barbelin had taught him that the most important thing was not what you say. It was not even what you do. Rather, the most important thing that should concern a man is who he is. All else would follow that.

Moss had recalled his promise to himself to never again get lost in an organization. It wasn't that he didn't appreciate teamwork. Instead, it was his firm belief that any team worth joining never asked an individual to forget who he was. That the best team thrived on the individuality with it.

But there was something else. Moss also felt that he now had a debt to pay. For him, that, too, was a matter of principle.

Between the police and the Rennert's people, Moss learned that the victim of the shooting was around thirty years old and had some business experience. He also had some scrapes with the law, mostly little stuff like check kiting and shoplifting. Given the man's history, one of the cops' theories on motive for the shooting was that it was over an unpaid debt.

It was difficult to get the information, but Baltimore City Hospital eventually told him that, although their patient was in critical condition, he was likely to survive. When Moss hinted that he might be in a position to cover the costs of the indigent patient, the hospital became very open and friendly. The only condition imposed was that the patient be told that it was the Rennert paying the bills.

Moss also searched for a way to help the young man get on his feet once he recovered. An opportunity arose in a conversation with a wealthy businessman who had befriended the budding engineer during one of the civil construction projects a few years earlier. The contact was considering providing capital for the start of a restaurant with a new idea. The only problem was that the would-be owner/operators had little business experience.

Moss had a solution for his friend. If he would allow Moss a small share of the investment, in turn, Moss would provide someone with business experience who would function as a minority equity partner in order to assure good practices were established and maintained. Because Moss wanted to remain anonymous, the minority partner would be told that his equity share was set up to help secure the larger investment. Aside from reducing the capital requirement, having someone who knew his way around finance and accounting principles directly involved in ownership would certainly reduce some of the risk.

Before the two men shook hands on the arrangement, Moss had one more condition he wished to put in place. His exact words were, "Harry, I'd appreciate it if you'd recommended me as the cook for the new restaurant."

CHAPTER 29

1897
A MATCHED PAIR

Winter in Baltimore is a sneaky thing, not to be trusted. No year seems to be like any other. And those who make a dubious living predicting what the weather will be often end their careers prematurely, leaving a copy of *The Farmer's Almanac* behind them as they are hooted out of town.

We who live here have become cautious about winter, to the amusement and often annoyance of those who know more consistently colder climes. These people often curse us in frustration as they try to maneuver their carriages, buggies, and bicycles around we slower traveling natives who are just doing our best to get home in the snow.

Those who normally live in warmer parts of the country look at us and shake their heads in wonder as to why we do it at all. Is it penance for some real or imagined fault that we have? I've heard some say that we should have taken a side in the war, and that the reason we live here is to prove that we can take a stand. Others have speculated that our weather is God's way of counterbalancing his bountiful gift of the Chesapeake Bay.

Whatever motivates the average Baltimorean to stay here in winter, I have my own reasons. I like the feeling of sitting in front of the Diamond's big fireplace while snow is falling on Howard Street outside our window. I like putting my wool socks up against the grate until I can't hold them there any longer. I like watching the steam rise from a fresh mug of coffee and the feeling of just having eaten a full breakfast of bacon and eggs with one or two of Moss's buttered biscuits. I like the comfortable way we sit snugly in our empty café and gab about what has happened during the year and what we want to happen in the next.

"Well, I guess it's been a good year overall for the Orioles. We came so close to winning four in a row."

"Tough to do," Moss said, rattling his newspaper as he turned the page. "Hard to expect a team to maintain the standards this team has for so long. How about either putting your feet down or changing your socks? This place is starting to smell like a rendering plant."

"Rumors are that Harry Von Der Horst and Hanlon are going to break up the Big Four," I said, removing my toes from the fire.

"I wouldn't be surprised, now that Harry has a stake in that New York club."

"I hate what baseball is becoming," I said, knowing that I really didn't and that, whatever it was becoming, I'd still be a crank.

"Becoming?" he asked.

"Yeah, it's all just a business now. Just a way of making the most bucks you can."

Moss looked at me in that way he does: "Frank, once it became professional, that's all it ever was or could be. Otherwise, it wouldn't be. If you want sport for the sake of sport, there's always Hopkins or the Maryland Aggies. Besides, aren't you a businessman? What's wrong with business?"

"Nothing, nothing at all," I backpedaled. "I know it isn't logical, but baseball has a way of making cranks like me forget that."

Moss bore in: "You mean you have an illogical sense about the game?"

Damn. I was not going to let him pummel me again with his favorite weapon. My comfortable morning was not going to be interrupted by the same old Mossonian lecture.

I stood, stretched and asked him if he wanted another cup of joe.

When he nodded his thanks, I took his mug and padded my way into the kitchen. Upon returning, I asked, "Do you think we'll ever hear from Fanny again?"

"I know I won't, but who knows, you might," Moss said. "Do you want to?"

"Probably not. But she was one beautiful woman."

"Indeed she was. Beautiful and dangerous."

"I know that's what you think," I said. "But I'm not so sure."

"I am," he said.

"You two were like two dogs who didn't like each other's smells."

"Dogs are very perceptive," he replied.

Spotting yet another potential door to the conversation about his well-developed right brain, I swerved and asked Moss if he had spoken to Detective O'Donnell recently.

"Not recently. Not for a couple of months now. I guess he's satisfied with Gatch put away where he can't hurt anyone, Spittle gone, and Dr. Munsch dead. I assume he's got more pressing things to do than chase Fanny with little or no evidence."

"You're probably right. Plus, I don't think his bosses want him to stir the whole thing up again. The Hopkins people got something of a black eye for their hiring of Dr. Munsch, and you know they have pull downtown. What a piece of work he was."

"A real mad scientist," Moss said offhandedly, folding the paper again with that distinctive rustle.

What has slowly materialized for me over the last few months is the fact that I got a bad feeling about Dr. Munsch from the moment I saw him in the train station. Sure, I already thought of him as a suspect at that point, but that wasn't enough to account for my immediate, gut-level awareness of the man's villainy. This is something I will never admit to Moss. But it remains that my right brain was trying to tell me something. And that something could have been used to avoid that terrifying moment in Munsch's hallway.

"That mad man scared the hell out of me."

"I bet he did," Moss answered, half-listening.

"You saved me."

"I guess. It probably just wasn't your time. You must have something else you're supposed to do."

"I doubt it." Then, still thinking about the muzzle of that gun pointed at me, I asked, "You ever been shot before? It doesn't feel so hot."

"Oh?"

"Yeah, I got shot once. Twice, actually. Some crazy man. I didn't know him from Adam. I was sitting in the crapper, just minding my own business."

"Yeah?" Moss was now looking up from the paper.

"You bet. There's not much to tell. Spent some time in the hospital. I don't even know what happened to the guy. Put away somewhere or hung, I guess. All I have is a couple of scars and a bad memory. The fact is that it just must have been a case of mistaken identity."

"Wasn't it your man Holmes who said, 'There is nothing more deceptive than an obvious fact?'" Moss asked.

"Now, what's that supposed to mean?" I countered.

"Never mind, I'm just trying to be clever," the cook said. "I see that the Auditorium is showing a documentary film on the Fitzsimmons-Corbett fight. Want to go?"

THE END

Appendix I
Author's Note

No Slave to Reason is a work of fiction. My hope was to entertain and to offer readers a sense of the time, not to establish a historical record. While some of the occurrences and characters employed in the novel are the product of my imagination, many have been drawn from the history of Maryland, the City of Baltimore, and other places.

The non-fictional characters play key roles in the plot, provide context for the action, and, hopefully, increase interest in the story. At times, I have taken liberty with their personal histories, but I believe that I have not created anything that would be outside of the realm of possibility.

Appendix II provides a sizable list of the non-fictional characters referenced or used in the novel. The reader may find some of the same minor amusement that I did when I developed the list and alphabetized it. As an example, it struck me as fun to see such dissimilar personages as Frederick Douglass, Sir Arthur Conan Doyle, and Dirty Jack Doyle residing next to each other in the lineup.

The idea for *No Slave to Reason* arose while I was researching the Diamond Café for my first novel, *Plug Ugly Ball.* I found it interesting that it's location at 519 N. Howard Street was situated right in the middle of Baltimore's old theater district. That sparked speculation on what the area must have been like in its heyday. So, with the help of the Maryland Historical Society, I began to reconstruct the occupants on both sides of the street between Franklin and what today is Center Street. What I found was an amazing bifurcation of enterprises that had art and intuition resident on the west side of the street (the theaters, e.g.) and science and reason on the east side (the Johns Hopkins University, Baltimore City College, and various professional offices).

The exception to this seemed to be the Diamond Café, situated on the east side of Howard Street—the scientific side, if you'd like. It was at that point that I realized the tavern was owned by Baltimore Oriole baseball players who, according to the sports writers of the day, played the "scientific" baseball of Ned Hanlon.

With the stars now in alignment, I began to think of Howard Street as a corpus callosum, separating the left and right hemispheres of a great urban brain of sorts. That happy thought led me to a murder mystery that would not be solved until the logical or reasonable side worked together with the intuitive or "unreasonable" side to unravel the facts of the case. While this belies the logical methods of the great Sherlock Holmes, the reader should think more in terms of the ubiquitous franchise, *Star Trek*. The late Leonard Nimoy's perfectly logical Mr. Spock resolved few crises without teaming with the very human intuition of Captain James T. Kirk. It was this idea which in turn led me to create the character, Moss Tilghman, who is obviously adept at using both sides of his brain.

Today's neuroscience has long left theories of strict right- and left-brain lateralization of function in humans behind, but that was not the case in 1897. In addition, there are examples in the historical record of extraordinary feats by individuals who have been forced to compensate for injuries to one side of the brain or the other. Mrs. Flannigan's and Mr. Johnson's stories, however, are figments of my imagination.

The Diamond Cafe (sometimes referred to as the Diamond Tavern) was owned and operated jointly by Hall of Fame players Wilbert Robinson and John McGraw. While McGraw eventually sold his interest in the enterprise at 519 North Howard Street, Robinson continued to operate the saloon well after his retirement from baseball in 1902. According to the Maryland Historical Society archives, the building had multiple owners over time, but was always operated as a tavern in Baltimore's old theater district until its demolition in 2004. Unfortunately, with the exception of a few, thin newspaper articles, there is little in the known historical record about the business. Photographs of the building's exterior or the interior of the place have been described by collectors of such things as "the Holy Grail" of Baltimore photographs.

While the bar's description is fictional, the activities and entertainments offered by the Diamond are not. It also may be of interest that the invention of duckpin bowling is credited to one of the tavern's managers (Frank Van Sant) who was said to have cut down damaged tenpins in an effort to save expense. The credit for the name "duckpins," however, goes to McGraw and Robinson who, as Frank mentions in the story, somehow put the sound of bowling pins and ducks together.

This version of the origin of the game comes from the archives of the *Baltimore Sun*. However, it should be noted that there are several others who claim the sport was played in Lowell, Massachusetts as early as 1893.

The name "Frank Van Sant" is mentioned in a 1955 retrospective article in *The Baltimore Sun* as the manager of the Diamond's bowling alleys. His central role in the story as a minority owner of the Diamond and close associate with the Orioles players of 1897 is invention on my part. I found no connection between the Diamond's Frank Van Sant and Joshua Van Sant, who was Mayor of Baltimore between 1871 and 1875.

The character Moss Tilghman is fictional, as is the story of his escape from slavery, his education, his time on the Chesapeake Bay and in Europe, the development of his circle of friends, and his general erudition. Moss's story provided an opportunity to offer a snapshot of some the difficulty of life as a black man before and after the Civil War. Moss does not represent the typical freed slave, nor am I in a position personally to suggest expertise in what that life was like. Just the same, no story of the time could ignore the major issue that America was struggling to resolve. For me, Moss represents an individual's triumph over the era's prejudice, and is not meant to suggest that what was available to Moss was available to all. At times, I was concerned that Moss's personal growth was unrealistic; however, I kept reminding myself of the accomplishments of Frederick Douglass, and that allowed me to plow on with my character's development.

The Von Der Horst family (often written as Vonderhorst) was, in fact, a very prominent Baltimore family, owners of the Eagle Brewery and Malt Works, investors in insurance and railroads, and the original owners of the early Baltimore Orioles. Harry Von Der Horst, according to numerous accounts in *The Baltimore Sun*, was quite an accomplished bowler and, like his father, John, a pillar of the large German community in the city.

The Baltimore Orioles of 1897 were, as Moss suggests, invincible on paper, but vulnerable on the field. Their role as one of the three main storylines exists to reinforce the concept that art and science must work in conjunction to resolve the knottiest of problems—problems like how to win something as difficult and elusive as a baseball championship.

I have attempted to capture the Baltimore Orioles' 1897 season accurately, as reported in a number of respected histories and in the archives of both Baltimore and Boston newspapers. Even minor instances, like the shower fight between John McGraw and Willie Keeler or the fistfight between Jack Doyle and umpire Tim Hurst, were found in these histories. One source, Bill Felber's *A Game of Brawl*, was particularly useful for its excellent research and almost season-long, game-by-game level of detail. As good as Felber's book is, however, its Boston slant makes it difficult for a true Orioles crank (fan) to read.

I have attempted to capture the personalities and antics of each of the players as they have been drawn in a number of respected baseball histories. Readers wanting more of what I have merely introduced have a world of resources available to them, some of which I've captured in the section "Contributors, Sources and Suggested Reading."

Baseball purists may chafe at my implication that the final series between Baltimore and Boston was the last of the 1897 season. In fact, there was a four-game series with the Washington Senators remaining in the 136 games played that year. But, for all intents and purposes, the season had been decided the week before in the epic three games between the Orioles and the Beaneaters, described in the novel.

Researching the Academy of Music, the Auditorium Music Hall, Ford's Theater, and the other playhouses in Baltimore in 1897 was spectacular fun. Not only were the buildings themselves architectural wonders, but the acts, plays, operas, and other entertainments staged within them made me want to go back to the time. The boxes and boxes of articles, playbills, photographs, and personal scrapbooks resident in the Maryland Historical Society and the huge newspaper archive of the Enoch Pratt Library, which offered critical reviews of the entertainment, were my resources. All acts, actors, or actresses mentioned in *No Slave to Reason* were gleaned from these precious repositories. The major exception to this was the fictional character Fanny Darlington, who was herself modeled in part on a well-known actress of the era, Fanny Davenport.

The comedienne, Edna May, was found among the Maryland Historical Society's archives and was a regular in the vaudeville shows staged at the Auditorium Theater. I was never able to discover the entertainer's surname or her personal history. As a result, the name I gave her (Klara Drambauer) is fictitious and used because I liked the sound of it. I cannot say that the jokes I ascribed to Edna May were actually used by her. However, they well could have been, given her act. I also can't say that the gags are of my own invention. They were gleaned from an archive of old, bawdy postcards from the 1920s that I came across in my research. They seemed to fit nicely, however, since they were every bit as corny and innocent as the numerous jokes I found printed as filler in the playbills from 1897. (Admittedly, the playbill jokes were not as ribald.)

Another rich source of personal amusement was my research on the patent medicines of the time. While there was nothing humorous about the widespread use of opiates and cocaine, the imaginations and claims of the producers of these curatives was only matched by the gullibility of those buying them. Readers wanting a quick lesson in advertising creativity should Google the Sears catalogue of 1897 and turn to the "drug store" section.

I found the real Thomas P. O'Donnell, Baltimore City Police detective, on a website that is well worth a visit: www.baltimorecitypolicehistory.com. (Click on "Our Police," then "1800–1900.") There, you will find a photograph of a handsome man, a brief summary of his long, decorated career, and an outline of one of his more well-documented cases. The following note on Detective O'Donnell seemed to describe a dedicated, even heroic public servant: "…retired after forty-eight years of continuous service, 1890–1938, during which he was commended a total of thirty-five times."

The Emory family held Poplar Grove Plantation in Queen Anne's County, Maryland, for nearly 300 years. The three Emorys mentioned in the novel were an integral part of Eastern Shore aristocracy and public service. John and Thomas were decorated generals in two different wars against the British and William served in the State Legislature in Annapolis. The Emory who the novel described as the captain of the pilot schooner *Mary Kate* is a product of my imagination. At the time, the Emory and Tilghman surnames permeated the population of Maryland's Eastern Shore counties, as they do today.

Those readers with a passing interest in the Chesapeake Bay and the craft that sailed its waters may be surprised at my omission of the famous "skipjack" schooner. Using Geoffrey Footner's wonderful history, *Tidewater Triumph: The Development and Worldwide Success of the Chesapeake Bay Pilot Schooner*, I learned that beginning in the 1880s, Bay captains went through a transition that corresponded with the diminishing of the oyster beds. As oysters became scarcer, boats got bigger and faster. As a result, baycraft evolved from log canoes to pungies (pilot schooners) to bugeyes and eventually later to the skipjack. There was a wider range of boats used, of course, but these four seem to capture the majority sailed by the oystermen. The timing of my story corresponded to the period when the pungy was the craft of choice.

Today, Crisfield, Maryland, located on the Tangier Sound, is a pleasant and nostalgic town of about 2,700 souls. It still supports the activities of Chesapeake watermen, but is just as familiar with artists and tourists. My description of the place as "a boomtown" in the middle of the nineteenth century is a far cry from what a visitor might experience today, yet it is nonetheless accurate for the period.

The City of Baltimore was a very dangerous place just before the Civil War. Municipal protection services were in a nascent state, including its police and fire services. As a result, the city suffered from widespread lawlessness and riot. It earned the nickname "Mobtown," as street gangs, affiliated with local, volunteer firehouses, ran its streets, corrupted law enforcement, and supported political parties with violence and intimidation. Readers who want to understand more of this time will find it all in a very well-researched historical work by Tracy Matthew Melton, *Hanging Henry Gambrill: The Violent Career of Baltimore's Plug Uglies, 1854–1860*. Or, if your preference is for historical fiction, my own *Plug Ugly Ball* will provide a degree of insight.

In the years before the war, Baltimore was home to the largest population of freedmen in the United States, with estimates as high as fifty thousand. The city was a pivotal demarcation point for the slave trade and, at the same time, a key stop in escape routes to the North. When the Fugitive Slave Law was passed in 1850, Baltimore's black population was not safe on the streets, whether freed, escaping, or in bondage.

Readers may note that the term "Underground Railroad" is not used in the novel. The reason for that is the growing number of historians who believe that routes taken by escaping slaves, safe houses used along the way, and the many others who may have provided support for those fleeing north were never organized to the point that warranted a specific name. Rather, they believe the term has come into being as a catchall for the overall abolitionist effort that was made across a broad spectrum.

The history of the Garrett family is well documented and its male members rode the heights of American business, society and wealth. Their story, however, often overshadows that of the Garrett women of the same period, namely Mary Elizabeth and her estranged sister-in-law, Mary Sloan Frick Garrett, wife of Robert Garrett II. The two women were only close in terms of where they lived in Mount Vernon Square, and opposed each other regularly on the use and distribution of the family estate and fortune. Mary Frick Garrett was the undisputed *grande dame* of Baltimore society, maintaining the largest and most opulent home on the Square, which she used to its fullest advantage for hosting and entertaining. Mary Elizabeth, on the other hand, had no desire to play that societal role, preferring instead to devote her time to activist causes. Just the same, Mary Frick Garrett fought Mary Elizabeth on most, if not all of her endeavors, including the funding of the Johns Hopkins Medical School, the inclusion of women in the school, the construction of Bryn Mawr, women's suffrage, and women's rights issues in general.

Thomas Garrett, whose role in the novel was to assist Moss in his escape, is not to be confused with the Baltimore Garretts. Thomas was a Pennsylvania Quaker, businessman, and a leader of the abolitionist movement from 1827 to the end of the Civil War. It is said that he helped over 2,700 people to freedom during that time.

The Metropolitan Methodist Episcopal Church, now known as the Orchard Street United Methodist Church, was founded in 1825 and constructed in 1837. It is the oldest standing structure built by African Americans in the city of Baltimore and is today the home of the Baltimore Urban League. It is thought to have been an important stop in Baltimore on the way to freedom. In the 1970s, workmen uncovered a hidden tunnel underneath the church that suggests its role in assisting escaping slaves, although there are contradictory reports that claim the tunnel is simply part of the church's heating system.

I found it of interest that Baltimore's press in the mid-1890s anointed two very different groups as the city's "Big Four." In the medical world, the founders of Johns Hopkins Hospital (pathologist William Henry Welch, surgeon William Stewart Halsted, internist William Osler, and gynecologist Howard Kelly) were some of the most respected medical men of the era. Simultaneously, sports writers named their own "Big Four," specifically the Baltimore Orioles' third baseman John McGraw, shortstop Hughie Jennings, left fielder Joe Kelley and right fielder Willie Keeler. I believe it to be safe speculation that if the average Baltimorean on the street in 1896 when asked to name the "Big Four," their answer would have little to do with medicine and everything to do with batting averages.

For plot purposes, *No Slave to Reason* assigns ownership of the area theaters to one man, James L. Kernan. While Kernan did build and own the Maryland

Theater, the Auditorium Music Hall, and the Kernan Hotel (later, the now defunct Congress Hotel), I found no evidence that he was directly involved with the Academy of Music. According to the archives of *The Baltimore Sun*, the Academy was owned by a partnership of national and local investors. Tunis F. Dean was mentioned in those same archives as the managing director in 1897, but there was no indication that the enterprise made use of a "Board of Sponsors" as described in the novel. Nor was there any indication found that the Academy made use of charitable fundraising to support their endeavors. Finally, the idea that Mary Elizabeth Garrett was interested in using the Academy of Music for a national convention on women's suffrage is an invention of my own.

Hopefully, readers got a smile from my fiction describing John McGraw balling up and throwing the woman's hat over the balcony at the Academy. In truth, the subject of women wearing hats in the theater seemed to be quite a thing of controversy in 1897. *The Sun* not only reported incidences of annoyed men and outraged women, but also wrote editorials on the subject. Millenaries advertised less ostentatious "theater wear," and physicians weighed in on the pros and cons of women's hats in general, some suggesting that women required hats for "proper health."

The incident in the novel describing the young man falling through the glass dome of the Auditorium is my invention. However, it was drawn from an article in an 1897 issue of *The Baltimore Sun* which described a horrific accident involving a twelve-year-old boy falling through the dome into the orchestra pit below during a performance.

I cannot support through research my use of St. Joseph's College in Philadelphia as a terminus for runaway slaves. Its plausibility, however, allowed me to assign the role in support of the plot. The idea that the school educated my fictional character, Moss, but refused to grant him a degree was also developed in support of the story.

It is, of course, fiction that Loyola College in Baltimore (now Loyola University Maryland) and the Johns Hopkins University educated Moss Tilghman. My point in having the schools require that his education be "informal" was an attempt to capture the discriminatory attitudes prevalent across the established society before and after the Civil War. My character's earning of a master's degree in civil engineering from Loyola is pure imagination. These were plot devices intended only to support my character, and were not meant to comment on St. Joseph's, Loyola's, or Johns Hopkins's actual attitudes toward people of color or slavery itself.

The history of the Union Army's 54th Massachusetts Infantry Regiment is a great American story that has been told numerous times, yet its impact is never diminished in its retelling. The men who led the regiment and those who fought in it demonstrated a level of commitment and bravery that cannot be eclipsed. My character's eventual dissatisfaction with the Army and the war in general is in no way intended to diminish what the 54th accomplished in their sacrifice. The names of the regiment's soldiers in my story are all drawn from the historical record, including Sergeant William H. Carney, winner of a United States Medal of Honor for bravery during the storming of Battery Wagner.

The Chesapeake Marine Railway and Dry Dock Company, founded in 1866 by Isaac Myers and John Locks, was the most successful black-owned business in Baltimore City at the time. It employed both black and white workers and served as a center of the city's shipbuilding industry. I could not resist allowing Moss Tilghman to connect with these entrepreneurs, nor could I avoid the historical irony that the business was situated on the former site of the center of Baltimore's slave trade (Kennard's Wharf).

While it is fact that Wilbert Robinson decorated the Diamond Café with a wide range of sports memorabilia, the means with which he and John McGraw collected the materials in the novel is fiction.

Readers may find disconcerting my reference to the fare at Union Park as "sausages" or "weckers," instead of "hotdogs." In fact, the history of the hotdog is both convoluted and controversial, with numerous claimants to its invention. The only common denominator among its histories is that it seems to have emigrated from Germany. The edible has as many names as it does supposed originators, including wiener, frankfurter, dachshund sandwiches, sausages, wurst, dogs, hotdogs, and, in 1897 Baltimore, weckers. If H. L. Mencken can be believed, in *Happy Days* (1936), he claimed that he was eating weckers as far back as 1886. In those days, the Bard wrote that the meat itself was "the same rubbery, indigestible pseudo-sausage that millions of Americans now eat." The difference, the humorist wrote, was that they came not in buns, but wrapped in a baked German wheat flour pastry called "wecke."

My story takes considerable liberty with the history of the Reverend Felix-Joseph Barbelin, S.J. I believe I have captured the Jesuit's spirituality, personality, and drive accurately enough from the biographies I've read, but I have altered some of the man's true biography in support of the story. Father Barbelin was born in Lunéville, France in 1808 and died in Philadelphia, Pennsylvania in 1869, not in 1884, not in Paris, and not from tuberculosis, as reported in the novel. While he did hold the presidency of St. Joseph's College in Philadelphia (now St. Joseph's University), among numerous other positions in various American Jesuit schools, including Georgetown University, I was never able to place him in Loyola College in Baltimore. Also, the priest's education was in philosophy and theology, not in engineering. Finally, the idea that Fr. Barbelin allowed a moral imperative to supersede federal law by aiding and abetting a runaway slave is yet another plausible, dramatic invention on my part.

Father Barbelin was every bit of the champion of the poor as described in my story. He labored for over a third of a century, providing both religious and humanitarian service to those in need.

I believe I have been authentic in summarizing the evolution of French cooking during the time of Georges Auguste Escoffier. While I did not ascribe the reorganization of the professional kitchen to the chef, specialization within culinary tasks was, in fact, his brainchild as well. Because the elite French culinary school, Le Cordon Bleu, was not opened until 1895, I created my own for Moss to attend: La Main Légère (The Light Hand).

Finally, I was accurate in my description of Baltimore's hotels and their reputation for good food in the Gilded Age. Barnum's City Hotel reigned supreme in the early half of the century, but was eventually eclipsed by those others mentioned in the novel. The Rennert House, particularly, is mentioned in the archives as representative of the best the Chesapeake Region had to offer.

JTE
November 2017

Appendix II
Non-Fictional Characters Appearing or Referenced in *No Slave to Reason*

A	John A. Andrew	Governor, Massachusetts
	Cap Anson	First baseman/manager, Chicago et al, HOF
	Susan B. Anthony	Social reformer/feminist
B	Dorothea Baird	Actress, multi-genre
	Francis Baldwin	Architect, B&O Railroad
	Felix-Joseph Barbelin	Jesuit priest, president St. Joseph's College
	Walter Barnes	News reporter, sports
	Alexander Graham Bell	Scientist, inventor, engineer, and innovator
	Digby Bell	Entertainer, vaudeville
	Frank Bowerman	Catcher, Baltimore
	Haynie Bradshaw	Boxer, bare-knuckle, Smith Island, Maryland
	Dan Brouthers	First baseman, Baltimore et al, HOF
	Abraham F. Brown	Private, U.S. Army (54th Mass.)
	William Jennings Bryan	U.S. Sec. of State/presidential candidate
C	William H. Carney	Sergeant, U.S. Army (54th Mass.), MOH

	Sigmund Freud	Neurologist, Vienna
	Emma Maddox Funck	Social activist/feminist
G	Joe (the Old Master) Gans	Boxer, gloved, LC 1902–1908
	Harrison (Harry) Garrett	Businessman/philanthropist
	John Work Garrett	Businessman/President, B&O Railroad
	Mary Elizabeth Garrett	Social activist/feminist/philanthropist
	Mary Sloan Frick Garrett	Socialite/philanthropist
	Robert Garrett II	Businessman/philanthropist
	Thomas G. Garrett	Abolitionist, Quaker, Delaware/Pennsylvania
	Daniel Coit Gilman	Educator/academic/president JHU
	John Gooseberry	Private, U.S. Army (54th Mass.)
	Jason (Jay) Gould	Industrialist
	Ulysses S. Grant	U.S. President, eighteenth
H	William Stewart Halstead	Surgeon/founder JHH
	Billy Hamilton	Outfielder, Boston, HOF
	Ned Hanlon	Manager, Baltimore, HOF
	Bill Hoffer	Pitcher, Baltimore
	Alcaeus Hooper	Mayor, Baltimore City
	Tim Hurst	NL umpire
J	Thomas J. (Stonewall) Jackson	General, CSA
	Hugh A. (Hughie) Jennings	Shortstop, Baltimore, HOF
	Joseph E. Johnston	General, CSA
K	William E. (Wee Willie) Keeler	Right fielder, Baltimore, HOF
	Joseph J. (Joe) Kelley	Left fielder, Baltimore, HOF
	Michael J. (King) Kelley	Outfielder/catcher/manager, Boston, HOF
	Howard A. Kelly	Gynecologist, founder JHH
	Stephen Kelly	Jesuit priest, president Loyola College

	James L Kernan	Theater manager/philanthropist
	Francis Scott Key	Lawyer/poet
	Frederick A. (Duke) Klobedanz	Pitcher, Boston
L	Lao Tzu	Philosopher/poet
	Robert E. Lee	General, CSA
	Abraham Lincoln	U.S. President, sixteenth
	John Locks	Businessman/shipbuilder
	Tom Lynch	NL Umpire
M	Edouard Manet	Artist, modern/innovator
	George B. McClellan	General, U.S. Army
	John J. (Muggsy) McGraw	Third baseman, Baltimore, HOF
	Minnie McGraw	Spouse, first, John McGraw
	William McKinley	U.S. President, twenty-fifth
	Miss Edna May	Comedienne, vaudeville
	John F. Morrill	Infielder, Boston
	Albert Mott	Writer, sports
	Ren Mulford	Writer, sports
	Tom Murphy	Groundskeeper, Union Park
	Isaac Myers	Businessman/shipbuilder
N	Horatio Nelson	Lord, Vice Admiral, British Royal Navy
	Charles A. (Kid) Nichols	Pitcher, Boston, HOF
	Jerry Nops	Pitcher, Baltimore
O	Tom O'Brien	Utility outfielder/first baseman, Baltimore
	Thomas P. O'Donnell	Detective, Baltimore City Police
	William Osler	Internist, founder JHH
P	Homer A. Plessey	Social activist, freedman
	Erasmus A. (Arlie) Pond	Physician/pitcher, Baltimore
	Jack Powell	Pitcher, Cleveland

Q	Joe Quinn	Second baseman, Baltimore
R	Henry P. (Heinie) Reitz	Second baseman, Baltimore
	Wilbert (Uncle Robbie) Robinson	Catcher, Baltimore, HOF
	Amos W. Rusie	Pitcher, New York, HOF
S	Leland Stanford	Industrialist/politician, founder Stanford U.
	John Singer Sargent	Artist, portraitist
	Frank G. Selee	Manager, Boston, HOF
	Robert Gould Shaw	Colonel, U.S. Army
	Jack Sheradin	NL Umpire
	William Tecumseh Sherman	General, U.S. Army
	Willie Simms	Jockey, ATR HOF
	William Smallwood	Planter/soldier/politician, Maryland
	Louis F. Sockalexis	Right fielder, Cleveland
	John Philip Sousa	Composer/conductor
	Martin John Spalding	Catholic priest, Archbishop of Baltimore
	Elizabeth Cady Stanton	Social activist/abolitionist/feminist
	Jacob C. (Jake) Stenzel	Center fielder, Baltimore
	George Crocket Strong	General, U.S. Army
	John L. Sullivan	Boxer, bare-knuckle/gloved, HC 1882–1892
T	Israel (Izzy) Tatter	Newstand, bookstore owner/curmudgeon
	Oliver Wendell (Patsy) Tebeau	Manager, first/third baseman, Cleveland
	Fred Tenney	First baseman, Boston
	Martha Carey Thomas	Educator/suffragist, president Bryn Mawr Coll.
	John Edgar Thomson	Industrialist/engineer, president Penn. R.R.

V	Cornelius Vanderbilt	Industrialist/philanthropist
	Frank Van Sant	Manager, the Diamond Café, Baltimore
	Joe Villa	Writer, sports
	Harry Von Der Horst	Owner, Eagle Brewery/Baltimore Orioles
W	Henry Walters	Businessman/art collector/philanthropist
	William Thompson Walters	Businessman/art collector
	George Washington	U.S. President, first
	Charles Watts	Private, U.S. Army (54th Mass.)
	William H. Welsh	Pathologist, founder JHH
	Herbert G. (H.G.) Wells	Author, multi-genre
	August Williams	Chef, the Rennert Hotel, Baltimore
	Austin Woolfolk	Slave trader, Maryland
Y	Denton True (Cy) Young	Pitcher, Cleveland, HOF

Abbreviations

ATR HOF	American Thoroughbred Racing Hall of Fame
B&O	Baltimore & Ohio Railroad
Coll.	College
CSA	Confederate States of America
HC	Heavyweight Championship
HOF	ML Baseball Hall of Fame
JHH	Johns Hopkins Hospital
JHU	Johns Hopkins University
LC	Lightweight Champion
MOH	U.S. Medal of Honor
NL	National League
Penn.	Pennsylvania
R.R.	Railroad
U.	University
U.S.	United States

Appendix III
Contributors, Sources and Suggested Reading

Alexander, Charles C. *John McGraw.* New York, NY: Viking, 1988.

Baseball Almanac; Baseball Almanac is a privately held web site located at 8263 SW 107th Avenue Miami, FL 33173-3740; www.baseball-almanac.com, 2011.

Bradshaw, Timothy E., Jr. *Battery Wagner: The Siege, the Men Who Fought, and the Casualties.* Charleston, NC: Palmetto Historical Works, 1993.

Bready, James H. *Baseball in Baltimore: The First Hundred Years.* Baltimore, MD: The Johns Hopkins University Press, 1998.

Dixon, Zachary J. *Man in the Street, From Dirt Roads to Blacktop: A History of Baltimore Street Names.* La Vergne, TN: Lightning Source, Inc., The Baltimore Sun, 2014.

Dudley, Allen Sargent. *Life and Reminiscences of a 19th Century Gladiator.* Boston, MA: J.A. Hearn & Co., 1892.

Duncan, Russell. *Where Death and Glory Meet: Colonel Robert Gould Shaw and the 54th Massachusetts Infantry.* Atlanta, Georgia: University of Georgia Press, 1999.

Emilio, Luis F. *A Brave Black Regiment: the History of the Fifty-Fourth Regiment of Massachusetts Volunteer Infantry.* Boston MA: Da Capo Press, 1995.

Felber, Bill. *A Game of Brawl: The Orioles, the Beaneaters & the Battle for the 1897 Pennant.* Lincoln, NE: University of Nebraska Press, 2007.

Footner, Geoffrey M. *Tidewater Triumph: The Development and Worldwide Success of the Chesapeake Bay Pilot Schooner.* Mystic, CN: Mystic Seaport Museum, 1998.

Hayward, Mary Ellen and Shivers, Jr., Frank R. *The Architecture of Baltimore: An Illustrated History*. Baltimore, MD: The Johns Hopkins University Press, 2004.

Hipp, Scott F. *Old Line Divided: Maryland in the Civil War: Volume I: Antebellum to 1862*. Baltimore, MD: The Baltimore Bookworks, LLC, 2011.

Liebling, A.J. *The Sweet Science*. New York, NY: North Point Press, 2004.

Melton, Tracy Matthew. *Hanging Henry Gambrill: The Violent Career of Baltimore's Plug Uglies, 1854–1860*. Baltimore, MD: The Press at the Maryland Historical Society, 2005.

McPherson, James M. *The Negro's Civil War: How American Blacks Felt and Acted During the War for the Union*. New York, NY: Vintage, Knopf Doubleday Publishing 2003

Sander, Kathleen Waters. *Mary Elizabeth Garrett: Society and Philanthropy in the Gilded Age*. Baltimore, MD: The Johns Hopkins University Press, 2008.

Scharf, Col. J. Thomas. *The Chronicles of Baltimore: Being a Complete History of "Baltimore Town" and Baltimore City from the Earliest Period to the Present Time*. Baltimore, MD: Turnbull Brothers, 1874.

Scharf, Col. J. Thomas. *History of Baltimore City and County: From the Earliest Period to the Present Day*. Philadelphia, PA: Press of J. B. Lippencott & Co., 1881.

Sherr, Lynn. *Failure Is Impossible: Susan B. Anthony in Her Own Words*. New York, NY: Crown/Archetype, A Division of Random House, Inc., 2010

Solomon, Burt. *Where They Ain't: The Fabled Life and Untimely Death of the Original Baltimore Orioles, the Team That Gave Birth to Modern Baseball*. New York, NY: A Main Street Book, Doubleday, a division of Random House, Inc., 1999.

Wennersten, John R. *The Oyster Wars of Chesapeake Bay*. Centerville, MD: Tidewater Publishers, 1981.

**THE THOUSAND YEAR REICH MAY BE
ONLY BEGINNING...**

ALLAN LEVERONE

A Tracie Tanner Thriller

www.braveshipbooks.com

WHO IS HUNTER? WHO IS PREY?
WHO WILL SURVIVE?

ROBERT BIDINOTTO

In a world without justice, sometimes you have to make your own...

**A VICIOUS DRUG CARTEL IS ABOUT
TO LEARN THE HARD WAY...**

TED NULTY

...there's no such thing as an ex-Marine.

www.braveshipbooks.com

www.ingramcontent.com/pod-product-compliance
Lightning Source LLC
Chambersburg PA
CBHW052032240626
47153CB00006B/2051